CW0051 7284

Florence Wilford

Dominie Freylinghausen

Anatiposi

Florence Wilford

Dominie Freylinghausen

Reprint of the original, first published in 1875.

1st Edition 2024 | ISBN: 978-3-38283-128-8

Anatiposi Verlag is an imprint of Outlook Verlagsgesellschaft mbH.

Verlag (Publisher): Outlook Verlag GmbH, Zeilweg 44, 60439 Frankfurt, Deutschland
Vertretungsberechtigt (Authorized to represent): E. Roepke, Zeilweg 44, 60439 Frankfurt, Deutschland
Druck (Print): Books on Demand GmbH, In de Tarpen 42, 22848 Norderstedt, Deutschland

Dominie Freylinghausen.

Dominie Freylinghausen.

BY

FLORENCE WILFORD,

AUTHOR OF "NIGEL BARTRAM'S IDEAL," "VIVIA," ETC.

LONDON:

MOZLEY AND SMITH.

6, PATERNOSTER ROW.

1875.

CHAPTER IX.

CHAPTER X.

CHAPTER XI.

CHAPTER XII.

CHAPTER XIII.

CHAPTER XIV.

CHAPTER XV.

CHAPTER XVI.

CHAPTER XVII.

CHAPTER XVIII.

DOMINIE FREYLINGHAUSEN.[1]

CHAPTER I.

𝕿𝖍𝖊 𝕯𝖔𝖒𝖎𝖓𝖎𝖊'𝖘 𝕻𝖚𝖕𝖎𝖑.

PACING up and down a little grass-plot at the back of a quaint house in Albany (U.S.) one afternoon more than a hundred years ago, was a young girl, whose real age was barely sixteen years, but whose fair, large, well-developed beauty gave her the appearance of being at least twelve months older. She was a native of the state of New York ; but, belonging to a Dutch colony which adhered faithfully to the traditions it had brought with it from Holland, her dress was that of a Dutchwoman of the period ; and the plain stuff bodice and kirtle, striped petticoat, and black ribbon passed through the flaxen hair, seemed almost too prim and sombre apparel to har-monize with the rich character of her loveliness. She had a book in her hand, and was learning something by heart —studying it with childish intentness, and now and then

---

[1] Mrs. Grant's spelling has been followed with regard to this name, but probably it would be more correct if spelt "Freling-huysen."

repeating the words aloud, as if hoping so to impress them more distinctly on her memory.

Presently she sat down in a stiff green arbour, which was placed with its back to the house, looking over a strip of very unpicturesque vegetable beds towards the broad waters of the Hudson, which swept along at the end of the garden ; and then for a moment her hold on the book relaxed, and her mind wandered off into reverie.

"Your lessons grow harder and harder, Dominie !" she said mentally ; "and my time for learning seems to grow less and less. Mother will be wanting me for the cake-making soon, but I *must* get this perfect first. It will never do to miss another class day, nor to go to the class with my lesson half learnt. How angry you were with Anna Gerritse, when she had not that table of references perfect ! "

She leant her head back against the green wall of the arbour, and her lips unclosed in a smile—such a happy smile ! assuredly not because Anna Gerritse had been scolded, but because on the same occasion somebody else had been praised, or rather tacitly approved of, after the fashion of the stern, reserved Dominie, from whom actual words of praise came but rarely.

It was a great surprise, when her eyes came down from their happy musings, to see standing before her the very person whom she had been so lately apostrophizing. He had come across the grass at the back of the arbour, unseen therefore by her, and now appeared suddenly at the entrance, its arched opening framing him round as in a picture, but scarcely leaving sufficient margin at the top to give full effect to the striking, almost colossal figure, so full of dignity and grandeur that it seemed to need the worthier setting of some lofty Gothic doorway.

He was of middle age, with regular features, a powerful

brow, and a face altogether far more noble and intellectual than the ordinary Dutch type; his expression was very fine—sternly thoughtful, yet tempered by benevolence, and with a certain visionary outlook in the eyes which often made his simple congregation wonder of what their pastor could be thinking. It was not a calm face, however—only one that struggled after calmness; and though he spoke slowly and distinctly, with deliberation and decision, it was not a calm voice either, but one subdued by a strong will into this mechanical composure. Self-mastery seemed his prevailing characteristic; he looked like one who was always doing battle with himself and always conquering, and who would have small mercy on those who were either too indolent to attempt such an encounter, or too weak to come off victorious.

"What! giving way to idleness, Child?" he said; "with your book in your lap, and your mouth open, and your eyes I know not where. I shall not have a perfect lesson to-day, I see."

At the sound of his voice she started up, curtseying in confusion. "Indeed, I believe I know it fairly well, Sir," she said, blushing; "but I did not expect it to be heard till next class-day."

"No? I thought, as I was coming here to speak with your mother, I would hear this, and set you another lesson for next time—the same that your companions have; but I fear you have little zeal for learning."

Her blue eyes ranged along the garden beds as if seeking an excuse, and then came timidly back to his face. "I have so much to do, Dominie," she said.

"So much, that in the golden hours of the day you can sit idle here, with your thoughts I know not where," he replied sarcastically.

Ah! if he had but seen her diligence as she walked to

and fro, conning her lesson! thought she; but she only
said, "Will you sit down, Dominie, and let me try to
say it?"

He sat down, and took the book—a sort of lengthy
catechism, with illustrative quotations from standard Dutch
divines; and she stood in front of him, repeating her task
in a cadence too monotonous and measured for the mind
to have had full share in the performance, but still with
almost perfect accuracy as far as the words went.

As she stood there, just outside the arbour, in the full
light of day, so exceeding fair, so unconscious of her fairness, the Dominie must have been blind indeed if he had
not noted into what a beautiful woman this child of his
teaching was ripening. He did note it, but with a certain regret, springing from a source of which she knew
nothing.

"Fairly well learnt," he remarked, when she had finished;
"but I wish you had given your mind more to the repeti-
tion. What have you been thinking of all this time?"

She played with her apron-string, and made no answer.

"Tell me," he added authoritatively.

For a moment she averted her face shyly, but a reaction
of courage followed; with a smile that was quite brilliant
in the bravery of its innocence, her blue eyes glanced up
at him with the honest answer, " I was wondering if you
would be pleased with me, and would see that I need not
be chidden for idleness."

"Child, you live too much for praise," he said, with
rather melancholy gravity.

" But it is just what I do not get, Dominie," she answered
quaintly and demurely.

He smiled in spite of himself for an instant, but rejoined very gravely, "Better if you do not; what can
man's praise do for us, but lift us up and feed our self-

conceit? He who toils for *man's* 'well done,' will never attain to *God's*." His voice dropped low in the last sentence, as if he were speaking to himself almost more than to her; and for a few seconds he seemed lost in thought. Then he roused himself, and said drily, "You will do well to get by heart the contents of the next two pages—see, from here to here,"—indicating the place with his finger.

She came to his side, and stooped down to look at the book, her fresh peach-like cheek quite close to him, the sun glinting on her long dark eyelashes and making them as radiant as her hair. It was as if a bright sun-ray had come between him and the printed lines: he was dazzled just for a moment; then he remembered that this beautiful creature was no pagan goddess to inspire a mistaken worship, she was just "one of the flock," one of his own young people, to be instructed, warned, comforted, or lectured, just as seemed to him best.

"Assuredly she is very beautiful!" he said to himself; "but better for her, perhaps, if she were not."

"My child," he said aloud, "you have heard, no doubt, that the orderly peacefulness of our town is to be broken to-day by the arrival of an English regiment. It need, I trust, make no material difference in our quiet lives; but there will be the more need that we should all walk steadily in the good ways which strangers in their folly are apt to sneer at, and that the maidens of the flock in particular should keep the veil of a perfect modesty and discretion around themselves and their comings and goings, so as to give no sort of occasion for them to be lightly spoken of."

"The soldiers will make the town look gay," she said musingly, with innocent lack of comprehension of the Dominie's exordium.

"A small benefit that!" he rejoined scornfully. "I

trust I shall not see our lads and lasses' gaping after them, as I have seen in other places before now. You, in particular, Franzje—since I must speak plainly, it seems—I would wish you not to go abroad for the future, save under your father's or mother's protection; it will not be fitting for you to walk alone."

"I may go to Cornelia's, may I not?" she asked, her eyes dilating with the utmost wonder and dismay.

"Not unless accompanied by one of your parents, or at any rate by one of your brothers—the elder ones, Evert or Jan."

"Then I shall scarcely ever go at all," she said sorrowfully; 'for my father and mother have too much to do to go visiting often, and in this fine weather the boys are off to the woods all day long."

"I cannot help it; the adjutant of this regiment is to be billeted on the Bankers, and it will not be well for you to go in and out there, as you have done hitherto."

"Cornelia will think I do not care for her; she is always vexed if I stay away a single day," she said in a low voice.

"Cornelia will find consolations," he replied, with rather sarcastic emphasis; then, more gently, he added, "I have good reasons for giving you this prohibition; you may trust me, Franzje."

"Oh, I do!" she said readily, with such dutiful reliance as was particularly welcome to him at that moment; and though the sweet serenity of her face was still a little troubled, she made no further objection, but followed him into the house—for he had risen to go while she was speaking—without another word.

He had not particularly desired her attendance, for he had wished to say a few private words to her mother, a hard-featured yet not uncomely dame, whom they found in the handsome wainscoted parlour, turning out the con-

tents of an oaken press which stood at one corner of the
fire-place. There was no need, however, of scheming to
secure a *tête-à-tête* ; neither the Dutch pastor nor the estimable matron had the least idea of treating the beautiful
young lady whom they both addressed as " Child," with
any degree of ceremony.

" I was wishing to say a few words to you, Madame
Ryckman," began the pastor at once.

" To be sure, Dominie.—Dear child, go up to your
room, and put your drawers to rights. I have been looking at them, and they are not quite in such fair order as
should be."

Franzje, thus dismissed, went straight to her room as
bidden, and without pausing to take that look in the
glass which is supposed to be the primary business of
every pretty girl on entering her bed-chamber, advanced
to the. tall chest-of-drawers which stood between the
windows, and addressed herself to the task of re--
arranging its contents.

It was rather a gravely pleasant place—this room of
hers—scrupulously clean, primly in order, with the chairs
in rows against the wall, and the carved wood-work of
the old four-poster shining with extremest polish, and
the Dutch-tiled fire-place, on which was represented the
story of Tobit, as white and bright as could be, and the
carpetless floor looking redolent of bees' wax and frequent rubbings.

There was nothing straggling or out of place, but a
rich spray of some creeping plant, which had made bold
to look in at the open window, and even to stretch itself
across the sill with a sort of defiant grace ; and there was
nothing to suggest the idea that the occupant of the room
was young and light-hearted, till Franzje pulled open a
drawer in which was a motley collection of coloured

breast-knots, embroidered aprons, quaint high combs, queer-shaped pincushions, half-finished knitting, and scraps of ribbon—all the little belongings which girls love to accumulate, and which are apt to get into dire confusion from a few vigorous routings of the young fingers when in eager search of some lost article.

There was a certain "order in disorder" observable even here, however ; there was nothing sordid or slovenly in the possessions thus exposed to view—nothing which was out of harmony with the fresh, bright, whole-some look of the owner. The Ryckmans were thriving people, and Franzje was one of the best-dressed, neatest, most-refined, of the maidens of the little colony, and was thought to have the best dowry. She had a number of brothers, certainly—one older, five younger; but Baas[1] Ryckman, as his dependants called him, had made a good deal of money in his earlier days by trading with the Indians, and had also inherited some property from his father, one of the original band of colonists who had settled in Albany in the previous century ; so that he would be able to put his sons out into the world, and yet to portion his daughter comfortably too. Her mother was already beginning to get together a store of household linen for her ; and it was considered quite a settled thing that she should marry in a few years' time, though at present she was a child, whose duty was to think of home tasks, and not of suitors. The education she had received had been rather of a desultory description, but compared with most of her companions of her own sex she was a marvel of intellectual prowess ; for few of them could do more than just read and write, or had a notion of any language except Dutch and English, both of which they learned almost insensibly as soon as they could speak.

[1] A Dutch term, signifying master.

Franzje had had the advantage of stray lessons from the
two most accomplished people in Albany, namely, the
Dominie—who was not a native of America, but had
come from Holland, and from a brilliant university career,
to take the charge of this expatriated flock—and Madame
Schuyler, a clever, cultivated, elderly woman, the wife of
a Colonel Schuyler, who lived at the "Flats," a country
place a mile or two from the town ; and with their help
she had acquired some knowledge of history and geo-
graphy and French, and some acquaintance with general
literature. In theology she was perhaps better versed
than most girls of her age in our own day ; but it must
be confessed that it was more for the sake of pleasing the
Dominie than for any innate preference for the study,
that she plodded so diligently through the laborious com-
mentaries of Dutch divines with which he abundantly
supplied her, and took such pains in preparing for the
weekly catechisings, which she still was considered young
enough to attend. Not that she was an irreligious girl—
far from it ; but the hard dogmatic teaching which she
received from books, side by side with the tender, practical teaching of simple home life, seemed to her something inseparably distinct : it was like the difference
between a science and a handicraft ; and she had not yet
learned to see that the latter might be founded on the
former, that "theology" was in any way to help her in
loving God, and being dutiful to her parents, and patient
with her younger brothers, and reverential towards the
Dominie.

Baas Ryckman was one of the elders of the Dutch
church, and being a thoroughly good man, and somewhat
better educated than most of his colleagues, had been
singled out for special friendship by the pastor, who was
on more intimate terms with him and his family than with

almost any other people in the place except the Schuylers.
Franzje and Evert Ryckman, an orphan lad by name
Killian Barentse, and two or three young Schuylers and
Cuylers, nephews and nieces of the worthy owners of the
"Flats," were supposed to be the Dominie's special favourites among the younger members of his congregation ; and
though he would totally have disclaimed the charge of
favouritism, it was certainly on them that he had placed
his brightest hopes, and to them that he looked to give a
tone to the others.

Perhaps the privilege—like most privileges—was not
quite without its drawbacks : Franzje, as she sorted her
laces and ribbons, wondered to herself whether the Dominie had cut short all the other girls' independent pro-
menades in the same way as hers; and having a shrewd
suspicion that he had not, could not quite bring herself
to be grateful for his special care of her. It was all
right, of course; "the Dominie had said it," and so it
must be ; but it was something new and inexplicable to
the simple-minded, unconscious girl, and she was just a
little inclined to be dolorous over it.

"Franzje!" called a boy's voice from the stairs, "the
soldiers are coming! I saw them in the far distance as
I stood on the roof just now, and I can hear the band.
Look out of your window."

The dismal train of her thoughts was interrupted ; she
ran to the window, and, leaning forward, could just catch
the distant strains of military music. Gradually it drew
nearer and nearer, and became mingled with the steady
tramp of advancing feet ; and as the regiment came in
sight, other heads began to appear at other windows ;
but still the one charming flaxen head, the one rich,
radiant face all aglow with this new excitement, that
peeped out from the bower of twining creepers, was the

loveliest of any, the most attractive sight for the soldiers marching in—at least for those of them that had any taste.

Most of the officers were on foot, like the men; but the colonel and the adjutant were mounted, and of course had a better view in consequence, though the curvetting of their impatient steeds somewhat hindered their attention. As they passed the Ryckmans' house, the adjutant—a young and handsome man—looked up; and evidently something that he saw there fascinated him, for he checked his horse a little, and his dark face wore its most gallant smile.

At this moment the Dominie, who had finished his conversation, issued from the doorway, and seeing the direction of the officer's gaze, he too looked up, turning round to do so. Instantly Franzje drew in her head, her fair open countenance—in which there had been no trace of self-consciousness before, only eager childish delight and curiosity—growing crimson all at once with a burning, painful blush; for was not this the "gaping after the soldiers" which the Dominie had so sternly deprecated?

Yet in that brief moment, the picture that the two men saw had stamped itself in their memory; the picture that *she* saw, in hers. Often, very often afterwards, as she stood musing at that window, would she seem to see again the slight, graceful, and yet haughty figure of the officer on horseback—the vivid scarlet and gold of his uniform, the handsome, brilliant, aristocratic face under the jaunty little cocked hat; and then from the porch below there would seem to issue, hat in hand, the tall, massive, gloomy form of the pastor; and she would see the sunlight falling on his gray uncovered head, and feel once more the grave reproach in his deep thoughtful eyes, which had driven her into the shadow of her room, away

from the soldiers and the music and the bright outside
world—from all which had so pleasantly absorbed her
but a minute before.

She could not forget the young English officer—his
proud, graceful bearing, his smiling glance at her; and yet
she had rather a grudge against him, and all his men, for
having been the unconscious means of depriving her of
her independence, and more especially of her constant
visits to her friend Cornelia.

"It's very tiresome of them to come here," she said to
herself, thinking of the soldiers, before she went to sleep
that night; "but they didn't look as if they would be
rude, and it seems hard that I may not go to Madame
Banker's because of them. I think it was rather crabbed
of the Dominie——" Then she stopped herself. "Oh !
what am I saying? If I were good I should never even
think disrespect. He knows best; he told me to trust
him; so I ought, so I will !"

Her sweet lips parted in oh such a smile ! the little
rosy mouth fixed, as it were, for a moment in a dimpled
trance, the tender filial light growing and growing in the
large starry eyes. Certainly, if Dominie Freylinghausen
were the autocrat of the little community, this was one of
the most confiding and most loyal of his subjects.

CHAPTER II.

Albany.

THE first hours of the summer evening were usually the
pleasantest time in Albany : it was the custom then for
most of the citizens to sit outside their doors in sociable

groups, while young men, old bachelors, and visitors to
the town sauntered up and down, and joined first one
party and then another, as choice or courtesy dictated.

The principal street ran along parallel with the river,
to which the gardens at the back of the houses stretched
away; and from a small steep hill, crowned by a fort,
which rose above the centre of the town, another street,
broader but less long, sloped down, and joined the first.
In this shorter street were the market-place, the guard-
house, the town-hall, and the English and Dutch churches;
but the dwellings of the citizens were mostly in the longer
one; and very comfortable, home-like places they were,
each with its open portico, over which some stately tree
threw a pleasant shade. The trees had been planted in
the early days of the settlement, and were of various
kinds and growths—some quite majestic in their spread-
ing grandeur, others less remarkable, but all combining
to give a pleasant countrified air to the place.

So the English adjutant thought, as he strolled down
the street on the evening of the day after his arrival in
Albany, accompanied by the son of the rich contractor on
whom he had been quartered: but he scanned the groups
under the porticos with a critical, half-disdainful eye,
making comments almost unintelligible to the homely
youth at his side, and not even condescending to pause
for more than a minute before what this latter individual
considered the most attractive party of all.

It was a group of young men and maidens, laughing,
talking, and singing with a simple, easy familiarity, which
never degenerated into rudeness. Some of the girls had
fair, comely faces and pleasant voices, though neither their
figure nor their attire was remarkable for elegance; but
the young officer included them all in one lofty, supercilious stare, and then with the remark, " Rustic, very

rustic," saantered on, careless of the feelings of the lad, who was longing to have a share in the merriment.

"We might as well have stopped and spoken to them," grumbled he. "I know them all : they belong to my Company."

Mr. Vyvian opened his fine dark eyes in amazement. "Pardon me, I scarcely understand your use of that regimental term. May I ask you to explain it, my young friend ? "

" I am called Cornelius," said the boy stoutly, not relishing apparently the linesman's patronizing epithet ; "and I thought everyone knew about the Companies. There are numbers in the town, of one age and another : each contains an equal number of boys and girls—in some they are all children, but in mine they are all nearly grown up, of course. We meet at each other's houses ; and once a year we all go to the hills to gather berries ; and my Company always gathers more than any of the others. We always choose our friends out of our own Company, and generally marry in the Company too. I have settled whom to marry when I come back from my trading voyage."

" You !" said Mr. Vyvian, looking down at the stripling with not altogether unkindly surprise. " Why, it would be time enough to talk of matrimony when you come to my age."

"We marry early in Albany," said the lad phlegmatically. "I expect my sister will be married as soon as Jansen Bleeker comes back from his voyage."

" Is he a sailor ? " asked the adjutant, carelessly.

"Oh no : he has gone on a trading voyage towards the frontier of Canada. He has got lots of guns and powder and beads and blankets, in his canoe, and he will exchange them with the Indians for furs and so on ; then of course he will sell those to advantage, and if he makes enough by the affair, he will set up housekeeping when he comes back."

"You seem to manage matters easily here," said Mr. Vyvian, laughing. "In the old country marriage is quite an affair of state. We have nothing like your Companies either. Are they old institutions among you?"

"I don't know," said Cornelius. "I only know I have belonged to a Company ever since I can remember, and that my younger brothers belong to another. There are better Heads to my Company than to any other in the place."

"Heads!"

"Yes; we always choose out a boy and girl to be our heads—our leaders, as it were. Killian Barentse is one, but he is quite grown up, and won't be here much longer; and Franzje Ryckman is the other. She——"

"Excuse me," said the polished soldier, interrupting, "but whose house are we opposite now? That group would make a picture. I wish I had an artist on the spot."

They were standing opposite the house from whose windows had dawned upon him such a radiant vision on his entrance into the town. On the benches under the large porch now sat the father and mother, and one of the elder sons; while in the corner was a very old man of picturesque and venerable aspect, clad in a sombre suit of almost monastic cut. On the steps the children of the family were at play with two or three little negroes about their own age. And standing with her back to the lookers-on, apparently soothing some little one that had fallen down and hurt itself, was a young girl of noble figure, and with an abundance of shining flaxen hair.

"Can you tell me who these people are?" continued the young man, eagerly.

" Of course; they are the Ryckmans. That is Franzje
standing with her back to us. I was just going to tell
you so when you interrupted me."

" Do you know her ? "

" Why, of course I do," said the young Albanian, exas-
perated by what he thought the Englishman's obtuseness.
" Didn't I tell you she was the Head of my Company ?
Shall we go and speak to them ? Not that we shall have
half the fun here that we should have had at the Waldrons, where you wouldn't stop."

" Let us speak to them, by all means," said the officer,
crossing the street as he spoke. " You must introduce me."

Cornelius Banker had very primitive notions of an
introduction. " Good evening, Franzje ! " he said, as they
came up to her. " This is Lieutenant Vyvian : he is
billeted at our house, you know."

Franzje turned round, still holding the frightened child
by one hand, and greeted Mr. Vyvian with a curtsey
which was a little too stiff for grace. Her father and
mother then came forward, and received him with kindly
dignity, but not in the cordial easy, manner with which
they would have welcomed one of their own townsmen.
" Will you be seated ? " they said courteously, yet not as if
very anxious to detain him.—" And you, Cornelius, are
you come to tell us when the berry-picking is to be ? "

" I should think about the week after next.—Shall we
stay, Sir ? "

And as the young officer seemed nothing loth, they
went up the steps,—the children huddling together out of
the way,—and seated themselves on the bench beside
Madame Ryckman. The old man in the corner bowed
slightly, but did not rise or speak; and Mr. Vyvian
hastily set him down as imbecile, though there was no
trace of such an infirmity in his grave sensible face.

Franzje sat down, with her little brother on her knee, but evidently did not take the compliment of the stranger's visit to herself. He was quite content to look at her merely; she was so like a lovely Madonna, as she bent over the child, and cherished its small tear-stained face between her fair plump hands.

"What do you think of the prospects of the war, sir ?" asked M. Ryckman, alluding not to the war of Independence, which had not yet begun, but to the struggle between the French and the English, and their respective allies among the natives and settlers, for the possession of Canada and the neighbouring States.

"I am very hopeful. Loudun, our new general, is a first-rate soldier—more than a match for Montcalm, I believe."

"So people say. When do you expect to be called to the front ?"

The young officer shrugged his shoulders. "Impossible to tell. For the present we seem destined to be the guests of your hospitable town, sir. I hope our presence here imparts a feeling of additional security to the ladies. The Indians would find my men pretty tough customers, I can tell them."

"The only Indians that come here are the Mohawks, and they are our very good friends," said Evert Ryckman, with a smile.

"I thought I saw one hanging about the town this afternoon ; but he was dressed in good broadcloth, and looked almost like a gentleman."

"Then he was not a Mohawk—I mean a Mohawk would not have appeared in broadcloth. You must mean Killian Barentse, I should think : some people think him like an Indian." And Evert exchanged looks with his sister.

"He is handsomer than any Indian I have ever seen," said she, in her gentle voice : "and so is Cortlandt Cuyler, who is generally thonght like an Indian too."

"Well, I suppose it must have been one or the other. The Cuylers are some of the principal people here, are they not?"

"Yes, M. Cuyler is our mayor; and there is no one more thought of than they," said Madame Ryckman, "except perhaps the Schuylers, and our Patroon and his family, the Renselaers. The Philipses and the Cortlandts are indeed very much respected; but we do not see much of them in Albany, their lands lie half way down the river, towards New York."

"Where do the Schuylers live? I have heard of them before. Colonel Schuyler has extraordinary influence among the Indians, has he not?"

"He has indeed, and so had his father before him." M. Ryckman answered this time. "He is a wonderful man; and his wife, Aunt Schuyler, as we call her, is a wonderful woman. They live at the Flats, a country place about two miles from here; but they are at New York at present."

"That is a pity : I was counting on them for society. They are above the usual run of people here, are they not?"

"They are both very highly educated," was the answer, somewhat stiffly given; "though perhaps not so learned as our pastor, M. Freylinghausen."

"And, my father, you should say how delightful Aunt Schuyler is," said Franzje, looking up brightly : "there is nobody like her."

"Such a testimony from *you* makes me indeed regret her absence at this time," said Mr. Vyvian gallantly.

Her great blue eyes were lifted and lowered again in

silence. She looked as if she did not quite comprehend him.

"The Schuylers are very hospitable to the military," said Evert.

"Hospitality is one of the Albanian virtues, I am sure," rejoined the Englishman, with an agreeable smile.

"I don't know," said M. Ryckman honestly : "we are very sociable among ourselves, but I am not sure that we take to strangers much—it depends on how we find them. The Royal American Company, who are quartered in the fort, are quiet decent people, and have become respected among us."

There was a certain awkwardness in this speech, which all felt, except the silent old man, who seemed in a state of abstraction. Just at this moment, however, Mr. Vyvian's attention was diverted by a sound of tinkling bells, and there came in sight a large herd of cows, pacing soberly along, apparently without any driver to direct their movements. As they passed the Ryckmans' door, two among them, fine gentle-looking creatures, detached themselves from the herd, and came and stood quietly under the large tree close to the porch.

And then—oh, the laughing and chattering and scudding about that began among the children, both white and black. "Now I can have my supper!" "Oh, I hope they'll give plenty of milk to-night!" "Call Deborah to milk them!" "Let's run and fetch some vegetables for my dear *dear* brown cow!"

Such were the shouts and exclamations ; and in another minute two tall negresses, with milking-pails, came out of the house, and proceeded to their task, surrounded, watched, and pestered by the crew of lively children.

Very much the same scene was soon repeated at the doors of other houses all down the street ; and the fastidious soldier looked on, half amused, half contemptuous, but could not find it in his heart to decline the goblet of fresh frothing milk, which Franzje presently tendered to him.

Dishes of crisp brown cakes were soon after handed round ; and the children sat down on the steps again to eat their homely supper, talking merrily between each mouthful.

It was a little bit of Arcadia ; but it would not have had much charm for Russell Vyvian but for the presiding nymph. She was one of those people who adorn common life, but never seem to belong to it ; her grand noble style of beauty, all the more remarkable from her extreme youth, associated her involuntarily in his mind with some of the heroines of history—the queens regnant of European *salons :* when she spoke, the fresh young tones, the childish unstudied sentiments, almost startled him.

Cornelius Banker had a high respect for her as being one of the Heads of his Company, and, in fact, respect was exactly the feeling which the whole Ryckman family inspired ; but he was not on such easy terms with her as with some of the other damsels of the place ; and as the hour drew nigh for the substantial supper, of which all who were beyond childhood in Albany were accustomed to partake, he threw out strong hints that it was time for his guest and himself to be returning home.

The Englishman rose reluctantly, shook hands all round, except with the grey-beard, whose quiet bow was repelling ; and they turned homewards, accompanied part of the way by Evert Ryckman, a tall, bright-faced youth, whom Mr. Vyvian secretly much preferred to his young friend Cornelius.

As soon as Evert had left them, he began to put the said young friend through a sort of catechism.

" How old is Mademoiselle Ryckman ? "

" Franzje ? Oh, about sixteen. Isn't she big ? "

The young officer drew back in half real half simulated
horror. " Big ! Is that the way you describe her ? She
is tall, grand, magnificent ; but I should never think of
calling her big."

" Oh, but she is big, though ! She's bigger than any
girl in the Company ; and she doesn't look well beside
any of us but Killian Barentse. He's big too."

" What, the young Indian ? Yes, he's a fine tall fellow.
I suppose those two always dance together ? "

" Dance ! " said Cornelius, making his eyes very round.

" Yes ; why not ? Don't you ever have balls and parties ? "

" We have parties ; but we don't dance. I never heard
of such a thing."

" Never heard of dancing ? "

" No—oh yes, though, there's something in the Bible
about it, isn't there ? David danced before the Ark, didn't
he ? The Dominie says that was in a sort of sacred rapture."

" So you are all waiting to dance till you feel yourselves
similarly inspired, eh ? " sneered the young man contemptuously.

" I don't know what you mean," said the blunt Cornelius.

" Get the Dominie to explain it," laughed Mr. Vyvian.
" I suppose it was he that I saw coming out of the Ryckmans' yesterday. Does the fair Franzje attend his ministrations ? "

" Does she go to the Dutch church, do you mean ? Of
course she does. Her father is an elder, and so is mine.
She is always at the catechising too, and answers—why,
it is like a book to hear her ! "

" She is as wise as she is fair, then ? "

" Well, she is too clever for most of us. Aunt Schuyler
and the Dominie, between them, have fairly crammed her
with learning."

" She speaks English perfectly, I perceive. Who was
that old man in the corner, who never opened his lips !
Is he childish, or dumb ? or did he hold his tongue because he can only speak Dutch ? "

" That was old Jan Ryckman, Franzje's great-uncle.
He could talk as well as anybody if he chose ; but he
never speaks unless he is addressed—they never do."

" *Who* never do ? "

" Those who have joined the Society. There is a set of
old people among us who live in a retired kind of way,
never talk except to each other, and then all about religion. They meet sometimes, and sing psalms. I should
think it must be dull ; but they seem to like it."

" Are they monks ? Do they live all together ? "

" Oh no ; they live with their relations. They are
mostly old bachelors or widowers. Aunt Schuyler says
they are a kind of lay-brothers—whatever that may be."

" I comprehend. But altogether you seem to have an
odd set of arrangements here, what with your Companies,
and so on. What have you by way of amusement ? "

" Oh, there is the berry-picking, and the meetings at
one another's houses, and the going out in a canoe to one
of the islands, or driving out into the bush ; and better
than all, there is the wild-duck shooting in spring and
autumn, and the sturgeon fishing ; and in winter the
skating and sleighing. Besides, if the town gets dull,
one can take one's gun and one's slave, and go off to the
woods. I was just thinking of going off, when I heard
your regiment was coming."

" And you believed we should dissipate the dullness ?

I shall certainly do my best towards that result. We must see if we cannot make your good steady-going Albanians open their eyes a little."

Cornelius did not seem altogether grateful for this promise. "We have done very well," he replied rather sulkily. "Albany is a nice place enough for those who are used to it. I don't like New York half as well, though we go there almost every year."

The Englishman smiled to himself: he was thinking of the gay capitals of the old world; and, compared with them, Albany seemed to him dull and primitive indeed. But he revealed no more of his sentiments, and did justice to the homely but ample supper which he was invited to share on his return to the Bankers', not forgetting to treat with all due gallantry the fair daughters of the house, Franzje's friend, Cornelia, or Keetje as she was generally called in the family circle, and a younger maiden, Engeltje by name, who was desperately afraid of him, and could not speak without blushing, but whose sweet shy eyes, of a soft grey, attracted him more than Cornelia's unflinching black ones.

So attentive and so flattering was he, that Keetje's silly heart bounded, and she began to compare him mentally with Jansen Bleeker, rather to the disadvantage of the latter; but for all that, his dreams were haunted not by either of these two bonnie damsels, with their somewhat bourgeoise prettiness, but by a glorious girl with flaxen locks, and the calm bearing of a queen.

CHAPTER III.

On the Hills.

TIME passed rather heavily for the young officers of the
British regiment in Albany. They happened to be what
now-a-days would be called a fast set, though the phrase
was not invented then; and the simple pleasures of the
citizens were not much to their taste. Whenever Mr.
Vyvian looked dull, Cornelius or Cornelia were sure to
try to cheer him by telling him they would take him to
the berry-picking; and they had no conception how mild
and pitiable a bit of dissipation this great gala of theirs
appeared to him.

It was thought a marked favour to invite any one not
belonging to one of the Companies, and Killian Barentse,
in his position as Head of Cornelius's Company, rather
demurred to the invitation.

" We don't want this dandified officer, do we, Franzje ?"
said he at one of the private meetings of the Company.
" I am sure he will be only in the way."

" I suppose Cornelius will take care of him," she said,
indifferently, while the fine Indian face of Killian was
bent eagerly on her, waiting for her words.

" Or Cornelia," said he rather maliciously. " They must
promise to walk one on each side of him, and take all the
burden of entertainment on their shoulders."

" You mean, we mustn't let him speak ·a word to
Franzje. I understand your tactics very well," said Cornelius, with a sage nod and chuckle.

Killian's dark cheek flushed with a sudden glow.

" Of course," went on Cornelius, seeing the shot had

told, "we know who it is keeps Franzje away from
our house now Mr. Vyvian is there; but no one can
prevent his thinking her the most beautiful girl in
Albany."

"I don't want to prevent him," said Killian, angrily;
"but he need not think we look to him to tell us whom to
admire. As for Franzje's going to your house, you know
very well that I never presume to interfere with her
movements. I have not the shadow of a right to do so,"
he added rather bitterly.

She glanced up at him kindly with a sweet and sooth-
ing smile, though a startled blush was on her cheek.
"Never mind, Killian," she said softly; "we all know
Cornelius is only joking."

But the pretty Cornelia, whose feelings had been considerably ruffled by her brother's reference to Mr. Vyvian's
admiration of Franzje, here broke in pettishly, "It is all
very well to call it a joke, Franzje; but you know yourself you have never been inside our doors since Mr.
Vyvian came. Some people would call that modesty,
I suppose; but I think to be always afraid of people's
falling in love with one is almost as bad as wishing that
they should."

It was a sight to see the grand beautiful eyes opening
wide in their amazed innocence; but Franzje was still
enough of a child to take the accusation in a very matter-
of-fact way. "If you mean that for me, Cornelia," she
said, with the childish dignity which sat so prettily on
her, "you must know it is all quite nonsense. I have
stayed at home more lately because the Dominie wished
it; that is the whole and sole reason."

"And so you are to drop your friends whenever the
Dominie chooses," said Cornelia, pouting. "I call it very
unkind. After all, too, I don't know what reward you

get for your obedience; I thought the Dominie seemed
quite put out with you last Sunday."

There was no doubt that Franzje was really wounded
now. She drooped her stately head, and could scarcely
keep the tears from rushing to her eyes. It was true
that, spite of her dutiful obedience to his wishes, the
Dominie had not been half so benignant to her as usual
since the officers arrived in the town, and her loyal little
heart was sorely troubled by it.

"For shame, for shame!" said several of the company in
a breath. And Killian Barentse came to the rescue yet
more boldly.

"You have no right to speak in that way to your Head,
Cornelia," he said severely. "I should like to hear what
the Dominie would say to some of your remarks. I
believe all of us, except Franzje, have been talking foolishly since the name of Mr. Vyvian came up, and that
makes me the more sorry that he is coming to the berry-
picking. You know we have scarcely ever had any one
but ourselves—not even the Dominie."

"I should hope not; *he would* spoil sport," said Cornelius Banker.

Killian looked at him steadily. "I don't know what
is come over you two," he said. "It must be pretty sort
of sport if our Dominie's presence would spoil it. Of
course, he is older and graver than we are; but you know
very well he never objects to innocent mirth."

"Spoken like the Dominie himself!" said Cornelius,
with a bow of mock homage.

But here some of the other lads of the Company laid
hold of him, and half in jest, half in earnest, forced him
down on his knees, and made him beg Killian's pardon
for all his impertinence.

"They are not like themselves now, those two," said

Killian, when the meeting had broken up, and he was walking home with Franzje and her brother Evert. "I wish these officers had never come into the town. The Dominie says he thinks they are a bad set."

"He made up his mind they were going to be," said Franzje, a little petulantly.

Killian glanced at her in surprise. "I do believe you wish Mr. Vyvian to come to the berry-picking," he remarked, with keen jealousy in his tone.

"I wish it because Cornelia and Cornelius wish it. I do not see that it need make much difference to anyone. We can get our berries all the same, Killian; I am determined that our Company shall pick the most of all. Last year the Company of the Red outdid us; but they shall not this time, shall they?" And she looked so eager and animated over this trifling ambition of hers, that Killian was reassured.

"She is thinking more about the berries, and the honour of the Company, than about Mr. Vyvian," he said to himself complacently. "That is well."

Killian Barentse was an orphan, and lived with his grandfather, an aged widower, who belonged to "the Society," and, like old Jan Ryckman, never spoke except when addressed, and though always cheerful and kind, took little interest in anything but subjects connected with religion.

It was but a dull home for the youth, and its silence and gravity had left their impress on his character. His appearance and manners had something of the dignified quiet of the people whom he so resembled in feature : he was brave and enterprising, but he was not gay; he was industrious and painstaking, but not intellectual, though he consorted much with the Dominie, seldom sought any relaxation but that afforded by his gun and the frequent

meetings of his Company, and never joined the band of
careless, dissipated youths who found their pleasure in
such strange exploits as stealing pigs or turkeys from
their neighbours after dark, and holding a grand midnight
carousal at one of the inns of the town on the strength of
the spoils thus accumulated.

Now that he was shooting up towards manhood, his love
for Franzje Ryckman had begun to be an acknowledged
fact in the place; and it was surmised that when he
returned from the trading voyage among the Indians,
upon which he was ‚ to start the next spring, he would
claim her as his bride ; some said with good probability of
success, as his character stood high, he was known to be
possessed of some means, and had always been a favourite
with all the Ryckmans, young and old.

He himself was doubtful and diffident. Franzje liked
him—yes, certainly liked him ; and it was just the sort
of quiet affectionate regard which frequently led on to
marriage in Albany, where no one thought of love as
a passion, and where courtship was almost always a very
simple and matter-of-fact affair ; but he had learnt to
feel that Franzje was not quite like other girls—that
there was a strength and depth in her nature which
made her love a great and precious thing, not so easily
to be gained, not so to be taken for granted as the less
discerning people around him judged.

"She is quite a child still," he said to himself, "and
loves her father and mother better than anybody else ;
it is quite natural that she should not care for me as I
do for her—I, who have no one else ; besides, I am not so
worth caring for. Perhaps in time she will come really
to care for me—perhaps when I go away, and come
back thoroughly a man, she will no longer think of me
as just like one of her brothers, as she does now. At

any rate, I will have patience. I would serve seven years
for her as cheerfully as ever Jacob did for Rachel."

Why he should feel an incipient jealousy of Mr. Vyvian
he could not tell; it was not the officer's good looks that
caused it; he was handsome enough himself for the matter
of that: it was perhaps, though Killian did not know it, a
feeling that in Mr. Vyvian's polish, in his ready cleverness
and abundant information, Franzje might find a something interesting from its novelty, and peculiarly attractive
to her from the natural bent of her mind.

She was better educated, as has been said, than most of
the maidens of Albany: she had a native grace and re-
finement about her which most of them lacked. She
read English books with avidity, liked poetry which
Killian thought insufferable, and had tastes and aspira-
tions which had never yet been gratified. The Dominie
and Aunt Schuyler had combined to make her what she
was; and yet she was different from both of them, with
that distinct individuality which no one can give or take
away. The Dominie had occasionally tried to repress it,
when it interfered with his views for her; but even he
could not eradicate it; and Killian, whose intellect was
not so profound, but whose sympathies were quicker,
felt perhaps better than any one what Franzje was, and
how little he himself could suffice to her, even though
she liked him. But even he did not know Franzje
thoroughly—the beautiful child, whose face was a prophecy of something to which the soul within had not
yet attained.

The sun rose gloriously on the day of the berry-picking;
and the hickory and maple trees that lined the road up
to the hills, were splendid in their flush of autumn
colouring. Early in the morning, groups of youths and
maidens, big and little children, began to assemble in the

principal street; and as each Company was to start
together in a body, the Ryckmans and the Bankers, with
Mr. Vyvian, soon found themselves side by side. "The
Ryckmans," however, only meant in this instance, Franzje,
Evert, and Jan; the younger children belonged to a
different Company, and had already started, as they were
likely to be longer on the road. Each member of each
Company was provided with a covered basket of Indian
manufacture, the handle of which was tastefully adorned
with ribbons, red, blue, yellow, white, or green, according to the insignia of their particular company. Franzje's
and Killian's was known as the Company of the Blue,
so the baskets of all their party were tied up with blue
ribbons; and Mr. Vyvian had been presented by Cornelia with a similar one, decorated with her own fair
hands. He walked along swinging it on one finger
with an air of half-disdainful good nature; while a young
ensign of his regiment, who had been likewise invited,
pretended to be overwhelmed by the weight of *his* basket,
and empty though it was, hung it on the end of a walk-
ing-stick, and carried it across his shoulders with many
professions of intense fatigue.

Franzje and some young friends of hers, with her
brothers and Killian, started off at a brisk pace directly
the Company was pronounced complete, and soon out-
stripped Cornelia and the young officers, who were acting
as her attendant squires. "Keetje" was more gaily dressed
than most of the maidens; and her decided prettiness in
some degree palliated the foolish hoydenish airs which
amused the young Englishmen, but certainly did not
captivate them. The ensign said to himself that she was
much easier to get on with than any other girl he had
met in Albany, and was so far content; but Mr. Vyvian,
though he was very gallant towards her, and paid her

outrageous compliments, vowed to himself that he would
not dance attendance upon her longer than he could
help.

"It is very well for the beautiful shy creature up there
to run away from me," he soliloquized, as a turn in the
winding hilly road showed him a glimpse of Franzje and
her party far in advance; "it is much better than this
other girl's coquettish forwardness; but I can tell her
she shall not escape me so easily. When once we arrive
at our destination, I will see if I cannot contrive to cut
out the young Indian."

It was easier said than done; for Killian seemed like
Franzje's shadow throughout the day, and was so intent
on filling her basket, that he almost forgot his own.
Even during the sociable mid-day meal, which they ate
pic-nic fashion, seated on the ground, the young queen of
the Blue Company was so hemmed in by her affectionate
subjects, so guarded by her fellow-sovereign, that Mr.
Vyvian found it almost impossible to get speech of her
without being heard by the whole assemblage. She was
very quietly, even' plainly, dressed—indeed, scarcely any
of the maidens, but Cornelia, had attempted anything like
a gala costume—but she looked radiant; all the sunshine
of the day seemed reflected in those glorious blue eyes, in
"the red young mouth, and the hair's young gold."

The Company hung upon her words as if they had been
rubies and diamonds; though, truth to say, they were not
remarkable for any portentous amount of wisdom. She
was childishly eager about the quantity of berries that
had been, or were likely to be, gathered; childishly proud
of the tasteful decorations of the Blue Company's baskets,
and nearly as ready as any of her companions to deride
the decorative efforts of the other Companies.

"Did you ever see anything so heavy and clumsy as

that great roll of red ribbons ? " she asked, indicating an unfortunate basket belonging to one of the Company of the Red who were camping near them.

"Never !" "It's hideous !" "That Red Company has not the slightest taste !" and so on, were the loyal responses from all sides.

But Mr. Vyvian, raising his musical voice a little, said distinctly, "Of course I am not so ungrateful and tasteless as to deny my preference to the blue, but may I be pardoned for thinking that that massive coil of scarlet is rather rich and good in its effect ? Is it heresy in your opinion, Mademoiselle Ryckman, to be able to admire the baskets of another Company ? I see everybody is beginning to look shocked."

Franzje's blush made her look more beautiful than ever. "I dare say we are prejudiced," she faltered. "We have a sort of little rivalry about these baskets ; but of course a stranger and a visitor can't be expected to enter into that."

"And of course Mr. Vyvian must be allowed to admire red," simpered Cornelia, with a glance at his handsome scarlet uniform.

"Nay, I don't admire it so much as blue," he said. "I fully admit that blue ribbons, blue eyes, blue flowers, are all more charming than any others."

A glance at the blue-eyed Franzje pointed his words ; but his gallantry might have been thrown away on the matter-of-fact young people around him, had not Cornelia's jealousy quickened her apprehension. "Perhaps you admire blue spectacles too," she said promptly, with a little toss of her head, and a saucy sparkle of her eyes, such as only dark eyes can give. "My mother says Franzje will have to take to glasses soon if she goes on wearing out her sight over big books."

There was a general laugh, for Franzje's learning was rather a joke among the not very intellectual young people of Albany. And before Mr. Vyvian could reply—

"Oh, defend us from anything of that sort!" cried out the young ensign, who had not heard of her fame in this respect. "I hoped we had left all the bookworms behind us in England."

"You certainly will not find them here," said Killian Barentse : "there are some well-read ladies among us, like Aunt Schuyler, but they do not shut themselves up to study, nor make any display of their learning. Shall we go and pick berries again, Franzje? Everyone seems to have done."

She thanked him with, oh! such a bright, grateful glance : he had turned off the allusion so beautifully, with such ready understanding of her distress, with such delightful tact.

"Killian, how good you are! I could have kissed you for saying that!" she said gaily, as they stooped together over a berry-bush, out of hearing of the others.

To her surprise the brown face became crimson ; he looked down at her with a strange glance, his lips quivering. "You shouldn't say that to me," he said, in an agitated voice. "You can't mean it—at least if you had you wouldn't have said it."

Her own cheeks were hot now with the terrible agonizing blush of maidenly shame and confusion. "I forgot you were not Evert," she stammered. "Killian, we used to be exactly like brother and sister ; I don't see why we shouldn't be still ; at least—oh, have I said something wrong again?—I mean, I don't see why we need either of us misunderstand a silly jesting phrase, which means nothing, except that one is grateful."

"You might be grateful to Mr. Vyvian, but you would not use it to him."

D

The blushes seemed to scorch her cheeks. "Use it to Mr. Vyvian! Killian, what do you take me for? Why do you say such strange things?"

"Nor would you to the Dominie," he pursued gravely and sadly.

"To the Dominie!" she rejoined, in a sort of terrified amazement, much as a young Roman Catholic might have said "To the Pope!" "No, of course not. Do you think it possible that anyone could take such a liberty?"

"Yet he kisses you sometimes—at least, I know he *has* done so."

A very sweet meditative smile moved the corners of her troubled mouth. "Yes," she said, quietly; "but that is quite a different thing; he treats me like a child, you know. Killian, why do you mystify me, and make me feel so ashamed and uncomfortable? I am sorry I have vexed you. I spoke foolishly, and without thought, just as I might have done to Evert or Jan."

"I know; that is what I complain of," said Killian bitterly.

She opened her large eyes silently, half offended, wholly puzzled.

"I want you to think of me not as you do of your brothers, nor yet quite as you do of Mr. Vyvian, or the Dominie, but—" he began haltingly, finding it difficult to explain himself. He was interrupted by a laugh from her, a clear, joyous laugh of irrepressible amusement.

"I am not to think of you quite as I do of the Dominie! O Killian, Killian, do you think there is any danger? Are you joking with me, or what?"

"It is you that are joking," he said coldly, "and will not see that I am in earnest. Can't you see that you are everything to me, and that I want to be something to you? That I don't want to be classed with Evert and

Jan? I know I am not your equal in many things; but at least no one can understand you better or prize you more than I do. Mr. Vyvian may admire your beauty, and the Dominie may praise your cleverness——"

"He never does," she said, indignantly; "he never praises me at all. And, Killian, I am sure he would not like you to flatter me, or to be always talking of Mr. Vyvian, and trying to make me think foolish things about him. I shall not stay to hear any more. I am sure I ought not." And closing down her basket-lid hastily, she ran away, seeking not only to escape Killian, but all her other young companions as well.

Poor little girl! she was waking up into womanhood, but waking painfully, feeling as if the self-conscious thoughts that had been aroused in her the last week or two must be wrong as well as perplexing, though they had been aroused by influences from without, and had not sprung spontaneously from within. She had had a happy, innocent, simple life, full of home indulgence and home love, with nothing more to hope or dread than approval or blame from the Dominie, with no whispers of flattery, no importunate admiration, nothing to excite premature feelings of any description. And now that Killian —her friend since babyhood, her pleasant play-fellow— should be the one to force new unwelcome exciting thoughts upon her, seemed to her very hard, very unjust.

Love-making at an early age was common in Albany: there had been instances of marriage between youths and maidens quite as young as Killian and Franzje; but, spite of the precocity of her beauty, she was unusually simple and child-like in mind, and no thought of love or lovers had come to trouble her peace, or arouse her share of woman's vanity, until now. An instinctive, ever-deepen-

ing, hero-worship occupied her heart, unsuspected even by
herself; and perhaps this had helped to keep her regard
for Killian from even the slightest tinge of romantic sentiment, and had blinded her to the touch of romance which
was creeping into the old familiar affection which he entertained towards her. She had seen other friendships ripen
into love, as Killian's friendship for her was ripening now;
but she had never expected this development in his case,
and was vexed and astonished to find it had already
begun.

She left the belt of shrubs, where the berry-pickers
were busy, behind her, and wandered into the dark pine-
wood which crowned the summit of the hill. She did
not penetrate very far into it, but walked along not far
from the edge, till she came to a place where a sort of
ravine opened, and a waterfall rushed down the precipi-
tous slope. The roar of the leaping, foaming water was
delightful to her; it brought a sense of freshness, of
liberty, an escape from the trouble of her own thoughts.
The little birch-trees that fringed each side of the ravine,
the lofty gloom of the pine-forest that stretched away
behind it, the gorgeous tawny gold of the shumach, with
its clusters of vivid scarlet berries, that here and there
sprang out like flames from the pines—all these things
gave her a keen sense of joy and relief, a feeling of unwonted admiration, which drew her mind quite away from
the small shadows that had crept into her life.

She sat down under a sycamore-tree, her hands folded
in her lap, her head a little thrown back—a very picture
of happy thoughtfulness, of thoughtful peace.

" It reminds me of that bit of Milton," she said to herself, " that the Dominie is so fond of."

She was still endeavouring to recall the lines exactly to
her memory, and hearing nothing but the roar of the

waterfall, when a shadow fell on the tufted grass at her feet, and looking up she saw Mr. Vyvian. If she had met him fresh from Killian's bewildering talk, she would have been annoyed and frightened; but now she was rapt away from all self-consciousness into a joyful calm. So she only lifted her eyes quietly and trustfully, and smilingly waved her hand towards the torrent as an apology for not hearing the words which he seemed to be addressing to her. He took the hint, and placed himself on the grass beside her in a careless, elegant attitude, watching as she did the swift descent of the foam-tossed waters, though with widely different thoughts.

He liked her for her calmness—for her apparent freedom from any suspicion that he had come there in search of her; but his vanity was mortified by her evident indifference to his presence, and he was not at all sorry when at length she rose to go. Not that he meant her to depart without him; but that, once away from the waterfall, he could exercise his eloquent tongue, and make her attend to him—make her listen and respond. It was very well to be lost in the contemplation of Nature, but not to the ignoring of his handsome self.

"Is this a favourite haunt of yours ? " he said, as they turned away from the ravine, and walked back together through the pine-glades to the scene of their day's industry.

"I like it very much," she said, shyly; "but I seldom go there, it is too far away from home."

"I am so glad my steps led me that way," he continued. "I got a little tired of stooping over bushes in search of berries, which I have bad taste enough to think most particularly unpleasant eating, so I thought I would explore the wood a little. Neither Cornelius nor his sister told me of the waterfall. I suppose they do not care much themselves for the beauties of Nature, and it never occurred to them that I might."

"On these days we think most of the berries," said Franzje, simply ; "we always want our Company to have more than any other. I came a good many years to the hills without ever going near the waterfall ; but one day, on our Dominie's birthday, he took Jan and me for a long walk, and brought us to this place, and since that I have always liked to come here when I could."

"And none of your companions share your taste ?"

"I don't know. I did not ask any of them to come with me, or no doubt they would."

"You seemed very happy all alone, smiling and dreaming to yourself, spinning a bridge of fancies over the torrent, I suppose. I ought to apologize for having interrupted the day-dream."

"There wasn't any day-dream, sir," she said, smiling. "I was only trying to remember some lines of poetry, but I could not get further than this." And she repeated a few of the lines to him.

"I am afraid I cannot help you," he said, surprised to hear her quote English poetry. "I do not even recognize the author."

She turned her serene eyes upon him with frankest wonder. An English gentleman who did not recognize Milton appeared to her a very marvellous phenomenon.

"They are from 'Paradise Lost,'" she said.

"Who taught you to like 'Paradise Lost ?' I did not know the British classics had found their way to Albany," he replied, with some amusement.

"I read it first with Aunt Schuyler ; and then the Dominie gave me a copy of it, a beautiful copy, for my very own."

"Indeed ! your Dominie must be a man of taste. I

suppose, however, he has not allowed you to read Shakespeare ? ”

“ I have read most of it at the Flats. Aunt Schuyler read a great deal of it aloud to me. She reads so beautifully, it makes one almost *see* the scenes ! ’

“ Ah, if you could see ‘ Hamlet ’ as we have it on the London boards—that would indeed make it real to you.”

The innocent eyes of the young American grew wide in mystified amazement.

“ See it *on the boards,* sir ? ” she repeated, uncomprehendingly.

“ On the stage, I mean. You know, of course, that these plays are acted sometimes ? ”

“ I don’t think I quite understand,” she said, still puzzled. “ Shakespeare’s Plays are poems, are they not ? ”

“ Yes ; but they were not written merely to be read—they were written for the stage. Shakespeare himself is thought to have been an actor. Ah,” added Mr. Vyvian, with a little laugh, “ I see I am still talking Greek to you. You must indeed have been brought up in Arcadian simplicity.”

“ I know I must seem very ignorant to you,” she said, blushing, and hanging her head a little, under the idea that he was laughing at her. “ I never knew that a play meant anything but a poem in dialogue.”

“ Then what enjoyments there are in store for you ! You say Madame Schuyler makes the plays seem real to you when she reads them ; but would they not seem ten times more real if you heard the different speeches delivered by different people, dressed to represent correctly the various characters, and on a stage, a raised place, with scenes painted to resemble those in which Shakespeare places his heroes ? It was for this kind of representation that

Shakespeare wrote them, and nothing else can give them their full force. Do you understand now what I mean?"

"Yes; I think I do," she said, her eyes kindling. "How strange and beautiful it must be! But we have nothing like that in Albany."

"No, you are centuries behind the rest of the world; but never mind that, you will not live here all your days, I suppose?"

She opened her eyes wider still than in her surprise of a few minutes before. "Why not? My father has promised to take me to New York some day; but we shall not stay there, you know; we shall come back here, of course."

"You may marry, and leave the place."

"No, we always marry here in the town," she answered, with grave simplicity, as if the question were one of mere ordinary routine, and admitted of no speculation.

"Does that mean young Barentse?" thought Mr. Vyvian to himself. "Hardly; she would not take the subject so coolly, if it were not still in the abstract." Aloud he said, "Well, if you are so determined on staying in Albany, if the mountain will not come to Mohammed, Mohammed must come to the mountain. What should you say to our getting up a theatre here?"

"A theatre, sir?"

"Yes—a place to act plays in; a large room, or covered place of some sort, with a stage raised at one end for the actors, and the rest of the space filled with chairs for the lookers-on. I wonder if that large barn of M. Banker's could be converted into one."

"The best barn of all is at the Flats: it is quite a beautiful place; but I should not think Colonel Schuyler could spare it. And besides, who could act? I know no one but Aunt Schuyler and the Dominie who can read Shakespeare well."

The young officer could not repress his amusement. "Old Madame Schuyler (who, by the by, I hear is very stout) and your gaunt austere Dominie as play-actors ! The idea is most delicious ! I had no idea you could be so satirical, Mademoiselle. They might possibly do to represent two of the witches in 'Macbeth,' and Freyling-hausen might perhaps make an effective Ghost in the apparition scene in 'Hamlet'—those are the only characters that occur to me as suitable."

"You would not say so if you had heard the Dominie read Henry the Fourth's speech about sleep, or some of Wolsey's," said Franzje, colouring. "I am sorry if what I said sounded disrespectful. I did not mean it so."

"I am sure you did not : you are the very perfection of innocence and propriety; the disrespect was mine. But seriously, without disparaging your good friends' talents, I do not think I could exactly invite them to join my theatrical company. When I started the plan, I was thinking that my brother officers and I could be the actors ; we have sometimes joined in such things before."

"Have you ?" said Franzje, with innocent respect, which would have been greater but for his patronizing flattery of herself. "And what play would you act ? I think I would almost rather see the 'Merchant of Venice' than any other."

"Oh, we must eschew Shakespeare altogether; he is beyond the reach of such tyros as we are. We must try some light comedy."

"Will it be at all like the 'Taming of the Shrew ?'"

"Well, not exactly ; the dialogue will be in prose, perhaps ; but I must not tell you more about it now. Only will you promise me that if I can arrange a play you will come and see it ?"

"Oh, I shall be only too glad! But might my father and mother and Jan and Evert come too? Perhaps, though, we shall fill up your room too much; everybody will want to see your play; there has never been anything like it in Albany before."

"Whoever comes, or does not come, I will engage that there shall be room for you, and as many of your family as you like to bring. But I want you to promise me one thing more—it is to keep this plan of mine secret for the present."

A vague trouble sprang into her face. "There is not anything wrong in it, is there?" she asked timidly.

"Nothing whatever; but I want to give your good townsfolk a surprise." And he added to himself, "I don't want to set any of the old Puritans meddling."

"Oh," she said, with a smile, which would not have shone out so brightly if she could have heard the unspoken as well as the spoken part of the sentence, "then of course I will not tell. But I thought you were going to ask M. Banker about the barn?"

"Yes, I must take the Bankers into the secret; but otherwise I shall confide in no one but you. How can I thank you enough for giving me this delightful stroll with you to relieve the tedium of the day?"

"I thought we met by chance," said the straightforward maiden, uneasy under his gallantry.

"It was chance on your side, no doubt; I will not say whether it was on mine. Mademoiselle Ryckman, I am anxious that we should be friends. It has pained me to hear that you avoid the Bankers' house on my account. Who has taught you to make such a bugbear of me?"

The lovely colour on her face deepened once more into a·burning, painful glow. "No one has taught me," she stammered. "I was told not to go to the Bankers' alone before I ever saw you—before you came."

"But the prohibition had some reference to my coming?"

She was too true to say it had not.

"And may I ask *whose* command it is that you go on obeying so implicitly?"

An older or more sophisticated maiden would have questioned his right to ask anything about it. Franzje, with a strange tortured humiliated feeling, for which she could not quite account, answered reluctantly, "It was the Dominie." And then, as the smile on his face stung her into pride, she added, almost haughtily, "The Dominie's counsel to us is always good, and we consider ourselves bound to follow it."

"How I wish I were the Dominie for a little while!" said Mr. Vyvian emphatically.

She did not answer; and in another minute they emerged from the shadow of the pines upon the open hill-side.

Franzje's brothers rushed up to her open-mouthed. "Franzje, we could not think what had become of you; and Killian has been looking for you everywhere. Cornelia said you must be with Mr. Vyvian, but we did not believe her."

The transparent ingenuous face was clouded over now.

"I met Mr. Vyvian at the waterfall, and we have walked back together," she answered, with a deprecating glance at him, and a feeling of annoyance with her too out-spoken brothers. "Killian had no occasion to search for me; I was quite safe." She added to herself, "It was from him that I ran away."

And though scarcely anyone suspected it, the result of that autumn berry-picking was an estrangement, destined to grow wider, between the young king and queen of the Company of the Blue.

Had Mr. Vyvian any hand in this, consciously as well as unconsciously ?

Time would prove.

CHAPTER IV.

Stir and Quiet.

"THE birds! the birds! the birds! the birds! the birds !"

It was Evert's voice rising in rapid crescendo as he thumped at each bedroom door in turn, and roused up the sleepers ; and as this was in the earliest dawn of the morning after the berry-picking, and most of the young people were very tired, from some of the rooms issued only dissatisfied grunts, and sleepy inquiries, " What did you say ? "

"The birds! the pigeons!" reiterated Evert in the passage.

Then there came a delighted " Oh ! " from the younger boys, and a sound as if they were all jumping out of bed at once ; and Franzje's sweet clear voice was heard, " I'll be down as quick as possible, and see to breakfast for you, Evert. Don't let mother hurry herself. Are the maids up ? " Whereupon Evert rejoined that breakfast was of no consequence at all, and he was going to see after the guns.

Franzje thought it was of consequence, at least that it would be better for the boys to have some warm chocolate and cakes to begin the day upon ; so she called her own especial slave, Maria—who slept in a room adjoining, and

was almost more a friend and companion than a servant
—and made her own toilet very speedily.

All gradually became bustle and excitement in the
street—men and boys rushing along with guns, women
and girls running after them with provisions, or with am-
munition forgotten by them in their excitement; and
patches of the sky overhead were dark with birds sailing
southwards to their winter quarters. Franzje ran singing down stairs, and found the cook coaxing the kettle to
boil in the kitchen, and Maria hastily laying out the
breakfast in the parlour. Evert sat on one of the deep
window-seats, cleaning a gun ; and a negro lad was standing beside him, filling some little bags with shot.

"I wish those boys would come!" he exclaimed, as his
sister entered ; "Kilian's off already. I fancy he was the
first in the town to see the birds ; you know what a way
he has of getting up before dawn, as if it were never
possible to be at work too early. He came and threw a
stone up at my window to wake me, that was how I knew."

" I wonder if the Bankers know?" said Franzje, beginning to butter cakes for the brothers as she spoke.

"I dare say they do ; I hope Cornelius will come with
us ; but as for that lazy Mr. Vyvian, they won't get him
out yet a while, he never comes down till nine whatever's
on foot ; though, to be sure, the birds are something out
of the common way."

"To us," said Franzje. "Evert, I am beginning to
think that our excitements may seem small to other
people."

"Well, I dare say pigeon-shooting might not seem much
to the excitement of war," pondered Evert reflectively ;
"but I am not sure that Mr. Vyvian has ever been in a
battle yet. I'll ask him next time I see him."

"But without battles, I think there must be things in

Europe, things we never heard of,"—she was thinking of
what the adjutant had told her of the delights of the
stage—" which make life different somehow there from
here. I know some of us seem ignorant to Aunt Schuyler
even, because she has been more about in the world ; so
what must we seem to——"

She left her sentence unfinished.

"The Dominie, do you mean ?" said Evert rather mis-
chievously ; " it must have been a change to him, coming
here from Holland ; but I never heard him find any
fault with the place."

"Ah yes, the Dominie has been in Europe too, of
course ; I forgot that," rejoined Franzje, with a sudden
start ; "and yet he seems quite one of us in some ways,
though so above us in others. I never feel——"

"Is breakfast ready yet ?" interrupted Evert, with all
the natural indifference of a brother to a sister's sentiments. "I shall not wait for those youngsters if they
—oh, here's Jan ! "

Yes, Jan and the chocolate came in together, and
Franzje put aside her perplexities and hastened to pour it
out. New thoughts were stirring in her mind, a new influence had come into her life, but the dear old simple
home duties had the strongest claim of all.

"Maaike, you are the dearest of girls ; how quick you
have been," she said, gaily.

Whereupon 'Maaike'—otherwise Maria—grinned from
ear to ear, and with a modest " Cooky, she done the most,
Ma'mselle Franzje ; and Dinah, she down stairs now,"
rushed away to give the younger boys a call.

They soon came clustering in, and quite rivalled Americans of the present day in the speed with which they
despatched their breakfast, though before it was ended
the father and mother appeared, looking as neat and pre-

cise and unhurried as if breakfast had only been at the
usual hour.

"So thou'rt down with the first, my queen," said M.
Ryckman, kissing his tall daughter fondly, "not too tired
with the day on the hills?"

"I haven't had time to think whether I am tired or
not," she said, laughing; "it is rather nice to be made to
get up early, it gives one such a famous long day."

"You'll come out and see the fun, Franzje?" said Jan,
jumping up.

"Franzje has her home duties," put in the mother,
gently.

"Lots of time for them after ten o'clock," he rejoined;
"and the birds will all be gone by that time.—Do come,
Franzje.—Hurrah! we're off!" And with a shout of
ecstasy the whole troop of boys rushed out of the house
and away to their sport.

"I think I'll take some chocolate up to Uncle Jan,"
said Franzje, when they were gone; "he will not think of
being down yet a while, though I dare say he was up before
any of us."

"And then shall you go out?" said the mother, who,
following the easy discipline common in Albany, had no
intention of insisting upon those home duties she had
spoken of.

Franzje's bright eyes turned a little longingly to the
bustling street, where a company of young girls, attended
by their slaves, were just hurrying past. "No," she said,
slowly, "I don't think I shall; I have some reading to do
up stairs till you are ready for me, mother. Please let
Maaike go out a bit if she likes; she has been as busy as
a bee this morning."

Then she turned and went up to her uncle's room, taking
a little breakfast-tray with her. Her tap was answered

by a ready " Come in ;" and when she entered, she found
the old man seated at his table, with the large Bible in
which he read so constantly open before him.. He scarcely
ever made his appearance down stairs till dinner-time, and
seldom admitted anyone to his room but Franzje, and an
old negro who each morning became a sort of amateur
housemaid for his benefit though usually employed in the
garden.

The room was almost destitute of furniture; besides
the table, there was a grand old carved bedstead—the
pride of the family—the chair he was sitting on, some
simple necessaries of the toilet, but nothing more.
Franzje, when she had set down the tray, perched herself
on one corner of the table, and sat waiting till her uncle
should close his book and speak to her, or rather should
look as if he were ready to be spoken to, which at present
he did not.

For some minutes she sat there with her head drooped
thoughtfully, struck by the contrast of the busy life in
the street and the quiet seclusion that prevailed in this
room ; and pondering, as she had often pondered before,
on the calm, monotonous, unruffled, existence led by her
great-uncle and many of the old people in the town.
Would her merry young brothers, would Killian, would
the Dominie even, ever settle down into an old age so
utterly calm as this—in which all emotion seemed past,
all interest in the outer world gone by, in which there
was strictness without asceticism, days methodically por-
tioned out though with no written rule to appeal to, devotion without fervour, the life of a mystic without its
enthusiasm ?

She could understand a repressed life, a strong nature kept
under with a strong hand ; but a dead calm, a piety so tame
that it was almost commonplace—something in her revolted

from that. Quietly as she sat there, her heart seemed to throb like a wild thing in her breast at the mere notion of ever settling down to that contentedly. "It is because I am not good," she said to herself; for her ideal of goodness was a Dutch ideal—very orderly, very prosaic, rather stupid. She had quite a reverence for people who could sit with their hands before them, and speak in a measured tone, and read so many chapters, and say so many prayers, by clock-work, as it were; the stolidity which she saw around her, and which she did not possess, seemed to her a kind of *merit;* it was unnatural to have those reachings forth of the soul towards a different state of things which she felt in herself; goodness meant, above all things, contentment, simplicity of mind, well-regulated feelings, a certain dulness, perhaps,—bah! how she hated it!—ah! how wicked she was! She rose with a kind of shudder at herself; and as she did so, the old man closed his book and looked up at her, though without opening his lips.

"I want you to lend me the great Commentary, Uncle, if you are not going to use it," she said; "I have a little time to myself now, being up so early, and I want to read a bit till Mother is ready for me. I had just got to the part last time where Moses looks at the Promised Land but must not go over into it; and I want to see what they say about it. Uncle, don't you think Moses must have *longed* to go? Why didn't God let him, I wonder?"

"We need not seek to inquire, my child," said the old man, slowly; "it was the Almighty's Will."

"Oh, I know, and I know His Will is always best; but, Uncle, don't you ever want to know *why* such and such things are His Will? I know we must submit, whether we understand or no; but don't you think He *means* us to think over it, to learn to understand sometimes, that we may adore it all the more?"

The old man looked troubled, as if he thought she were trying to lead him out of his depth. "You had better ask the Dominie," he said.

"Uncle, I think if the Dominie had been Moses he would have broken his heart with longing to see the people safe in the Promised Land before God called him away."

"He was going to a better Canaan, that is, an heavenly," said the old man, in his deep low voice; "he had no need to long for the earthly."

"Not for himself, but his people—the people that were always going wrong, that he had had to bear with so patiently through all that weary wilderness—if he could only have seen them safe there——"

"He left them to God," said the recluse, quietly; "they were God's people even more than his."

Franzje's eyes caught the deep beautiful look of an adoring saint in one of Fra Angelico's pictures. She folded her hands together and seemed to gaze out far away. "I see," she said, "he loved them, but God loved them better still; the poor, foolish, wilful people that were so hard to guide were God's own people. Ah! he could trust them to God, as you say; that must have made his heart calm again. Uncle, I am glad you have made me think of that."

"Do not forget it, child," said Jan Ryckman, with more animation in his manner than Franzje had ever seen in it before; "and what is more, pray that our young Dominie"—the elderly minister really seemed young to this patriarch—"may not forget it either; he will always have his flock to serve God *his* way, and I don't say but what it is a right way, but yet there may be more ways than one of serving God; and I think we may trust Him to know best how to guide His own people. There have been many, who, in making God's cause theirs, have sometimes forgotten that their cause might not be always God's. It seems to me our Dominie is one of them."

"He is very good, though," said Franzje, a little reproachfully, still looking out into the far distance, searching into this new problem which was being set before her.

"Truly he is," assented the old man heartily; "but this mistake that I spoke of, my child, is especially a *good man's* mistake."

She did not attempt to gainsay it; he was speaking out of his experience, and experience carries a weight with it beneath which young people, if they are thoughtful, instinctively bow. The silent, secluded life of the old man did not seem to Franzje so dreary, so vapid, as it had appeared a few minutes ago; he had learnt wisdom, as it seemed, in this stillness; and, child as she was almost, it seemed to her that for wisdom's sake much might be foregone.

She kissed one of the wrinkled old hands, and said tenderly, "Now, dear Uncle, drink the chocolate, and let me sit close by thee on this little stool and read the Commentary. I can be quieter here than anywhere."

He made no objection; so she took down the great folio from the shelf, and was soon absorbed in it—her ears covered with her hands, that the gay sounds in the streets might not distract her.

Her uncle sipped his chocolate and watched her attentively. A girl who could sit down to study at seven o'clock in the morning seemed to him rather an anomaly; he was inclined to look npon the intellectual training which the Dominie bestowed upon his niece as a newfangled notion, which was not likely to come to good; but he could tolerate what he thought a mistake much more easily than the Dominie could have done in his place. "It may be all right," he said; "the girl's a good girl, and the Dominie is a good man and would not wilfully mislead her, and they are both in God's Hand—God's Hand—and they will be guided safe."

No Quietist of the seventeenth century ever stilled himself into a simpler serenity, a more tranquil faith, than this old Dutch recluse; though it is well, perhaps, for the mission work of the world that hearts are found with as firm a trust, as wide a charity, but with greater zeal.

Zeal without love! ah, the mischief it has worked, ah, the rents that have divided Christendom! But love without zeal! ah, the failure, and the loss, and the terrible ranks of heathendom that might have been won to Christ and are not!

Franzje read on for a good while in silence, then suddenly closed the book, and sprang up in her bright youthfulness ready for the work-a-day world. "Now for Mother and the preserving," she said cheerily; "we brought home *such* baskets of berries yesterday, Uncle; our Company picked more than any."

"So this is your way, my child," said the patriarch; "you read good books, and then you rush away and forget them. It is by meditating on what we read that we really learn."

"I do not quite forget," she said, blushing; "it all gets worked up into my life somehow; it is not good for me to think too much, it gives me a pain in my head."

The old man smiled, and let her go without more remonstrance.

About ten o'clock the boys came rushing back with their spoil; and for the next few days, roast pigeons, stewed pigeons, pigeon pies, and even pigeon soup, were

the order of the day. It was much the same thing in
other houses; and some of the dainty English officers
grumbled to each other at the monotony of the fare, and
wished, with all the energy of philanthropists, that the
pigeons were safe in the myrtle groves of sunny Florida,
instead of having been slaughtered for their benefit.

The following week flocks of wild ducks passed over
the town in the same way, and again a gun was in the
hands of every man and boy, and the same excitement
prevailed. It was "more slaughter than sport," and the
young Englishmen rather despised it on that account;
but wild ducks being somewhat nobler game than pigeons,
the lazy Mr. Vyvian did bestir himself a little on this
occasion, and was rewarded by Cornelia's rather loudly expressed admiration of his unerring skill as a marksman.

It was a stirring scene : the common just outside the
town was alive with people—white men and red, great
big lads and small sturdy boys in jackets, young girls
fair and rosy, and stout negresses armed with huge baskets wherein to collect the game—all mingled together
in confused motley groups, surrounded by a band of
bewildered cattle (this being the usual pasture of each
family's cows), who felt obliged to pause in their grazing
and ruminating, to add their bellowings to the general
confusion, and wonder what especial form of madness
had taken possession of their owners. Beyond flowed
the stately waters of the Hudson, broad and bright—
a sort of Rubicon to the poor winged fugitives, who,
when once across that, might feel themselves free and
safe ; and above was the blue sky, clouded as it were by
a storm of birds, sweeping on in great compact masses,
too often broken by the shots of their enemies below,
and adding by the flutter of their wings to the strange
medley of sounds which was filling the air.

Mr. Vyvian, even in this *mêlée*, thought of Franzje, and on meeting young Jan Ryckman, who was reloading at the moment, and so had leisure for speech, asked him why his sister was not there.

"Oh, I don't know," said Jan rather surlily, "she is getting quite a stay-at-home ; and besides, she never did care for the shooting much, she is so fond of birds and creatures of all sorts."

"No marvel then this wholesale murder is not much to her taste. I wonder your Dominie does not deliver a discourse on cruelty to the brute creation."

"Cruelty ! where's the cruelty ?" said Jan astonished ; "we do it every year."

"Does that make it any better ?" asked the adjutant dryly, as he took another of his deliberate and invariably successful aims.

He was inclined always to do at Rome as the Romans did, and yet to reserve to himself the right of criticising the Romans' customs.

A little later in the day, when the hubbub had subsided, Franzje and Maria, each with a small basket on the arm, were walking up the street past the Dutch church and the Dominie's house, when the Dominie himself came out and stopped them.

"Franzje, I want you just to look with what a prodigality of good nature my wants have been anticipated this morning," he said, with a pleasant inflection of amusement in his usual grave tones. "I can live upon salted wild duck for the whole winter if I choose, and yet have plenty to give away if I can find anyone that wants them."

He led the way through the hall, not into the accustomed sitting-room, where any of his flock who wished to speak with him could always find audience, but into the kitchen, where—piled on the table, on the chairs, even on the dresser with its grand array of Dutch crockery, and hung from hooks upon the wall—were wild ducks innumerable, poor pretty dead things whose travels had been stopped prematurely.

"You come look at larder, Ma'mselle Ryckman, dat cram full of pigeon," said the Dominie's black cook, showing all her white teeth in a grin of delight; "people love Massa well, me tell him; don't let him want for anyting to eat—eh? Your broder brought some, dat dey did—see, dem by de fire-place; dey been well brought down, not riddled wid shot like some of de poor tings."

Franzje shuddered, and the Dominie looked grave and rather disgusted; he had accepted this annual sport as one of the customs of the place, and though of course he had never himself joined in it, had always been rather amused and pleased by the eagerness of his people to share its results with him; but old Dinah's words associated a thought of suffering with the poor feathered victims, and his appetite for wild duck seemed to desert him on the spot. Like Franzje, he was sensitive to the pain of all dumb creatures, though he never sentimentalized over it as people sometimes do nowadays.

"It is rather as if I had brought you to look at a battle-field," he said half apologetically to his young visitor. "But I wanted to ask if you are any of you likely to be driving out this afternoon. Everyone in Albany is sure to be well supplied; but I thought the Bleekers and some of the other wood-settlers might be glad of some of these birds."

"Mother did talk of our taking some to the Renselaers—not that they want for anything, but rather as a compliment, you know; we could drive on to the woods afterwards if you want some of these taken there, or "—rather timidly—" would you like to come with us, Sir?"

The Dominie began to consider of his engagements. "The Elders are to come to me at two, and consult about the repairs of the church roof; and then I was thinking of going to read to old Vrow Dorckman—she will be expecting me; but still I do want to see the Padroon, and to pay a pastoral visit to the Wendels and the Bleekers; so perhaps, my child, it might be as well to accept your offer."

"Ma'mselle Franzje," whispered Maria, pulling her young mistress's sleeve, "if Dominie liked, you might take tea out and have it in the woods, and then you need not start too early"—*Too* being used by the negroes in the sense of *very*.

Franzje rather shyly repeated the suggestion aloud, adding, "And we are just going to Vrow Dorckman's with some preserves, so we could take her a message from you if you liked, Sir."

"You are smoothing all my difficulties," he said pleasantly. "Yes, you shall tell her my plan for this afternoon, and that I will visit her to-morrow instead. If you have time, you might stay and read to her a little yourself."

It was not a task which Franzje much enjoyed, as the old woman was very deaf, and it required the utmost exertion to make her hear reading at all; but still she assented very readily. She was always willing to do a kindness to anybody, and moreover the Dominie's suggestions were equivalent to commands.

They had come out into the hall as they talked, and glancing through the open door of the study, the Dominie asked Franzje if she wanted any more books.

"No, thank you; I am reading Uncle Jan's big Commentary now."

"Can you follow it at all?"

" Not when it quotes Latin and Greek," she said, looking
up at him with a bright smile, afraid of the presumption
of affirming that she could pretty fairly in other respects ;
" but I like it very much, only—"

" Only what ? "

" The people don't seem so real in it as they do in the
Bible itself ; when I read it I don't feel so much as if they
really lived."

" That may be more your fault than the Commenta-
tor's," he said dryly.

" Yes," she said thoughtfully, with slow but not unwilling candour ; and then they shook hands, and the
two girls pursued their way.

" Oh, Ma'mselle Franzje," said Maaike, who had felt the
last little rebuff for her mistress more than Franzje did for
herself, "me glad me not born in *dat* house. Dominie
bery good man, bery ; Dinah, she pretty good woman ;
but dull, bery dull, both, house dull altogeder."

Franzje smiled, and looked back at the house—a tall,
square, stiff bit of masonry, its front a little redeemed
from bareness by the tree overshadowing the porch ; not
an unapt type of the Dominie himself, grave and rigid,
and uncompromising even to sternness, yet with a redeem-
ing touch of feeling and of kindliness which was as refreshing to the heart as his linden-tree to the eye.

" I like the house, and I like Dinah," she said. She did
not add "And I like the Dominie ;" but after a pause she
continued, "Maaike, if I were in any trouble I think I
should run straight there."

CHAPTER V.

𝖂𝖔𝖔𝖉 𝕾𝖊𝖙𝖙𝖑𝖊𝖗𝖘.

THE Wendels and the Bleekers were two young married couples, with a host of little children, and very straitened means.　They had both cleared for themselves a space in one of the charming little glens which diversified the somewhat barren heights to the westward of Albany ; and there, out of the reach of all town luxuries, and with scarcely any servants, they lived a frugal, hardy, independent life, cultivating maize and potatoes for home consumption, and sometimes selling their crops of wheat and hay to the citizens who had not farms of their own.

No one in Albany thought the worse of them for being poor : and they often received visits and presents from their town friends, who in the summer used occasionally to drive out to dine or drink tea with them, taking care to bring the materials of the repast—an arrangement so common that it gave no offence—and merely troubling Madame Wendel or Madame Bleeker, as the case might be, to boil her kettle for their benefit.

After the visit at M. Renselaer's, which—'Padroon' though he was, and owner of large landed estates—was no affair of ceremony, but a pleasant meeting of friends young and old, Madame Ryckman and the Dominie, accompanied by Franzje and two of her little brothers, drove through the barren hill country, till they reached the small inhabited dell to which they were bound.

They stopped first at the Bleekers', and here only the

Dominie and his offering of ducks went in; while Madame Ryckman drove on to the Wendels' to see about tea, after exacting a promise from the Dominie to join her there by the time that meal should be ready. The arrival of the carriage—a light, open vehicle, something like a double gig—at the Wendels' house, was the signal for the sudden irruption of a flock of small children, clad in loose cotton garments, merely confined at the waist with a string; and their eager cries of "How do you do?" "Are you come to tea?" "Our mother is in-doors, Madame Ryckman;"—"O Franzje, what have you brought me?" &c., were for the first minute or two perfectly deafening.

Albert and Dirk Ryckman had brought a splendid bow and arrows for the eldest boy of the party; and Franzje had a bag of cakes, of her own making, for all the children, greater and lesser, so these were immediately distributed. And then the hamper containing materials for the tea was taken out; and the horse was released from harness, and allowed to graze by the road side, while Madame Ryckman and her daughter went in-doors to find the mistress of the house. She was hard at work bread-making, and the fingers she extended in welcome were floury, and her face was flushed with her exertions; but the absence of all false shame or trace of discomposure in her manner was of the very essence of good breeding, and set her visitors at their ease at once. She was a comely young woman, with a fair fresh complexion, dark eyes and hair, and a figure too stout to be absolutely graceful, and yet not awkward. There was about both her and her house an air of plain, practical good sense, as if all the necessaries of life were duly attended to, and indulgences not even thought of. The rooms were rather bare of furniture, but beautifully clean and neat; the open windows and doors admitted plenty of the sweet fresh air

from the hills ; and the grass-plot in front of the house,
and the vegetable garden at the back, were well kept and
orderly, and bore witness to the labour expended upon
this clearing, which a few years before was but a bit of
woody glen covered with luxuriant chestnut-trees, like
those which now partially hemmed it in on two sides.

The soft sighing of the wind among the chestnuts
made a sort of under-song to the conversation—not very
remarkable or interesting—which went on in the little
kitchen between Madame Wendel and her guests. They
had both thrown aside their out-door things, and set to work
to help her to roll out and trim the paste for the goodly
supply of flat cakes, which she was bent upon making,
and which her tribe of little boys would no doubt soon
demolish.

" I shall get on bravely now you are come," she said,
heartily ; " and I hope we may have them all finished
before the Dominie arrives. I must go on with them now
I have begun, for it does not do to heat the great oven
for nothing."

So they all worked away with a will ; and Franzje's
cheeks grew flushed with heat, as she helped Madame
Wendel to put in one set of cakes to bake and take out
another. She liked it though,—there was something in
the bright warmth of the oven, as she stood looking into
it, which took her fancy ; and the smell of the hot cakes
was appetizing enough. She had not the faintest shadow
of contempt for household employments, much as she
liked intellectual pursuits.

Before they had quite " cleared up," as Madame Wendel
expressed it, the Dominie's tall form came in sight ; and
then there was just the least bit of a panic. To the
settlers, who saw him but rarely, a visit from him was
rather an affair of state.

"Franzje, do ask him to sit down in the porch, or the parlour, while I wash my hands, and put on my best apron," said the rosy matron a little piteously.

"Oh, and I must stay and unpack the hamper," said Madame Ryckman, in the same breath. "There are the things for tea to be got out; and I have brought you a ham, and a few preserves for the boys."

Franzje broke into Madame Wendel's "Oh, how kind! but there's the Dominie coming up the steps!" with a reassuring "He will like to see the children, I think; I will ask him if I may take him in search of them;" and tying her cloak loosely round her, went to meet him at the door.

"She is a handsome girl," said Madame Wendel, looking at her from the window, as she was seen conducting the Dominie towards the thicket where the children had disappeared; "and what is more, she is a sweet pleasant girl too. I almost wish I had a daughter instead of such a handful of sons."

"I have got the handful of sons as well," said Madame Ryckman, with a smile; "but Franzje does help me with them nicely. I only hope she will not be drawn off into any of the gaieties the Bankers and the Gerritses are setting on foot to please these fine English officers. The Dominie tells me he has heard some talk of getting up a dance—a ball, I think they call it; but I have not said a word to Franzje about it."

"She would not care for such things, I should think," rejoined Madame Wendel placidly.

"I am not sure. Do you remember going with us, some years ago, to the Mohawk village, and the Indian children having a sort of queer dance of their own, and my Franzje and Jan joining with them? How angry the Dominie was, to be sure! And the worst of it was,

Franzje never would own she was wrong. I can see her now, as she stood up to be scolded, looking down at her pinafore as modest as you please, but with such a naughty little questioning smile upon her lips. Jan gave in, put his knuckles in his eyes, and cried, and said he would never do it again ; but Franzje would not say a word, and I had to punish her. It is almost the only time in her life that I ever did ; and perhaps I should not have done it then, if the Dominie had not made me see that it was my duty. She cried when she saw how much in earnest I was—for it always does break her heart to vex me, dear child ! and after a bit she begged my pardon and the Dominie's for having displeased us ; but she never said in so many words she had been naughty, and never promised not to do it again, as Jan did. It is my belief she did not see any harm in it, for all our talking."

Madame Ryckman had hit the truth : this one severely visited fault of her childish life had never dwelt on Franzje's conscience as a fault at all. She had felt a vague sense of guilt in having made the Dominie and her mother angry, and had been unhappy till she received their forgiveness ; but for all that, the dance round the Indian camp-fire with the dusky graceful little Mohawks, all bedight in beads and coloured shells, had remained in her memory as something utterly innocent, which was never to be repeated perhaps, but which she could not wish undone.

She was not thinking of this, nor of herself in any way, as she strolled further into the glen with M. Frey-linghausen, looking for the children, and every now and then waking the echoes by a shout of " Dirk, Marte, Peterkin ! where have you hid yourselves ? Come and speak to the Dominie ! "

Her respect and liking for her pastor were not tempered

with any uncomfortable amount of fear, though whatever
exceptions there had been in the general indulgence
shown to her had either come from him, or been due to
his influence. She was very happy this afternoon, and
had forgotten bygone troubles altogether.

The Dominie, however, looked grave, and seemed full
of thought. "Shall we rest a few minutes?" he said,
when they had gone a little way, and a beautiful soft
gloom of foliage was all round them, nearly shutting out
the sky. "This trunk will make you a nice seat; and
as the children come back to their tea they will find
us."

"Oh yes," said Franzje willingly; "I called them because I thought you wanted to question them a little."

"So I do; but I am weary," he answered, with unusual
listlessness in his tone. "Those Bleekers are good honest
people; but it is always the same story over again : they
must get the corn in, or the children must gather the
hickory-nuts, or there are fresh crops to sow. No harm,
you will say, true; but it is always earth—earth first,
and chiefly; and Heaven only as an after-thought."

"These settlers must have less time than we of the
town," said Franzje. "With scarcely any servants, and
their living to get by downright labour, they cannot have
much leisure, I suppose, except now and then in the
winter, perhaps."

"No, I do not blame them; but there were fishers
once upon the lake of Galilee, poor hard-working men,
as we should say, who plied their task with thoughts of
the wonderful new Teacher that 'spake as never man
spake,' and who presently 'left the ship and their father,
and followed Him.'"

"It seems so different now," said Franzje, pondering. "Do such calls ever come to Christians now-a-

days, do you think, Sir ? Mr. Stuart, the 'Father of the
Deserts,' as people call him, *he* left, as it were, 'the ship
and his father,' his home and all its comforts, didn't
he ? "

" Yes, and I honour him for it. When I see those
Indians of his gathering into the town for their Easter
Communion at the English church, when I hear them
singing their hymns at good Colonel Schuyler's, I wish
that one from among *us* would go forth in like manner,
and bring some more of those scattered sheep to a knowledge of the truth."

" I suppose Father Rallé did among the Iroquois something like what Mr. Stuart is doing for the Mohawks,"
said Franzje, still in the same meditative way.

" He was a very devoted man, doubtless," rejoined the
Dominie, dryly.

He had not much admiration to spare for the French
missionary, the zealous Jesuit priest, the determined
enemy of the English and Dutch settlers, who had been
martyred some said, righteously slain said others, among
his band of faithful Indians, when Norridgwog was taken
and burnt by the people of York.

" I sometimes wish Killian could be a missionary," said
Franzje; " he has a good deal of influence with the Indians
already—partly because he is like them, perhaps. When
they are at the Flats, they always ask for him and for
Cortlandt Schuyler."

" Yes, he is one who would be fitted to respond to such a
call ; but I fear me he does not listen for it, and is setting
his heart upon an earthly prize."

Franzje's cheeks had been flushed when she came out
of Madame Wendel's warm kitchen, and were so still in
a degree, but the flush did not deepen in the least. The
Dominie was looking straight at her ; and her eyes, as

they met his, seemed to him like deep, clear wells, into which you could look down and see truth: pure simple truth, without a shadow of artifice or equivocation.

" One who would be a real devoted missionary," he went on, "must forego many things besides the home of his boyhood: he must give up the hope of ever making to himself a home of his own ; he must be content to live a solitary life, with ' the Lord for his inheritance,' in a fuller sense than even the Levites of old."

" That makes it all the better," said she, with her eyes kindling.

" My child," he answered, despondingly, " not one in a thousand feels that."

No shade came over the brightness of her eager face.

"*You* felt it, Dominie, didn't you," she said, " when you left your own people, and your father's house, and came out here to teach us ? "

" I *thought* so," he said bitterly.

She looked troubled now. She did not understand the bitter self-accusation that lurked beneath the brief reply ; she thought perhaps he answered shortly because she had been presuming—had spoken amiss.

" I beg your pardon," she stammered. " Evert said something the other day that made me think how much you must have given up in coming here, how stupid and ignorant we must seem to you, and I——"

She hesitated. And he said gravely, " And you thought perhaps that this ' made it all the better,' as you said just now ; that if there were a sacrifice—I do not say there was, mind—something made me glad to make it. What was it, child, do you think, that made me happy in coming here ? "

" Was it not, sir, that God said to you, as He did to Moses, ' My Presence shall go with thee ; and I will give thee rest ' ? " she answered, in a low voice.

F

He almost shrank from the tender reverence of her upward glance.

"Was it?" he said. "Or was it that I thought I could do what never man had done before—that here was a field which Holland could not afford? Had I coveted the things of this world, I might have had them there, it is true : my ambition reached beyond that. But what if it were but ambition still?"

She could not follow the train of his thoughts ; to her, as to most of his simple flock, he seemed an embodiment of severe perfection : she could not imagine for a moment that he had really anything wherewith to reproach himself. She saw that he was disheartened—that he had been plain at the very beginning of the conversation—but she thought it was the result of his *people's* shortcomings, her own included, and she answered humbly and deprecatingly, "I know we ought to be much better than we are. Aunt Schuyler says, with such teaching as we have, we ought to be very different from other people."

"Well," he said, "Albany has hitherto been simple and primitive, free from the vices of larger cities. There has been little zeal amongst us ; we have been dead and flat as the fields of my own Holland ; but at least we have been kept from the evils that infest many other places. So far I have had cause to be thankful. But if even *that* fails —if the simplicity of the young people, the young people in whom I have placed my hope, whom I have myself helped to mould—if *that* should be tainted, where can I look for consolation then ?—of what use will my ministry have been ?"

Franzje guessed to what he was alluding now, and was too true to pretend that she did not.

"Is everything that is new wrong, Dominie?" she asked, with a puzzled look.

"I do not say that; but when novelties are introduced, we should look to the character of those who introduce them. Have you remembered what I said about not going to the Bankers'?"

"Yes; I have been there once with Evert—never alone," said Franzje, colouring at the remembrance of what Mr. Vyvian had said on this subject.

"Do you not. begin to see a difference in Cornelia already? If you have any influence with her, and with the other girls of your Company, as I suppose you have, use it on the right side—be sure that you do. *You*, at least, child, must never give me cause for displeasure."

There was a kind of appeal mingled with the authority of his tone, which was utterly strange.

She was silent from a sort of awe; and he did not press for any promise, but sat looking dreamily on into the dark recesses of the glen, as though he saw there a presage of evil—of evil which he could not avert.

It was a grand face in the mingled melancholy and fire of its glance; and the soul within was a grand soul, vast in its capacities for good, but rising too high in its hopes, sinking too low in its despair, to be well fitted for the wear and tear of common life. The fault of his character, the fault of his teaching, was, perhaps, that it was too self-conscious—there was too much "I" in it; and the Calvinistic training he had received had rather fostered than checked this. Taught to think of himself more as an individual than as the organ of a Church, to feel himself more like one of the olden prophets—a direct exponent of God's Will—than one of a divinely-appointed band of interpreters of the Catholic faith, it seemed to him as if God's cause must stand or fall with him; as if he were the Elijah whom not to follow was of necessity to follow the priests of Baal.

There was a pause, and then Franzje said gently, " I wish Annt Schuyler would come home."

" I wish so, too," said the Dominie, rousing himself from his abstraction ; " I regret their absence now for the sake of others, as well as for my own. But these children, Franzje, they do not seem to be coming, and it is getting late."

" I thought I heard their voices a minute ago—to the right there, among the trees. I will go and look for them."

And Franzje plunged in among the branches, and presently emerged with a troop of little merry sunburnt children hanging round her.

Their hands were full of nuts, which they had been gathering in honour of Albert and Dirk, their faces were not over clean, and a little dismay had fallen on them at the thought of being catechised by the Dominie then and there.

" We must go and wash our hands first, at any rate," said the oldest boy. " Just whisper me the first word of the answers that come to my turn," said the second. " Oh, yes, Franzje, stay with us, and help us," entreated one of the little ones, clinging tight to Franzje's skirts as he spoke. And so, all talking at once, they came into the presence of the Dominie, who was still sitting on the fallen trunk, and still looking weary.

Franzje agreed with them in the wish that they should be made clean and tidy before they came to him for their lesson. A vast amount of scrubbing and rubbing and vigorous hair-brushing, had always fallen to her share in childhood, before she was started off for the weekly catechising, and it did not seem respectful to the Dominie to omit this preparation.

Apparently, however, he did not very much care about

it, but thought that these wild little children of the
woods, having been caught, had better be attended to
immediately. He greeted them all by name, patted some
of the little rough heads, and then bade them stand in
order before him, that he might hear how much they had
learnt since he was there last.

There was a solemn pouring out of nuts from tumbled
pinafores on to a soft patch of grass beneath the trees, a
primming up of little laughing faces into a correct
gravity of expression; and then the six small Wendels
took their places in a straight row in front of the Dominie, their hands behind them, and the six pair of blue
eyes fixed steadily upon him to begin with, though by
and by glances wandered in desperation up to the trees,
down upon the ground, and round to Franzje, in hopes of
obtaining a clue to the words of those difficult answers,
which somehow *would* always come to the turn of those
who knew them least perfectly.

Franzje stood a little to one side, leaning against a tree,
with Dirk and Albert standing close to her, and listening
far more critically than she did to the mistakes made by
their play-mates. She was obliged to catch at their small
brown hands sometimes, or cover their rosy mouths with
her fingers, so eager were they to display their superior
knowledge, and set the little Wendels right. Perhaps it
might have been better for them if she had let them do
it; the setting-down they would then have got from the
Dominie would have utterly quenched for the time the
small men's conceit; but she was too tender a sister to
wish to expose them to this, and anxious also to spare the
supposed feelings of the little ignoramuses.

The Dominie was very patient with the mistakes, very
clear in his explanations of the hard words, over which
the children stumbled; years afterwards, when more im-

portant things had faded from her memory, this little
scene would rise before Franzje's mind. Back her
thoughts would fly to that woody glen, the dark, soft
masses of chestnut-trees, with here and there a fiery
gleam darted through them from the afternoon sun on
the long grass at their feet; the little group of ruddy
children, picturesque in their untidiness; the stately
figure of the Dominie, and the intent face, turning now
on one, now on another, of his little disciples—his eagerness to teach far outstripping their eagerness to learn;—
back it would all come before her eyes, eyes which used
to fill with tears then at the remembrance, because this
scene belonged to the dear old time, which had slipped
past, unprized perhaps, but was yearned after when it had
gone by for ever.

"Franzje! Children! where have you hid yourselves?
What have you done with the Dominie?"

It was a man's voice breaking in upon the children's
sing-song; and the group was joined by the father of the
six urchins, Marte Wendel, a broad-shouldered, hearty
Dutch-American, who had been called off from field-
labours by his spouse to meet the Dominie at tea.

"The wife and Madame Ryckman have got the tea all
ready," he said, as he shook hands with his pastor; "and
there is a rare feast of good things of your mother's providing, Franzje. Will you come and take some chocolate,
Dominie? Catechism is but dry work."

The Dominie's brow clouded a little; but the children,
apparently agreeing with their father's sentiments, broke
into sudden smiles, made a series of awkward bows, as an
intimation that they considered the lesson finished, and
scuttled off to get their share of the good things.

"How is old Peter?" Franzje asked, alluding to an old
crippled negro, whom the Wendels kept, and tenderly

nursed, though they considered themselves too poor for
the luxury of ordinary servants.

The man's somewhat coarse face softened into a kindly
expression at once.

"He's but ailing, poor old fellow ! He has not left his
room this week past ; though I tell him this fine autumn
sun would warm him up, and drive away his aches and
pains, if he could but sit out on the grass a bit. He'd
like to see you, Dominie, after tea, I dare say, if you can
spare time for him. His head-piece is not what it was,
but he maunders out bits of texts and hymns that he picked
up in his younger days, and they seem to comfort him."

"I will gladly visit him, whenever you like to show me
the way to his room," said the Dominie readily, registering
a mental determination to address a few earnest words to
the negro's rather ignorant master as they went.

Franzje, who knew every shade of his expression, could
see how Marte's mode of talking jarred upon him ; but in
her young hopefulness felt a conviction that old Peter's
texts and hymns, "maundered out" though they might
be, were making a deeper impression on Baas Wendel
than he cared to show.

She even ventured to hint as much, when they came
upon the grass-plot, and Marte hurried forward to get the
Dominie a seat ; and her hint was not taken amiss.

A smile came into the Dominie's sombre eyes. "You
may be right, child," he said kindly. "'Charity hopeth
all things.'"

So it was in a hopeful, happy mood that they sat down
to tea ; and never had cakes and cream, chocolate and
preserves,' tasted nicer than they did on this particular
occasion, partaken of on the grass in the sweet country
air, amid the cheerful talk of the seniors, and the light-
hearted laughter of the children.

"I wish you came every day," said the goodwife heartily to her guests.

"Nay, nay, wife, that sounds rather greedy," said her husband, looking at the provisions, which perhaps really were to *him* as well as to the little ones almost the most welcome part of the visit.

"I meant for their own sakes, not for what they brought," she said, colouring, and glancing deprecatingly at them.

And one of her little sons looked up, and said quickly, "Mother's never greedy; she gave old Peter the very last bit of the ham Madame Ryckman brought last time, though she had never so much as tasted it herself."

"That's right, little Jan, speak up for mother," said the Dominie kindly; "and tell me, are not these hot cakes that I am eating of mother's making? I do not think they came in the hamper; I am sure they could not have been kept hot all this time, unless Dirk had them in his pockets."

Dirk, who had come forth that day in the glory of a new suit, with particularly capacious pockets, chuckled over this supposition; while Madame Wendel felt grateful to the Dominie for having singled out almost the only item of the feast which was really of her providing, and pressed more hot cakes upon him with such hospitable assiduity—seconded by Madame Ryckman, who was pleased to make the most of her friend's culinary feats—that he was obliged rather abruptly to announce his intention of going to see old Peter, to escape from the necessity of taking more than his usual frugal portion of food.

What a drive home it was on that September evening! What a cool soft splendour was upon everything! how the Hudson gleamed in the tranquil golden light! how the distant hills caught the last rosy tints, and grew like

the wonderful glorified Mount Sinai in Uncle Jan's pic-
ture-Bible! And the Dominie was so kind and so gentle,
with all the gloom passed away. If his ministrations had
been wasted on the Bleekers and the Wendels, at least
old Peter had welcomed them thankfully: and perhaps,
too, they had *not* been wasted; if he had met with
stolidity and want of sympathy, a chance word here
and there might still have sunk into the listeners' hearts;
and at any rate, difficulty was but a call to persevere,
and made his work, as Franzje would have said, "all
the better."

CHAPTER VI.

Franzje's First Minuet.

"MA'M'SELLE," said the coaxing voice of the little slave-
girl Maria, whispering to Franzje, who was seated at work
in the parlour by her mother's side, "you come to de door
one minute, somebody want to see you."

"Who is it?" said Franzje aloud, disdainful of mystery;
but Maaike only retreated hastily into the hall, and her
young mistress was obliged to follow and find out for
herself.

At the door was no more wonderful a personage than
Cornelius Banker; but he, too, had a mysterious air that
afternoon; and when Franzje asked, smiling, "What is
it, Cornelius? won't you come in?" he merely beckoned
her out into the porch, and not till she had come there to
him would deliver his message.

"Cornelia wants to know if you can meet her at the
Gerritses' after tea? Madame Gerritse told her to ask you.
Evert can come too, if he likes, but we don't want Jan."

" Why do you want any of us ? " questioned the girl;
"is it a meeting of the Company ? "

" No ; but there's something you'll like to hear about;
mind you come—Mr. Vyvian wants you."

Franzje drew herself up rather stiffly. " I am busy;
mother and I have work in hand to-day, Cornelius, thank
you," she said.

" Nonsense ; Keetje and Engelt will cry their eyes out
if you don't come. It's no harm, I tell you—only something new that M. Gerritse is helping to get up. I would
not have broiled down here in the sun if I had thought
you would have said no after all."

" It was very good of you ; I will see if Evert would
like to go," she said, relenting ; and with this half-accept-
ance Cornelius was obliged to be content.

Evert *did* wish to go, and overruled Franzje's scruples,
which increased considerably on finding that her mother
did not quite like the idea.

" Anna is but a foolish idle maiden," said the good
housewife to her daughter ; " and the Gerritses are more
apt to take up with new-comers than your father and I
can think wise. See how intimate they became with the
Waldrons all at once ; and now they are making as much
of this English colonel as if they had never seen his like
before."

" Perhaps they never had," said Franzje, not pertly, but
as if the matter were one which perplexed her ; " there is a
something, mother, in those English officers which our
young men have not. I don't quite know what it is."

" They have got a polish on them, and perhaps look all
the better for it, like our bed-posts when they have been
well rubbed," replied Madame Ryckman, reflectively; "but
maybe one can judge better of a person who has not so
much—who shows the grain of the wood, as it were. I

would rather have Killian Barentse for a son than that young Mr. Vyvian."

"And I would rather have him for a brother," said Franzje readily; "but—" and then she stopped, and a blush overspread her face.

"What are you doing with that seam, child?" said the mother, sharply, so sharply, that Franzje, who had been most tenderly nurtured, looked up in amazement. "You are sewing it all awry, and must unrip it again. That comes of letting your mind run after strangers with whom you have naught to do."

"I was not thinking of them till you began to speak of them, mother," rejoined the girl, with a sudden sense of injury which was perhaps natural in one who had been accustomed to so much indulgence.

"Don't argue in that way," said Madame Ryckman, still severely; "remember, you are only a child, as the Dominie says, and have to be taught your duty like other children. Unpick that seam at once, and see if you can do it better."

Franzje hung down her stately head, and did as she was bidden; but perhaps she had never felt more completely a woman than at that moment. The sudden tightening of the easy rein in which she had been held all her life had come just at the wrong moment; it formed such a sharp contrast to the deferential admiring tone which the English officers adopted towards her, that it forced her to think about herself, to question if she were indeed such a child, and inspired her with a vague inclination for revolt, such as she had never felt before.

At present she crushed this down as undutiful, and would have given up going to the Gerritses altogether if Evert had not pressed it. Madame Ryckman never could withstand her son's coaxing, and in this instance was all

the more inclined to yield because in her motherly heart
a certain relenting had followed upon her momentary
harshness. "She is such a good girl, I don't think the
Dominie need fear for her," she said to herself. "I may
as well let her go this once."

Yet when Franzje came down after the early tea with a
bright blue breast-knot illumining her sombre dress,
Madame Ryckman, in accordance with her new ideas of
duty, bade her take it off, and likewise put on her old
hood and cape instead of her new ones. "It is not necessary to bedizen one's self just to visit one's neighbours,"
she ended, with assumed displeasure; "and as you are
not grown up, your dress can be of no consequence to
anybody."

"I don't mind what it is like, if only you will not be
vexed with me, mother," said the poor child, with great
tears rushing to her eyes; and so carelessly did she cast
aside the obnoxious bow, that her mother—convinced she
was not quite given over to vanities—gave her a hearty
kiss, and in quite a natural voice told her not to fret, that
all would be well so long as she did as she was told, and
did not set up for a fine lady.

But perhaps the admiration she received that evening
would not have been quite so dangerous to her as it was,
if this little bit of so-called "wholesome repression" had
not been exercised previously. The best way to prevent
a girl's being vain of her natural advantages is surely not
to ignore them, or to endeavour to hide them, but to treat
them as simple matters of course. To have it suddenly
impressed on her at home that she was a mere child,
and her appearance of no consequence to anybody, only
made poor little Franzje all at once keenly alive to the
fact that the English strangers treated her as a woman,
and a very beautiful woman too.

Adrian Gerritse's house was quite at the further end of
the town, and besides the large garden, the grass-plot, and
the well, which it had in common with all the other
dwellings in Albany, was surrounded at the back by farm
buildings, among which a large barn stood conspicuous.

Much to the young Ryckmans' surprise, there was no
one sitting in the portico, as was usual at this hour; and
when they entered the wide-open door no one was visible
in the hall, and no voices were to be heard in the parlour.
They were standing near the threshold in doubt and perplexity—for neither knocker nor bell was to be found in
the primitive mansion—when a consequential-looking old
negress popped her head out of the kitchen, and said in a
tone of friendly familiarity, "Just step out to de barn,
my dears; you'll find 'em all dere. We begun to be afraid
you weren't coming, and such a syllabub as you would
have missed! I be going to make it as soon as ever de
cows come home."

"Mind it froths well," said Evert, laughing. "But
what on earth have they gone to the barn for? Have
they turned it into a withdrawing room for the English
quality?"

"Oh, dey're up to all sorts of pranks," said the old
woman, grinning; "I haven't seen 'em so merry all dese
years I've been wid 'em. The Dominie called here just
now, but I asked him to step round another day; he
could see for himself dat dere wasn't a soul in de house,
and I couldn't send *him* out to de barn, you know. I
expect he came to see what was going on, for he's not
been nigh us above once since his last house-visit."[1]

"I wonder what we are to see," laughed Evert to his

---

[1] A visit paid by Dutch pastors to each householder among their
flock just before Easter, the purpose being to invite him and his
dependants to the Easter Communion.

sister, as they crossed the garden, and went through a side-
door into the yard, " I don't think Colonel Trelawny can
have been taken to the barn simply to look at the horses."

Yet the Gerritses' barn was in itself something of a
sight. It was a large wooden structure, about ninety feet
long and fifty wide ; the walls not more than ten feet
high, but the roof raised to a great height in the middle,
and forming, by the help of cross-beams, and long poles
stretched from one to the other, a sort of vast open loft
for the reception of the summer crops. The building was
raised nearly three feet from the ground, supported by
large beams resting on stone, and down the middle of it
ran from end to end a solid flooring of oak. On either
side were stalls for cattle, arranged so that the creatures
should stand with their backs to the wall, and their heads
turned towards the threshing-floor ; and though most of
these were empty when the young Ryckmans entered,
some fine horses and a few young heifers were in the
stalls nearest the door, and stretched out their noses in a
friendly way, as if expecting notice. The sweet fragrance
of newly-stored hay seemed to pervade the building ;
busy martins skimmed about outside and in, as if they
were as much at home there as the owners ; and altogether,
in the dim October twilight, it seemed on first entrance
completely a rural scene : but at the other end of the
building a wonderful transformation had been effected.
There the stalls had been removed, and a wooden stage
erected, curtained in at each side and at the back, and
artificially lighted by lanterns suspended from the roof.
Upon this moved about some figures, strangely apparelled ;
and in front of it, at a little distance, had been placed a
double row of benches, on which sat the Gerritses and a
good many of their *young* neighbours, laughing and talking in a lively excited way.

Anna sprang up as she caught sight of fresh guests approaching, and came forward to meet them. "I am so glad you are come, you two," she said. "Is not this charming?"

"What are they doing?" asked Evert stolidly, not altogether as if he were prepared to admire.

"They are acting—pretending to be other people, you know; but this is only a sort of rehearsal, they haven't got up their parts yet," replied Anna, with the air of one who had been behind the scenes, and knew all about it. "You remember that little lean-to at the end of the barn, Franzje? we have made it into such a famous green-room, and cut a door through."

"A *green* room! what is that?" pursued the mystified Evert; "and who are those dressed-up people? The officers? What makes them want to pretend to be any-one else?"

Anna gave her shoulders a little shrug, which was a bad imitation of Russell Vyvian's. "Did you never hear of a play before? *You* understand, don't you, Franzje?"

"Mr. Vyvian explained to me a little about plays once; is it going to be Shakespeare?"

"What's that?" said Anna, puzzled in her turn; and then, before Franzje could answer, she added, "Come nearer the stage," and taking her hand, pulled her forward to the foremost row of benches.

Madame Gerritse was sitting there in state, with two or three young girls on either side of her. Franzje dropped a low curtsey to her, and was sitting down at the further end of the bench, without raising her eyes, when a voice, which seemed to come from the air, said, "How do you do, Mademoiselle Ryckman? You have *more* than kept your word. You promised to come and see our play, and now you are honouring even this poor attempt at a rehearsal by your presence. I am afraid this dumb show will not answer your high expectations."

Looking up, she saw she was addressed by one of the actors, who was leaning forward from the stage towards her, and talking over the heads of the regimental bandsmen, who formed a sort of orchestra between the stage and the spectators. By the voice she knew it must be Mr. Vyvian, but otherwise she would scarcely have recognized him; for he was dressed in a costume of Charles the Second's time, and a quantity of long curling hair, *un*-powdered, covered his head and shoulders, while a sort of unnatural fairness had come over his dark complexion.

She bowed gravely and courteously, but said nothing; and seeing she had not courage to carry on a conversation in this prominent fashion, he bowed also and retired, reappearing, however, in a moment, at the top of a small flight of steps at the side of the barn, which led down from the stage to the part occupied by the spectators.

"We have just been trying on our dresses, which have come from Boston," he said, when he had reached Franzje's side; "the 52nd have been giving theatrical representations there, but are now on the march, and so have made over to us some of their stage properties. The play is still in embryo; but now that we have made fools of ourselves for a few minutes to please these good people,"—this was said *sotto voce*, with a sly glance towards portly Madame Gerritse—"we are going to turn the remainder of to-night's entertainment into a miniature fancy ball. May I ask the honour of your hand for the first minuet?"

"I do not know what it is, sir, thank you," said Franzje, gravely.

"It is a dance much in vogue at the English court,

and in all good society," said the young officer, demurely. "You will permit me the pleasure of teaching
you ?"

"It is not like the Indian dances, is it?" she asked,
with a sudden rush of colour, called up by the remembrance of that dance of hers with the Mohawk children,
which had made the Dominie so angry.

"Not in the least," said Mr. Vyvian, with a gleam of
amusement at her *naïveté;* "it is the most correct of all
possible performances."

Franzje found it very difficult to tell whether Mr.
Vyvian were speaking in jest or earnest; but she had
not much time to ponder over the matter, for there was a
great stir around her at this moment. The actors—all in
male costume of a picturesque character—had followed
Mr. Vyvian's example, and were mingling with the spectators, and selecting each some favoured damsel as a companion in the dance. Anna was singled out by the
handsome colonel, who assisted her up the steps with
an air of half-mocking gallantry; Cornelia and Engeltje
followed with other officers, and as the couples increased,
Franzje began to see that everybody was going to dance
except Madame Gerritse and her husband, and Evert and
Cornelius, for whom there seemed to be no partners left.

"You do not mind our dancing, then, Madame?" she
said, drawing near to her portly hostess for a moment, and
speaking in a low voice.

"Not at all," replied the stout dame, placidly; "it is
an English fashion. The colonel tells me they dance at
court, and in the most respectable circles."

Franzje longed to ask if the Dominie would be likely
to object: but in the first place, she knew that Madame
Gerritse was scarcely to be depended on as a faithful exponent of the Dominie's sentiments; and, in the second,

she was sure from Mr. Vyvian's face that he overheard
her whispers, and she felt a shyness about mentioning the
Dominie before him, after what he had said at the berry-
gathering.

So when the young adjutant offered his hand to lead
her up to the stage, she accepted it gracefully, though with
a little inward reluctance, and found herself conducted
along a side passage to the green-room, which was full of
young Albanian ladies and their partners, who were going
through some preliminary, apparently, before passing on
to the stage itself.

"See, Franzje," said Anna, rushing up to her, "we are
each to wear one of these scarfs from Boston. Here is a
rose-coloured one for you. Colonel Trelawny gave me first
choice, so I have chosen a blue one, but you will like this
just as well, won't you?"

It was a broad silk sash of as bright a pink as could be
had before our modern dyes were invented; and though
it looked rather out of place on Franzje's stuff dress, its
hue "suggested rose-buds," as Mr. Vyvian whispered,
and when tied across one shoulder in a fashion which the
colonel had introduced, it was far from unbecoming. But
would her mother have liked it? Franzje wondered.

The dance which followed was a curious affair. The
colonel acted the part of dancing-master most efficiently,
and was ably seconded by Mr. Vyvian; but the young
Dutch maidens were not remarkable for either intelligence or grace, and Franzje and the little shy Engeltje
were the only two who performed their part in the minuet
with marked success.

Franzje's swan-like movements were full of unconscious ease and dignity, and as she began to enter into
the spirit of the thing, her blue eyes brightened into
splendour, and the soft colour in her cheeks deepened

to the sweetest carmine flush; so that with the rosy
scarf floating round her, she looked not unlike a picture
of Aurora—at least, just sufficiently like to put the
comparison into Mr. Vyvian's head. Fortunately he·
kept it to himself; he had perception enough of Franzje's
notions to feel that she would not consider herself com-
plimented by being likened to a heathen goddess.

The musicians played their best, and the dancing, such
as it was, was kept up with spirit. Colonel Trelawny,
finding minuets not successful, bethought himself of
trying country dances, which proved to be better suited
to the capacities of the rustic belles. After the first
minuet he had decided to be only master of the ceremonies, and, giving Anna over to one of his subalterns,
beckoned Evert on to the stage; but Cornelius was still
left among the spectators, and his round eyes watching
the proceedings with a sort of stolid wonder not unmixed
with contempt, were the one thing that detracted from
Franzje's sense of enjoyment. The grapes being out of
reach, he decided that they were sour; and though he had
been the very one to bring Franzje there, he now seemed
to express by his countenance a sort of sullen disapproval
of the part she was taking in the prevailing gaiety.

Once, when she was resting for a few moments on a
bench at the side of the stage, he drew near to it—getting
past the bandsmen—and said in a gruff way, "Killian is
reading Hebrew with the Dominie this evening. Madame
Gerritse asked him, but he would not come."

"I dare say he likes the Hebrew best," she returned
quietly.

"That doesn't seem to be your case."

"I haven't had the choice offered me," she said, with
a smile.

"But you like all this jumping about?"

"The dancing? Yes, I like it very much."

The sweet frank tone, the unabashed glance of the blue eyes, seemed to astonish the Dutch boy. Franzje's innocent taste for enjoyment appeared to him inconsistent with her learning, and her position as the Dominie's favourite.

Mr. Vyvian, who had been Franzje's partner from the first, came up at that moment to claim her once more. "Well, my young friend," he said, patronizingly to Cornelius, "so you despise dancing? Are you waiting for the afflatus to come upon you—that 'sacred rapture' that you talked of?"

"There isn't a girl for me to dance with," said Cornelius, grumpily.

"Try Major Berkeley's partner; he has just retired behind the scenes, worn out."

"Not I! she dances like a pig. If the girls could sit where I sat, and see themselves, they wouldn't be such fools again in a hurry—turning about like great pumpkins that have been set rolling."

"Do you make no exceptions?" said Mr. Vyvian, with a little arch bow towards Franzje.

"Oh, Franzje's not so bad.—I say, will you dance with me, Franzje, if I come up on the stage?"

"Remember that you belong to me this evening, Mademoiselle," put in Mr. Vyvian, hastily, his dark eyes gleaming at her strangely from under the overhanging cloud of light brown hair, and a sort of right of possession in his tone.

"And _I_ have a petition to advance," said the colonel gallantly. "I think it is your turn now to be master of the ceremonies, Vyvian, and mine to enjoy myself. Permit me, Mademoiselle Ryckman."

"I should like to dance with Cornelius, please, if

you will let him come up on the stage," she said, gently.

"With that lout!" said the colonel, in surprise, as Cornelius, waiting for no permission, ran round to the steps.

"He has been sitting still, and it is so dull for him," she said.

"And evidently you prefer native produce to imported articles," said Mr. Vyvian, laughing; "how do you propose to teach our young friend his steps?"

"Yes, what will you do with your Caliban when you have got him?" continued the colonel.

"Try to spirit him along in Ariel's fashion, if I were not too clumsy myself," she answered gaily.

Colonel Trelawny arched his eyebrows, and glanced at Russell Vyvian; it was a surprise to him to find an Albanian young lady who understood an allusion to the "Tempest."

"I shall sit and watch the process," said he, dropping on to the bench from which Franzje was rising.

"I shall stand and watch it," said Mr. Vyvian; but he saw a bright indignant glow mount in Franzje's cheek, and instead of carrying out his intention, he went and took pity on the awkward damsel whom Cornelius had likened to a pig, and led her to a place opposite to that which Franzje and her partner were taking.

If the girls danced like pumpkins, Cornelius danced like a sack of potatoes, and spite of Franzje's careful prompting, made so many mistakes, that his performance elicited continual laughter, his own sister Cornelia's giggle being heard among the loudest.

"Do you call that manners?" said he crossly to Franzje. "I am sure the last meeting of our Company was much pleasanter than this."

"It is the girls that laugh so," she answered apologetically; "they make much more noise than the officers; I wish they would not."

"Are you all ready for the catechising to-morrow?" he asked suddenly.

"Quite!" said she, astonished at the introduction of this subject.

"I'm not; I think I must go home and finish learning that chapter of Genesis. If only I can get Keetje and Engelt to come away!"

"Is it late?" said Franzje, with whom time had passed unnoticed.

"I heard Madame Gerritse say half an hour ago that it was past eight o'clock."

To Franzje's primitive mind this seemed a very dissipated hour indeed, though a modern young lady would think it a much more natural hour to *begin* dancing than to leave off. "Oh, then indeed I must go!" she said. "Just cross over and tell Evert so for me. Mother bade us not be late."

Evert when summoned, declared there was no hurry, and the officers remonstrated vehemently against any one's leaving the dance; but Franzje was firm. How could treats like this be enjoyed safely if they were allowed to lead to undutifulness to parents?

She divested herself of her rosy scarf more gaily than she had put it on, and with curtseys and thanks to Colonel Trelawny and Madame Gerritse, took her way out of the barn, followed by the unwilling Evert; while Cornelius was left with the unlearnt chapter of Genesis on his mind, to wait the pleasure of the giddy Cornelia.

But as the brother and sister passed through the house, the old cook insisted on their pausing to eat some corn-cakes made after a particular recipe of her own—though syllabub, and some other light refreshments, had been handed round during the intervals of dancing.

"What would missis say if I let you go out of de house widout one bit of supper?" gabbled she. "Mamselle Ryckman, you right to keep good hours; don't let dem young English gentlemen turn your head. Dey're sure to talk nonsense to you, 'cause you're a pretty one; but don't you tink too much of what dey say."

CHAPTER VII.

𝕮𝖍𝖊 𝕮𝖆𝖙𝖊𝖈𝖍𝖎𝖘𝖎𝖓𝖌.

THE regiment attended morning service every Sunday at the Episcopal Church in Albany; and the incumbent—Dr. Ogilvie, who enjoyed a tolerable salary from the English government as "chaplain to the Indians," but really had very little to say to the Indians at all except when they flocked into the town for their Easter Communion—was not sorry for the addition to his rather scanty congregation, though the behaviour of some of the officers was not quite so reverent—or, to use his own word, "decorous"—as he could have desired. However, on the Sunday following the dance in the Gerritses' barn —which had been kept up long after Franzje and Evert left it—very few of the officers accompanied the soldiers to Church; some mysterious indisposition seemed to have taken possession of them, which made it desirable for them to linger in bed, or dawdle over their breakfast; and various excuses were devised for non-attendance at church-parade, the colonel himself setting the example of absenteeism, and leaving his place to be filled by the senior major. But in the afternoon the invalids revived, and might be seen strolling forth in pairs by the river side, or lolling out of the windows of the houses in which they were billeted, and chatting with those of the passers-by whose respect for "the Sabbath" did not cause them to look upon idle gossip as one of the things prohibited by the Fourth Commandment.

Most of the Albanians, however, had gone to the Catechising, and the bell of the English Church was booming forth a summons to three-o'clock Evensong, when Mr. Gardiner, the young ensign who had accompanied Russell Vyvian to the berry-picking, stopped just outside the Bankers' house, and accosted the adjutant, who was sitting on the parlour window-sill smoking.

"I say, Vyvian," he began, "I think I shall go to Church, as I did not go in the morning; will you come with me?"

"No, thank you; I have just scandalized my worthy host by anouncing my intention of making an expedition to the woods. He went off to his prayers in a state of internal combustion, the signs of which were only too visible in his puffy countenance."

"Suppose we look in at the Dutch Tabernacle, and see how he is getting on. Seriously, I have rather a curiosity to hear that Dominie of theirs hold forth; but I daren't face him by myself, particularly as I shall have lost so many heads of his discourse by not getting there in time. Come along, there's a good fellow."

"It's Catechising in the afternoon," said Mr. Vyvian, yawning; "my young friend Cornelius has been gabbling over something which he said was the Dutch for Sodom and Gomorrah, in preparation for it. No, if I go any-

where I'll go to Church ; I was always brought up to a
veneration for Church and King."

" I didn't know you had got such a thing as veneration
in you, except for Lady Mary," said Mr. Gardiner, alluding to his friend's mother, a good and noble woman.

" Well, for her sake I have a certain lurking respect
for all that is good, even though it be a little dull, Yes,
let us go to Church. Just wait two minutes, and I'll be
with you."

He got up and put aside his pipe, and presently issued
forth in his best regimentals—officers did not think of
wearing plain clothes in those days—looking very handsome and very spruce, and carrying a large Prayer-Book
which his mother had given him.

They strolled along the pavement leisurely, though the
bell was giving its last stroke ; and as they turned into the
cross-street which led up to the church, and were passing
the door of the Dutch chapel, Mr. Gardiner arrested his
companion's steps.

" Do let us look in here," he said, " and see what they
are all about."

Russell was going to object, but it occurred to him
suddenly that he should like to see whether Franzje were
there, and so he yielded to the suggestion and went in.

Franzje was the first person who caught his eye on
entering. She was standing at one end of a semicircle con-
sisting half of maidens and half of lads, who were gathered
in front of the Dominie's pulpit, and were evidently, as
the young ensign whispered, being "put through their
facings" by him. She did not look like the floating
Aurora now ; her dress was of the soberest, her hands
folded together, her bright hair smoothed down demurely
under a white hood. But the upturned face was quite a
study in its intentness, and she was so quaintly lovely in

her Sunday apparel and with her good-child expression,
that Mr. Vyvian forgot all about the English service, and
drawing his companion into a pew near the door, pro-
fessed himself content to remain and listen.

Franzje did not see them, but the Dominie did instantly,
and a restless glance flashed out upon them from under
his powerful brows, though he did not pause even for a
second in what he was saying. One or two of the lads
turned round to gaze at them stolidly, but were immediately recalled to attention by a question from their
pastor; and though some of the older people in the pews
near them showed a little sense of discomfort at their
presence, it might have done no harm, had not the Dominie happened to look rather pointedly towards them
when he was impressing upon his youthful audience the
exceeding wickedness of the city from which righteous
Lot escaped.

"I'm Sodom, and you're Gomorrah, evidently," whispered Mr. Vyvian to his brother officer, catching by instinct the drift of the Dominie's discourse, though unable
to follow it word by word; and the Dutch lads seemed to
think so too, for they all turned their heads round for a
stare at the red-coated intruders. Then the lasses, not
unnaturally, must needs look to see what the boys were
looking at; and though Russell Vyvian was not sorry,
since it gave him a sudden glimpse of Franzje's full face
instead of her profile, the proceeding was to the last
extent exasperating to the Dominie. With a stern word
and sterner gesture he recalled the little band to order,
and kept their attention by a shower of questions addressed first to one and then to another with a quickness
which seemed to send the slow young intellects to the
right-about, and brought forth nothing but a set of confused and hopelessly irrelevant answers.

Franzje was the only one who preserved her presence of mind, but the silvery tones were low, and seemed to tremble a little, and the Dominie bade her speak louder, and then chid her for not immediately obeying. Russell saw the red lips close firmly on one another, and guessed something of the struggle which was going on in the young heart; but he was not prepared for the clear, ringing sweetness of the voice which at length gave the answer for which the Dominie was waiting. Even Dutch was musical in those accents, he thought; but they did not seem to melt the heart of M. Freylinghausen, who saw in Franzje's transparent face a sort of consciousness of the Englishmen's presence, and was more annoyed with her for it than was perhaps quite reasonable. He went on with his catechising more slowly again, giving the heavy lads time to recover their faculties, but his eye seemed to rest sternly on Franzje and her female companions; and once, when he saw a glance of intelligence pass between Cornelia and her, at something which the young people took as a side hit at the dissipations introduced by the officers, he rebuked both girls authoritatively, and perhaps all the more unsparingly because he divined that the presence of the young English gentlemen made the public reproof especially humiliating.

Cornelia twisted her shoulders, and looked more pert than she had ever dared to look before within range of the Dominie's eyes; probably in any other place she would even have ventured on a saucy rejoinder. Franzje drooped her stately head with a kind of proud, grave humility, which made Russell feel savage, and long to take up arms in her defence. Nevertheless, the Dominie was much more inwardly perturbed at Franzje's demeanour than at Cornelia's. He knew he could crush Keetje's pertness any day, if he took the trouble; but Franzje's

proud submission gave him a sense of something uncon-
quered within her, with which it was more difficult to
deal.   He could not read the expression of the resolutely
drooped eyes now, as he had so often read it before, when
after a reproof they had been raised to him swimming in
tears, but full of trusting filial appeal ; it seemed as if she
were no longer quite his own child to do with just as he
liked, but rather as if she were withdrawing part of her
mind from his allegiance—submitting still, it is true, but
with a mental reservation.

A little sadness mingled with the sternness when he
spoke to her next, and if he could have known how
Franzje's heart throbbed when she detected the change of
tone, he would certainly not have despaired of her ; but
her face told nothing, and he brought the lesson to a close
in a dissatisfied mood, meditating how he could keep the
English officers out of his church for the future.

When he went to the vestry, M. Ryckman followed him,
and one or two other elders bustled in after him with
rather an important air, as if they had something very
particular to communicate.   Meantime the congregation
left the building ; and as Madame Ryckman had stayed
at home that afternoon, there was no duenna to daunt Mr.
Vyvian, and prevent his walking beside Franzje if he
liked.   He was waiting for her outside the door—alone,
for Mr. Gardiner had joined Cornelia—and greeted her in
a bright, familiar, yet not disrespectful tone, as if he felt
himself already almost an old acquaintance.

He did not make any allusion to what he had just seen
and heard, but talked over the preceding evening, and
brought in a delicate compliment here and there, in a way
which was rather soothing to a little girl who had just
been publicly snubbed.   He was very pleasant and friendly
to her brothers, too, and she quite wished Jan would not

have answered him in such a short, bearish tone. Jan
was a good boy, very good, and answered much better at
the catechising than Evert; but certainly Evert's manners
were far pleasanter—far more like Mr. Vyvian's, Franzje
thought. Already Mr. Vyvian was becoming a kind of
standard to her.

They had not gone far, and were but just beginning
thoroughly to enjoy their chat, when a voice behind them
called, " Franzje! Franzje!" and she stopped abruptly and
turned round.

" Who wants you?" said Mr. Vyvian, turning also.
" Oh, the Dominie! Has he all the young demoiselles of
Albany at his beck and call?"

" It was my father," said Franzje; " that is he walking
with the Dominie. See, he is beckoning to me; I must
go back."

She made a little hurried curtsey, and retraced her steps
till she had joined her father and the minister, who were
walking very slowly and talking together. Mr. Vyvian
watched her quick, youthful, and yet not undignified pace.
" She has still the instinct of running when she is called,
like a child," he said to himself; " I wonder exactly how
much of the child and how much of the woman there is
underneath that precocious beauty. If she were but more
becomingly dressed, she would be the very type of beautiful girlhood; even my mother would not be able to
see a fault in her."

. He did not attempt to follow her, not having courage
to face the Dominie and his elder in what seemed to be
their present mood, but strolled along with Evert, and
finally enticed him for a walk upon the river bank, while
Jan ran off without even saying good-day.

Franzje was left to pace along soberly by her father's
side till they reached the Manse, and then was told to

come in there with him, though no explanation was
given as to why he desired her presence. He had merely
nodded in answer to her " Do you want me, father ? "
when she first joined him, and had gone on talking to the
Dominie ; so she could only conclude that she had been
summoned in order to prevent Mr. Vyvian's walking with
her.

They went into the Dominie's study, and he and M.
Ryckman seated themselves at the table, and began to
look over some papers together, and discuss something
about the admission of new " Church-members " the
following Easter. Franzje sat down in the window-seat,
not wholly uninterested, because she was anxious to
know whether the Dominie meant to admit *her* as a
Church-member—but feeling herself rather *de trop*, and
wondering at intervals how Mr. Vyvian and the boys were
getting on together, and what he had thought of the
rebukes she had got from the Dominie that afternoon.

Presently, some words of M. Freylinghausen's startled
her into fuller attention. " On one thing I have quite
determined," he was saying ; "that no one shall be admitted as a Church-member who takes any part in the
worldly amusements which these young Englishmen are
introducing. My people shall choose whom they will
serve—God or the devil ; I will have no trying to reconcile
both services."

M. Ryckman made a doubtful murmur, something between assent and dissent, which only set the Dominie off
on a more elaborate explanation of his intentions. Franzje
listened, amazed, doubtful, almost rebellious—the old old
conflict between Puritan principles and natural instincts
going on within her. Were all amusements wrong except
exactly such as had been common at Albany hitherto ? Had
the dance she had joined in the night before really made

her unfit for the Easter Communion? were youthful
spirits and laughter, and bright colours, and gay music,
indeed displeasing to God? Was Mr. Vyvian wicked, because he liked acting plays and doing things that Killian
and his compeers never dreamed of? Some inward voice
cried out No! no! to all these questions; her heart beat
with a rapid pulse, her face glowed under the white hood,
her little feet—cased in ugly thick shoes—began an impatient pit-a-pat on the floor; she was almost ready to
speak out, and assert an opinion of her own, there in the
Dominie's very sanctum!

And all the while he never so much as glanced towards
her.

M. Ryckman, who was calm and cautious, was not altogether carried along by the Dominie's zeal. "I have
heard the Schuylers say that social amusements of a more
lively character than those to which we have been accustomed are not altogether to be condemned," he said; "I
am not sure that if all well-meaning people withdraw their
countenance from these officers, they may not do more
harm than if tolerated to a certain extent, and kept within the bounds of moderation by the advice of prudent
persons."

"Do you flatter yourself that Colonel Trelawny, or
that light-minded young adjutant, are in the least inclined to take advice from you?" asked the Dominie
sarcastically.

"I don't see why they should not," said Franzje, suddenly firing up, both for her father's sake and Mr.
Vyvian's.

The Dominie just looked at her with a sort of lofty
surprise, and went on as if he had not heard. "I tell
you, Ryckman, that these Englishmen make a god of
their amusement: and you can no more hope to confine it

within reasonable bounds by your counsel than you might
hope to dam up the Hudson by sinking a few hedge-
stakes. Those who lend themselves to their wishes—the
Bankers and the Gerritses more particularly—will have
cause to rue it. Remember my words a year hence, and
see if they have not then come true."

"What would you have, Dominie?" rejoined M. Ryckman, with rather a perplexed air. "I invite none of them
to my house; but must we needs keep away from all the
houses where they are to be met? It is true, I am as well
content to smoke my pipe at home as with my neighbours;
but it seems hard upon the young people to be so restrained."

"*Hard*, to keep them from evil; hard, to keep them
pure; hard, to save their souls for God!" said the
Dominie earnestly. "Eli's sons would perhaps have
thought it hard if he had checked them in their sinful pleasures; yet wherefore came the wrath of God
upon him? Because his sons made themselves vile, and
he restrained them not. Was it better to let them
have their way? Did it seem better in that day when
Hophni and Phinehas died both of them? Nay, had
they not brought woe upon the whole nation? was not
the Ark of God taken? The sins of individuals may
bring danger to the whole Church."

It was impossible not to be impressed with the fiery
energy with which the Pastor spoke; the strength of his
convictions gave a degree of force to his manner which
exercised a well-nigh irresistible sway over the half-
convinced mind of his elder. But Franzje, while grant-
ing fully that if the pleasures the officers were setting on
foot *were* sinful, then it was the right and true and loyal
part to keep away from them, could not lay the ghost of
a doubt as to whether this were indeed the case—whether
the Dominie were not condemning from hearsay things

which, had he seen them, would have appeared to him
innocent enough.

"We let our Franzje and Evert go to the Gerritses' last
evening," said good Baas Ryckman, with a glance towards
his daughter; "I thought it had been a harmless merry-
making enough, from what they told us of it, but young
folks are not the best judges, no doubt. I suppose we had
better keep them away for the future—eh, Dominie?"

"Certainly," said the Dominie, gravely.

Franzje turned her face to the window, and struggled
with herself. It did, it *would* seem hard to be cut off by
a word from all that she had so enjoyed, and had meant
to enjoy for the future; to see her father content to abridge
his children's pleasure merely because the Dominie stigma-
tized as 'wicked' amusements which he had not seen, and
of which therefore he could not fairly judge. And yet,
and yet—was not the Dominie always right? was it not
the wildest presumption to think that he could be mistaken and prejudiced, that her father could be wrong in
submitting implicitly to his guidance?

She did not see that there was another side to the question; that it was not necessary to suppose the Dominie
infallible in order to submit cheerfully to his decrees;
that it might be that he and her father were wrong—and
yet that her part all the same was to obey, that the sacri-
fices of obedience are never lost, even though they may
be in themselves unessential. In after years, when Franzje
thought all over the matter, she used to date the beginning of her mistakes from that Sunday afternoon, on which
she had put aside the simple question, "What is *my* duty,
the Dominie's and my father's decision being what it is?"
and had perplexed herself with thoughts of what was
their duty, and whether they were really acting in the
best and wisest way.

H

She hardly heard the next few words of her father and the pastor, so full was she of her own thoughts, but was roused by M. Ryckman's getting up to go.

"Well, good-day, Dominie," he said, as he prepared to depart; "I am on your side, of course, whatever happens; and we must see if we cannot bring our townsfolk to reason."

"Good-day," replied the Dominie, in a friendly and satisfied tone, holding out his hand as he spoke.

Franzje rose and curtsied, but before she could utter any verbal farewell, the Dominie turned away, and began arranging the papers on the table.

So he was going to let her leave his house without one word of good-bye! Her heart swelled, her lips quivered, but she followed her father mutely to the door, and they were half way home before she spoke.

"Father," she said timidly at last, "*you* are not vexed with me, are you?"

"No, except that you should not have spoken just now when the Dominie asked if I thought the officers would take my advice; it was not your part to interrupt."

"But I could not bear the Dominie's tone, Father; it seemed to disparage you and the officers both."

"'Could not bear,'—that is a new way of speaking for thee, little one. Tut, tut, thou must be a good child, and not fancy thou knowest better than the Dominie, but be content to hold thy tongue, and sit at home with thy mother, and think no more of these officers."

"I don't think of them,—not in any wrong way, I mean—and we didn't do anything wrong at the Gerritses'; if the Dominie had asked me, I would have told him all about it; at least—" for she suddenly remembered her promise to Mr. Vyvian not to betray his theatrical plans —"I would have described to him the dancing and everything I joined in."

"Dancing! ay, that is just what the Dominie objects to; and from what Elder Jansen told him, it seems it was kept up long after you two were at home and in bed. I wish I had thought to tell him that *you* came away in decent time, but even that would not have made him think it right for you to be there. You must keep away from all such merry-makings for the future; you understand that, I hope, my Franzje?"

"Father, you would not have said so if it had not been for the Dominie."

There was some bitterness in her tone, and the worthy elder turned round and looked at her in surprise.

"Softly, softly, Franzje!" he said, admonishingly.

She fell a little behind him, and was silent again, all sorts of contrary emotions fighting a battle within her.

When they reached their own door, she said in quite an altered voice, "Father, why wouldn't the Dominie speak to me?"

"He is disappointed in you, child, I think; but never mind, be a good girl, and it will all come right."

The words in the glen came back to her—"*You*, at least, child, must never give me cause for displeasure,"—spoken in that strange appealing tone. Already she had given him cause, or at least he thought so; he was *disappointed* in her, her father said; the still loyal heart thrilled with pain at the thought.

"Father, I am sorry now," she said; "let me go back and tell the Dominie so. I sha'n't be able to go to sleep to-night if I think he has not forgiven me."

"Best not trouble him now, my girl, had you?" said her father, irresolutely.

"Oh, I don't think he will mind; I will not stay long. Father, I can't rest till I think he is not angry with me, and that he will let me be a Church-member at Easter."

M. Ryckman said no more; and taking silence for consent, Franzje turned and walked back quickly in the direction from which they had come, a sudden rush of earnest remorseful devotion to her pastor filling her heart, and leaving no room for the questioning criticising thoughts which had troubled her such a little while before. She had not gone very far, however, before she met Mr. Vyvian and her brother, returning from their stroll.

"Where are you going in such a hurry, Franz?" said Evert, stopping her as she was trying to pass them.

"What have you done with your father and the revered Dominie?" struck in Mr. Vyvian before she had found words to reply.

Oh, if she had only had courage to say straight out, "I am going back to M. Freylinghausen now, you will find my father at home!" but the sneer in Mr. Vyvian's tone as he mentioned the pastor made her feel doubly shy and embarrassed, and she merely faltered, "I have just left my father; I am going a little way up the street," and again tried to pass on.

"I'll come with you," said Evert, turning; and to her dismay, Mr. Vyvian must needs turn too, and walk beside her.

He was very agreeable, even more so perhaps than he had been when her father had called her away from him; but his presence was torture to Franzje just now. If she had been less unsophisticated, and had had more of the assurance of a modern young lady, she would have known perhaps how to get rid of him; but spite of her womanly appearance, she was but a child in many points still, and could think of no courteous mode of implying that she would rather be without him.

They were nearing the pastor's house, and she was beginning to form a desperate resolution of avowing that to

be her destination, when who should come forth but the
Dominie himself! He seldom went out after the Sunday
services were over, unless some sick person happened to
send for him, so Franzje had never reckoned on such a
contingency; and the notion of what he would think at
seeing her again with Mr. Vyvian, and without her father,
flashed upon her with a sudden shock.

In another minute they had met face to face; and
though he uttered no word of surprise or annoyance,
Franzje knew by the hard expression of his mouth and
eyes that he had judged and condemned her, and that
nothing but a frank and prompt explanation could remove
the false impression that he had conceived. And how
was she to give that, with Mr. Vyvian standing by?

"Where have you left your father, Franzje?" inquired
the Dominie, when he had exchanged a stiff greeting with
the young officer.

"He is at home, Sir," she answered in a quiet constrained voice.

"And you have not had walking enough, it seems?"

"Oh yes, I was not going any further; at least—" and
there she paused. "Only to the Manse," was the real end
of the sentence; but something between timidity and
pride prevented her from uttering it.

"Then perhaps you will turn with me," pursued the
Dominie, gravely; "I am going past your house."

Oh! if Mr. Vyvian and Evert would only have gone
on and left her with the Dominie, all might yet have
been well; but Russell firmly believed that by deserting
her he should leave her exposed to the full outpouring of
the Dominie's wrath, and therefore determined to accompany her to her door, no matter what hints he might
receive to depart. He would not even walk behind or
before with Evert, but resolutely kept his ground beside

her; and as the Dominie walked closely on the other side,
Evert found himself of no account, and was perhaps
almost as uncomfortable as any of the party.

Mr. Vyvian made a few nonchalant efforts to keep up
a conversation, which were rather baulked by Franzje's
monosyllables and the Dominie's dry rejoinders. As for
Evert, he could not think of a word to say. Oh, what a
long way it seemed to M. Ryckman's door!

Franzje had a lingering hope that the Dominie would
come in with her, or would wait at any rate till Mr.
Vyvian had taken leave, and so give her the chance of a
confidential word with him. She no longer felt the impulse to open her heart to him, which she had felt when
she set out for his house; her whole soul was chilled by
the harshness of his manner; but something she might
and would have said if the opportunity had been given
her. It was, however, denied her, in this way. As they
approached the house, the Dominie turned suddenly to
Evert, who was lagging behind a little. " I cannot come
in," he said, " I have to proceed further. Go on before
us, if you please, and ask your father to come to the door.
I have a word to say to him."

Evert obeyed; and the father, with a long pipe in his
mouth, made his appearance in the door-way just as they
reached the steps. The Dominie ascended them solemnly,
still by Franzje's side; while Mr. Vyvian stood below,
waiting to catch a parting look from her if possible before
she disappeared.

" I have brought your daughter home, Ryckman; keep
watch over her for the future," said the pastor sternly;
and then, before the slow Dutchman or the astonished
girl could speak, he hurried away, and was seen striding
off down the street at an unusually rapid pace.

Mr. Vyvian lingered for one graceful bow, which

Franzje scarcely returned, and for a half-comical half-supercilious smile, which she did not return at all; and then he too turned away in the opposite direction, and Franzje followed her father into the house.

"What is it about, my girl? what have you been doing?" said M. Ryckman, removing his pipe for a moment, and puffing out a volume of smoke as he did so.

Franzje drew up her head with the air of an offended queen. "I have done nothing," was all she said, was all she *could* say at the moment; and then she went slowly up the stairs, and into her own room.

Her father looked after her with a puzzled, dissatisfied air; then he glanced round for Evert, meaning to question him, but Evert had disappeared; so he put his pipe between his lips again, and with a muttered "I will get the wife to find out what is amiss, and set it to rights," enveloped himself in clouds of fragrant tobacco, and mightily soothed himself thereby.

Perhaps he would scarcely have taken the matter so placidly, however, if he had heard the agony of sobs into which Franzje broke when she was safe within the shelter of her room. A terrible feeling of shame, of humiliation, overwhelmed her, and yet her innocence asserted itself indignantly against it. "She had done no harm, the Dominie had misjudged her; it was very hard, very unjust." But still all the time her heart cried out to him with something of the old filial devotion; his hard judgement of her was so unbearable, just because her reverence for him was so great. But could they ever go back to the old happy relations after what had passed that day? In her strong youthful tempest of misery, Franzje thought not.

CHAPTER VIII.

A Christmas Gift.

AUTUMN had gone by, and winter had come ; the Hudson was frozen over, and skating and sleighing were the order of the day ; the Albanian youths were in the highest spirits, and prided themselves on outdoing the English officers by their prowess on the ice ; and the Albanian maidens went about wrapped in furs, looking very blooming and bright, and showing themselves by no means insensible to the charms of a moonlit drive along the frozen river, with the sleigh bells tinkling a refrain to their animated remarks. All this belonged to Albanian manners, and was not frowned on by the elders ; nay, even a grand stolen supper at the King's Arms, in which some of the most daring of the youths indulged towards Christmas time, was winked at by the civic authorities as a mere youthful folly, and allowed to escape punishment. Such things were wont to happen on winter nights, "it had always been so," and the good folks of Albany knew how to be indulgent to freaks which had been common to their fathers before them; but the new diversions introduced by the English regiment stood upon different grounds. It was quite strange and wrong, according to their primitive notions, that a sleighing-expedition should be wound up by a dance instead of a friendly tea at some hospitable mansion along the river ; and the announcement of a play which was to be performed in the Gerritses' barn during the first week of the new year, excited the greatest surprise and misgiving among all the respectable citizens. Most of them did not clearly know what a "play" meant.

so a spice of curiosity was mingled with their alarm; and even some of those who were perfectly convinced that they should not like it, and quite ready to say, " Yes, yes, to be sure, Dominie," when their pastor denounced the intended diversion, cherished a secret wish to see the spectacle, and judge for themselves whether it were indeed at once so bewitching and so wicked as it was represented to be. It happened that M. Ryckman had to go to New York on business, just as the play began to be publicly talked about, and therefore he did not hear so much of the Dominie's views on the subject as he would otherwise have done; but his worthy spouse echoed her pastor's sentiments with true feminine fidelity, and forbade her children to say a word about the play in her hearing, or entertain an idea of going to it.

Franzje had been kept away from all dances that had been deliberately planned, but had come in for one which had been got up *impromptu* at the close of a sleighing-expedition, and had found a strange mixture of excitement and unhappiness in joining for once in an amusement of which she now *knew* the Dominie most distinctly disapproved. Life had become wonderfully changed for her since the Christmas of the year before; *then* it was with a calm untroubled heart that she had listened for the echoes of the angels' song, and her only anxiety had been as to whether the Dominie would like a Christmas present, on which she had been bestowing much time and pains; *now* she would not have ventured to ask him to accept any such offering, and though she lent her voice to the Christmas hymns, it was with a sad misgiving that she was not worthy to sing them, that she had perhaps begun, as the Dominie said, to " love the world," and was not pure enough to stand even in thought by the Manger Cradle. And yet that world, how attractive it

was, how innocent it seemed to one who was ready to
enjoy it innocently! What did it mean but a little
amusement, a little novelty, a little admiration and encouragement, a little new wonderful unexpected love?
Yes, *love*, for she felt now, though she never put it to
herself in so many words, why Mr. Vyvian's dark eyes
softened into reverential tenderness sometimes as they
looked at her, why his light tones grew earnest when he
talked to her; she knew that though in the Dominie's
judgment she was wicked and worldly and undeserving
of notice, in that of Mr. Vyvian, she was peerless in
innocence, stainless as a saint, his very ideal of perfect
maidenhood, the brightest and noblest influence, so he
said, of his whole life. She had been feeling this instinctively for some time, and on Christmas Day he made
her sure of it.

There was no Catechising that afternoon, and it was
rather the custom for people to pay each other friendly
visits, drink coffee together, and exchange the compliments of the season. Franzje prevailed on her mother
to call on Madame Banker, a thing which she had not
done for some time, and to take her—Franjze—to see
Cornelia. The visit was quite honestly to Cornelia, for
there was Evensong at the English Church that day as on
Sunday, and Franzje imagined Mr. Vyvian would attend
it. He had been in the morning, however, and thought
a second service unnecessary, so though he was not to
be found in the parlour, where Madame Banker was sitting
in state to receive her guests, he soon made his appearance among the gay group of younger people who were
gathered round the wood fire in the hall. Cornelia was in
boisterous spirits, and instead of drawing Franzje apart
for a friendly talk, such as they used to have in old times,
jested and giggled with Anna Gerritse and Mr. Gardiner,

who were both of the party, in a way that was more amusing than polite or refined. Engeltje, however, had a special greeting for her sister's friend; and the two girls were standing together at one side of the fire, the little one's arm passed lovingly round the elder's waist, when Mr. Vyvian joined them.

Engeltje blushed scarlet, and seemed ready to fly as he approached, but Franzje held her fast; she loved the little thing, and wondered why she should still be so scared at Mr. Vyvian, now that he had been for so long an inmate of her father's house. *He* did not appear at all embarrassed by *her* presence.

"It is an unexpected pleasure to see you here, Mademoiselle," he said, turning on Franzje one of his most ardent glances. "I was just wondering whether it would be thought presumptuous if I were to call at your house to offer you all my Christmas wishes."

"You would find no one at home just now," said Franzje; "my mother is here in the parlour, and my father has not come back from New York, and my brothers have gone out skating."

"There is no longer any need for me to go, since *you* are here," he returned. "I like your Albanian Christmas very much, everybody visiting everybody, and gifts passing from hand to hand. I wonder how many you have had to-day?"

"Not one in this house yet," said Engeltje, with a start of compunction. "Keetje began a purse for you, dear, but what with driving out in the sleigh so often, and going up street to see the boys slide down hill, she has not finished it. Cornelius says you will be lucky if you get it by Vrowen Dag."[1]

Franzje laughed, and disclaimed any desire for a present,

[1] Feast of the Purification.

at the same time producing two pretty little bags which she had worked for Engeltje and Cornelia. "It is quite pleasure enough to see you, dear Engeltje," she said.

"You like giving better than receiving," remarked Mr. Vyvian, and the subject dropped; but when coffee and cakes had been handed round, and the young people were busy partaking of them, he disappeared, and presently was heard calling from the stairs, "Mademoiselle Engeltje!"

Engeltje looked fluttered and frightened again, but ran off to him; and there was a whispered consultation, which ended in their both going up-stairs together. In a few minutes she came back alone. "Franz," she said, twining her arm in that of her friend, and speaking coaxingly, "I want you to come into my father's little account-room. I have something to show you."

She marched Franzje away with the would-be careless air of the small conspirator that she was, and took her into a room near the back door, where M. Banker paid his servants, and the labourers from his farm.

On the table, supported in an upright position by some books placed behind it, was a small painting of the Madonna and Child, the loveliest thing that Franzje had ever seen. It had no frame, but a few frosted twigs, very white and sparkling, had been tastefully placed round it so as to form a sort of natural bordering, and the holy mother's face looked out from them with a sweet pure wistful look that went to Franzje's heart. She leant on the table gazing at it without a word; it seemed the most beautiful bit of Christmas teaching that had ever come to her. How her heart yearned towards that Divine Child with the wonderful sorrowful eyes that seemed already to discern the future Cross; to her,— unused to the sight of good sacred pictures, except a few possessed by the Schuylers, among which this subject did not happen to be,—He was very very real; if she had been quite alone, she would perhaps have knelt. As it was, she only continued to bend over the picture in silent delight till Engeltje roused her by asking, "Do you like it ?"

"I never thought there could be anything so lovely," said Franzje earnestly; and she was going on to ask where it had come from, when Engeltje cut her short by the. eagerness with which she rejoined, "It is for *you.*"

"For me ?" said Franzje, startled; "oh no; what can you mean, Engelt ? Is it M. Banker's ?"

"No, it was mine, and now it is yours; it was given me to give you, and you cannot refuse it. There is no one so fit to have it as you, Franzje."

There was a little *soupçon* of natural envy in the admiring tones, but not unkind envy; and Engeltje's face was very pretty and touching in its wistfulness as she raised her lips to Franzje's to be kissed. She did not guess the secret of her own feelings, nor did Franzje; but Russell Vyvian, as he entered the room—having stolen down the back-stairs to join them—said to himself complacently, "Poor little thing! she is half in love with me herself, and yet grateful for being made a confidante of my love for another girl. What little weak tender simpletons some women are !"

It was well for him that Franzje could not read his thoughts, well perhaps too that she did not know that he had picked up the picture dirt cheap from.a poor German at New York, and had bought it, not because he cared for the subject, but because it was a pretty thing in its way, and might be worth taking home to his mother. When he saw her rapt gaze, he would not break the spell by a light word, and only said, "Mademoiselle Engeltje has found a gift to please you, I see. She could not bear you to leave the house without a single Christmas offering."

"But this is too good for me, too beautiful!" said Franzje, scarcely withdrawing her eyes from it even when she spoke.

"As if beautiful things and good things did not belong to you by right," he answered, in a low tender tone which thrilled Engeltje to the very heart.

Franzje only thought with a sudden pang, "And yet the Dominie will not speak to me because I am so bad!"

"If you gave this to Engelt, she ought to keep it," she said, too straightforward to disguise her conviction that the picture was Mr. Vyvian's in the first instance.

"It was given to her that she might make it acceptable to you," he said, smiling. "*Angel's* gifts can never be refused, you know, and most especially at Christmas."

The little shy maiden coloured at the play upon her name. Franzje said gravely, "Engelt does not need it to make her good, but still I should like her to keep it, Sir, if you please, and she will let me come and look at it sometimes."

Something in this speech gave little Engeltje pain. "Franz, you *must* take it," she whispered; "it was only meant for you, and if you love me, you will not try to refuse it any more. I shall go and look for something to wrap it up in;" and she ran away.

"I wish this diamond frosting on the twigs were all real jewel-work for your sake," said Mr. Vyvian when she was gone.

"I should not like it so well then," returned Franzje simply.

"And perhaps it would not then have come so naturally as little Engelt's gift," continued Russell, with a smile;

"will you think of me as well as of her sometimes, Mademoiselle, when you look at this picture? I see that you will look at it often, by the way in which you gaze at it now."

"I should like to show it to the—" began Franzje; then her face grew changed and sad, and she added, "I shall show it to Uncle Jan."

"Has he a soul for art?" inquired Mr. Vyvian, not very sympathizingly.

"I don't know; but he loves our Lord," said Franzje, in a soft voice of reverence.

He had very little faith, this heedless young officer, but he could feel what faith was in another; he saw that religion was not to Franzje a thing in the abstract, to be treated with a certain distant respect, but the worship of a Divine Person, a real living love.

"If we could be all like you," he murmured under his breath, and his dark eyes in their liquid splendour were full of a strange eloquence which thrilled the girl's soul with an emotion which she could not define. They spoke a language which is understood all the world over, and which leaves a far deeper impression than any audible speech.

She cast down her own eyes when she had read his, and he stood watching the fair modest face in silence for a moment, and then said in a lighter tone, "You have not so given your heart to heaven as not to leave a little corner for earth, I trust? You are not thinking of joining 'the society,' as you call it?"

She looked up at him once more, with a little amusement, and yet a little trouble in her face. "Oh, no," she said, "I never can feel as if I should like that, though it is very bad of me."

"It is a delightful badness," he rejoined; "you cannot

street, adding by their lively comments to the hilarity of the scene.

"There are Killian and Arij," shouted the boys ; and truly among the foremost of the sledges was one in which sat young Barentse, most charmingly at his ease, and with little Arij Ryckman propped up in front of him.

Killian stopped his sledge exactly at the right moment, and jumped lightly out, and drew it to one side before it could be overwhelmed by the torrent of other sleighs which accomplished their descent almost simultaneously. There was a glow of exercise on his dark cheek, and he looked very manly and handsome as he came up to wish Madame Ryckman and Franzje a happy Christmas, little fair-haired Arij capering by his side.

Madame Ryckman smiled on Killian as she always did, thanked him for taking care of Arij, and asked after his grandfather. Franzje said but little, and looked about with rather a dreamy air in the midst of the merry throng.

"Mother, come to the top and see us get in," clamoured Dirk and Albert, bringing out their sledges from under the shelter of a friendly door-way, and proceeding to drag them up the hill by the bit of rope in front of them.

" Oh yes, Mother," said Arij, pulling her hand, " I'm going to ride with Killian again—ain't I, Killian ? "

" No, no, Arij, he must be quite tired of you ; you had better go home with Franzje," said Madame Ryckman ; and a little altercation began between the mother and her darling, under cover of which Killian approached Franzje, and walked beside her up the hill, dragging his sledge after him.

"How dull the Dominie looks this Christmas," he began ; " he came to eat his Christmas dinner with Grandfather to-day, but he had no appetite, and gave such

heavy sighs now and then, as if things were altogether
wrong."

" I thought he looked tired this morning," said Franzje,
feeling rather guilty, but trying not to show it. "Mother
thinks he sits up too late at night studying."

"Oh, he always did that, but he used not to look
so worn and sad. Franzje,"—he paused, and then went
on hurriedly, " you are not going to see this play, are you?"

"I don't know, I suppose not; but I should *like* to
go, Killian."

" I ought not to be surprised at your saying so," said
Killian, " for nearly every young person in the town says
the same; but somehow I thought *you* were different.
Franzje, how can you like those officers? They are *not*
a good set; they can only do you harm."

Franzje clasped Mr. Vyvian's present closer to her under
her cloak. "I don't think they do me any harm at all,"
she answered.

" Franzje, don't be angry with me if I tell you that
things are said—that people are beginning to talk about
you and Mr. Vyvian."

"People talk about everything under the sun," rejoined
Franzje, with sudden petulance ; "but it does not follow
that there is any meaning in their words. It is the gossips
and the tale-bearers that make half the mischief in the
world. I wonder you listen to them, Killian. Though
indeed," she added, with some pain in her tone, "it is
not wonderful, perhaps, that you should, since even our
Dominie does."

" It is right that the Dominie should know what goes
on," said Killian, stanchly.

" But if he would see with his own eyes and not with
Elder Jansen's, he might judge of things differently," replied Franzje.

"It must be the English officers that have taught you to criticise the Dominie," said Killian.

She made a little impatient movement with her shoulders, and there was something almost like scorn upon the wide brow. "It is you who do me harm, Killian," she said. "You make me feel cross and wicked, even on Christmas Day."

"Yes, it is my fault, I suppose; somehow, I can never talk to you now without offending you, Franzje," replied Killian, sadly. "I must try to hold my tongue for the future."

They were jostled apart for a moment by the throng, and it was a bitter moment to Killian, full of pain and wrath and self-reproach and disappointed love. But when they came together again, Franzje's mood had changed.

"Don't let's quarrel," she said, with rather a tremulous smile upon her sweet mouth; "I am glad you are what you are—that there is *one* person in whom the Dominie is not disappointed."

"O Franzje, you could please him much better than I if you would," returned the youth, eagerly. "He does not care for me as he does for you, who have been like his own child almost."

"I could not please him now except by being a hypocrite," said Franzje, with the smile growing still more tremulous. "He will never be satisfied with me till I hate what I don't hate, and think what I don't think. *You* cau please him and yet be honest, but I could not now."

"Are you so changed as all that, Franzje?"

A little of the petulance came back. "No, I am just what I always was; I never pretended to think everything wrong, but just the very things we were accustomed to. Killian, how is all this sliding and dashing down hill in a sledge so much more sensible than dancing, or making beautiful poems seem real by saying the speeches in character ? "

Franzje's idea of a play was still wholly drawn from Shakespeare; not wonderful, perhaps, since she had read no other.

"It's silly enough, I dare say," said Killian, colouring a little; "but at least it does nobody any harm; and see, Franzje, there are two of the officers going to try, so they don't despise it."

"They'll tumble out, most likely," rejoined Franzje, with a bright gleam of fun in her eyes. Her supposed devotion to the officers by no means blinded her to the fact that the two young ensigns who were just embarking, in little sledges at the top of the hill were not likely to exhibit such expertness as her young townsmen, to whom this was an annual diversion. One of them could not even get under weigh, it seemed, and Franzje was still more amused when she got near enough to hear the exhortations which Dirk and Albert were addressing to him.

"You ought to have a stick," said Dirk, "to push yourself off with. I wonder you did not think of it. I'd lend you mine, only I want it myself."

"You shall have mine," said the more good-natured Albert, "if you'll promise to let me have it back when you've had one turn. See, you must give the sledge a push, so ! and then——"

And then, before Albert could finish his sentence, off went the sledge like a shot down the slippery hill, and the young officer, not being skilled in guiding it, came to grief half way, and not only tumbled out himself, but descended like an avalanche on top of the other ensign, who, but for this catastrophe, might have fared more prosperously.

There was a tremendous shout of laughter among the bystanders ; they meant no incivility, and would have been quite as ready to laugh if the accident had happened to Killian ; but perhaps the Englishman's clumsiness was rather more delightful to them than native clumsiness would have been, and they did not make much allowance for his not having had similar opportunities for practice.

" I'm glad *he's* had a tumble," said little Arij, dancing about ; and even his quiet kindly mother did not reprove the sentiment.

" I hope he has not broken my stick," said Albert, ruefully. " Killian, lend me yours, will you ? It's no use to you if you're only going to talk to Franzje."

" O Killian, you *must* take me down the hill once more," pleaded Arij. " Franzje can wait for me, can't you, Franz ? "

" You will tire Killian's patience out," said Madame Ryckman : but the Indian face was lit up with a good-natured smile, and Arij was placed in the sledge and taken down the hill " like a flash of lightning," as the boys had said, before any further objection could be made.

Madam Ryckman stood at the top, shivering. " I wish Vrow Banker would not keep her rooms so hot," she said ; " it makes one feel the cold so when one stands about."

" Had not you better come home, Mother ? Killian will see to the boys," said Franzje.

" Ah, yes, that's very fine ! " returned her mother, quickly. " You can scarcely speak a kind word to him ; but when you want anything done, then it's ' Oh, Killian can do it.' "

Franzje blushed, and attempted no self-defence. " Then will you take Arij home, Mother ? and shall I see to Dirk and Albert ? " was all she said.

" Well—" began Madame Ryckman, half-assentingly. She was very cold indeed, and the thought of the warm stove at home was very comfortable, and to leave Franzje under Killian's protection, as it were, was a thing not repugnant to Albanian notions of propriety, and might be the means of bringing about a better understanding between them. She was just going to say yes, when she caught sight of a bevy of officers, among whom were Colonel Trelawny and Mr. Vivian, advancing up the street; and then she changed her mind all in a hurry, and became anxious to despatch Franzje home as fast as possible.

She would have taken her into the middle of the road out of the way of the gentlemen, had it been possible to keep clear of the sledges that were rushing down or being slowly dragged up ; as it was, she hurried her so quickly along the crowded pavement, that she had nearly precipitated her into Mr. Vyvian's arms. He moved aside most courteously, but looked surprised and amused. " A second meeting to-day ! that is an unlooked-for pleasure," he said quickly.

Colonel Trelawny would have spoken to her, but she only curtsied and passed on, her mother panting behind.

By going out into the road, Mr. Vyvian managed to get near her again for an instant, and whispered, " Remember the 7th, and your promise."

On the 7th, the theatricals were to take place.

Arij was found, and Franzje and he were sent home together as quickly as possibly, Madame Ryckman remaining to shiver, though the glow of excitement she had felt about the officers and her daughter had warmed her up just for the moment. The consequence was, she caught cold, and though she persisted in what she called shaking it off for several days, it mastered her at last, and brought

a sort of feverish attack in its train. On New Year's
Eve she took to her bed, and for a day or two was really
ill—so ill as to make her children uneasy at the absence
of their father. She would not hear of his being alarmed
about her, however, or summoned home. "Business must
be attended to," she said ; and by the 7th she was really
a good deal better, though in that weak, uncomfortable
irritable state, which sometimes makes the beginning of
recovery more trying than the illness itself. Franzje was
very tender and devoted in her attendance, but Madame
Ryckman seemed almost to prefer the services of a middle-
aged negress, who had been with her since her babyhood,
and so the girl's chief business lay in overlooking her
little brothers, and making her Uncle Jan comfortable.

One of her special occupations was to soothe and
sympathize with Evert, who was in a very discontented,
unsettled frame of mind. He had rebelled against his
father's decree with regard to not joining in the officers'
amusements much more decidedly than Franzje had done ;
had even stolen off to one ball without leave, braving M.
Ryckman's short-lived anger and the Dominie's lasting
displeasure, and now openly declared that he meant to
attend the theatricals, and saw no harm at all in doing so.

"Father never has *forbidden* them, you know ; how
could he, when he never heard of them ? " said the lad,
coming and leaning his elbows on a little table in the
kitchen, where Franzje and the faithful Maria were making
cakes together. " It's my belief, if he were here he would
want to see the play himself."

"I don't think he would go to it, though," said
Franzje.

"No, because of the Dominie. Isn't it unbearable,
Franz, that the Dominie should set himself against everything that is amusing ? "

"Oh, but he does not; not against *everything*, I mean," corrected his sister.

"Well, not against skating, and so on, perhaps, but against everything that is introduced by the officers. Do you know, Franz, the Cuylers are going to the play. Madame Cuyler says she will not judge without seeing, but that if she does not like this one, she shall never go to another. I am going with them; I promised Cortlandt I would."

"Oh, Mamselle Franzje, you go too," broke in Maaike. "Madame Cuyler, she very good lady, it quite safe to go wid her anywhere. Monsieur Evert, you ask de mistress to let Mamselle Franzje go."

"Oh no, no, Evert. I can't have Mother worried,' said Franzje, warmly.

Maria and he only exchanged smiles; and he proceeded to unfold before the girls a printed play-bill which set forth that on such a day and at such an hour a comedy called "The Beaux' Stratagem" was to be acted by "the Royal Company of Players;" and there followed a list of the characters, though not the names of those who were going to take them, as the actors expected much amusement in puzzling the good towns-folk as to their identity. The paper was dingy, and the printing imperfect, compared with the marvels of modern typography; but it had been printed at New York on purpose for the officers, and wa the best thing of the kind that the period could produce.

To those young people, who had never seen anything of the sort before, it was something very wonderful and fascinating; and Franzje and the little slave-girl suspended their cake-making, and hung over it together. Franzje was thinking of her promise to Mr. Vyvian, and longing to keep it, though feeling half ashamed of the longing, since her duty seemed to be to stay at home.

" What is a comedy, Mamselle ? " queried Maria, as she plunged her hands into the flour again.

"Something funny," responded Evert briskly.

Maaike's black eyes glittered, and she showed all her white teeth ; but Franzje said meditatively, " It must be witty, of course, but I don't know that it need be exactly what you would call funny, Evert, though it is not like a tragedy, there are no deaths in it. I hope Mr. Vyvian won't have any funny speeches to make."

" Franzje, you are a sort of she-Dominie at heart, after all ; you don't really care for fun," said Evert.

" Oh yes, I do, in its way ; but I don't like people I care about to be ridiculous. I should not like to see Mr. Vyvian sliding down hill in a sledge, even if he did it as well as Killian."

When she had said this, she got hot and confused at the admission she had made. She had implied that she cared for Mr. Vyvian, cared for him more than for Killian.

Maria, woman-like, caught the force of the remark ; but Evert did not seem to notice it. " Would you rather see a trage—what d'ye call it, Franz, then ? " was all he said.

" Oh no ; I like things to be happy and to end well," she answered. " I want it to be so in real life as well as in poetry."

With her bright face raised, with her soft eyes gleaming, and her fresh lips parting in a smile, she looked the very picture of joyful anticipation. She liked life to be happy, and it was going to be so, she believed, spite of little passing cares and contrarieties. And all the while there was a tragic future waiting—a future which she herself was unconsciously helping to mould.

When she had finished her cakes, she made some thick milk for Madame Ryckman's dinner, and took it up to

her ; but though she had taken pains with it, her mother
was not at all satisfied. The poor lady was out of sorts,
and nothing seemed nice or comfortable to her. She was
too amiable by nature, and too self-restrained, to make
much complaint; but she declined to eat, and told Franzje
to let her be quiet and go to sleep, affirming that that
was all she wanted.

The boys went out after the early dinner, Maaike was
kept busy by the cook, and the afternoon seemed very
long to Franzje sitting alone in the parlour with her sewing. Once she would have passed it in learning page after
page of "theology" for the Dominie, but she had missed
his last week-day lesson through her mother's illness, and
besides, he scarcely seemed to care to set her any tasks
now.

Just as it was getting dusk, Evert returned, accompanied by no less a personage than Madame Cuyler. He
had been working on her feelings with regard to Franzje's
loneliness and dulness now that the mother was ill and
the father away, and she had come to see if the girl would
go to the play with her.

"I have told my husband that _I_ shall go and take my
children for this once," said the mayor's wife in her
stately manner ; "if we do not like it, we can but come
away again."

"I should think you are sure to like it," said Franzje
fervently. She had such a beautiful ideal of what it was
going to be, that she would not admit the notion that it
might turn out something reprehensible.

Madame Cuyler had designs of seeing Madame Ryckman and persuading her into giving leave for Franzje to
go; but Franzje was sure that her mother would not see
any visitor, and at last it was agreed that Evert should
steal up and try what his eloquence could effect.

He went, and returned in a marvellously short time, waving his cap in the air, and calling out, "Victory! victory! You are to go with Madame Cuyler if you like."

To Franzje the news seemed too good to be true. "Are you sure, Evert?" she said doubtfully. "I don't think mother can have meant it. You know she would not let us talk of the play even. I must go and speak to her."

But Evert caught hold of her, and held her fast. "No, no, you must not go near her. She said she was sound asleep when I went in, and that we must not disturb her again. I tell you, she said as plainly as words could speak, that you might go with Madame Cuyler."

He did not explain the ambiguous tactics by which he had won this consent. All he had said to Madame Ryckman was, "Madame Cuyler has come to fetch Franzje; she wants her and me both; will you mind our going, Mother?" without any mention of the play at all. It is true that Madame Ryckman knew that the play was to be on the 7th, but having forbidden the subject to be mentioned before her, the date was not nearly so strongly impressed on her memory as on that of the young people; and now, when occupied by her own ailments, it had passed from her mind. Had Madame Gerritse or Madame Banker been mentioned as calling for Franzje, her suspicions would have been aroused; but the mayor's wife was looked up to as a most sensible, superior person, and nothing but the notion of a friendly tea-party suggested itself in connection with her.

"Of course you may both go; I don't want anybody but Jettje," Madame Ryckman had said; and Evert had jumped at the ready permission, and not thought it necessary to explain the real state of affairs, though he saw his mother was under a misconception. It was not honourable or dutiful, and Franzje herself would never so have acted; but Evert's leading idea at the moment was to give her pleasure, and he was not so strictly truthful or upright by nature as either she or Jan.

His wish to please her had an immediate fulfilment. Franzje's face, as she rose up to go and dress for the evening, was like a sunbeam for radiance. "She is the most beautiful girl in Albany," said Madame Cuyler to herself, which, for the mother of two or three good-looking daughters, was quite a triumph of impartiality. Oh, how gaily she decked herself in her gala dress, such as it was! how deftly she coiled round her thick plaits of flaxen hair! what a happy thing it was to be young and to be beautiful, and to have a whole evening's pleasure before her, and to know how one face would brighten when she appeared! How kind it was of Madame Cuyler to come for her, of her mother to let her go! how nicely everything had turned out! In her foolish, girlish, natural gladness, she nearly forgot the Dominie, and did not pause to think whether it could be right to do in her father's absence what he would certainly not have allowed her to do had he been at home.

Before she left the chamber, she gave one rapid glance at the little picture of the Madonna and Infant Saviour, which she had hung in a recess at one side of the fireplace; but she was thinking of it more just then as Mr. Vyvian's gift than as the holy messenger which it sometimes was to her. The wistful look on the spotless mother's face haunted her as she went down the stair, but she did not read in it either warning or rebuke, she was too gay of spirit at that moment to be troubled with any misgivings. The "little corner for earth," which she had left in her heart was widening.

CHAPTER IX.

"The Beaux' Stratagem."

THE Gerritses' barn presented a different aspect when Franzje entered it this evening with Madame Cuyler, from that which it had borne on the night of the dance. There were no busy martins skimming about now, no friendly heifers in stalls near the door—all vestiges of the real purposes of the building had disappeared, and rows of benches extended from the orchestra to the very entrance; while the open loft above was draped with gay-coloured flags and festoons of white and scarlet cloth. Lights abounded, crowds of people both young and old were gradually filling the benches, the bandsmen were tuning their instruments for an opening piece, and altogether the scene was so lively and so unlike anything to which the good townsfolk were accustomed, that it was not wonderful if an unusual feeling of excitement took possession of them. There was a little sensation when Madame Cuyler and her bevy of young people appeared; the mayor's wife was felt to be rather a distinguished personage; and when Franzje Ryckman, with her graceful figure drawn up to its full height, and her cheeks glowing like bright carnations, was seen to be of the party, there was a little buzz of surprise and comment, not unmingled with admiration. Seen where she was not expected, and with her beauty heightened by animation, she made an unwonted impression even on those who had known her all her life, and were not accustomed to think of her as anything out of the common.

But after a short overture the curtain drew up, and then all eyes were turned towards the stage, and all minds

were occupied with the problem of what " The Beaux'
Stratagem " might prove to be.

There was not much that was poetical in the first scene,
which represented the parlour of an inn ; but the portly
landlord reminded Franzje of Falstaff, and she was very
much interested and puzzled by his coquettish little
daughter, Cherry, with her frilled muslin apron, and her
smart little cap trimmed with flowers. Somehow, though
she had seen in the play-bill that there were female parts
in the play, she had never realized till now that those
who acted them would be women, or dressed to look like
women. She could not think where Cherry had sprung
from, and could almost have fancied her to be Anna
Gerritse in disguise, if Anna had not been sitting a little
way from her among the spectators. Presently a gentleman and his servant came upon the stage, and then the
real excitement of the play began for Franzje, for in the
gentleman she recognized Mr. Vyvian.

He was booted and spurred as if just off a journey, and
his blue coat, yellow waistcoat, and drab pantaloons, made
him look very different from what he usually did ; but
spite of this and some artificial changes in his complexion
and hair, Franzje could not mistake him. Those dark
eyes, and the sudden bright glance which—forgetful of
his part for one instant—he allowed to fall on her, were
unmistakeable. She did not at once recognize Colonel
Trelawny in the smart, saucy footman, but she took an
objection to that character from the very first, and even
when he turned out to be a gentleman, and came on in
the later scenes looking like his own splendid self in
scarlet uniform and cocked hat and feathers, she felt no
sort of admiration for him. When, in his *rôle* of footman,
he bantered wittily but not very delicately with the landlord's pretty daughter, she scarcely even listened, but was

wondering all the time when his master would reappear.
The master was supposed to be gone to Church, and
though it had been plain from his conversation with his
servant that he was going only to see the belles of Lich-
field, and try to captivate one of them, Franzje's thoughts
would follow him admiringly; and certainly he had looked
the very prince of *élégants* as he set out, in his full-dress
blue coat and white waistcoat and silk stockings, with a
sort of confident killing air about him, which belonged to
his own natural self as well as to his part. She was not
surprised when it appeared that he had bewitched the
Lady Bountiful's fair daughter, Dorinda, a blooming
young lady in white muslin with very short sleeves,
though who Dorinda could be was a sore perplexity to
her; but when in the next scene he avowed himself to
be madly in love with this susceptible young creature, a
strange, childish jealousy took possession of her, of which
she was herself ashamed.

Henceforth the play became to her a sort of bewildering dream, in which Mr. Vyvian moved about, and looked
at and spoke to another woman something as he had
looked at and spoken to her, Franzje, only more unre-
strainedly. Aimwell and Dorinda engrossed her whole
thoughts; and when they were not upon the stage her
attention was listless. The coarse bickering of Dorinda's
half-brother and sister-in-law, Mr. and Mrs. Sullen; the
jovial talk of the sham French priest, Foigard; the plot-
ting of the highwaymen—reached her ears indeed, and
aroused a certain sentiment of disappointment and dis-
like; but for her the whole interest of the play centred
in the hero and the heroine, and except that she was
amused by the kind fussiness of Lady Bountiful and her
wonderful remedies, she could scarcely be said to take
heed of anyone but them. The extraordinary arrange-

ment at the end of the piece, by which Mrs. Sullen was given as a bride to the pretended footman, Archer, who had just rescued her from the robbers, while Mr. Sullen calmly sat down to drink, after merely stipulating that he should be allowed to retain his wife's marriage portion, only made Franzje open her great blue eyes in astonishment and mystification. She did not comprehend it in the least. All she understood and cared about was that (by a lucky chance) Aimwell turned out to be really a viscount, and not merely an usurper of his brother's title, that Dorinda was going to marry him, and that he was so disinterested as to be willing to give up all her fortune to his dissipated ex-footman. He looked so gloriously handsome, so noble, so triumphant, as he stood holding Dorinda's hand and gazing at her with proud loving eyes, that poor little Franzje wondered how anybody could care to hear or see any more of the play after that, and wished the curtain would fall and leave those two standing there together in their beautiful happiness.

Other people who were not dazzled and engrossed by a special regard for one of the actors, had looked at the performance with very different eyes, and listened with different ears. Some of the worthy townsfolk had sat through the whole with a bewildered stare upon their faces, and had neither laughed at the jokes, nor frowned at the oaths, but seen and heard everything in one unbroken maze of surprise, while others had been partly amused and partly scandalized, and others again wholly the one or wholly the other, according to their age, disposition, and principles.

The young people had mostly enjoyed it, and, like Franzje, had scarcely taken in the worst points; it was all very new and very odd, and it had made them laugh— that was the general result of their impressions. They

had felt nothing of the fascination, half pleasure, half
pain, with which Franzje had followed every word and
movement of Aimwell and Dorinda, but they had been
entertained by the fat landlord, and Lady Bountiful's
funny old servant, Scrub, in his faded livery; and fashionable Mrs. Sullen, in her white satin, had set the girls'
fancies going, while Captain Gibbet, the merry highway-
man, had rather reigned over the imagination of the boys,
till he proved himself such an arrant coward when Archer's
pistol was at his ear. One or two of the elder people,
among whom was Madame Cuyler, had shown signs of dis-
approbation as the play went on, and had looked specially
disgusted at Dorinda with her short sleeves, and marvelled
to each other what girl could have been got to appear
"with so little clothing," even though she had the protection of long fair ringlets to take off the unclothed
effect. Madame Gerritse had had some secret to impart,
apparently, with regard to Dorinda and Mrs. Sullen, for,
when they appeared, she had whispered something to one
or two of her neighbours which had made them first
draw back with an incredulous air, and then nod and
laugh, and ejaculate, "Is it possible ?" "Well, I never
could have thought it !" and so on. Whatever the secret
was, it had not reached Madame Cuyler or Franzje : they
were both equally mystified as to who were taking the
female parts, and Madame Gerritse knew better than to
enlighten them. When she looked round now and then,
and caught a glimpse of Madame Cuyler's shocked face,
she was half afraid that even as it was the mayor's wife
would get up and depart ; and she was more distressed
than surprised when at Archer's sudden appearance from
a cupboard in Mrs. Sullen's room, Madame Cuyler with
nervous haste turned and sat with her back to the stage—
rather to the discomfort of the people behind her—

desiring her daughters to do the same. They did not
obey, but only turned their heads and whispered petitions
and remonstrances to their mother, without passing on
the order to Franzje, who sat between Evert and Cornelius Cuyler, and was too engrossed in watching for
Aimwell's reappearance either to be aware of what was
passing round her, or to care for anything that was said
and done by Archer. When the curtain fell, and she
looked round, she was surprised to see her kind chaperone's position, and felt a sudden embarrassed consciousness that there must have been something reprehensible
in what had passed, to call forth this demonstration.

. "I am sorry to have brought you here, Franzje," said
Madame Cuyler, in a distressed voice, when the girl left
her place and came to her; "we will go home at once."

But here Madame Gerritse interfered. "There was
supper laid out in the house; she had actually had a wall
taken down, and thrown parlour and hall into one, at
Colonel Trelawny's suggestion, to make a supper-room
worthy of the occasion; she should never forgive herself
if Madame Cuyler"—the first lady in the place in the
absence of the Padroon's wife—"were to go away supperless; M. Gerritse would make a point of himself conducting her to the humble banquet."

She was so pressing, that Madame Cuyler could not
have persisted in her intention without the greatest un-
friendliness, and the young people were not sorry for it.
They had got over the sleepiness which had attacked
them a little at their usual bed-time, and were all alive,
and ready for anything that offered itself in the shape of
enjoyment.

Such a supper as Madame Gerritse's had never been
seen in Albany before. Not that the ampleness of the
provision was in itself anything remarkable; but the

number of guests provided for, the long range of loaded
tables, the choice delicacies that had been procured from
New York for the occasion, the display of plate and
crockery, all marked it as something quite out of the common way, and excited loudly-expressed wonder and admiration. There was a row of seats all round the walls as well
as round the tables; and while Madame Cuyler was conducted to a place of honour at the principal table, Franzje
and her younger companions were invited to sit on one
of the side-benches, and there, with their plates in their
lap, made their supper as best they could, talking and
laughing over it all the more because of the slight inconveniences which followed upon this arrangement.

But though Franzje's attention was partly at the service
of her friends, it must be owned that she answered
a little absently, and that her gaze wandered frequently
in search of the actors, none of whom had as yet appeared upon the scene. Some few of the officers who
had not taken part in the performance might be seen at
the supper-table, but the meal was almost ended before
the majority of them appeared. Then in they flocked, in
uniform, looking quite like their usual selves, except that
they were manifestly somewhat excited, and came in
laughing together in a noisy reckless way, which made
everybody turn round and look at them, and brought an
expression of alarm on the faces of the Albanian matrons.
Franzje's eyes singled out Mr. Vyvian at once; but her
anxiety was not so much whether he would discover her,
as what he had done with Dorinda. That lovely lady,
with the white dress and the long curling hair, was
nowhere to be seen. What had Mr. Vyvian done with
her? And could he really care so very much for
her, if he left her alone and supperless while he came
to take his share in the general festivity? What was

very strange—Franzje thought—was, that *none* of the
ladies who had appeared on the stage accompanied the
officers into the supper-room. What had become of them
all? Other girls besides Franzje longed to know.

Her suspense at any rate seemed likely to end soon, for
Mr. Vyvian no sooner caught sight of her than he came
up and spoke to her; but when, after making some shy
inarticulate answer to his eager thanks to her for keeping
her promise, she ventured to say, "Are not the ladies
coming to take any supper, Sir?" he first asked, in surprise, "What ladies?" and then, when she had explained,
laughed to himself in a provoking way, and declared they
had vanished, and left their costumes behind them. "Did
you want to make their acquaintance?" he asked, half
mockingly.

"I should like to have seen Miss Dorinda closer, sir;
she was very beautiful," said Franzje, frankly, yet with
half-grudging admiration.

"She will be much flattered to hear that you thought
so," said Mr. Vyvian, looking round as he spoke, as if
somehow Dorinda were in the room after all.

"Are the young English ladies all like that?" continued Franzje, timidly. "And have they all white dresses
and curls?"

"Well, as to that—yes, I think most of them have;
but I can't say they are all like Dorinda," he answered,
smothering a laugh. "How could one expect them to
be?" he added. "Isn't she 'the peerless Dorinda?' I
called her peerless in the play, didn't I?"

"I don't remember, but I thought you thought she was
very beautiful," said Franzje, in a puzzled tone.

"That shows that I acted my part with due fervour;
you don't suppose it was more than acting, do you?"

"I don't know, Sir," said Franzje, rather stiffly.

He laughed with an air of most enjoyable amusement; and why such fun and malice should dance in his dark eyes, Franzje could not at all understand. Had she betrayed the little sore jealous feeling that lingered at her heart, and was he laughing at it?

She drew up her graceful neck with a sudden haughtiness which made her look really superb; and all at once Mr. Vyvian left off laughing, and said, in a low, silvery whisper, "To my thinking, the *belle* of the evening was off the stage, not on it, and her unconsciousness made her charms the greater. It was so evident that she came to see and not to be seen. *She* is the one peerless pearl, in my estimation."

He was looking at her much as he had looked at Dorinda; and was this true passion, while the other was feigned, or was it all acting alike?

Franzje could not decide, and was silent; but the proud expression died away in a soft, womanly blush, and the rich firm lips parted in a sort of sweet confusion, as if from *him* she half liked compliments, though they made her shy.

At this moment, Madame Cuyler rose, and began to collect her little flock previous to departure. She was not comforted by the good supper which she had been induced to make against her will, and it was in rather a grave voice that she said, " Now, Franzje, I am going," as she swept past, with quiet dignity, towards the door.

"I am afraid we have scandalized your estimable *chaperone*," said Mr. Vyvian, laughingly, to Franzje, as she rose to follow. "You may expect to hear a great outcry against us to-morrow; indignant virtue will be running all about the place in a few hours' time, but I rely upon your generosity to defend us."

She made no promise, but the curtsey with which

she took leave of him was as gracious as it was stately, and the trusting innocent look of the blue eyes lingered with him, and kept him from joining in the too boisterous conviviality, which was indulged in by some of his brother officers during the small hours of the morning. More than once a speech addressed by Archer to Cherry in the play, "You have a pair of delicate eyes, but you don't know how to use them," had come into his head while he was talking to Franzje; but, after all, no coquettish glances could have gone to his heart, as did that clear, star-like gaze. There dawned on him even a faint perception that the evening's entertainment had *not* been worthy of her presence, though he did not believe that it would harm her. "Nothing could," he said to himself.

It was in a strange whirl of excitement, disappointment, and pleasure, all mingled together, that Franzje, wrapped in her great fur mantle, walked home with her brother over the crisp, firm snow. She had not found what she had expected in the play; it had not been in the least like Shakespeare—the higher, nobler, more poetical part of her nature remained unsatisfied; but there had been keen interest of a certain sort, and the girl's head was a little bewildered for the moment, so that she was incapable of framing a dispassionate judgment on all that she had heard and seen. The house door was sure to be closed ere this, though not barred or bolted, for such precautions were seldom taken in Albany; and Franzje had forgotten to ask any of the servants to sit up for them; but Evert's knock was answered so rapidly, that it was evident someone had been on the watch.

Maaike, in a sort of *déshabille*, opened the door in a cautious and mysterious manner, and laying her black hand on Franzje's arm, said, in a tragic whisper, "Don't go in parlour, Mamselle; Baas dere! Madame, she very bad, and send for Dominie; den Baas he come home. Everybody angry. Jettje, she send me to bed, but I not go to sleep, watch for you. Come straight away upstairs, deary; everyone be better in morning."

"Mother worse, and Father come home!" said Franzje, quite sobered by the unexpected news. "Don't hold me, Maaike, I must go and speak to Father."

"Dominie been talking to him," persisted Maria, with a gesture of awe.

Franzje gave a little sad proud smile, and went on all the same.

She ran straight to her father; and at any other time the good elder would have clasped the bright, beautiful, blooming creature to him in a hearty embrace; but now when Franzje would have kissed him he repulsed her, and turned away his head. "Don't come and kiss me, child," he said; "and you, sir," to Evert, who was following his sister slowly, "don't pretend you're glad to see me back. You have been taking advantage of my absence to play your own pranks, and here have you left your poor mother as ill as she can be, and gone off to see a parcel of madcap officers make fools and knaves of themselves! I am ashamed of you both, I am ashamed that you belong to me. Go to your rooms, and stay there: you will force me to turn the key upon you, I suppose, before I've done."

It was a strange humiliating reception for the belle of Albany, but Franzje was too fond of her father and too anxious about her mother to resent it. "Is Mother really so ill?" she asked, tremblingly. "She said she was much better to-day, and only wanted to be quiet."

"Ah! and a fine way, truly, to keep her quiet, to go

off to the play without her knowledge !" said M. Ryckman, indignantly.

"She knew; she gave me leave," pleaded Franzje, in
surprise.

But M. Ryckman turned on her with a sudden sternness
of wrath. "Have they taught you to tell lies, girl?" he
said fiercely.

A scarlet flame sprang into Franzje's cheek. Never in
all her life had such an accusation been brought against
her; she was even more astonished than hurt.

"Madame Cuyler came for me, and Evert asked Mother's
leave for me to go with her," she said, in as calm a voice
as she could command. She looked round for Evert to
corroborate the assertion, but he had made off and left her
to defend herself. It was rather a cowardly proceeding,
but he glossed it over in his own mind, by saying that
"Franzje would be sure to manage Father when she had
him alone."

She could have done so on an ordinary occasion, but
M. Ryckman had been worked up by what had passed
between him and his wife and the Dominie before the
young people returned, and was really angry now, with
the sharp short-lived anger of a naturally good-tempered
person.

"I won't hear a word," he rejoined; "you are only
trying to deceive me. I could not have believed it of
you, Franzje. Go to your bed, and do not come near me
again till I send for you. A day or two in your own room
will give you time to think, and you will be just as useful
there as gadding about over the town. Go at once," he
added, still more angrily, as Franzje stood hesitating, not
feeling as if she could bear to go and leave him so displeased with her. "I told the Dominie I would find some
means of punishing you. As for Evert, I shall send hi

your uncle at New York; a little drudgery in a merchant's
office will keep him out of mischief, perhaps."

Franzje's heart gave a proud rebellious throb at the
sound of punishment. She—a woman, as she now felt—
to be treated like a naughty child !

Nevertheless, she saw that words were useless, and
turned to go, only pausing at the door to ask, " May I not
see how Mother is ? I will go in very softly."

" No, no, I won't have her disturbed ; do as I bid you,
and go straight to bed; you ought to have been there
hours ago."

The Dutch clock in the hall struck twelve as she went
up the stairs; and though she was too excited to feel
weary, there did indeed seem something unnatural and
dissipated in keeping such hours for the first time in her
life.

Evert came out of his room as she passed it. " Have
you made it right with Father, Franz ?" he asked. " Jan
says there has been a terrible to-do. Perhaps I brought
you in for it rather, but never mind ; you have had your
treat, and Father won't be angry for long. It's only that
tiresome old Dominie that makes him so particular."

" I suppose it was he who wished me to be punished,"
thought Franzje to herself, and her heart swelled so that
she could not speak.

"I wish we could get rid of him and his preachings, that
I do," continued Evert vehemently, but Franzje started as
if the idea were treason, and with a shocked " O Evert !"
disappeared within her own room.

It was a troubled wakeful night that succeeded this
eventful evening ; and it was followed by a long dull
solitary day, unlike anything in Franzje's previous experience. There was nothing to break the loneliness but the
appearance of old Jettje bringing her breakfast and dinner ;

and to feel that her mother was ill close at hand, and that
she might not go to her, was very painful to the tender-
hearted girl. She had plenty of time to think, as her
father had said ; but her head ached after her sleepless
night, and her thoughts would not come clearly or collect-
edly. Mr. Vyviau's gallant compliments and her father's
angry reproaches rang in her ears by turns, and her puzzled
endeavours to find out how far she had been wrong were
mingled with surmises as to who Dorinda could be, and
wonderings whether she should ever see her again.

Late in the afternoon Jettje popped her head in
suddenly.

"Dominie want you, Mamselle ; you to go to him in
Madame's room."

Franzje dashed away some idle tears that had begun to
fall, and rose up, half trembling, half defiant. With the
old childish instinct of making herself tidy before entering the Dominie's presence, she bathed her face and
smoothed her hair and settled her apron, and then took
her way to her mother's room.

The negress had vanished, and Madame Ryckman's
door was shut, so Franzje gave a gentle tap and waited
for permission to enter. None came ; and as she heard the
Dominie talking with her mother, she thought her soft
knock might have passed unnoticed, and tapped again.

This time there was a slight pause in the voices, and
she was sure it must have been heard, but no one opened
the door, nor said "Come in." The nursery door, which
was just opposite, was open, and the room was empty, for
the children were running riot in the kitchen, so she sat
down on the step and waited, at first with an anxious
beating heart, then with a sort of hardening of indifference, till finally weariness overpowered her and she
dropped asleep.

How long she slept she did not know—not more than a few minutes really—but she was roused by the soft touch of a hand on her head. So soft, so caressing it seemed, that she woke with a smile on her face like the waking smile of a little child that has felt its slumbers watched by loving eyes. And a strange confusion, part surprise, part shame, part hope, took possession of her when she looked up and saw that it was the Dominie who stood before her. Had she gone back in sleep to the old days when she was, as Killian had said, like the Dominie's own child, and had all the intervening time passed away like a feverish dream ?

The illusion only lasted for a minute, the first sound of the Dominie's voice dispelled it, and yet he spoke more gently than Franzje had any cause to expect.

"Poor child!" he said, in a pitying tone, "you are weary after your last night's pleasuring, and there is nothing like disappointment for producing this lassitude both of body and mind ; when we find we have sinned for nought, we begin to feel weary of everything, and of ourselves most of all."

She rose up while he was speaking, and it was indeed rather a languid face which she raised to his, but she did not give the answer that seemed to be expected from her.

"I was very happy till I found Father was angry, sir," she said.

"Come in here," said the Dominie, beckoning her into the empty nursery, not into the room he had just left.

She followed him in, gave him a chair, and then stood in front of him to hear what he had to say. How like and yet unlike it seemed to the day when she had stood before him to repeat her lesson, and he had told her that the regiment was coming, and cautioned her about her behaviour ! Then all had been sunshine round her, and there had been sunshine in her heart too; now there were shadows creeping about the large bare room, and some shadows within her as well, though not enough to put out the light.

"You have disobeyed me, and pained and surprised me," said the Dominie, "and have been persistently blind to the dangers of the course you have entered on; but I will not wrong you, my child, by supposing that last night's doings have not opened your eyes. No Christian maiden could be present at such a spectacle, and not feel deeply ashamed of herself and of those who had brought it before her."

Franzje was silent; she had been disappointed, it was true, and at moments even disgusted; but she had not felt that amount of horror and virtuous indignation which the Dominie seemed to take for granted.

"You could not see Christian men—Christian in *name* at least—acting the part of fools and knaves, strutting about with painted faces, and uttering line after line of contemptible jargon, without blushing for them, I am sure," continued the pastor. "Still less could you see men in women's garb without turning away your head and wishing with all your heart that you had never come."

"Oh! was Dorinda a man?" asked Franzje, with a sudden start.

He did not reply; the eagerness of the tone puzzled him, as well it might, and for the first moment, too, he thought her innocence assumed; but there was unmistakeable truth in the accents of her voice, as she went on, "They were not the officers, were they, sir? those ladies on the stage?" and he was obliged to believe that of this portion of the iniquity she had really not been cognizant.

"The ensigns of the regiment and one captain under-

took the female parts, I am informed," he answered, with
grave distinctness.

"Oh," said the girl softly. There was great surprise,
not untinged with disapproval, in the tone in which she
breathed this "oh," but yet there was a sound of relief in
it too, which did not escape the Dominie's ear.

"Who was this Dorinda that you mentioned just now?"
he asked sternly.

"She was the young lady that Mr. Vyv— that Aimwell married, Sir," returned Franzje simply, but with
rising colour.

"Am I to understand that there was the mockery of a
wedding?"

"Oh no, Sir! but I mean, he asked her to marry him,
and she said she would."

"And you thought her a very happy young lady," said
the Dominie, with a smile, in which there was even more
pathos than satire. "Oh, child! child! what can I say
that will open your eyes before it be quite too late?"

"I am sorry that I went to the play when Mother was
ill, Sir," said Franzje, finding courage and humility enough
to own what did really appear to herself as a fault.

"And is that the extent of your sorrow?" questioned
the Dominie gravely. "Have you no other pardon to
ask than your mother's?"

Her colour went and came, but she said nothing; and
it was in a sterner tone that the pastor continued, "Have
you no sorrow to express for all that has come and gone
since we last talked together alone?—in the little chestnut
wood, do you remember it as you ought?—nothing to say
about all the self-will and the going after vanities, no
contrition to tell me of, no counsel to ask? Are you
stifling the voice of conscience, or is it really dead within
you?"

A slight tremor passed over the girl's frame, and her hands clasped and unclasped themselves together nervously. She was not unmoved—oh! far from it; but yet she did not speak.

He gave her a little time, but when still there came no word, not so much as a sob to break the silence, he rose and walked to the door. On the threshold he turned and said, in a deep, still voice, " I leave you for the present, Franzje ; when you awake to a better mind, and find you have awoke too late, then remember that the least expression of penitence would have been accepted had it been offered now."

Again he waited a moment, but surprise and perplexity and a sort of awe chained the girl's tongue, and in another minute, he was on his way downstairs, hiding his sadness under a mask of additional sternness, and bestowing on Evert, whom he found in the parlour, the sharp rebuke which Franzje had expected, and which, in her case, for some reason or other, he had forborne to give.

When she was left alone, she stood a little while with her hands clasped in a sort of painful reverie ; then she ran to her mother, and found some relief to one of her anxieties in seeing her look rather better than she had expected. Madame Ryckman could not help looking glad at the sight of her, and giving her one motherly hug ; but after that she seemed to remember Franzje's misdemeanours, and to try to be distant and repressive. What appeared to vex her most was, that her husband had found no one to welcome him after his long, cold journey, or to see to his wants, but Jan ; and she would scarcely listen to Franzje's real regret ; but after saying what she had to say, closed her eyes wearily, and desired to be left alone.

" Am I to go back to my room, mother ? " asked the

girl, not unsubmissively, though with a little proud lifting of her queenly head.

"Not unless your father sends you. I would rather you saw to him and the house and the children and your Uncle Jan. Go and tell your uncle I am better, and sit with him a little bit till your father comes in."

Franzje was not at all sorry to have this command given her; she wanted counsel, sympathy, someone to tell her how and why she had been wrong, someone who would be satisfied with something short of unconditional submission, someone who would not wound her by implying harsh things of Mr. Vyvian; and her heart turned yearningly towards her old uncle, as more likely than anyone else to afford her what she needed. When she entered his room, however, he was leaning back in his chair with his arms folded, and seemed engaged in placid meditation, so that after watching him for a little while, all that she had meant to say died away upon her lips, and she told herself that it would be cruel to trouble his peace. She did not turn away though, but went softly forward, knelt down beside him, and laid her head upon his knee.

He did not say a word, nor even stretch out his hand, but neither did he repulse her, so at least the flaxen head had found a rest, and the young heart a haven of stillness where it might soothe itself into calm.

CHAPTER X.

Aunt Schuyler.

"THE FLATS, *January 7th.*

"MY DEAR FRANZJE,

"I dare say you have heard from your father that the Colonel and I travelled home with him; it was indeed what he told us of

the state of things here which induced us to return at once, instead
of passing the whole of the winter at New York, as we had intended.
I am suffering with my rheumatism from the cold journey, and
cannot go out ; but if your mother can spare you, I shall be happy
to see you here, and hope you will be able to stay the night. How
have your French studies been progressing during my absence !
Present our kindest compliments to your mother, and believe me
to remain,
"Your affectionate old friend,
"CATALINA SCHUYLER."

Madame Schuyler penned this note on the afternoon of
the 7th, sitting in what was called the winter-house, a small
snug sort of cottage adjoining the back of the large three-
storied brick mansion, which was the nominal residence of
the family. The wide airy rooms and polished floors were
too cold for winter comfort, and the smoke of the great wood
fires that it was necessary to keep up would have injured
the elegant furniture and the paintings that hung round
the walls ; so whenever they happened to be at home in
severe weather, Colonel Schuyler and his wife retreated
into the little house at the back, which was warm and cosy,
and comfortably carpeted, and furnished in a plain but
convenient way. They lost the lovely view of the river
which they had from their summer parlour ; but the windows looked towards steep, picturesque, pine-crowned hills,
which were beautiful even when covered with snow, and
made the bright fire-lit room seem all the cosier from the
contrast with their white desolation.

Aunt Schuyler, as her friends called her, was a comely,
middle-aged woman, tall and stout, with a remarkably
pleasant, sensible countenance, and the manner of one
who felt herself a person of importance, and yet was far
from feeling any contempt for others, or any wish to
dictate to them. When she had despatched her note
the next morning by one of the many willing negroes who

were about the place, she sat by the fire knitting and
thinking; and, to judge by the grave expression which
her kind face took, her thoughts must have been rather
of an anxious character. Colonel Schuyler had been into
Albany the day before, seen the Dominie, and heard
something of his troubles; and good Madame Schuyler—
who had a great regard for her pastor, and yet thought
him somewhat too narrow and uncompromising—was
perplexed as to how far her friends and neighbours
had really been going wrong in her absence, and what
could be done to help them to get right again. Looking
on the young people of the town as so many nieces and
nephews, she naturally felt a keener interest in their mis-
doings, real or imaginary, than is usually felt by a childless
woman about the faults of the boys and girls of her
acquaintance; and what she had heard from M. Ryckman
at New York, had made her fear that they had really been
led astray in some degree by the English officers, though
she was not prepared to pass sentence on them at once as
irreclaimable, because she was told that they had suddenly
developed a taste for dancing.

"I hope Franzje will come," she said to herself; "the
child has great good sense, and I know I could trust her
view of affairs, even though her father did seem to say
that she had not escaped the Anglomania altogether. I
should like to have a talk with her before I send for my
nieces"—she meant her real nieces, the Cuylers, now—
"*one* girl can give a coherent account of things, but two
or three girls together always get confused and contradictory. I wonder if Cornelia really did take those dear
girls to the play; Philip understood her to say so, and
that she very much repented it now. I must hear what
she and her husband say of the officers before I decide to
show them any civilities. Trelawny is a good name, and

so is Vyvian ; but it is not uncommon to meet with degenerate scions of honourable houses."

Her meditations were interrupted by a little stir in the lobby outside ; and feeling sure it portended the arrival of visitors—M. and Madame Cuyler, of whom she had been thinking, perhaps—she got up and went to meet them. It was not her brother and sister-in-law, but the Dominie and M. Jansen, the elder whose constant tale-bearing had excited Franzje's indignation. Madame welcomed them with great cordiality and respect ; and though she would rather have seen the Dominie alone, she was much too hospitable to betray the least annoyance at his having brought a companion with him. She pressed them to sit near the fire, and to remain to dinner, telling them that the Colonel had but gone to see his brother Peter, who lived close by, and would be sure to be home by the time the meal was ready.

Elder Jansen, who was a fat, puffy little man, of true Dutch build, showed a certain quiet satisfaction at the idea of dinner ; but the Dominie gave no definite acceptance, and glanced round restlessly, as if he were impatient to be doing something, without knowing exactly what.

Madame Schuyler thought to herself that nowhere during her absence had she seen anything so fine as that broad intellectual brow, and those deep-set, piercing eyes ; but she missed the kindly smile which was wont to light up the pastor's face when in company with real friends, and was struck with the worn and wasted look on his handsome features, which even those who saw him every day had begun to notice.

"You have not been taking care of yourself while we have been away, Dominie, I am afraid," she said, presently ; "you should give yourself a little holiday at this festival season, and come and spend a few days with us. You know well what pleasure it would confer on my husband and me."

"Thank you, you are very good," replied the Dominie, gravely; "but I cannot be absent from the town at present; and there are things which call upon us rather to fast and pray than to feast and make merry just now, Christmas-tide though it be."

He did not seem inclined to explain what the things were, but M. Jansen volunteered the explanation.

"You have been away from home, Madame, and don't know all that our Dominie has had to try him," he said; "those English officers have turned our good city upside down, and not content with introducing balls and all manner of worldly amusements, they have now gone so far as to act what they call a play. I can assure you that not only did these young men, who are familiar with every vice and every disguise, spend the whole night in telling lies in a counterfeited place, but they actually degraded manhood, and broke through an express prohibition of Scripture, by assuming female habits. Female habits!" repeated the little man, impressively, as if the full horror of the statement might have escaped Aunt Schuyler's perception. "Moreover, they painted their faces—*painted their faces!* think of that, Madame! and strutted about on the stage like so many Jezebels; cursing and swearing, and assuming the characters of knaves, fools, and robbers, such as every good man would have held in detestation."

"I wonder you could bear to see it, M. Jansen," said the good lady, demurely.

"See it!" cried the elder, his round, red face growing purple with indignation; "*see* it, Madame! what do you take me for? I was not there; I was where a Christian ought to be at such an hour, in my bed asleep."

A faint smile, barely perceptible, moved the lips of the Dominie at his elder's definition of sleep as the only Christian occupation for midnight hours. When he had left Madame Ryckman on the night of the 7th, it had not been to retire to rest, but to wear out the hours in prayer for his misguided people, till the slow daylight dawned, and he could believe the revels over; but of course he said nothing of this, and it was Madame Schuyler who replied, "I beg your pardon, I am sure, but you described it all so vividly, that I could not suppose you were speaking only from hearsay. Are you certain that you have been rightly informed about it? My sister, Madame Cuyler, was there, I understand; and I scarcely think if the spectacle had been so revolting she would have remained to witness it."

"Do not quote Madame Cuyler's presence at the play as sanctioning what went on there, dear friend," said the Dominie, suddenly taking up the word; "she has expressed to me the greatest regret at her rashness in going and taking her young people with her. You, who know her gentle and retiring nature, will believe how reprehensible the thing must have been, when I tell you that one scene was so gross that she felt obliged to turn her back upon the stage altogether, and look the other way. Had she done what she ought, she would have left the barn, but it seems she had not courage for that."

"I am sorry that she should have gone," said Madame Schuyler, much more convinced by the Dominie's calm statements than by Elder Jansen's vehemence.

"Yes, it is much to be regretted, and she will have cause to rue it many a day. The misfortune is, that the young people who accompanied her do not all see the

matter in the same light that she does ; one would think
they had been familiarized with evil, so callously do some
of them speak of it."

" I am told Franzje Ryckman sat and looked on as
coolly as possible," said M. Jansen, with what Aunt
Schuyler could not but think spitefulness in his tone.

" May it not have been their innocence that prevented
the young things from understanding all that was amiss ?"
said she, in her tender wisdom. " I doubt whether there
are better maidens anywhere than Franzje and my nieces,
though perhaps it is not for me to say it, as I have had
some share in their bringing up."

" Ah, you've been deceived in the young Ryckmans,
Madame !" said M. Jansen, solemnly ; " as for *Mamselle*
Franzje, as she likes to be called, she goes about as proud
as a peacock, and sets the Dominie at defiance. It's a
scandal to the whole place to see it."

Madame Schuyler, though nominally holding rather a
harsh and narrow creed, was above all things large-hearted,
and had in perfection that "graceful perversity of in-
credulousness about scandals" which Faber calls "the
temper and genius of saints and saint-like men."

" I dare say Franzje is a little apt to be captivated with
novelties, like other young people," she said, with a smile ;
"but I think better of Albany than to suppose it is
taken up with the doings of a young girl of sixteen ;
and I don't think a little girlish wilfulness, if there has
been such, need be construed into defiance,—do you,
Dominie ?"

That touch of fatherly tenderness towards Franzje which
lingered in the Dominie's heart, made him more disposed
to side with his charitable friend in this case than with
the zealous elder ; but just *because* of this feeling he
braced himself up to impartial severity, and answered,

"It is true, however, that Franzje and Evert have both
set at naught my clearly-expressed wishes. In public
and in private I have exhorted my flock—the younger
members more especially—to take no part in the dissipations introduced by these officers ; yet on the evening of
the 7th, the Gerritses' barn was crowded with the youth
of the town of both sexes, and among them were my
own elder's children—Franzje and Evert Ryckman."

"And my nieces and nephews too ; I am really sorry,"
said Madame Schuyler thoughtfully. "I can quite imagine
how that giddy fellow Cornelius talked over his poor
mother. Was his stolid namesake, Cornelius Banker,
one of the party ?"

"No ; Cornelius Banker and Killian Barentse stood
firm against temptation, and for that I am thankful," said
the Dominie. "Cornelius was especially tried, for his
parents and sisters went ; but ever since a dance at the
Gerritses' last autumn he has kept aloof from dissipation."

"I do think having a thick head makes it easier to be
good sometimes," rejoined Madame Schuyler pleasantly,
with no wish to under-rate young Banker's virtue, but
longing greatly to excuse all the culprits a little ; "would
it not be possible, Dominie, for my husband and others to
take these young officers in hand, and win them to keep
their amusements within due bounds ?"

"No, it would not!" said the Dominie, rather exaspe-
rated at hearing from the lips of the woman whom of all
others he most esteemed, the same proposition which he
had already combated when advanced by M. Ryckman
and divers of the "moderate" party ; then, in a gentler
tone, he added, "These men do not look on pleasure as an
occasional relaxation—a refreshment to make them fitter
for duty ; they consider it the business of their lives, and

therefore there is no possibility of coming to terms with them on the subject."

"I should have been glad if it could have been done, for the sake of our own young people," said Madame Schuyler; "they, at least cannot be yet such votaries of pleasure as not to be easily persuaded to moderation; and surely a little dancing, for instance, *might* be indulged in in a harmless way. Even our great master, Calvin, allowed that 'dances and cards were not in themselves evil,' did he not?"

"He put the wife of the ex-syndic in prison for a few days because she went to a ball, and showed no sense of her error in doing so," remarked the Dominie, rather grimly; and perhaps he himself would nowise have objected to pop that recalcitrant female Madame Gerritse in prison if he had had the power—all for her real good, as he firmly believed—though he did not give expression to any such desire.

If Madame Schuyler had been thoroughly up in the history of Calvin and the Geneva of Calvin's day, she might have rejoined that the dances performed at the ball in question had been inconsistent with propriety, and that Madame Perrin had not only "shown no sense of her error," but attacked her pastor with violent invective and abuse; as it was, however, she merely answered mildly, "I did not know that; but I have heard Calvin quoted as not condemning amusements altogether, and as once even putting off a sermon for the convenience of those who were attending at a *play*." She could not help glancing at Elder Jansen as she said this, with a little quiet humour in her eyes; but her triumph—if triumph it were—was short-lived.

"You are not perhaps aware," said the Dominie, "that this play was intended to be of an improving character, and was entitled 'A History for the Edification of the People,' and that it was, moreover, the only theatrical piece which Calvin sanctioned. When a second piece was about to be performed, called 'The Acts of the Apostles,' he upheld one of his colleagues in opposing it; and I believe it was the last that was given at Geneva during his ministry there."

There was no disputing the calm positiveness with which the Dominie spoke; and Madame Schuyler gave in at once, with a respectful good humour which was unconsciously soothing.

His stern face relaxed into a smile that was almost playful, as he said, "I will be content to go as far in toleration as my master, and if you can get hold of this 'History for the Edification of the People,' and persuade the officers to act *that*, I will promise to make no objection."

Madame Schuyler smiled, and took the jest as it was meant; but M. Jansen gave a significant snort, and observed sneeringly, "You will be clever indeed if you get edification of any sort out of this godless regiment—they are a set of rakes from beginning to end. I could tell you fine tales of them, if I were not afraid of shocking your ears, Madame; and when you see the terms that two of them are on with Anna Gerritse and Franzje Ryckman, you will agree with me that the sooner they are out of the place the better."

He was about to add more, but at this point the Dominie checked him. "We must beware of rash judgments, my friend," he said, "especially where young maidens are in question.—Neither would I have you believe," he continued, now addressing Madame Schuyler, "that Franzje and Evert Ryckman have gone all the lengths of the Gerritses and their set. You will use your

influence with them, I trust, and perhaps they may even
yet be brought to a better mind."

"I am hoping to see Franzje here to-day. I have
written to ask her to come," was the reply.

"You will not see her," said the Dominie, gravely;
"it was her father's intention, I know, to confine her to
her room for a few days, on account of her insubordinate
conduct with regard to the play-acting, and this will of
course prevent her accepting your kind invitation."

Madame Schuyler let her knitting fall in her lap with
a sudden movement of surprise—of shocked surprise, it
seemed. She awoke all at once to a perception that her
kindly longings to reconcile the opposing parties in the
town, by preaching toleration to the one set and moderation to the other, were by no means likely to be realized;
that the war between them had become already interne-
cine. If such a fond, easy-tempered parent as M. Ryckman felt it necessary to go to such lengths with an almost
grown-up daughter, things must indeed have come to
a bad pass! "Quite beyond my mending, or even
Philip's!" thought good Aunt Schuyler, in momentary
despair.

She took refuge in a hope that the regiment would not
remain long in the town. "There is to be another attack
on Crown Point in the spring, is there not? My husband attended the Congress at which it was proposed,
and we heard much talk of it at New York. Surely
Colonel Trelawny and his men will be wanted then!"

"I hope so; but nothing can be done till the frost
breaks up," said the Dominie, gloomily, "and between
January and April a great deal of mischief may be
wrought."

"It must be our part to try and prevent it," said
Madame Schuyler, with an effort to appear cheerful and

hopeful still.—"Oh! you are not going, surely, Dominie?
I expect Colonel Schuyler in every minute."

But the Dominie persisted in taking leave, spite of M.
Jansen's evident willingness to remain; and Madame
Schuyler accompanied them, not only to the door of the
winter-house, but through a passage which led to the hall
of the other house, and so out at the great porch, which
was the more dignified way of exit.

As they were passing along, with M. Jansen a little
in the rear, Madame Schuyler thought she would say a
good word for Franzje. "I hope M. Ryckman won't be
too hard on my little friend Franzje," she said; "she is
so gentle and sensible, that I should think reasoning with
her would have quite as much effect as punishment might
have on others."

"It has been tried," said the Dominie, in a tone that
sounded harsh and abrupt, because it was so full of pain;
"her parents have dealt very tenderly with her hitherto;
we must now see what severity will effect."

He fancied her sitting lonely in her room, with the
pale, languid look that he had remarked the day before;
and Madame Schuyler's mental image of her was not very
dissimilar. What was their surprise when, just as they
came out into the porch, a sledge drew up at the steps,
and from out of a cloud of furs appeared a bright, blooming face all glowing from the frosty air, while a sweet, gay
voice exclaimed, "Oh! Aunt Schuyler, how glad I am to
see you again!" and behold there was Franzje, not a
prisoner at all, but abroad taking her pleasure, and with
her father sitting beside her, and looking almost as pleased
as herself! When she ran up the steps and caught sight
of the Dominie and M. Jansen, her expression changed a
little, it is true, and she kissed Madame Schuyler silently,
and made rather a shy, constrained curtsey to her pastor;

but still what a scandal it was—according to Elder Jansen's
notions—that she should be there at all, and just in time
for the good dinner that he was missing, when she ought
to have been locked up at home, with bread and water
for her fare!

Madame Schuyler could not help being glad to see her,
spite of the Dominie's grave looks, and pressed M. Ryckman to come in too; but he declined, and after handing
up to Franzje a parcel which contained her provision for
the night, announced that he must get back to Albany
as quickly as possible, and offered the Dominie a seat in
his sledge.   He knew that he was laying himself open to
a lecture by doing so, but he had a great deal too much
respect for his pastor to neglect to show him this very
natural piece of courtesy, and would not acknowledge to
himself how relieved he felt when it was refused.

"You will give M. Jansen a lift, perhaps; but for myself, I would rather walk," said the Dominie, glancing at
his snow-shoes as he spoke, and rather ignoring the prof-
ferred hand of his elder—a weak-minded elder, who had
no proper ideas of parental discipline!   "Good-bye,
Madame.—Good-bye, Jansen; you will dine with me, I
hope.   I shall be home nearly as soon as you."   And
then away he strode, in his determined fashion, with an
air which forbade even M. Jansen to follow him, so
plainly did it say, "I am in haste to be alone."

The two elders drove off together; and when everybody
was out of sight, Madame Schuyler gave her young friend
a real comfortable hug; and then putting her a little
away, said rather drily, "And so your father has brought
you to the old aunt to be scolded.   What am I to do to
you, child, to make you good?"

"Have they made you think me so bad then, Aunt?"
replied Franzje, with a playfulness that was half wistful.

"I don't know what to think; after dinner we will have one of our long talks, and you shall tell me what has been going on while I have been away. I should like to arrive at an understanding of how much is right and how much is wrong in all these novelties that I hear of."

"That is just what I can't be sure of," said Franzje, with a sigh which came from the very depths of her heart; but it was something to have to do with a person who had not already prejudged the case, and in another minute she looked up, and said hopefully, "O Aunt Schuyler, I think everything will be better now that you have come home!"

Madame Schuyler was chirruping to the birds who had found winter quarters in the shelter of her friendly porch, and for whose accommodation a small shelf had been erected, upon which they nestled; but she turned round with the cheery answer, "Well, we will see what can be done, though I am afraid of turning into an old busybody, and making things worse than I find them." And then, taking her guest's hand kindly in her own, she conducted her to the winter-house, and up into a small but comfortable bedroom, which was to be hers for the night.

"Now I will leave you to get ready for dinner," she said, "for I hear the Colonel's step in the lobby; but by and by, when he has gone out again, we will have our long talk, and see what we can make of it all."

Spite of these good intentions, twice expressed, the "long talk" did *not* come off that afternoon. Just as Madame Schuyler and Franzje were settling down to it, —the girl sitting on a low stool at her friend's feet—the bustle of an arrival was heard, and no less than four officers—Colonel Trelawny, Major Berkeley, Mr. Vyvian, and Mr. Gardiner—were ushered in with some ceremony by the gray-haired negro who believed himself to be Colonel Schuyler's butler, though no one else in the primitive mansion was conscious of the existence of such a functionary. They had driven out to pay their respects to the owners of the Flats ; and spite of what she had heard against them, the aristocratic appearance of the commanding officer and his adjutant did impress Madame Schuyler favourably, though she liked Colonel Trelawny less and less as the visit went on. He was extremely courteous on the surface, but his scarcely-disguised superciliousness and frivolity were not congenial to the good-hearted, sensible lady ; and it was a great relief to her when her husband—summoned from his barn—came in, and she had leisure to talk a little to the others, and prevent Mr. Vyvian's colloquy with Franzje from becoming a complete *tête-à-tête.*

Franzje had risen up in haste when the visitors entered, and modestly withdrawn to a seat near the window. *Artfully,* Elder Jansen would have said, for it gave Mr. Vyvian the opportunity of taking a large arm-chair which was close to her, and so rather cutting her off from the rest of the party.

"I am so relieved to find you here!" said he, when they had exchanged greetings ; "I had heard all sorts of dreadful tales about you, and pictured you to myself immured in some secret dungeon beneath the floor of the Manse."

Franzje coloured painfully. Somehow, though she had borne her brief disgrace very patiently on the whole, it was intolerable to her that Mr. Vyvian should know of it. "I have been at home quite safe," she said, "till my father brought me here this morning : it is so pleasant to have Aunt Schuyler back ! "

"Yes, I dare say," he answered, with a rather critical though not unkindly glance towards that worthy lady; "but, Mademoiselle, have you really been quite well and happy since we parted on Monday night? I can't tell you what uneasiness I have been suffering on your account. Report said that the Dominie was looking up all the lambs who were beguiled into straying in the direction of Babylon on the evening of the 7th, and was driving them back into the fold by main force. No words can describe how it pained me to think of *you* given over to his tender mercies."

Womanly pride, as well as the remains of her old trusting loyalty, came to Franzje's aid at this moment. "I should have had no cause to be afraid if I had been," she said; "but you have not been quite rightly informed, Sir."

He admired her kindling glance, and the momentary hauteur of her manner, and took his cue from her immediately. It was just the facility with which he did so that made his admiration dangerous to her. She scarcely ever saw him as he was in himself, but only as he *could* be under her influence.

"So you trust your formidable Dominie more than you fear him?" he said. "Well, I dare say the trust is not misplaced. I can fancy he is too grand-natured to be a thorough tyrant—not weak enough to be cruel, I mean."

Her glance kindled now in a brighter and sweeter fashion. "I am so glad you don't think cruelty goes with strength! I do like what is strong, even when it is against me."

He looked hard at her as she spoke, reading every line of the brightening face, and well divining her capacity for hero-worship, and also the sort of character that was likely to be heroic in her eyes : not his own, he knew, and yet he meant to win her for himself all the same.

"So do I like strength when it is allied with gentleness," he said ; "and I always think there must be something very strong and reliable in a person who continues to stand one's friend spite of all adverse influences. Mademoiselle, if anything were needed to increase my regard for you, it would be increased tenfold by the generosity of your partisanship ! Now if you can only get Madame Schuyler on our side, we shall have a chance of organizing a really enlightened, liberal-minded circle, that will be able to stand its ground against the narrowness of Elder Jansen and his set."

"I don't want you to act any more plays, Sir," said Franzje, colouring very much, but getting the words out bravely. "I was interested in that one, but I would rather not see any more."

"You were scandalized at my love-making to Dorinda, I know," he said, secretly very much flattered at what he thought her jealousy. "I will promise you to take no lover's part for the future ; one does not enjoy the mockery of a thing when one knows what the thing itself is."

She had meant something quite different, for since her discovery that Dorinda was a man her little foolish jealousy had all died away, and she had been able to take a much more dispassionate view of what she had heard and seen ; but just as she opened her lips to speak again, Colonel Schuyler came in, and Mr. Vyvian had to go forward and be introduced to him, and then Madame Schuyler changed her seat and came nearer to the window, and it was no longer possible to say anything without being overheard.

Mr. Vyvian did not seem at all put out at having his

conversation with Franzje interrupted, but good-humouredly set to work to ingratiate himself with her old friend, and was so agreeable that Madame Schuyler could not help being somewhat taken with him, and feeling glad that she was not bound to accept as just M. Jansen's sweeping condemnation of the whole of the officers. He declared that he remembered hearing his mother talk of having met old Colonel Schuyler—Madame's uncle, now dead—when he brought the Mohawk chief, "King Hendrick," to England, and insinuated that she would be much charmed to hear of her son having made acquaintance with the family at the Flats. He admired the beauty of the scenery, told how he had enjoyed the berry-picking in the autumn, expatiated on the delights of sleighing, and altogether exhibited so little of that contempt for the pleasures Albany could offer, which had been discernible in him when he first came to the place, that Madame Schuyler set him down as a very sensible young man, and Franzje said to herself, "He has got to like us, and to enter into our ways. I wonder whether any of the other officers care for us as he does! At any rate, I don't think Aunt Schuyler will be able to help liking him better than the rest."

Certainly Major Berkeley and Mr. Gardiner would not bear comparison with him. The former did indeed try to get up a little interest in farm matters, and asked Colonel Schuyler how his sheep were housed in the winter, and remarked on the great size of the barn, which was considerably larger even than the Gerritses'; but Mr. Gardiner did nothing but yawn, and stare at Franzje, wondering to himself how it was that her eyes looked all the bluer for the blue ribbon in her hair, though they couldn't be said to match, and whether

M

Vyvian would not find it a great bore if his flirtation with her should end in his having to marry her. "And I think it will," concluded the sapient young fellow, "if he goes on at this rate; though I'm sure we've all done our best to laugh him out of it; and Trelawny has given him fair warning that he won't have a married man in the regiment."

Franzje thought her old friend Colonel Schuyler a great contrast to the three empty-headed men around him, with his manly, resolute bearing, and grave, intelligent face. She took to listening, half to him, half to Mr. Vyvian, and was very happy and comfortable, very grateful to her father for forgiving her, and bringing her to enjoy herself at the Flats, and only just a little troubled, deep down in her heart, at the thought of how sad and stern the Dominie had looked as he had hurried down the snowy path alone.

CHAPTER XI.

Invitations.

THE Schuylers had not been long at home before they became fully convinced that matters in Albany were past their mending, and that the only hope of restored harmony lay in the probability that Colonel Trelawny's regiment would be called into action as soon as the frost broke up. The struggle between the French and English subjects in America had been going on in a tedious, lingering way for some time; but in the previous year greater energy had been put forth on the English side than before, and important operations were in prospect for the year which had just begun—1757. The limits of the territories of the two nations had been left undetermined at the Treaty of Aix-la-Chapelle; and though commissioners chosen by both had met at Paris, in 1748, to determine the boundaries, no decision had been arrived at. Pending this settlement, it was the policy of each to gain possession of all the important places to which they had any pretensions, and hold them until actually forced to give them up. The French had planned to join their distant settlements in Canada and Louisiana by a chain of forts and posts, extending from the St. Lawrence to the Mississippi, and also to advance their possessions in the eastern part of Canada, so as to command navigation in the winter, when the St. Lawrence was impassable. This double claim interfered with English rights not a little; and the colonies of Nova Scotia, New York, and Virginia, which were chiefly encroached upon, had made their complaints known in the mother country.

The English Government was inclined at first to leave the colonists to fight their own battle, but finally gave some limited assistance; though it was not till 1758, when Pitt took the matter in hand, that a really considerable British force was sent out to attack the French at once by sea and land.

Albany, which in the early days of its settlement had owned allegiance to Holland, had been taken by the English in 1664, and obliged to exchange its Dutch title of Oranienburgh for its present one, in compliment to the English Duke and had ever since remained, like the rest of the New Netherlands, in loyal subjection to the British crown. Since the commencement of the war with the French, it had risen in importance; the commissioners from the various states had met there in 1754, to consider their project of union; the regiments raised in New Hampshire had passed through it on their

M 2

way to attack Crown Point, and a good many hangers-on
of the army had taken up their residence there, though,
except the regiment of American militia which was quartered in the fort, no soldiers had been actually stationed
in the town till the coming of Colonel Trelawny and his
men.

The old people who remembered Albany as it used to
be sixty or seventy years before, felt that it could never
be quite the same again, even if the English soldiers were
got rid of; the new residents were of a different stamp
from the original inhabitants of the place, and their style
of dress and manners was not without its influence on
the rising generation, which was prone to be attracted
by novelties in other things besides amusements. Old
Barentse, and a good many other members of "the
Society," shook their heads over the inevitable degene-
racy of the place; but Colonel Schuyler and his wife,
who were not so wedded to antique fashions, and believed
to a certain extent in progress, felt that they could be
satisfied to see a little more independence of judgment—
a little more life and liberty—among the younger citizens,
if only they could put away from them temptations to
licence. Without adopting the harsh, sweeping judgments of Elder Jansen, they had come to believe in
the worthlessness of *some* at least among the officers;
and when Madame saw Anna Gerritse's complacency
under Colonel Trelawny's bold glances, she was half inclined to echo the elder's sentiment, that the sooner he
was out of the place the better. But Franzje and Mr.
Vyvian! she could by no means find it in her heart to
fear for them, or condemn them in anything like the same
degree. The girl was so little altered, as far as Aunt
Schuyler's charitable eyes could discern, by the admiration she had received; so simple and so true; so open

and so loving; so nobly superior to the small coquettish
arts in which Anna and others indulged, that it was
impossible to believe her admirer had done her any
harm; it was a thousand times easier to fancy that she
had done *him* good.

" I really believe that he is a great deal better than the
rest," said Madame, in confidence, to her husband; "and
I am quite sure there is no use in abusing him to my
little Franz; it only enlists her generosity on his side,
and makes her like him all the better. I wish I could
bring our Dominie and him together, without Marte
Jansen to make mischief between them; I really think
it might be the means of removing prejudice on both sides.
I give up the officers as a body; but I still fancy that Mr.
Vyvian and Major Berkeley, and that bashful young
ensign—is not his name Charlwood?—might become
worthy members of society, if our best and most cultivated citizens would take them in hand, instead of turning
their backs upon them."

So, as a last attempt at achieving in a small way what
she found impossible on a large scale, and reconciling a
portion, at least, of the opposing parties, Madame planned
a sleighing expedition, which should end in a grand tea-
drinking at the Flats, promising that her company should
be very select, and that all should be conducted in a
friendly, but at the same time, unexceptionable manner.

M. and Madame Cuyler and their family; M. and
Madame Ryckman, Franzje and Evert; the Renselaers,
and one or two other dwellers in the country; the three
officers she had named; and last, but not least, the
Dominie—were the guests whom she at once decided to
invite; but by-and-bye she made up her mind that she
must ask one or two others, whose presence she less
desired. She had always been on friendly terms with

the Bankers; and though she did not approve all their
recent doings, nor admire Cornelia's manners, she felt
it would be scarcely possible to invite Mr. Vyvian, who
was living in their house, without including them in the
invitation. Then Killian Barentse—he was such a good,
pleasant fellow, so perfectly unexceptionable, and such a
favourite with the Dominie—it would be difficult to leave
him out, and yet she doubted whether Mr. Vyvian and he
ever appeared to advantage in each other's company. It
would not do to have them showing off their rivalry about
Franzje under the Dominie's very nose. After some cogi-
tation, she decided to [let Killian's invitation wait, but to
make sure at once of the people she chiefly wanted—the
Ryckmans, Mr. Vyvian, and the Dominie; and for this
purpose she determined to spend the next day with the
Cuylers, in Albany, and go about and invite her friends
herself. " And then, if one day does not suit them, I can
fix another; my convenience can easily be made to defer
to theirs," she said, cheerily, to her husband, as she set
forth on her drive the next morning, her face beaming
with benevolence.

Just before she got to M. Cuyler's door, she met
Mr. Vyvian walking alone, and stopped the sleigh to
speak to him: it was as well not to lose the opportunity
of securing one of the indispensable elements of her
party.

He accepted most politely—eagerly even—and declared
himself quite disengaged for the day she named; so, encouraged by her success, she said, with a sudden impulse,
" I am on my way to my sister's, but I have a great mind
to drive on to Madame Ryckman's first, and ascertain that
Wednesday will suit *them*."

A smile came into his eyes as he answered, " I was
just going there myself—to the door, at any rate. Old

Jan Ryckman slipped down on the pavement yesterday, and I had the honour of picking him up and helping him home; so I thought it would be but civil to go and inquire after his bruises."

Was it wonderful that Madame Schuyler thought him a very kind-hearted young man, and did not at once remember that being in love with a young lady often makes men singularly considerate towards the young lady's relations? And could she do less than offer him a seat in her sleigh, even though it was possible that they might meet the Dominie and Elder Jansen as they drove along the street?

He made himself very agreeable on the way, and though it was rather early for calls, and she was not quite sure how it would be taken, she felt as if she could hardly avoid asking him to come into the house with her. The Ryckmans could scarcely be offended at her doing so, since he had been of such service to their uncle.

There was no one in the parlour when they were shown in; and though Madame Ryckman soon appeared, and was very gracious and kindly, they seemed likely at first to see no one else; but, in a few minutes, in rushed Arij.

" Uncle Jan wants to thank Mr. Vyvian, so he is to come up stairs, please!" he shouted; and then, as the young officer readily rose, he continued, " I'll show you the way; I saw you from the window driving up with Aunt Schuyler, so I ran straight off to tell Franzje; but I couldn't find her till I thought of looking in Uncle Jan's room, and then he said you were to come up."

Good, proper, demure Madame Ryckman felt her darling to be somewhat of an *enfant terrible* at this moment. " Tell Franzje to come down and see Aunt Schuyler," she said, with as much composure as she could command.

"She's coming!" shouted Arij, who was out of the room again before his mother had finished speaking; and then he ran up stairs as fast as he could go; and Mr. Vyvian, who did not wish to lose sight of his guide, was obliged to run after him.

And so, instead of meeting Franzje on her way down, they found her re-adjusting some bandages on her uncle's head, and trying to make him look more presentable for his visitor. She had not reckoned on Arij's extreme haste; and some writing, on which she had been engaged, was still scattered about the table, together with some little girlish belongings which she had meant to remove; so when she had shaken hands with Mr. Vyvian, she paused to gather up these, her cheek tinged with a soft flush of embarrassment which was exquisitely becoming to her. She thought she had never seen Mr. Vyvian look more elegant—more splendid even—than he did as he came, all in brilliant uniform, into the bare, carpetless room; but to him the room was not bare by any means. He scarcely noticed how little furniture there was, and what a quaint, dismal figure old Jan Ryckman looked as he sat in his arm-chair, wrapped up in a cloak, with his head enveloped in linen bandages; his young love, with her sweet, noble presence, made the whole scene delightful to him—his one thought was only how to detain her for a while.

He spoke kindly to the old man, and asked after his hurts; then waiving aside, as it were, his grave, courteous thanks, he turned to the table, and offered to assist Franzje in her task.

"Let me put these papers together," he said, taking some scattered pages in his hand as he spoke. "French! what, are you a French scholar, mademoiselle? There is no end to your accomplishments."

"Aunt Schuyler has taught me a little," said Franzje, modestly; "perhaps if I take these exercises down to her, she will be kind enough to point out some of my blunders now."

"Would you trust me, I wonder?" said Russell, in the tone of gentle familiarity which he had learnt to assume in speaking to her. "I have forgotten most of my French, I fear, but I should enjoy rubbing it up in your service. I made the grand tour once when I was young, and could speak glibly enough then."

Her eyes glanced up at him with such a bright, wondering smile at the words "when I was young," it made him quite smile at himself; and he continued, "I am not so *very* old now, it is true, but I feel old beside you, Mademoiselle. Can't you imagine me to be 'Aunt Schuyler' for a few minutes, and let me have the pleasant task of correcting some of these mistakes? Surely you have used the wrong tense here."

He pointed to one of the words with his finger, and she came a little closer, and looked over the page. The proximity of the peach-like cheek was far less indifferent to him than it had been to the Dominie in like case; perhaps if Uncle Jan and Arij had not been there, even his respect for her fearless innocence would not have kept him from taking an ungenerous advantage of the opportunity. As it was, he only gazed his fill, and said, softly, "How I envy Madame Schuyler! Has she been your principal teacher?"

"No, I think I have learnt most from the Dominie," said Franzje, suddenly taking up a pen and busying herself in correcting the mistake which Mr. Vyvian had pointed out.

"I shouldn't like the Dominie to teach me," broke in Arij, who had been hitherto absorbed in trying to climb

up the back of Uncle Jan's high chair. 'Ain't you glad
he does not come now, Franz?"

"No," said she, in a low tone.

Mr. Vyvian looked at her with a jealous, troubled
glance; and Uncle Jan pushed up the bandage which
partially covered one of his eyes, and looked at them
both. They were very pleasant to look upon in their perfection of form and feature, and the old man might well
have envied them their youthful brightness and vigour;
but there was more of pity than of anything else in his
heart as he gazed. "It won't come to good," he said to
himself; " he has come and troubled my little maid's life,
and turned her ideas upside down, and half persuaded
her into caring for him; and by-and-bye he will go away,
and be shot by the French, or scalped by the Indians, or
else he will live to go home and marry some fine English
lady; and what will he have done for Franzje, but just
spoiled her innocent peace, and prevented her being
happy with Killian, and submissive to the Dominie? I
wish I had not asked him to come up, though I *did* want
to thank him."

Meanwhile Mr. Vyvian had begun to point out some
more mistakes in Franzje's French, and she had actually
sat down to correct them, though under protest, as it
were. "Will you let me be your teacher," he said, "now
that the Dominie proves neglectful? I cannot promise
to teach any catechism—you are much more fit to teach
me in all those matters—but in lighter things I might
perhaps be able to help you."

As she did not immediately answer, he added, "Will
you try me? I will promise not to be hard upon you:
on the contrary, you shall be as idle as ever you like."

"Then, *no*," said Franzje, getting up, and laying down
the pen; and with a gay, arch glance at him she con-

tinued, " I want to learn, and not to play at learning ; so
I will go on with Aunt Schuyler, if you please, Sir. I
shouldn't like to be idle and not be scolded for it."

" We don't scold divinities," said he, in a voice that
was only meant for her ears ; and really, as she stood
before him in her grand beauty, it seemed to him incredible that even the Dominie could find it possible to
reprove her. But her azure eyes turned from him with a
displeased expression, as if she thought him at once
ridiculous and profane.

" I am going down, dear Uncle," she said, addressing the
silent patriarch. " I will bring you some fresh bandages
by-and-bye.—Come with me, Arij ; you make uncle uncomfortable when you shake his chair so."

She bowed to Mr. Vyvian with a slightly heightened
colour, and turned to go ; but finding that he was following her, she paused to say, " You will stay a little while
with my uncle, will you not, Sir? He has been wishing
to see you—and indeed, we have all wished to thank you
for your kindness to him."

" Will you give me a reward beyond my deserts, and
promise to let me drive you at the sleighing party which
Madame Schuyler is arranging ? " he answered, intercept-
ing her progress towards the door.

" I cannot say anything yet, Sir ; this is the first I
have heard of the party," said she in surprise. " I do
not even know that Mother will let me go."

" Will you at least promise not to give the preference
to young Barentse, as you did the last time I had the
pleasure of meeting you on one of these excursions ? "

" Franz has quarrelled with Killian," burst forth Arij,
pulling at the hand by which his sister held him. " I
shall run this minute and ask Aunt Schuyler if *I* may
go, and then Killian shall drive *me*."

"I will not grudge him that honour," laughed the young officer; "but, Mademoiselle Ryckman, you are not going to refuse me my one little petition? If you will not have me as your preceptor, you cannot be so hard-hearted as to say that I am not to be your charioteer either."

His eyes were full of the most eloquent beseeching; and Franzje—who could not bear to coquet about the matter, nor to make a greater favour of it than she really thought it—answered quietly, "If Aunt Schuyler likes me to go with you, I will go; but I have not quarrelled with Killian, please do not believe that, Sir."

And then, yielding to Arij's efforts, she moved again towards the door, and with a triumphant smile and courteous bow Russell stepped aside and let her pass.

When she was gone, he took the one spare chair—which Franzje had brought there that morning for her own use—and sat down beside the old man, without having the vaguest idea how to draw him into conversation. To his surprise, Jan Ryckman was the first to speak.

"I am glad you are going to stay with me a little," he said, in the grave, measured tone in which he always spoke. "I am very grateful to you, Sir, for the service you did me yesterday, and I want to say a few words about a matter which is very near my heart. You will pardon an old man's plainness of speech, I hope, if I venture to ask you what is to come of all this?"

"Of all what, Sir?" rejoined the young man, carelessly, though he knew well enough what the recluse meant, and at once gave him credit for more observation than he had looked for from him.

"I have not heard all that has passed between you and my little Franzje," continued Uncle Jan quietly, ignoring the question; "but I am not blind though my eyes are

weak, and I see that you think her fair and sweet, and
take pains to show her that you do. I am not her father,
to call you to account, nor shall I make any use of what
you tell me; but as one who loves the child dearly, I ask
you, what end do you propose to yourself in your dealings with her?"

"This is plain speaking with a vengeance!" thought
Russell to himself. Aloud he said, "Really, Sir, it is so
natural to admire a beautiful young lady, and to show
that one admires her, that one may do so, I think, without any very deep-laid plan of any kind."

"Then so long as my niece knows that you think her
fair, you are satisfied? you do not wish to make any
further impression on her than that?"

The young man bit his lip, and looked and felt annoyed;
but there was a sort of spell in the old man's calmness
and gentleness, which prevented his giving voice to any
of the angry answers which rose to his lips.

"I think her much more than fair," he said, after
chafing for a moment in silence. "I think her one in a
thousand, infinitely superior to her surroundings, infinitely
too good for that Indian-faced young Barentse, or for such
a harsh old Puritan as your worthy Dominie."

Uncle Jan gave a slight but rather meaning smile, and
probably considered himself included in the surroundings
of which the young Englishman spoke so contemptuously;
but his tone was gentle as before, as he rejoined, "It may
be that my dear little maid is too good for Killian, worthy
young man though he be; but I do not know why you
couple our Dominie's name with his. M. Freylinghausen
has given you no reason to look upon him as a rival; his
interest in Franzje is merely that of a pastor in one of
the lambs of his flock."

"Stimulated by a tolerably lively perception of the

charms of the lamb in question," sneered the handsome
soldier. "If M. Freylinghausen does not care for
Mademoiselle Franzje, why does he look ready to kill
me when I speak a civil word to her ?"

"Because he loves her soul," replied the patriarch
gravely.

"And thinks that she perils it by being five minutes
in my company? Hem, I can't say much for his charity,"
said Russell, with a contemptuous laugh ; then, finding
his remark unanswered, he continued in a more amiable
tone, "I wonder how you contrived to endure my talking
to her just now, Sir."

"I do not say that I liked it," said the old man
candidly ; "but I cannot think you so black as you are
painted—your kind courtesy to me alone forbids that ;
nay, I even think you better than you yourself would have
me believe. Did I consider you what you seem to wish
to appear,—a mere thoughtless rake—I should not speak
to you as I have spoken just now."

"He is not such a bad old soul after all," said Russell
patronizingly to himself ; "nay, ridiculous as it seems to
say it of such a poor old broken-down creature, he
reminds me somehow of Franzje when he looks up in
that innocent, trustful way."

"Your kind heart makes you judge kindly of others,
M. Ryckman," he said courteously ; "I hope I shall
never give you any reason to consider me the consummate
villain which some of your excellent fellow-citizens
would fain make me out. I have no feeling for your
niece which I should blush to avow ; though I cannot
precisely undertake to say how it will all end, since that is
a matter which must partly depend upon herself. I have
no wish to sully what I find stainless—you may be sure
of that, whatever your Dominie may be pleased to think."

"And perhaps," said the old man—lifting the pale blue eyes, which certainly, in their trustful purity, *had* a look of Franzje's—"perhaps, Sir,—you will forgive my saying it—you may be a better man all your days for finding that there *are* such souls as my child's in the world, and may be glad that you came among us simple, unpolished folk, if only for that reason."

"God bless him, and lead him into the right path," he continued to himself, as after shaking hands heartily with him, and wishing him a speedy recovery, Russell took a somewhat speedy departure; "I was wrong to think he would forget my Franzje—even if he *does* marry a fine English lady he will not do that; but yet I would rather he had never come here. We may think a flower the loveliest we ever saw, and it may give us some grateful thoughts of the God who made it, such as we never had before; and yet the touch of our hot hands may wither it, and it may not bloom on as it would have bloomed if we had not chanced to pass that way." And then again he stilled his fears and anxieties with the old unfailing panacea: "But the child is in God's Hand—God's Hand; and she'll be guided safe."

Madame Schuyler had had the courtesy to wait for Mr. Vyvian, but rose up to go directly he appeared, so that he had no opportunity for any more talk with Franzje. He went as far as M. Cuyler's in the sleigh, and there parted from Madame, after having helped her to alight, and made her some very gallant speeches, with which she would willingly have dispensed; she decided that the young Englishman was "too much of a courtier;" but yet owned to feeling a sort of fascination in his company, and readily forgave Franzje for having lingered a little while to talk to him before coming down to welcome her.

The rest of the morning was given to her sister and

nieces, one of whom she was going to take back with her to the Flats for a long visit; but after the early dinner, she sallied forth to give some more invitations, and betook herself first of all to the Manse, in order to undertake the difficult task of persuading the Dominie to join her party.

She had chosen the best hour for her visit, for the pastor usually studied or wrote sermons or held conference with his elders in the morning, and then allowed himself about an hour for dinner and relaxation before setting out to visit his flock or attend to any necessary business in the town; and during this brief interval he was particularly easy of access to those who came on mere friendly errands such as Madame Schuyler's. His frugal meal had long been over, and he was seated in the nearest approach to an easy chair which his study could boast, turning over the leaves of a volume of the *Spectator*, which Madame herself had lent him, when she was shown in. His sombre face lit up with evident pleasure at seeing her, and he came forward cordially to greet her, and made her sit down in the chair from which he had just risen, while he took a less comfortable one, nearer to the table.

"I am glad to see you in Albany again," he said, when they were seated; "it is a token, I hope, that you have lost your rheumatism."

"Yes, I am much better, thank you, Dominie; and freedom from pain has put me in first-rate spirits. The Colonel and I are actually meditating a little piece of gaiety; but nothing of which you could disapprove— nothing, in fact, but a sleighing-party such as we gave two years ago. I remember you gave us the pleasure of your company then, and I am hoping you will not refuse it to us on this occasion."

"You are very good," said he politely, but with a little

abatement of his previous cordiality. "You are perhaps aware, however, that sleighing parties have lately been made the excuse for unseemly dissipation, and therefore can scarcely be looked upon any longer as opportunities for purely innocent enjoyment."

"But I think, as the Colonel says, we should not abandon all our resources to the enemy," rejoined Madame Schuyler, with a pleasant smile; "my party is to be one of the good old sort; we will drive up the river beyond Stonehook, perhaps take some refreshment with our good friends there, and then return to the Flats for a substantial tea; there shall be plenty of sociability and cheerfulness, but nothing that deserves the name of dissipation; and we will break up early, and retire to our beds like good Christians, as M. Jansen would say."

"You must be careful, then, whom you invite, dear friend, or this judicious programme of yours will be overturned in spite of you. Your brother and sister, and the Renselaers, and a few others such as our worthy friend Jansen, whom you have just mentioned, would be abundantly content with what you propose; but I fear most of our *young* townspeople would try to engraft upon it some undesirable excitement. You do not, of course, think of asking any of the English officers?"

Aunt Schuyler looked a little bit dismayed—she feared that the Dominie was going to make the selection of the other guests the condition of his presence; and she was vexed with herself for having brought forward M. Jansen's name—M. Jansen, whom of all people she least wished to invite on this particular occasion. She occupied herself for a moment in drawing out her handkerchief from a little reticule woven of Indian grasses which she held in her hand; and then she recovered her presence of mind, and in the sort of elder-sisterly tone which she

N

sometimes adopted towards the Dominie, who was some
eight years younger, hastened to answer, " It would defeat
my object of drawing back the young people to their former
harmless amusements if I included none of them in my
company ; and the old aunt is never happy, you know,
but when she has some young folks round her. I will
be very careful, however, whom I invite ; and if you will
come, Dominie, your presence will be an effectual check to
any frivolity."

" And a damper to cheerfulness as well, perhaps," he
said bitterly ; " I scarcely know how it has come to pass,
but I am looked upon as a sort of kill-joy now by all our
lads and lasses ; yes, even by some whom I love as my
own children, and who, when they were little, used to
come running to my knee as if they looked upon me as
their own especial friend."

" I think you mistake shyness for aversion," said his
friend, with kindly eagerness ; " a few young people here
and there who know themselves to be much to blame,
may try to think you over-strict by way of self-excuse ;
but depend upon it, the general feeling of respect and
affection for you is as strong as ever. It is only the fear
that you are displeased with them that makes my nieces
and Franzje Ryckman and such as they shrink away
when you approach. If they did not love and honour
you, they would not care for your displeasure as they
do."

" They care for it just enough to make them shy and
sullen in my presence, but the fear of it does not deter
them from joining in sinful amusements. No, I would
not give much for the love and honour of children who
prefer the example of a parcel of worthless young officers
to that of their parents and ministers."

" Poor children ! it is only a passing epidemic ! " said

Aunt Schuyler, compassionately, as if she had been speaking of measles or scarlet-fever.

"We shall see," returned the Dominie, despondently; "but even the comforting fact of which you so often remind me, that this regiment will soon be going away does not altogether console me. It will go, but the mischief it has worked will remain. Do you think minds that have lost their soberness, hearts that have lost their purity, can ever be made what they were before? Do you think young ears that have ever heard such words as these,"—and he suddenly lifted a small, grey-coloured pamphlet from the table and hastily turned over the leaves—"can ever again be unconscious of evil? Do you know what this is? It is a play-book, and contains the words of a play which I am told the officers are going to act in a little while. I will just show you one passage in it—not the worst—and leave you to judge of the rest from that specimen."

She read it, and though she was a middle-aged, or as she would have said, an *old* woman, a blush mounted to her cheek as vivid as any girl's. Then she turned to the first page, looked at the title—"The Recruiting Officer" —and laid the book down again on the table.

"On one thing I am determined," she said, impetuously, "that Mr. Vyvian shall not act in it, and that none of the young people I care for shall go to see it."

"Nevertheless you will find that he *will* act, and that most, if not all of your favourites, will be there to see," rejoined the Dominie, with a chilling certainty of conviction which quite oppressed her for the moment with a sense of the inevitable.

"Oh, you will not let them!" she said, earnestly; "you will try to win them to submission, will you not, Dominie?"

"I shall warn them," said he, gloomily; "and if they will not be warned they must take the consequences."

She had meant more than mere warning, and St. Paul's words about being all things to all men that he might by all means save some, were ringing in her ears. "You will let them see that it is in *love* that you hold them back from such false pleasure as this?" she said, with her kind face kindling; "and first of all, you will try—will you not? or let my husband try—to persuade the officers to drop this play altogether? I daresay they do not see it as we do; I have been told that in Europe much license of language is permitted on the stage; they cannot tell how it sounds to us, who, thank God! have been trained to look on immorality with the horror it deserves."

"You say truly that they do not see it as we do. So little do they blush for it, that the subalterns who are billeted in Jansen's house leave this book about within reach of his young nieces. He took it from the hands of one of the girls when he brought it here this morning."

"That is very inexcusable, but still perhaps it is only carelessness on the young men's part," said Madame Schuyler, with a sudden change of tone, and a rising hope that this rumour that the play was to be acted might prove a mare's nest of M. Jansen's after all. "These lieutenants may talk of acting this, but it does not follow that the better men in the regiment will sanction it;" and she thought of Mr. Vyvian.

The Dominie read her thought, and with sarcastic emphasis inquired if she had noticed the name written on the cover. It was "Russell Vyvian."

"Yes, I see it is his book," she said, as he pointed to the writing; "but for all that, he may have too much good feeling to wish Franzje to see and hear what it contains. My dear friend, will you not sanction one last effort to win him and one or two others over to the right side ? I own to you that I have asked him to my party ; will you forgive that, and come and meet him, and lend the colonel and me your powerful countenance in our poor attempt to set things straight by gentle means ? I ask it as an old friend who has always wished to be loyal to you."

" And for your sake, dear madame, I will not refuse," said he, touched by her persistent benevolence ; " but all the same I know your efforts will be useless."

She would not risk losing the point she had gained by any approach to contradiction ; but though she left the house with a certain sense of triumph, she was very sad at heart. " Was ever a cause gained by one who despaired ? " she said to herself. " I wish I had some of the Dominie's goodness, and that in return I could give him my belief in the possible goodness of other people."

CHAPTER XII.

A Love-Dream.

THE sleighing-party did not come off after all on the day originally fixed for it. The niece whom Madame Schuyler took home on a visit fell dangerously ill; and though her mother went at once to the Flats to assist in nursing her, and her illness lasted but a short time, it was of course out of the question for the kind aunt to leave her, or to have anything like gaiety in the house till she had recovered.

It seemed a light matter, this postponement of the party, in comparison with the more distressing consequences of Catalina Cuyler's illness; but yet the results were not altogether unimportant. In the first place, all hopes of bringing the Dominie's influence to bear upon Mr. Vyvian, with regard to the objectionable play which his regiment proposed to act, were frustrated by it; for before the party took place a performance of "The Recruiting Officer" had been publicly announced for the ensuing week, and one of the principal parts in it assigned to him; so that there was no longer the least likelihood of his being persuaded to draw back, even if the Dominie could be induced to condescend to persuasion. Moreover, such slight chance as there might have been of the Dominie's acting towards him in a conciliatory spirit was now quite gone by; and it was only by reminding M. Freylinghausen of his *promise*, and treating the fulfilment of it as something absolutely due to his old friendship for the Colonel and herself, that Madame Schuyler got him to the party at all. She felt as if she were going to lead a forlorn hope, when she ordered her sleigh to the door that bright March afternoon, and set forth to welcome her guests from the city, who had agreed to meet her at a certain point on the river, and proceed at once to Stonehook, where they were to pause for refreshments.

It was a pretty sight, when the crowd of sleighs came gliding along over the firm ice; and the greetings were for the most part glad and eager, and the sleigh-bells tinkled merrily; but Madame was too anxious to see who had come, and how they had arranged themselves, to be able to take in all the pleasantness of the scene. Mr. Vyvian was driving Cornelia Banker, and Cornelia's loud giggle was heard even above the tinkling of the bells; Madame Ryckman had paired off with the Dominie, and Franzje was seated beside her brother Evert—M. Ryck- being nowhere to be seen. Madame Banker and

Killian, who had been invited after all—Engeltje and her
father—Major Berkeley and the eldest Mademoiselle
Cuyler—and shy Mr. Charlwood bringing up the rear
with Cornelius Banker, and casting admiring glances
from afar at Franzje—all these Madame took in with one
sweeping glance, and then her anxiety was in a measure
appeased, for how the other guests disposed of themselves
she did not very much care. There would be a fresh
arrangement made at Stonehook, where the Renselaers
and others would meet them (if indeed they did not join
them by the way); and then Madame Schuyler intended,
if possible, to get the Dominie to herself, and to give
Franzje *one* of the beaux, though not perhaps Mr. Vyvian,
as he was in her black books now, as well as the Dominie's, for having consented to take part in the impend-
ing theatricals. From Stonehook they were going to proceed further up the river, so whatever pairs were formed
there would remain together till they all got back to the
Flats in time for the substantial supper which was to be
the crown of the entertainment.

Franzje did not look at all unhappy in the companionship of her brother, and was talking to him with quite as
much animation as if he had been one of her devoted
admirers. Madame Schuyler thought it would be hard if
the infection of that innocent joyousness did not spread
even to the Dominie before the day was done; and by-
and-bye, when the party all found themselves together in
the state parlour at Stonehook, she was glad to see him
approach Franzje with something of the old paternal
friendliness in look and smile.

"Vrow Dorkman showed me the warm coverlet you
brought her this morning," he said; "I am glad to find
you do not forget her."

Spite of all that had come and gone, Franzje flushed

up with pleasure at the words. "I am sorry I did not finish it before," said she; "the south winds will be coming soon, and then good-bye to snow and frost. Perhaps, however, it will serve her for another winter."

"If she should live to see another; but she seems to me to be very near her rest. Near her *rest*," he repeated, absently, with a sort of soft, grave stress upon the words, as if the sound of them soothed him somehow.

Franzje looked up at him, then round at the large room full of guests of all ages, then out over the ice-bound river along which his gaze was travelling. "She said this morning that her work was done. It is not wrong for people who have not even *found* their work yet, to be more anxious to live than she is—is it, Dominie?"

It was just one of the old thoughtful questions in the simple, grave tone of appeal which had once been so familiar to the Dominie's ear; but something in it seemed to jar upon him, and he answered abruptly, 'Each of us has his work—we need not go far to find it; only some of us have been too busy with play lately to think of work at all."

"The play?" said Mr. Vyvian, catching up the word as he approached with a cup of chocolate for Franzje. "Have you heard the last proposal, Mademoiselle? It is that some of you young ladies should take the female parts—your friend Mademoiselle Gerritse, and others."

It was an audacious invention of his own, made up on the spot for the purpose of shocking the Dominie; but Franzje, who had not seen the book of the play, had no idea *how* outrageous the notion was, and was startled by the withering glance of indignation and contempt which the Dominie turned upon the jester.

"You need not give a thought to the matter, my child," he said, in a studiously calm tone, interposing his stately

person between the girl and her admirer, as if he thought
the latter unfit even to approach her; "fortunately
there is no maiden in the whole city so utterly lost to
a sense of modesty as to entertain the proposal for a
moment."

" I understood that it sprang from Mademoiselle Gerritse herself," said Russell, in his demurest voice, sitting
down on a chair at Franzje's elbow, and beginning to sip
the chocolate, as if it were merely his own cup which he
had brought in his hand, and not at all as if he had been
balked in his intention of offering it to Franzje.

He was not altogether slandering Anna, for she had
really expressed a great desire to appear on the stage,
and had bedecked herself one evening in Dorinda's garments for Colonel Trelawny's benefit, but she had never
seriously entertained any idea of acting in public; and
the Dominie, badly as he thought of her, did not give
credit for a moment to Mr. Vyvian's insinuation.

" We are not bound to believe such a monstrous assertion," he said, still addressing Franzje; "and we have both
known Anna somewhat longer than Lieutenant Vyvian."

" I wish you joy of the intimacy, Sir," said Russell,
with a supercilious curl of the lip. " Mademoiselle Ryckman, have you had any refreshment? No doubt M. Freylinghausen has been taking care of you."

Franzje looked around, aghast at the supposition. That
the pastor should wait upon her seemed too ridiculous an
idea even to require refutation; but apparently M. Freylinghausen himself did not resent the hint so much as
she did for him.

" You have nothing to eat ! " said he, as if suddenly
waking up to the perception. " Here, Cornelius, my lad,
bring some chocolate and cakes this way, if you please."

Cornelius Banker, who was creeping along with both

hands full, gave an awkward start at being thus hailed by
the Dominie; but having contrived to recover his balance before any harm was done, soon obeyed the summons; and so Franzje's wants were supplied without the
Dominie's having to budge an inch from his defensive
position.

As for his own refreshment, that was brought to him
by the hostess herself, with every manifestation of respectful solicitude; and Russell Vyvian, after standing
his ground for another minute or so, and hiding his dis-
comfiture under a nonchalant, satirical air, got up and
returned to the Demoiselles Banker, who received him
with very gratifying *empressement*, even the shy little Engeltje making room for him on the ottoman beside her.
He was horribly disgusted and out of temper, but he
resolved to avenge himself on the Dominie by making
violent love to Franzje as soon as he got her to himself.
"Madame Schuyler said the sleighs were to keep together," thought he; "but I'll see if I can't inspire my
trusty steed with a tendency to run away. No fear of
Franzje's being frightened; she has a good spirit of her
own, though she does look as demure as Goody Two-
Shoes herself when once the Dominie gets hold of her.
How shall I contrive to get rid of him when we start, I
wonder? I must get Madame Schuyler to help me; she
is a kind soul, though she did make the mistake of asking
this intolerable old tyrant to her party."

Madame Schuyler was to a certain extent playing into
his hands without knowing it, for when the refreshments
began to circulate less freely, and the time for departure
seemed drawing near, she said to her husband, "Suppose
you take some of the young people down with you,
Philip, and get them seated first. I want Franzje to have
one of the young men to drive her—not Mr. Vyvian,

perhaps, but Mr. Charlwood or Killian; and Evert can
have little Engeltje, they will make a nice pair."

So Franzje was borne off by the colonel, while the
Dominie was detained to listen to the compliments of the
lady of Stonehook, and her thanks for honouring her
with his presence; and Russell quickly followed in the
colonel's wake, and was at Franzje's side directly they
reached the porch. He had scarcely had time, however,
to remind her of her promise, before she was beset by
Killian, Cortlandt Cuyler, and Mr. Charlwood; and
though he quickly snubbed the latter, and sent him off
feeling that an ensign had no chance when his adjutant
was in the field, the two Albanian youths were not so
easily disposed of.

"You *must* come with me, Franzje," said young Cuyler,
who was afterwards known in his regiment by the
sobriquet of "the handsome savage;"—"I hate all
girls except you, and Mother only got me here by saying
no doubt you would let me drive you."

"Madame Ryckman gave me leave to ask you," pleaded
Killian on the other side; "and I have brought my new
sleigh, that I got from New York, on purpose for you."

"Mademoiselle Ryckman is engaged to me," asserted
Russell in his most imperious tone, but with a glance at
Franzje that was all gallant entreaty.—"You know,
Mademoiselle, I have your *promise*."

"I said if Aunt Schuyler liked," rejoined Franzje, perplexed between her real wish to give him the preference,
and her fear that all her elders and betters might be displeased if she did.

"Of course she likes—she asked me to come on purpose to meet you," he urged; and so he continued to
press her, while Killian and Cortlandt, from sheer rivalry,
would take no denial either; and at length it seemed as

if a brawl were about to commence among the three young men.

Colonel Schuyler thought it time to interpose; and very good-naturedly, but with all the authority which his age and position gave him, he said, "Come, Franzje, if you can put up with an old man instead of a young one, I think I must ask you to drive with me.—Excuse me, Sir," as Mr. Vyvian was about to remonstrate, "your turn will come another time, I daresay." And without waiting for more objections, he took Franzje's hand kindly within his own, and led her to the sleigh.

She made no resistance, she even gave a faint smile, as he tucked in the bearskin round her, and told her he would be as gallant as an old man knew how to be; but the smile was absent and forced, and the blue eyes seemed riveted to the spot where Mr. Vyvian stood, with clouded brow, apparently indifferent to the fact that ladies young and old were flocking past him, and that his sleigh was drawn up in readiness, and waiting to be occupied.

Presently, Aunt Schuyler went and spoke to him, and under her cheerful influence his gloom relaxed a little; but he seemed to negative one after the other the propositions she made, and at last, with an air of haughty condescension, marched up to one of the old country dames who was very deaf and very dull, and offered to be her charioteer.

Franzje looked just a little bit pleased, and then was ready to laugh at herself for feeling as if Mr. Vyvian's sulkiness were a kind of tribute to her. She had thought that he would console himself with the vivacious Cornelia, and it could not fail to be a little gratifying to her vanity to find that he refused to be consoled at all. She thought he was much worse off with regard to a companion than she was; for she had a really grateful affection for the good old colonel, and after a bit brightened up, and talked to him with all her own natural sweetness.

There was something exhilarating in the dashing speed at which they were going, in the clearness of the atmosphere, the brightness of the sunshine, and the mingled clamour of voices and bells; the frozen banks, and the snow-laden trees that crested them, seemed to be flying too, and Franzje's eyes sparkled and her colour rose with youthful, healthful enjoyment.

When they got near the Cohoes, a famous waterfall about ten miles above Albany, where three rivers united their streams, they were obliged to diverge from the ice and take to the road; and then the rate of progress was slower, and the occupants of some of the sleighs began to talk to each other.

"You seem well amused, Mademoiselle," said Russell Vyvian sarcastically, as he urged his sturdy little American horse to its fastest trot, and showed off his skill as a driver, rather to the terror of his elderly companion.

"She is longing to get past the portage[1] and take to the river again," answered the colonel for her, glancing down with a smile into the radiant face.

"I am so glad you are with the colonel, my dear," called out Madame Ryckman approvingly, as he in his turn showed off the paces of his steed, and passed the vehicle which contained the good lady and M. Cuyler.

"Do you call yourself 'one of the young men,' Philip?" asked Aunt Schuyler merrily of her husband, as the Dominie and she came for a moment side by side with Franzje and the colonel.

The Dominie said nothing, but gave Franzje a glance of dignified approval which she felt she did not deserve,

---

[1] The name given to any part of a river where a canoe cannot pass, but is obliged to be taken to the shore and carried.

and which somewhat nettled her. Approving looks from
the Dominie were rare now, but she did not feel as if she
could consent to win them at the price of giving up all
intercourse with Mr. Vyvian. Unconsciously to herself,
she wanted to bring the Dominie to admit that she could
enjoy that intercourse and yet be none the worse. That
he was so loth to admit it, seemed to her the result of his
narrowness—and so in a measure it was; nor, perhaps,
was she to blame for perceiving that narrowness as she
would not have done a year before.

A belief in the infallibility of pastors and teachers is
scarcely possible, perhaps, except in early youth, and
seldom survives the first contact with the world; but
happy those to whom maturer judgment brings no dimin-
ishing of the early loyalty; who do not come to think
lightly of the "treasure" because they realize that it is
contained "in earthen vessels;" who can allow for mistakes and imperfections in their guides as in themselves,
and not therefore refuse to be guided at all, but trust in
the unseen Hand which overrules such mistakes for their
good.

The colonel saw a half-vexed, half-determined expression settle down upon the girl's fair face, and said to
himself, "I shall be surprised if she and the handsome
young Englishman do not get a drive together before the
day is done. I wish I could think of him as charitably
as Catalina does! but I am afraid his merits begin and
end with his handsome person and distinguished air.
'Tis a pity, for he is a fair match for Franzje in looks;
and the army is not a bad profession to *my* thinking,
though my good friend Evert Ryckman might not relish
a military son-in-law."

The drive, though a long one, being chiefly on the ice,
was accomplished in a wonderfully short space of time;

and the party returned to the Flats before the sun had
set, and about half-past six sat down to a supper which
almost rivalled that of the Gerritses' in its abundance of
good things. It was served in what was called in homely
phrase "the eating-room" of the summer mansion, a
stately place, hung round with fine Scripture paintings,
and seldom used except for company. The pictures had
been brought from Holland by Colonel Schuyler's ancestor,
and were old and good. There was one representing Esau
coming to demand his father's blessing; and the fine,
bold figure of the hunter, and the anguish of rejection
depicted on his strongly-marked features, drew many eyes
to it, even though most of the guests had seen it at various
times before. Franzje, from her childhood up, had loved
to study that picture, and had always been haunted and
fascinated by the dark, splendid, despairing face.

"Oh! I am so sorry for Esau!" rose to her lips now,
as a hundred times before; and though she did not utter
it, her two neighbours—Mr. Vyvian on the one side, and
M. Cuyler on the other—both noticed her absorbed, regretful gaze; and while the latter only looked at her and
then went on quietly with his plate of roast pig, the
former said with a smile, "You seem very much taken
up with that picture, Mademoiselle. What is it meant
for? Is it Actæon coming home with his spoils? I suppose it must be a presentiment of his future fate that
makes him look so miserable."

The blue eyes turned to him with frankest wonder.
"It is Esau bringing the venison for his father, and finding he has been forestalled. Can you help being sorry
for his losing the blessing, even though he did not deserve it?"

"I am afraid I never thought about it enough to be
sorry. Jacob supplanted him, did he not? I wonder he

only talked about 'slaying' Jacob; I should have slain him outright if I had been he."

"You do not mean it," said the girl, tranquilly, too incredulous to be shocked.

"More than you think! I *hate* whatever comes between me and the objects on which I set my heart."

There was a force of passion in face and voice, which seemed to show that there were some subjects on which he could feel with an intensity which one could scarcely have looked for from the man's slight nature. A sense of keen personal animosity gave point and emphasis to his words; and Franzje shuddered and turned away from him, as if she had had a real glimpse of his soul, and did not like what she found there.

But then, in a low, soft tone, he murmured, "I believe my love is as intense as my hate, and that it is its nature to aspire; as Esau could sit down content with a daughter of Heth, and leave it to his brother to seek out a Rachel, no wonder he put up tamely with the loss of the birthright and the blessing. As for me, I mean to win *my* Rachel, let who will oppose me; and when I have won her, she shall make whatever she likes of me."

No one but herself heard the words; no one knew the foolish thrill, half exultation and half shrinking, which they sent through her; but she was aware of a sort of frowning watch kept upon her by the Dominie from his place at the opposite side of the table; and with an instinct of courageous openness not unmingled with perversity, she answered the eloquent glance that accompanied them by one of her own beautiful star-like looks of gratitude and trust, and such belief in the better nature of her imperious lover, as always raised him to her own level for the moment.

How he loved her for giving him that look under the

very eyes of his rival, as he still persisted in considering
the pastor. M. Cuyler spoke to her the next minute,
and there were no more asides while the meal lasted; but
Russell was now invincibly determined that nothing should
baulk him of the short drive homewards with Franzje from
the Flats to her own door. He had been disappointed of
her company twice that day, and it was only by a ruse
that he had managed to get the seat next her at supper;
but he would not be disappointed a third time. Not all
the Dominies in creation should snatch his good angel
from him; he meant to have her love to bless his life,
though all the forces of Puritanism were allied to keep
her out of his reach; and he meant to win some avowal
of it from her lips that very night. His colonel's sneers,
and the more good-natured ridicule of his younger com-
rades, had faded from his mind; he had ceased to think
of what Lady Mary would say when he presented her
with a Dutch-American for a daughter-in-law; he was
fully purposed now to make Franzje his wife, let the consequences be what they might.

The party that gathered round the wood fire after
supper was sociable, and even hilarious, in a mild kind
of way; but to Franzje it was something like the evening of the play over again. Aimwell and Dorinda had
engrossed her thoughts then, and she had cared little
what anybody else did or said; and now she herself was
Dorinda, and Aimwell's looks and words and meaning
tones were all for her; what passed among the rest of the
company was well-nigh indifferent to her.

How the finale was managed she never quite knew.
All at once, the Patroon and his wife rose up and asked
to have their sledge brought round to the door; and
then there was a sudden buzz of leave-taking, and with
scarcely an adieu to her kind host and hostess, she found

herself hurried out into the porch, her wraps produced
with marvellous celerity from a heap of others by a grinning negress, and a strong arm helping her down the steps,
and almost lifting her into a sleigh which stood in readiness at a short distance from the house.

The moon was shining in all its brightness; the stars
were looking down in. their stedfast splendour; and the
pure white snow, reflecting the moonlight and starlight,
was even more dazzling than it had been by day. Each
feature in the landscape—from the pine-crowned hills
in the distance, to the gleaming white railings which
bounded on each side the short piece of private road
leading from the Flats to the public highway—remained
fixed indelibly on Franzje's mind, though at the moment
she scarcely seemed to remark anything around her, or to
have a thought to spare for the beauty of the night.
Never could she forget how, when they came to the
high road, Mr. Vyvian checked his impatient horse, and
let some of the other sleighs pass him, apparently that
he might enjoy the baffled look of the Dominie and Killian; nor how, when they were gone by, he pushed on
with lightning speed and passed *them*, gazing down at her
with a proud air of possession as he dashed onwards
towards the town. The mere thought of that wild
drive, and her companion's eager, rapturous, burning
words, would set her heart beating for months afterwards, though yet the deepest emotions of her nature
remained unstirred. What there was in her of sentiment, of poetry, of a woman's natural craving for love
and service, awoke, and lent a softened beauty to her face
as she listened; and the spell of her young, fresh innocence was on him, and kept him from uttering a word
that would have wounded her sensitive modesty. He
loved her with the highest part of his nature, and in this

supreme moment the lowest was kept out of sight as by a natural instinct.

He did not ask her in so many words to be his wife ; he could not shape any formal proposal at the time ; but he implied that that was the hope he was setting before him, and probably she did not in the least expect anything more explicit. While it was considered allowable in Albany for young men and maidens freely to avow their mutual love, the actual terms of marriage were usually settled for them by their parents or guardians ; and Franzje only felt that the strange, unlooked-for romance which had come into her life was now advancing towards its height, and did not seek to hurry it to a practical conclusion. It was so very, *very* wonderful, that this clever, handsome, attractive Englishman should care for her ! She was lost in wonder and gratitude, and a girlish sense of triumph. When they reached her door, he drew her towards him for an instant, and, by an irresistible impulse, gave her one long kiss. It burned on her startled lips, this first lover's kiss, and her cheeks glowed as if the clear, cold, heavenly moonlight had turned to noonday heat. Would that glow have faded as quickly as it came, could she have known that that first kiss was also to be the last ; that the brief love-dream of that spring night was all she was ever to have of what makes so great a portion of the life of many women; that nobler, more satisfying things lay before her in the future ; but never again anything like the passionate sweetness of that moment, when she seemed to see her lover's face all glorified by the halo that her suddenly awakened devotion threw around it, when she still believed in him and in herself ?

To some the romance of life comes late—so late that it is marred by a fear of being ridiculous, and of what the

world will say : to others it comes prematurely, before
they have learnt to discern the true from the false; and
then it is apt to leave a sting behind it—a regret for
what no after-wisdom can undo. There came a day—
and that not very far in the future either—when Franzje
would fain have taken that kiss from off her lips, and unsaid the few sweet, low words which had given substance
to Mr. Vyvian's hopes. Romance is not a necessity of
existence; better to be without it, than to have it shorn
of its possible nobleness, its possible power of lifting us
into that pure region, where, through love of one worthy
to be loved, we are drawn upwards to the highest Love
of all !

Just for this one night, at least, there was no misgiving
and no repenting. When Madame Ryckman got home,
and went in search of Franzje, she found her standing
before her little oval mirror, not in a trance of vanity,
poor child ! but in order to settle that question, which
rises so instinctively in some hearts at such moments :
" Is this really me ?   Can it be me that he loves so, and
is ready to die for ?   What can he see in me to make him
care so much ? "

When she turned round, in all her glowing, bashful
beauty, at the sound of her mother's step, anyone but
herself could have answered the question; for hers was
not the loveliness of form and feature only—the whole
depths of her noble and tender soul were shining through
her eyes. Her mother looked at her with a startled and
confused air. She had come to rebuke; but something
in the girl's aspect made her forget the speech she had
been putting together on her way upstairs.

" Franzje, is it possible that you care for this man ? "
was all that she could say.

Her daughter did not answer, but came and put two

trembling hands in hers, and gave her one shy glance, and then turned away the beautiful blushing face.

" Oh, my dear child ! you have not let him think so ?" questioned the mother, in consternation at this mute response.

Still Franzje would not speak, and Madame Ryckman's fears were verging upon certainties.

" At least, you did not let him kiss you ? I told the Dominie I was certain you would not. Look up, and tell me that you did not ! "

" But I did," said Franzje, in a soft, sweet voice, that refused to be ashamed, though her eyes were still cast down in maidenly confusion.

And then she started at feeling her mother's tears upon her neck, as the good lady exclaimed in sorrow, " Oh ! my poor child ! my poor little, foolish, innocent - maid ! How came I ever to let you out of my sight ? O Franzje ! Franzje ! "

CHAPTER XIII.

𝔇𝔢𝔣𝔢𝔞𝔱𝔢𝔡.

IT was rather an anxious, uneasy congregation which gathered in the Dutch chapel on the following Sunday. A rumour had gone forth that the Dominie, being unable to stop the performance of what he considered an immoral play, had determined to make one last effort to prevent his flock from attending it ; and as many of the young people had set their heart upon the sight, and many of the old lacked the firmness to forbid their doing so, it was with far from a quiet conscience that they prepared themselves to listen to the Dominie's harangue. The metrical psalm which preceded the sermon was sung with quavering voices, and much wandering of mind; but when the discourse began the attention was breathless, and the pastor could not at least complain of having to preach to deaf ears. *Dull* ears perhaps they were, though, some of them, for his bursts of fervid eloquence seemed to meet with little response, and scarcely any expression could be read on the greater part of the faces upturned to him but one of uneasy apprehension or sullen dissent.

Several of the elder people, however, wore an air of grave satisfaction, as though they were mentally saying, "Ah, very true!" "Just what I have always thought!" especially when he dwelt on the hollowness and the fleeting nature of all worldly pleasure : and when from this he turned to speak of the joys with which God recompenses the souls that keep themselves unspotted from the world—the pleasures which are at His right Hand for evermore, not a few, even among the younger people, were visibly moved; and some good parents, such as. M. and Madame Ryckman, looked at each other as much as to say, "We love our children too well to let them risk the loss of these higher things by indulgence in the lower."

Evert listened with an air of half saucy defiance, Jan was stolidly attentive, the little boys were absorbed in watching the unusual vehemence of the Dominie's gesticulations; Franzje's face was set in its gentlest, gravest, most dreamy expression, and all through the sermon she never once looked up. Ah, how the old problem, which had haunted her so often before, would recur now; how she wondered whether there were indeed such a sharp line drawn between this and that amusement, this and that object of interest, as the pastor seemed to say—

whether all up to a certain point were indeed so innocent,
all beyond it so hopelessly wicked! It was not a mere
question of pleasure with her now; it went beyond that.
She was not hankering after the play—nay, so far from
intending to go and see it, she was nourishing a little
secret, triumphant hope, that now Mr. Vyvian was quite
her own, she should be able to prevail with him to give
up his part in it—perhaps to keep away from it altogether,
unless he could assure her that there were no such passages
in it as had jarred upon even her inattentive ear in the
performance of the "Beaux' Stratagem." The question
was, would they *let* him be her own? would her parents
give her in marriage to the Englishman? or would they—
acting under the Dominie's influence—insist on dividing
her from him for ever, and so take all the brightness and
romance out of her young life? Not worldly amusements
only, but worldly intercourse, the Dominie was inveigh-
ing against, as she sat thinking; not places and things
only, but people, were to be shunned, if they interfered
with that strictness of life which he represented as indispensable; the charity of prayers was the utmost that his
system accorded to worldlings; as for bestowing friendship or love upon them! he spoke of it with shuddering,
as a *crime*. It was not so much in the theory, as in its
application, though, that Franzje found herself unavoid-
ably differing from him. She had been long enough
under his teaching to be used to strict and stern views of
things; but she lacked courage to apply them to the
actual case before her. If Mr. Vyvian were indeed a
worldling, then it was no doubt her duty to sever herself
from him; but *was* he a worldling? The Dominie would
have unhesitatingly said "Yes." Franzje's innocent, trusting, hopeful heart cried out "No" with all its might.
Hers was not the mistake—the sad, but not uncommon

mistake—of thinking that she could make a wild man
steady, or convert a sceptic into a faithful believer; she
had no such confidence as regarded herself, no such discernment as regarded him. She was simply blind in
some degree to the faults she saw, incredulous about the
graver faults of which she only heard. To her thinking,
Russell Vyvian was different, but not inferior, to the
young men she had known from her childhood; less quiet
and guarded and respectful, perhaps—but then, on the
other hand, much more clever and interesting and fascinating; and the deficiency in his standard of right, compared
with her own, she attributed to the fact of his having been
differently trained—of his never having been taught by
the Dominie, for instance. Aunt Schuyler had said that
there were great allowances to be made for him; and
Franzje was ready to make all manner of allowance. There
was so much for him to forgive in *her*—such ignorance,
such rusticity, such a heap of real faults which he had
not found out, but which were patent to herself—why
should she not be content to forgive something in *him ?*

Poor little girl! spite of the maturity of her beauty,
she had but the immature judgement of not-yet-seventeen
to fall back upon; and moreover she was too dazzled just
now to be able to judge clearly at all. No fear of her
future fate, if she were allowed to marry Russell Vyvian,
troubled her; she was only half sickened by the pangs
of doubt as to whether that fate were ever to be hers.

Two nights before—the memorable night of her drive
with Mr. Vyvian—her mother had begged her with tears
to say nothing to anyone of what had passed between
her and him, and even to forget it herself if possible.
Since then she had not seen him, nor had any word been
said to her about him. Were they keeping him from her
purposely? had he offered himself as her suitor, and had

her father declined to receive him as such? She could
not tell. One' thing, however, she was sure of, namely,
that if M. Ryckman had been indisposed to listen to his
suit before, he would be ten times more so after this
sermon of the Dominie's. She knew well what the
pastor's influence on her parents was; and without seeing
the glances that passed between them, she guessed as
truly what feelings and resolves were rising in their minds,
as if those minds had been spread out before her like an
open book.

Quietly as she sat there, with her dark-fringed eyelids
lowered, and her perfect lips set in' an expression of
thoughtful repose, all sorts of painful and pleasurable
emotions were busy in her heart by turns. She was going
to belong to Mr. Vyvian somehow or other—that was the
predominant feeling at first; there would be difficulties,
no doubt, but they must be got over; there would be
opposition, of course, but it was born of narrow prejudice,
and could not in the nature of things be really invincible.
Yes, she did in a certain sense belong to him already, and
was not going to commit herself—even mentally—to any
line of argument which would lead to the conclusion that
it was her duty to give him up. She was tolerably comfortable while this feeling lasted, spite of instinctive fears,
spite of the stern denunciations thundered over-head.
But all at once there flashed in upon her a new thought, a
new dread, a new conviction that seemed unbearable, but
which none the less took possession of her, and asserted
its supremacy. What if after all she were setting her
will not against her father's and the Dominie's, but
against God's? What if, in permitting their prejudice
to form a barrier between her and the thing she coveted,
He were showing her that the thing was not for her,
calling her to renunciation and submission? What if,

without making pleasure and brightness and novelty
wrong *in themselves,* He had made them wrong for *her* by
the circumstances of her position ? What if He Himself
had made it impossible for her to have the joys she
longed for here, and yet also " the pleasures at His right
Hand for evermore " ?

A pang seized her, so keen that she could almost have
cried out with anguish ; but she only clasped her hands
tightly together under her cloak, and set herself steadily
to consider this new view, which she had not sought for,
but which some invisible influence had brought before
her mind. The truth which she had missed that day in
the Dominie's study, when she had listened to arguments
with which she *could* not agree, had flashed upon her now.
Ah ! how much depended on whether she were willing to
embrace it, or were minded to put it from her because of
the sacrifice it involved !

The flaxen head dropped lower in the earnestness o.
these thoughts, the sweet suggestion of a dimple about
the mouth died away, and the lips moved slightly and
then closed one on the other with a sort of sorrowful
firmness. When the sermon was over, and they all left
the chapel, she moved with even a more stately grace than
usual, as in the dignity of a new resolve ; but yet there
was a crushed, bewildered look in the eyes that were wont
to be so serene.

"Franzje," said Evert, pulling her by the arm, and
drawing her a little behind the others, "'if *you* can bear
all this tyranny any longer, *I* cannot. I mean to go to
the play, and I mean to tell Father so to his face ; and if
he has me up before the Dominie for undutifulness, why
I shall tell the Dominie so too. It is monstrous, as Gardiner says, that a man should be priest-ridden all his days.
I declare I won't go to the catechising this afternoon—

nothing shall make me! I am a great deal too old for it."

Franzje woke up from her dream, and looked anxiously and fondly at the boy at her side, who was strutting along with that air of sulky independence which a lad of fifteen is so apt to assume when he once begins to think himself a man.

"Dear Evert," she said, with a smile, "you are not so very much older than you were last Sunday, and how well you answered then! Mother was quite pleased."

"I was in a good humour then," said he; "I had the sleighing-party to look forward to; and I wasn't sure but what father would let me go to the play if I pleased him by my behaviour. He let me off going to New York, you know, though he vowed he would send me there in January."

"Evert, I don't feel as if we ought to think about the play, since Father and Mother are so set against it."

"Franzje!" said Evert, standing still in the street, and staring at her as if confounded by the desertion of his expected ally. "I know what it is," he added, more composedly; "it's all the Dominie, and the fire and brimstone he has been consigning us all to in his sermon. Dirk Wessels says the Dominie's sermons are just made for frightening women and children. They shan't frighten me, though!" and then out came a fashionable English oath, which he had learnt from the officers, and which shocked his sister beyond description.

She was just beginning a very gentle and earnest remonstrance with him—a remonstrance which from her, loving her as he did, he might have borne—when her father called to her rather sharply not to loiter, and so obviously waited for her, that she was obliged to go on and join him.

Evert ran off—probably to find Dirk Wessels, a good-for-nothing youngster, a little older than himself, and have out his grumble with him—while Franzje walked home demurely between her father and mother, and *felt* rather than saw that Mr. Vyvian was one of a group of officers which was assembled outside the Bankers' house. Amid all the talk and laughter and jingle of swords, she thought she could distinguish the tones of his voice, and his glance seemed to follow her as she went on her way, though she never so much as turned her head in his direction.

Evert came in late for dinner; and when it was time to go to the catechising, mumbled something about not being ready for it, and not meaning to go, but was peremptorily ordered there by his father, and went off obediently, though with a very bad grace. Franzje, when she was getting ready to accompany him, was told, to her great surprise, that she had better stay at home and take care of Arij, who was suffering from inflammation of the eyes, and was obliged to be kept in a darkened room; and though it was in some ways a relief to her, she could not help being a little uneasy as to the motive of the command. Was the Dominie's anger against her so pronounced, that her mother, with instinctive motherly tenderness, wanted to shield her from it? Some such suspicion occurred to her, as she saw the nervous haste with which Madame Ryckman helped her off with her cloak and hood; and she could not refrain from saying, "Mother, you have not told the Dominie anything about me and Mr. Vyvian, have you?"

Madame Ryckman occupied herself in folding up the cloak, and turned away to put it in the drawer, as she replied, ambiguously, "It is not a thing that needs much telling; when you went off with him in the sleigh, it was pretty plain what matters were coming to; but never mind, child, I did not come up to scold you, but only to tell you to go to Arij. I have given Jettje a holiday this afternoon."

She bustled off directly she had said this ; and Franzje prepared to go to her little brother, but first went to the casement and opened it, feeling as if she must have one fresh draught of air and sunshine before shutting herself up in the darkened nursery.

The south wind had come, and under its soft breath the snow was fast vanishing from the streets, and spring-like influences were beginning to be felt. As Franzje leaned her head out, the warm breeze that had come straight from the burning sands of Florida and Georgia seemed to caress her cheek ; and all the hard brilliance of the frost had disappeared, and given place to a soft, balmy brightness, which soothed her for the moment into a dreamy feeling of vague delight. Just for a minute or two she yielded to the enjoyment ; then there came back suddenly the remembrance of the day when she had stood at that window to watch the entrance of the regiment into the town, and as the gay pageant rose before her, so there rose also the dark, picturesque figure of the pastor and his disapproving glance ; and once more she drew her head in, and went back to her home duties, feeling as if his shadow had fallen between her and the brightness of the day. Was it a picture of her life ? Was duty, as represented by this stern disciple of a rigid school, always to scare her away from pleasure ? Must the light that had come upon her in the chapel that morning burn on till it had scorched up all her folly and frivolity, all her vain dreams of happiness, all her romantic longings ? Must she submit to suffer and be weary, and lapse into the dulness which was almost inseparable from her idea of goodness, and would the day indeed ever come, when she should look back tranquilly on her present feelings, and philosophize about them with the calm contentment of her Uncle Jan?

Decidedly the day was yet far off; for now she could scarcely still herself sufficiently to bear with patience the dreary afternoon, passed in artificial twilight, and in ministering to the fretful wants of poor little Arij, who was not by any means content to sit on her lap and be sung to as she had hoped, but who insisted on groping about and dragging her after him, asking meanwhile for all possible and impossible things, beginning with hickory nuts, and ending with "a long dangling sword, to come down from my waist and knock my heels as I walk—like Mr. Vyvian's, you know, Franzje."

The mother was the first to return, very much put out with Evert's bad behaviour at the catechising; then, when she was gone to take off her things, in came Evert himself, very much excited, and full of some plan, which he hinted at mysteriously but would not reveal. He teazed Arij till he made him unbearably cross, and then went away; but when Franzje was going downstairs to tea, he rushed out of his room after her, and said abruptly, "I want a bit of waste-paper to wrap something up in; may I take one of your old exercises, Franzje?"

"Oh yes; you will find them all on the middle shelf of my cupboard," she answered, with ready good-nature; "but are you not coming down to tea? Maaike says it is all ready; and Father must have come in, for I hear his voice in the parlour."

"You might have heard it all over the house five minutes ago," returned Evert indignantly; "he was in a fine rage with me. I have told him I shall go to the play, and he says if I do he will give me a thrashing. Fancy that to *me*, Franzje, who have never been beaten

in all my life ! " and the lad drew up his handsome head
with an air of such bitterly-insulted dignity, that his
sister scarcely knew what to say, fearing to make matters
worse by any attempt at preaching submission.

"I don't think Father can quite have meant that, he is
so kind," she murmured ; " but indeed, Evert, his wishes
ought to be enough for us ; we ought not to provoke him
to threats."

Even the sweet pleading voice did not suffice to make
the remonstrance palatable. Evert gave a snort of defiance, and with the angry exclamation, " Yes, talk away !
When we've got rid of the Dominie we'll give you his
pulpit, and you shall hold forth to your heart's content ! "
dashed off to his own room.

He did not make his appearance at the tea-table ; and
Franzje had sisterly compunctions about having irritated
him, instead of having soothed and persuaded him to
come down to tea with her, till she heard from Maaike
that he had carried off a lot of cakes to his den with the
express intention of avoiding the family meal, and had
announced his intention of going out again before the
others had finished.

He was gone by the time she got upstairs, and she
found some reason to repent of her permission to him to
search in her cupboard ; for her papers were all tossed
and tumbled about, the French exercises turned over in
one careless heap, as if for some reason or other they had
not suited his purpose and some answers to questions in
theology, which she had written for the Dominie the year
before, strewn hither and thither, as if he had chosen to
select his wrapping-sheet from among *them.* She was
vexed ; but as these answers were written on better and
larger pieces of paper than the French—for which she
had made use of any scraps that she could beg from her

father—she concluded that was his motive for the selection, and did not disquiet herself about it. She did not see her brother again that night, for he came in very late, and went straight to bed without saying a word to anybody; and her sleep was broken by restless dreams, in which his image and that of Mr. Vyvian recurred perpetually. Once, and only once, she dreamt of the Dominie. She thought that he came and put his hand on her head while she was asleep, just as he had done that January afternoon, and that no sooner did she wake to feel the touch than he was goné. She ran after him, but he vanished from her in a sort of long, subterranean passage; and as she stood looking down it, there came a strange noise like the roaring of the sea in her ears, and then she awoke—*really* awoke this time, and the fantastic dream was over.

The Dominie himself, meanwhile, was neither sleeping soundly nor dreaming; he was passing one of those long miserable, intensely wakeful nights, which of late had become frequent with him. Anyone but he would have complained of them, and sought medical advice, and would have told also of the strange, morbid, delirious fancies which were apt to haunt him at such times; but the Dominie breathed not a word to anyone, and simply set himself to bear them with the stoical endurance in which the stronger part of his nature asserted itself, as against that weaker side which left him a prey to the torments of wounded feeling, and the subtle miseries of injured self-love. He was ready to suffer—nay, to a certain extent, he even *liked* suffering, though not so much from the tender yearning, so characteristic of saints of old, to be made like unto the Lord by having a portion in His cross, as from a sort of natural heroism, and contempt for all personal inconveniences which might assail him while toiling in his Master's cause. He would have been content to suffer martyrdom itself without a groan, could he thereby have secured that a single one of the thoughtless young people who were grieving him should go to heaven in his track—in that straight, narrow path which he had marked out for himself and others, and in which alone, according to his thinking, salvation could be found.

He was hard and narrow and bigoted, and his mind was warped by the heretical teaching of his school, but he was true to what he thought the truth; he was thoroughly, even fiercely in earnest. He had that one vast superiority to his adversaries, that he was fighting for what he believed of the highest possible moment, while they were simply battling for the enjoyment of a few passing hours; and he loved them after his fashion, and would have died to save their souls, while they were grumbling about his harshness and his meddle-someness, and far from longing to do anything for him, were in some instances meditating how they could "pay him off" for having interfered with their amuse-ments.

As the sleepless hours rolled by, his thoughts went back to the earlier years of his ministry at Albany, and he re-called the enthusiasm with which he had entered on his charge, the success which had seemed to crown his efforts, and the popularity which he had soon acquired, and had enjoyed almost undiminished till the coming of the Eng-lish regiment into the city. It was true that those families who had settled in Albany since the com-mencement of the war scarcely looked upon him with the same veneration as the primitive inhabitants of the place, and had introduced some new and heterodox notions which he had felt obliged to combat; but still,

P

on the whole, his influence had been supreme, and till
bitter experience had convinced him of the contrary, he
had supposed it to be *permanent* also. He did not distinguish (which of us would have, in his place?) exactly
how much of his present regret was due to the waning of
his own popularity, and how much to the belief that those
who were deserting him were deserting their Heavenly
Master also. He had so identified himself with his
cause, that he felt as if they must stand or fall together, as if any triumphs won over him were neces-
sarily the triumphs of irreligion, as if he "did well to
be angry even unto death" at the destruction of what
had been his solace through all the burden and heat of
the day. No consciousness of just retribution in the
snapping of the bow which he had bent too tight, came
upon him even for a moment; he was not aware of
having exercised any tyranny over the consciences of his
flock. Those who talk of "priest-craft" as an instinct
confined to Catholicism, must ill have studied the history of Protestant sects. A rule all the more absolute
because it was mainly the rule of the individual and
not of the Church, seems to have prevailed in almost
all the first Protestant communities, and to have been
submitted to by the majority with a docility which now
seems incredible. Presbyterians in Scotland, Calvinists
in Holland and Switzerland, Puritan sectaries of all sorts
in America, burdened themselves with sumptuary laws
and minute social regulations—imposed sometimes by the
Consistory rather than by a single minister, but generally
at the instance of some one person more remarkable for
zeal than his fellows—such as the Catholic Church has at
no time laid upon the great body of the faithful. And
ministers who were no longer "priests," and who never
even *cared* to claim the priestly power of ministering to

burdened consciences, and speaking the "word of reconciliation" to penitent souls, committed themselves to a system of direction at which Catholic directors, whether Roman, Greek, or Anglican, would have stood aghast. Those lights of the Kirk who forbade mothers to kiss their children on Sunday surely out-did anything that has ever been attributed to the most despotic of spiritual rulers within the fold of the Church.

Is it not that priest-craft is one of those *exaggerations* of a thing right and good in itself—nay, directly ordained by God—which are incidental to human nature, whether orthodox or heterodox, and that those who think it is to be done away with by effacing the sacerdotal character of the ministry, are simply thinking to perfect the human element by getting rid of the divine, and leaving completely untouched the real root of the evil? It is not the dignity of Apostolic succession, nor the grace of the Divine Anointing, which puffs men up, and makes them sometimes act as "lords over God's heritage;" it is that human pride, that disposition to make their own will law, which is the snare of hundreds who are not in the ministry at all, and which remains (unsuspected perhaps) even in some of those whom God has called to that ineffable honour. They who feel the honour most, who most prize the supernatural powers conferred on them, are just those who think least of themselves, who, far from usurping undue personal authority, are content to be our "*servants* for Jesus' sake."

From the days of his popularity, the Dominie's thoughts soon returned to the time being, the constant mortifications and the loss of influence which he felt only too keenly, and the doubt whether he was doing any good in striving against the tide—whether anything but disappointment to himself and irritation to them would come out of his efforts to force back his straying sheep into the straight path. And then again they wandered to the old days in Holland, the old, calm, studious days, the delightful period of learned leisure which succeeded his early university triumphs; and almost he wished that there had never come upon him that sudden longing for Christian enterprise, that zeal for souls, which had sent him forth across the wide Atlantic to preach God's truth in a distant land.

Why not return? Why not re-visit, if only for a little while, his native country and the scenes of his youth? Why not leave his post for a short spell of rest, and come back to it after a time re-invigorated, and with fresh spirit to encounter opposition and revolt? A Dutch ship on its homeward way was even now at New York, for he had received an intimation from a friend there that an opportunity, which he had long been wanting, for sending some precious manuscripts to Holland, had suddenly arisen. Why not take them instead of sending them, and himself see to the publication of his cherished work— a work on which he had expended whole years of anxious thought, and which, perhaps, was destined to rival that "True Religion Delineated" of Dr. Bellamy of Connecticut, which was just now the favourite reading in New England homes? There was some attraction in the thought, and something soothing too in the notion of returning to Albany by-and-by, with all the prestige of a successful author added to his other titles to respect; but he put it from him as a temptation, and even said to himself that badly as his flock were behaving, it would be too heavy a punishment to deprive them of his ministrations altogether. "Even the worst of them do not absolutely wish to get rid of me, I think," soliloquised the Dominie, with that sort of saving clause which self-esteem puts

in after the first shock of finding oneself less regarded
than one thought has been got over.

The idea afforded some slight balm to his wounded
spirit, and he arose at his usual early hour, and braced
himself for a fresh day's work, trying with all his might
to shake off the lassitude engendered by total want of
rest. When he opened his chamber door to go forth to
his study, something fell to the ground with a loud noise.
In the dim light of the passage he could scarcely see what
it was, but he felt for it with his hand, and, in doing so,
touched one or two other objects, which seemed to be
ranged in order on the mat. He threw back the door so
as to gain the full light from his chamber window, and
there, lying before him, beheld, to his amazement, a club,
a pair of old shoes, a crust of black bread, and something
wrapped in paper, which, upon examination, proved to be
a dollar.

It was very enigmatical, but the Dominie's proud, sensitive nature rushed at once upon the true purport of this
emblematic message. He did not pause to call for Dinah,
and ask by whose instrumentality the things had come
there; he did not say to himself that at worst it was only
a boyish insult, unauthorized by any of the elder members of his congregation; he simply read by heart, as it
were, the meaning of each article—the stick to push him
away, the shoes to wear on the road, the bread and money
as provision for the journey—and then he went back into
the room he had just left, and sat himself down to face the
hard truth that his people *did* want to get rid of him, that
what he had been thinking of as a punishment they would
regard in the light of a *deliverance*. If ever anyone had a
" mauvais quart d'heure," the Dominie had it then with
a vengeance ! One drop was yet wanting in the bitterness
of his cup. It came when beginning half absently to

scrutinize the crumpled piece of paper in which the dollar had been wrapped, he saw that there was writing upon it, writing which he would easily have recognized as Franzje Ryckman's, even if her signature had not been the first thing that he lighted on, written in fair, clear, delicate characters, such as harmonized well with what he had once supposed to be the quality of her mind.

It was not a letter—she had not had the audacity to write to him—but it was what conveyed to him almost as definite a meaning as pointed words of insult might have done, for it was part of a theological exercise which she had written for him in the old happy time when he was her honoured teacher, and she the willing, grateful pupil, in whose abilities he felt a fatherly pride. There were his own marks of correction on it, correction which she had received with, oh! such loveable docility—and it was one of a certain set which he had bidden her always to keep, as he thought they might form a kind of text-book to help her in her future progress. It was bad enough that those dissipated Englishmen had turned against him the giddy lads and lasses, such as Dirk Wessels and Anna Gerritse, who, left to themselves, might have attained to better things in time; but that they should have stolen from him the very purest and sweetest of all the band, the one heart that had seemed to beat in truest accord with his own, was a cruel and unbearable wrong, against which his whole spirit revolted.

Must *she* indeed go to perdition—that fair, gentle girl, with her virgin grace, and the noble, candid, aspiring nature, which seemed meant for the appreciation of divine realities? Would they be satisfied with nothing short of that? and had they already brought her to such a reckless state as made her wish to drive from her the one person who was ready to interpose unhesitatingly between her and ruin?

The Dominie sat there defeated; he had identified *his* cause with God's, and he thought that they were lost together; all that was human in him rose up and tempted him to despair, and he mistook the voice of his own soul for the whispers of a Divine leading.

CHAPTER XIV.

In Vain.

THE second day of what was to prove in the end a most eventful week, passed heavily with Franzje, as the first had done. It was spent chiefly with Arij in the darkened nursery; and when she met her parents at meals they talked only on general subjects, and made not the slightest allusion to Mr. Vyvian. She was devoured by a fretting anxiety, and felt as if she would gladly have exchanged her state of suspense for any certainty, however painful; but yet, a very natural bashfulness kept her from approaching the subject herself, or even from leading the conversation in that direction.

It so happened that, after she had bidden her parents good-night that evening, she was sent back to the parlour by her uncle Jan, to fetch a book which he had left there; and when she entered it she found them deep in consultation, and overheard, without meaning to do so, a few words that were not intended for her ear.

"I begged him to defer the interview until next Wednesday," her father was saying; "I thought that would give me a clear day for reflection, and for consulting the Dominie."

"Yes, you must talk to the Dominie, of course ; though I know his opinion of the young man too well to doubt—" began the mother, cutting short her sentence, however, as she caught sight of Franzje, who purposely made a little noise in advancing to draw the eyes of the speakers to her.

No name had been mentioned, but the girl could not but conclude that "the young man" was Russell Vyvian, and felt with what justice she had supposed that it was practically the Dominie who would decide her fate.

"I knew how it would be," she said to herself ; "Father will do whatever the Dominie advises ; and of course, the Dominie will advise him to have nothing to do with Mr. Vyvian, and I shall have to submit, I suppose—and then what will become of me ? Mr. Vyvian will go away to the war, and forget me perhaps—it is so different for men ; but how can *I* ever forget, or be the same as I was before ? Oh ! it is cruel, *cruel*, when we cannot love and be happy without being wicked too !"

A weight of despair fell on her when she was once more alone in her own room ; and though she instinctively knelt, as if for help to bear her burden, she did not at first utter any words of prayer at all. She was clinging on to the right ; she had abandoned any idea of happiness which was to be won at the price of undutifulness, whether shown in deceit or in open rebellion. She felt that she must obey with honourable, faithful obedience, whatever it might cost her to do so, but she could not as yet feel any comfort in the decision. The peace of mind that is won through sacrifice seldom comes till the sacrifice is accomplished ; *desolate* hearts have to be offered to God, and then He fills them.

All at once a little hope sprang up—a new way of outlet, which she had not thought of before. Why should she despair so soon ? why should she accept as inevitable the sentence which the Dominie had not yet pronounced ? Since her fate rested with him, why should she not plead her cause with him before he was called on to decide it ? Hopeless as the case might seem, it was within the bounds of *possibility*, that face to face with him she might be able to make him see things in a different light—that if she could but find courage to bare her heart to him in some degree, she might awaken something of that fatherly compassion and sympathy which she knew to be latent in his nature, and of which she had sometimes made proof in the lighter troubles of her childish years.

. Harsh as he had been to her of late—firm and unrelenting as he was popularly supposed to be—she yet felt with ineradicable confidence that his inmost heart was tender and warm, and that if her appeal could but reach it, there still remained to her a chance of success.

" If I can only make him feel what Mr. Vyvian has been to me," she said to herself, " and how much goodness and nobleness there is in him which does not show, and if I can but make him understand what is implied in giving up all that has made my life so bright these last few months, I think I may be able to persuade him at least not to crush our hopes at once—to let me keep Mr. Vyvian's love as something to look forward to in the future, even if he counsels father to prevent our bethrothal now. And if not—if I can't convince him, if he still persists in thinking it a sin for me to care for Mr. Vyvian at all—still, if he will tell me *why* it is a sin, and if he seems only to deny me because he can't please me without displeasing God, it will not be *quite* so hard to submit as it is now. Oh ! how well I remember that day years ago,

when I was a little tiny child, and he would not let me
drink the molasses-and-water that Dinah brought me,
though I was so hot and tired and thirsty, because he
said it was a bad habit to take anything between meals ;
and it seemed so hard and cruel, till he took me up on
his knee, and let me lean my head against him, and then
all my angry feelings went away, and I did not mind any
more. I think it might be something like that now ; I
think I might bear my trouble better if he laid it on me
with his own hand, and helped me to bear it. Yes, I
will go to him ; I will not let fear or shyness keep me
away. I do trust him still, even though he is angry with
me ; if I speak to him truly and openly, soul to soul, I
do not believe he will misjudge me."

Then she folded her hands, and said her prayers re-
verently, and presently laid herself down to sleep, not very
happy or hopeful, but by no means *so* miserable as she had
been when she first came up-stairs. She was not troubled
by any thought of what Mr. Vyvian would say at her
selecting the Dominie as her *confidante ;* her feeling
towards her pastor was so simple and so filial, so free
from the slightest tinge of sentimentality, that it seemed
quite as natural and unobjectionable to open her heart to
him as to her father and mother—nay, in her case *more*
natural, because the Dominie had been more of a friend
to her than her parents had ever been, and had done far
more to form her character than they.

Her father and mother were very kind and good, and
she loved them dearly, with a far more intimate, sensible,
familiar fondness than she gave to the Dominie ; but
they were so accustomed to treat her as a child, and to
think she had all she wanted if they provided her with
food and clothes and other bodily comforts, and kissed
and praised her when she tried to be useful to them, that

she had learnt never to expect from them the same kind
of help and counsel and sympathy which she had been
wont to receive from Madame Schuyler and the Dominie.

They were not in the least jealous of the influence
which these good friends exercised over her ; and she did
not at all anticipate any opposition to her scheme of going
to the Manse the next morning, except that something in
her mother's manner on the past Sunday had made her
feel as if just at the present crisis they preferred to keep
her and the Dominie apart.

"Perhaps it was my fancy ; at any rate, I will pluck
up courage, and ask Mother to let me go to him as soon
as I have finished my home-tasks," she said to herself, as
she went down to breakfast ; "Father will probably
choose the leisure hour after dinner for his talk, and I
must speak to him *first*, if possible. Oh ! if he will only
be a little kind to me, and let me speak to him freely, as
I used ! "

During the meal a note was brought to M. Ryckman
which seemed to inspire him with a good deal of consternation ; and as soon as he had read it he got up and went
out, without giving a word of explanation, even to his wife.

Franzje waited till the boys had also left the table, and
then said gently, " Mother, I want very much to speak to
the Dominie. May I go and see him when you have
done with me ? "

Madame Ryckman looked as if she thought it a sort of
putting one's head into the lion's mouth, and answered
with manifest indecision, "I don't know what to say,
Franzje. I never do like your gadding about in the
morning ; and perhaps you may find your father there—
and altogether I think you might as well stay at home."

" I will only just go the Manse and back," rejoined the
girl. "Mother, I know you think the Dominie is angry

with me; and I daresay he is; but indeed, I am not afraid. I shall be happier if you will let me speak to him than if I have to sit quiet while the whole matter is decided over my head."

She did not explain what she meant by "the whole matter," but Madame Ryckman seemed to understand.

"You had better leave it to your father, I think," she said; "he will be gentler with you than the Dominie. Oh! my dear child, what a pity it is that you do look so like a woman! No man ever troubled his head about me when I was your age."

"I think I *feel* like a woman now, Mother," said poor Franzje, not without some pathos in face and voice, as she lifted her great steadfast eyes to her mother's anxious gaze. "I won't do anything you don't like; but if you would let me go to the Dominie, I should be very, very grateful."

Thus appealed to, Madame Ryckman gave way; and about an hour afterwards Franzje set forth in the direction of the Manse, accompanied by the faithful old negress Jettje, who was considered more of a protector than merry little Maaike, and whom she promised to keep close beside her all the way there and back. Once safe at the parsonage, Jettje could be dismissed to gossip with Dinah in the kitchen, while her mistress went in alone to the Dominie's study.

The old woman talked a good deal as they went along, expressing her opinions with all the freedom which was common among the household slaves in an Albanian family of the true primitive type; but Franzje, though she listened good-naturedly, and responded with a smile, had very little to say in return. She was thinking deeply; and as they drew near the house, a vivid recollection came back to her of the day when she had gone

there with Maaike in the autumn, and of her own words :
"If I were in any trouble, I think I should run straight
there."

She could not feel quite the same towards the Dominie
as she had felt when she said that; but still, a sort of
hope of finding something to lean on—a sense of having
got to the desired haven—came over her as she stood at
the Dominie's door waiting for her ring to be answered.
She waited a long time—much too long for Jettje's patience
—and at last rang again, but still with no response.

"Let me jus' open de door, and see if I can find Dinah,
Mamselle," said the old servant; "perhaps she jus' step
out a minute, and Dominie he deep in big book, and not
hear de ring at all. If I not find Dinah, s'pose I tap at
study, and say, 'Mamselle Ryckman she want to see you,
please Sir ?'"

Franzje preferred this to making a further and louder
ringing, which might startle the Dominie at his studies,
and bring him to the door himself; so the negress lifted
the latch without ceremony, and passed into the hall,
leaving her young mistress still standing in the porch.

A minute or two passed, and then came Jettje's voice
from some inner room in accents of alarm. "Mamselle,
you come here! Oh! whatever can it mean ? Mamselle,
you come and see !"

Franzje obeyed the summons with all the speed of
terror, picturing to herself the Dominie fallen in a fit, or
stark dead upon the study floor; but when she reached
the study—for it was from thence that Jettje had called·
her—she found no one there but Jettje herself, though
startling indeed was the scene that met her eyes. The
whole room was dismantled; pictures and books, and all
that had made it home-like and characteristic, were utterly
gone, and the chairs standing about here and there as if

pushed aside by an impatient hand. On the table were a pair of old shoes, a club, a crust of mouldy bread, and a little crumpled packet, which startled Franzje more than anything, because on the paper wrapper she recognised her own handwriting.

"What you tink it all mean, Mamselle?" said the negress, with a grin, apparently deriving some satisfaction from seeing Franzje as puzzled as herself.

"Perhaps Dinah is going to clean the study," suggested "Mamselle" doubtfully.

"Queer way to set about it," said Jettje contemptuously; "no brush, and no pail—not even duster! No Dinah neither. First I look in kitchen, but she not dere; den I call, but she not come."

"It is very strange, certainly," said Franzje, not knowing what further to suggest, and feeling a strange sinking of heart at finding only emptiness and disorder where she had come seeking rest and counsel.

She drew nearer the table, to have a closer look at the mysterious packet : and meanwhile, Jettje, who was not troubled with any very delicate feelings, nor fear of taking liberties, left the room to pursue her investigations, and presently returned, exclaiming, "Dominie gone! dat what 'tis, Mamselle! Me look in his room; no coat hanging on door, no shoes in cupboard—all gone! Dominie gone away and left us, and never come back no more!"

"O Jettje! it can't be; and you shouldn't have looked in his room!" cried out Franzje almost passionately. "He can't have gone away and left us! Perhaps he has just gone to the Flats for a night, while Dinah cleans the house."

"Then why don't she clean it?" retorted Jettje. "Me never did tink much of dat Dinah. She pull a long face, and Dominie tink her right-down Christian woman; but

no good Christian woman leave her master's shoes on de
study table—eh, Mamselle Franzje?"

"I don't think they are his shoes," said Franzje, de-
clining to enter into the abstract question of the anti-
Christian nature of such a proceeding. "I can't make
out how these things came here at all; that piece of paper
belonged to me, and Evert took it on Sunday to wrap up
something in. No, don't meddle with it, Jettje," as the
old woman stretched out her hand to take it. "We must
come away now; we have no business here while the Dominie and Dinah are out."

She walked towards the door, disappointed and perplexed, and Jettje followed her rather unwillingly; but
on the steps they met Dinah coming in.

A very untidy-looking Dinah it was, with the cotton
handkerchief which she wore on her head all awry, her
dress splashed with mud, and her whole appearance as of
one carried out of herself, and too agitated and exhausted
to care how she looked, or what was thought of her.

When she saw them she sank down on the seat in the
porch, and began rocking herself to and fro, and making
a sort of dismal howling, which rather put Jettje out of
patience.

"Oh," she sobbed, "'tis you, come to look at de empty
house, is it? Yes, Dominie's gone, and you can all make
merry; dere's no one to hinder you now. Oh! oh!
oh—o—o—o!"

Franzje had turned very pale, but she spoke quite calmly
and gently. "Gone? I don't understand, Dinah; has he
gone somewhere on a visit?"

"I mean what I say, Mamselle!" snapped the
Dominie's retainer; "he be gone right away—gone to
New York, to find de big ship to take him across de
seas. You've drove him away wid your jiggings and your

maskings; and he's gone to where dere's people as 'ill listen to him, and walk in de holy Gospel ways."

" Walk in 'em yourself, you Dinah ! " burst out Jettje, before her young mistress could speak. " Mamselle Franzje she know her duty as well as anybody ; and she come here dis mornin' to see Dominie, and speak good words wid him ; and fit to break her heart when she couldn't find him. You go 'long ! "

" We won't stay now ; Dinah is tired," said Franzje, with dignity. " But I believe the Dominie will come back to us, so don't cry," she added kindly to the weeping woman.

A deep, aching regret was gathering in her own heart, yet not a single tear rose to her eyes. She wanted to hear the facts of the case more clearly, and then go alone to think over them, and realize what it all meant, and what the loss that had come upon them involved.

" Tired ! ah, I be tired, Mamselle," said Dinah, a little mollified. " I've run after de carriage till all de breath be out of me ; and Dominie he wave his hand to me to bid me go back, but he not stop for me nor nobody.— Oh—o—o ! oh—o—o—o—o—o ! "

They left her still sitting in the porch and howling ostentatiously, and pursued their homeward way, but not without many interruptions. Dinah in returning had spread the news of her master's departure; and all along the street were gathered knots of people, discussing, with more or less excitement, the wonderful, and—to many—*disastrous* intelligence. The Dominie had sent away his trunks over-night, and had himself driven off early, before the town was fully astir ; so the secret had remained a secret to most of his flock for an hour or two, but now all the town was occupied either in telling or hearing it ; and while some were crying bitterly, and a few exulting, others were improving the occasion after Dinah's fashion, by taunting or rebuking those whom they believed to have been the cause of his departure.

Franzje felt a cowardly inclination to take to her heels, when she saw M. Jansen haranguing the passers-by from the steps of his door; but instead of yielding to it, she drew up her head and walked quietly along on the other side of the street, catching as she went a few words evidently levelled at her, about light-minded maidens, who had wearied out the Dominie's patience by their frivolity and obstinacy.

A little way further on she encountered a noisy group of youngsters, with Evert at their head, who greeted her with a shout of "Hurrah! the Dominie's gone! Now we can have as much fun as we like!" and a sudden "Hear, hear!" came from the windows of the Bankers' house, beneath which she was passing, though the speaker was invisible.

He was not invisible long; for while Franzje was trying to induce Evert to come home with her, and explain to her on the way the mystery of that piece of paper which she had seen on the Dominie's table, Mr. Vyvian, whose voice she had recognized, came out and joined her. She looked round for Jettje, but the old woman was in full chase after Dirk and Albert, who had excited her wrath by chorussing Evert's hurrah; and as Evert made off directly Mr. Vyvian appeared, she was left for just a few moments tête à-tête with him.

"You have heard the news, I see," he said, looking at her grave face, which lighted up for one instant at the sight of him, but speedily grew sad again. "I don't expect you to rejoice, like these madcap boys, but I think you and I have some real cause for being glad."

"Glad to have driven him away!" said she.

Q

There was a keener pathos in her tone than she was aware, and Mr. Vyvian's brow grew clouded. He hated to see her grieving after his "rival;" but at the same time he tried to adapt himself somewhat to her mood, as so often before.

"Well, that last stroke was too much, perhaps," he rejoined; "it must have been pretty clear to him that he was looked upon chiefly as an obstruction; and he might have been spared so palpable a hint as yesterday morning's performance. Still, if I had been he, I should have thought it beneath me to care about such a mere boyish joke."

"I don't know what you mean," said Franzje, breathlessly.

"What! didn't Evert let you into the secret? Have you really not heard of the fine outfit for his journey which the Dominie found at his bed-room door yesterday? I was told you contributed the paper that the dollar was wrapped in, but I can't say I ever fully believed it."

If he had, Franzje's face of startled distress would have convinced him to the contrary. She knew so much better than he did—so much better than her brother even—all the significance that that torn leaf of her theological exercise must have had for the Dominie, that she was struck dumb for the moment at the discovery of Evert's treachery, and let the indignant grief in her beautiful eyes speak for her as it listed.

"It was a very silly practical joke," said Russell, not thinking it necessary to mention that he and Mr. Gardiner had encouraged the boys thereto. "I don't wonder you are displeased at it; but, my own love, don't take such a gloomy view of the matter. The Dominie will come back some day; and meanwhile you and I are now free to be happy. Your father will surely not be able to stand out against us without his clerical dictator to second him."

"I cannot tell," said she, hurriedly, beginning to walk on at a rapid pace; "and oh! Sir, I cannot even tell now whether I really wish him to yield or not. I know it must seem very childish, and I must ask you to forgive me; but, indeed, I do not feel sure now what is right or what is wrong. I must have time to think."

She seemed a different woman from the one he had clasped in his arms but a few nights before; and he looked at her jealously and suspiciously as he rejoined, "Have you not had time for that already? What have you been doing all these days that they have kept you from me? Listening to ill-natured stories about me, perhaps, skilfully dished up by the Dominie and M. Jansen."

"I have not spoken to either of them!" said Franzje, indignantly; "I *wanted* to speak to the Dominie this morning, but when I got to the Manse he was gone."

Her heart was still quivering with the shock of that bitter disappointment, and a little sympathy—a little token that her feelings were understood and respected—would have been inexpressibly soothing; but Russell's mind was altogether out of harmony with hers on this subject, and so he only answered with a triumphant smile, "Yes, he has gone, and left you to me; there is no one to come between us now. Franzje, why do you call me 'sir,' and rush along as if you wanted to get away from me? If you knew how proud I am of your being mine, you would not be so unwilling even to seem to belong to me. Why can't you speak freely to me? me, who would do anything in the world for you! What made you want to speak to the Dominie?"

" It was about you," said she.

She had spoken quite simply and fearlessly ; but for an instant she almost quailed beneath the sudden glance of fierce, jealous wrath which her lover turned upon her.

" Is it usual in your country for a young gentlewoman to consult one of her admirers on the expediency of marrying another ? " he asked, sarcastically.

" Admirers ? " she repeated, in bewilderment ; " I thought we were speaking of the Dominie ! "

" Exactly ; but are you really so innocent as never to have discovered what it was that made M. Freylinghausen keep guard over you so jealously ? Don't you see that he was so determined not to let me have you because he wanted you for himself ? "

A strange thrill passed through her, and for one instant the young face was lifted with a sort of half-proud, half-trembling exultation, as though an undreamt-of honour had come upon her all at once ; but in another moment her eyes fell, and in a grave, humble tone, as if shrinking from the presumption of the thought he wished to force upon her, she answered, " Oh, no ! indeed you have misunderstood ! M. Freylinghausen cared for us all, because he was our pastor ; and once, when he used to teach Evert and me, and saw us trying to be good, I think perhaps he loved us a little more than the rest of the class, but oh ! there was never anything but that ; and since he thinks we have become wicked, I am afraid he has left off loving us at all."

" Afraid ! You care for his love, then ? " said Russell, angrily, and looking as if he would have liked to strangle the Dominie then and there.

She did not quail this time, but paused and fronted him steadily with her grand, clear gaze, as she exclaimed, " How shall I make you understand ? It is no question

of love and lovers. It was God who sent us the Dominie, and taught us to love and honour him ; do you
think we can help caring for having grieved him and
driven him away ? "

Even yet he did not understand ; his grosser and more
worldly mind could scarcely take in the notion of a love
distinct alike from sentimentality and from passion ; and
it was but natural that—looking at the Dominie as a
mere strait-laced old Calvinist—he should fail to comprehend the veneration which his character had inspired ;
but Franzje's face in its pathetic loveliness touched and
softened him, and he was beginning to murmur some fond,
soothing words, when up came old Jettje, panting mightily
after her long run, and dragging little Albert in her train.

" Ah, Mamselle, dis here naughty bad boy lead me such
a chase," panted she ; " but now me got him me not let
him go till Baas speak to him. Jus' you help me to bring
him 'long, Mamselle ! "

" You need not hold him, Jettje ; he will come with
me, I know," said the girl, in the gentle tone of command
which slaves and children alike had learned to obey. " I
must bid you good-day, Sir," she added, firmly, to Russell,
who was standing chafing at the interruption. " My mother
will be looking for us, for doubtless she has heard the
news ere this."

" Tell your father I shall not fail to keep my appointment with him to-morrow," rejoined the young man
haughtily, " and trust that on his part he will not fail me.
As for you, Mademoiselle, when you have a thought to
spare from the Dominie, I shall intreat you to give it
to me."

She felt the reproach conveyed in the words ; and all
at once a wistful, deprecating sweetness came into her
eyes as she said, " I am afraid I have indeed seemed cold

and ungrateful, Sir; I do not quite know myself to-day."

It was not so much re-awakened love, as the anxious humility of a child feeling itself wrong and asking for pardon, that spoke through her looks and tones; but the very least sign of tenderness towards him was enough to kindle afresh the man's passionate devotion, and he answered with a few burning, rapturous expressions of affection, couched in French, that they might be less intelligible to Jettje.

The sweet eyes fell, and that glow came to the delicate cheek which he most loved to call forth; but there was no nearer approach to him, no soft whisper of love in reply; the night when her heart had spoken in answer to his, when her lips had met his unabashed, seemed already far away.

Franzje returned, to find her mother in tears, and her father standing by the fire with his travelling-cloak on, as if equipped for a journey. They both saw by her face that she knew what they knew, and both seemed to have forgotten Mr. Vyvian, and to feel confident of their daughter's sympathy with all that they felt regarding the loss of their pastor.

"I have been longing for you to come back, my dear," said Madame Ryckman, holding out her hand and drawing Franzje towards her. "Did you really go on to the Manse, and find it empty? or did you hear the news on the way?"

"I could have saved you the fruitless walk," said M. Ryckman, "if I had known; for that note that was brought to me at breakfast was from M. Cuyler, telling me that he had got scent of the Dominie's departure, and begging me to come with him and intercept him at that bit of the road—"

"Oh! and did you?" interrupted Franzje, too eagerly anxious to wait with her usual respect for the close of her father's sentence.

"Yes, but it was all of no use; and though I offered to go on to New York with him, hoping at least to prevent his embarkation, it was only wasting my breath; he would neither turn back nor accept the company of anyone on the road. He has a will of iron, our Dominie. I always thought so."

"*Our* Dominie!" echoed Madame Ryckman. "Ah, we scarcely dare call him that, now that he has gone away and left us. I wonder what the Schuylers will say when they hear this terrible news. Your father wants you to drive out to the Flats with him, Franzje, and help him to break it to Madame."

"And leave you all alone, dear Mother?" said Franzje, tenderly.

"Oh, do not fear for me, I have no time to sit and grieve; I must see to Arij and your uncle Jan. I did just run up to him with the news; and I was almost provoked with him, dear good old man! for instead of seeming surprised, he said, calmly, 'I have been expecting this,' and then turned away, as if he wished to hear no more."

"I daresay he is praying for the Dominie, and for us," said Franzje, in a low voice, full of emotion.

"Yes," replied her mother, in rather a dissatisfied tone, as if just at that moment she would have preferred some more human manifestation of sympathy. "And now, child," she added, "you must have some hot chocolate before you set out on your drive; I told Maaike to bring you a cup before the carriage came round. Your father came in as jaded and disheartened as could be, and was for taking nothing; but a good glass of hollands-and-water has made him something like himself again."

Franzje felt scarcely able to swallow, but obediently
put her lips to the cup which Maria brought in at this
moment. While she raised it with one hand, the little
slave-girl took possession of the other, and covered it with
kisses. "Mamselle! dear, dear Mamselle!" was all she
said; but Franzje understood to the full what was implied
in this sudden outburst of tenderness, and putting down
the cup, bent forward and kissed the round black face
with a warm impulse of gratitude.

Ah! how sweet the home-kindness seemed now that
her heart was so torn and perplexed! She valued it so
much, that she could scarcely bear to risk the loss of it
by an untimely word; and as she drove along with her
father towards the Flats, delayed from minute to minute
the delivery of Mr. Vyvian's message, and at length determined to give it on their way back.

They found that the tidings they brought had reached
the Schuylers already, and that the Colonel had even set
off in pursuit of the Dominie, after the example of his
brother-in-law and M. Ryckman. Madame had been a
little hopeful about the result of his mission; but when
she heard of M. Ryckman's failure, she shook her head,
and said, sadly, "Then Philip has not much chance of
success. How I shall watch and weary for his return!
Could you not leave me Franzje? It is a comfort to
have someone to share one's anxiety—and I could send
her back to you to-morrow."

M. Ryckman looked half unwilling to consent; but
then a sudden idea seemed to strike him, and he said, "If
you will keep her till Thursday, I will come and fetch her
myself."

"Till Friday if you like," said Aunt Schuyler, thinking
of the play, which was to take place on Thursday night;
"but surely, my little Franzje—"

"She is a good girl," interrupted her father, hastily. "There is no need for keeping her out of the way; but it seems a pleasant change for her to be here with you; and I have business to-morrow, and altogether—yes, you will stay with Madame, Franzje," he concluded, turning to the girl, who was standing with parted lips and eager eyes, wondering what might be the real purport of this new arrangement.

He got up to go directly he had said this, as if he were in a hurry to escape any arguments to the contrary, and seemed to mean his hurried kiss as a final good-bye; but Franzje followed him to the door.

"Father," she said, breathlessly, "I met Mr. Vyvian, and he said he hoped you would not fail to keep your appointment with him to-morrow. I don't know what you are going to say to him, nor even what I want you to say—but oh! father, let me have a voice in the matter; don't settle it all without my knowing!"

"I must talk to your mother," said he, irresolutely; "and I shall hear what the young man says; but you know very well, my maid, what the Dominie thought of him, and that should be enough for us. Be a good girl, and don't fret about this young coxcomb; we have trouble enough in losing our Dominie."

"Yes, and oh! Father, I am glad to be with Aunt Schuyler for a bit; I do want to talk to her—but if you could send for me to-night? I am anxious about Evert; and there are so *many* things that make me want to be at home to-morrow. Please, Father, let me come home to-night!"

"No no," said he, breaking from her, just because he felt he could not resist her pleadings for long. "I have spoilt you all, and that is the truth of it. Evert will do very well—the young rascal!—there's no keeping him in order as I should like, with your mother always taking his part. I shall fetch you on Thursday or Friday, as seems best; and meantime you must be a good child, and try and cheer up Madame."

He drove off, and Franzje stood on the steps looking after him, feeling rather as if she had been trapped, though she did not for a moment suspect her father of any deep-laid design in bringing her to the Flats that morning. "Be a good child!" Oh! how easy it was to say! but who could make her feel like a child again? And was goodness possible, when her choice seemed only to lie between two evils—the being unfaithful to her lover, or unfaithful to the Dominie?

CHAPTER XV.

𝔗𝔥𝔢 𝔄𝔴𝔞𝔨𝔢𝔫𝔦𝔫𝔤.

A visit to the Flats had always appeared to Franzje in her childhood the very acme of delight; and even now that she was—to her own thinking—grown up, a certain prestige still hung about it which made her proud as well as pleased to be Aunt Schuyler's guest; but on this particular occasion, so much of her heart had been left behind her in the city, and such a tumult of conflicting feelings was going on within her, that she could only half appreciate the simple enjoyments into which she had been accustomed to enter with so much heartiness and zest. She remembered that she had been left to cheer Madame, and all through the first day made valiant efforts to take a hopeful view of the Dominie's proceedings, and suggest

that even if the Colonel did not succeed in persuading
him to turn back, a feeling of compassion for his pastorless
flock might at the last moment prevent his actually embarking; but in her own heart she did not believe that
any such change of purpose would take place. It was a
sort of relief to her restlessness to find that even her staid
old friend was restless also; and when Madame said,
"Come, Franzje, we must not give way; we must set
ourselves steadily to *do* something, it is better than talking and thinking," she gave a ready assent, and entered
upon the task proposed—the dusting and arranging of the
valuable china ornaments in the summer parlour—with
great goodwill, though not with the interest she would
once have felt. The queer-shaped bowls and quaint
figures, which at another time she would have paused to
examine and chat about, now passed through her listless
fingers with scarcely a word of comment; and even when
Madame proceeded to unveil all the great mirrors, and
give an air of habitation to the room, Franzje could
scarcely rouse herself to admire, or even to ask whether
the change from the winter to the summer house was
about to be effected. She half wanted to solicit
Madame's advice with regard to Mr. Vyvian, and yet she
could not bring herself to say a word upon the subject.
That yearning to open her heart, which had taken her to
the Manse in the morning, had met with such bitter disappointment, that her feelings now seemed frozen up and
incapable of expression.

"Besides, she will ask me, perhaps, whether I really
wish to marry him," said the girl to herself; "and just
now I do not seem to know whether I do or not. Only a
few hours ago I was wishing it with my whole heart, and
thinking to be able to win even the Dominie's consent;
but now I see that that could never have been—that it

was nothing but my foolish fancy which ever made it seem possible. Can I go on longing for what I can only have at the price of doing wrong? How can I be happy, or make him happy, if I am wicked and undutiful? No; if Father refuses his consent, I must take it as the Voice of God to me, telling me I am not to have the thing I had set my heart upon. Oh! it is no use asking advice, for I see the right at last only too plainly. If I could but speak to him, and make *him* see what it is that severs us, it might not be quite so hard to part as it seems at this moment!"

So she kept silence; and, when the weary afternoon wore to an end, and the colonel came back tired and dejected, with failure written on his frank open face, she heard the history of his fruitless mission without a word, and then crept apart to the little room in the winter house which Madame had assigned to her, feeling that she had always known it would be so, and that she was too heartsick to be capable of any fresh sense of disappointment.

She scarcely knew how the evening was got through: but with a new day came renewed energy and spirit, and she followed Madame from the parlour to the store-room, and from the store-room to the barn, the next morning, with somewhat of her old smiling helpfulness,, though now and then her manner grew a little absent as the thought came, "I wonder whether Mr. Vyvian is with Father now; I wonder what Father is saying to him."

After the early dinner, the Colonel rode into Albany to see M. Cuyler, and Madame announced her intention of taking a walk, and going to call on her sister-in-law, Madame Jeremiah Schuyler, who lived not far from the Flats. She invited Franzje to accompany her, and the girl herself could never tell *exactly* what it was that made her decline the invitation; for mingled with a vague longing for perfect quiet and solitude was a sort of instinctive feeling that it would not be well to be absent from the house that afternoon, and also a half-unconscious desire to avoid a *tête-à-tête* with her old friend. She had to endure a little playful scolding for her laziness, interspersed with some fragments of sound advice about not giving way to the luxury of woe; but finally she was left to wander at will about the large, bright rooms of the summer-house, while good Aunt Schuyler—her own heart heavy enough—trudged forth as briskly as her *embonpoint* would permit, with a little basket containing some delicacies for a sick nephew upon her arm. After she was gone, Franzje stood in the portico for a while, talking to the birds; and then went and had a long gaze at the picture of Esau in the dining-room; and finally took her knitting, and sat down for a while near one of the windows in the drawing-room, gazing out from time to time towards the river, and the tree-fringed line of the high-road which ran along its bank. The white railings that skirted the little bit of private road leading from the front-door of the Flats were gleaming now in the sunlight, though not so distinctly as they had gleamed in the moonlight on that memorable night of which Franzje was thinking; but suddenly the broad belt of sunshine between them was broken by a shadow, and a clatter of hoofs announced the approach of an equestrian. Franzje knew who it was even without looking, but almost involuntarily she started to her feet; and Mr. Vyvian caught the movement and the eager glance, and doffed his hat to her with gallant grace as he rode past the window. A flock of little negroes appeared as if by magic from some of the back regions directly he got to the door; and confiding his horse to one of them, he desired another to conduct him at once to Mademoiselle Ryckman; so that instead of being ushered in with great state by old Peter, his entrance was announced by a comical little black boy, who, throwing wide the door, bawled out, "Fine big gentleman to see Mamselle!" and then took to his heels precipitately, as if he feared the gentleman would demolish him.

Certainly the expression on Russell Vyvian's face that afternoon was not of the pleasantest; there was pride and pique in every curve of his handsome mouth; and underneath all the polish of his manner, as he exchanged greetings with Franzje, was an angry sense of injury, not allayed even by the unmistakeable interest and sympathy which he read in her transparent eyes.

"I have had my answer from your father," he said, hastily, as he took the chair she offered him; "the reason that I am here is, that I refuse to accept it as final—that I refuse to have my suit dismissed by anybody but yourself; though, of course, I conclude that you were purposely sent out of my way, or came out of it of your own accord."

"I do not think there was any set purpose in my coming," said the voice, which sounded clearer and sweeter than ever from the contrast with his own sharp, agitated tones; "I came with my father when he brought the news to Aunt Schuyler yesterday, and when she asked me to stay, he seemed to wish that I should."

She did not specify *what* news, something kept her from uttering the Dominie's name any more to those unsympathizing ears; and besides, her instinct was rather to soothe than to augment by an unnecessary word her proud suitor's irritation.

"And you have been very comfortable here, I suppose, and cared nothing about what has been going on in your absence?" he rejoined.

"Oh, if you did but know!" she cried out, with sudden emotion, a little, sad quiver breaking the sweet repose of her lips. "It has seemed so hard to stay here and be quiet while so much was being decided; only I tried to think it was best, and that perhaps you would not even care to see me again."

"Then you mean to force me to accept your father's decision—you mean to cast me off ? " he exclaimed, passionately; "and you would have me think it all filial duty, I suppose, and not the miserable result of your long bondage to the Dominie, whose cowardly departure even has not sufficed to set you free."

If he had meant to taunt her into relenting and compliance, he was not long in finding out his mistake ; the nature, so gratefully sensitive to the least touch of tenderness, was not to be moved by fierceness, was not even awed by it. There was brave determination in her voice as she replied, " I made up my mind last Sunday that I must do what was right, even if it led to giving you up, only it has taken me longer to see that it *does* lead to that. It is my shame and blame that I did not see it sooner, that I have misled you, Sir, and listened and been happy when I ought to have turned away, even at the risk of seeming ungrateful."

The speech that had begun with such a stately ring in it, faltered into self-accusing lowliness as she uttered this last sentence, and for an instant the flaxen head was bowed, so that he could not see her face. She had refused to be ashamed that night—that wonderful night, when love had stirred her soul, and seemed to her as innocent as it was sweet ; but now shame seized and covered her in the presence of the man whom she had allowed to love her, and whom she could never marry.

He saw his advantage, and was not slow to use it.

Rising from his seat, and standing close beside her, he said, earnestly, "I will not reproach you now with the misleading; Franzje, you admit that my love made you happy. Why not accept it once and for all, then, let who will say nay?"

He was looking down at her with a softened glance; and as he stood there leaning against the wall in all his handsome grace and bravery, he was the very ideal of a lover, the very embodiment of a girl's romantic image of the wonderful hero who is some day to win her heart. Perhaps there was scarcely another maiden in Albany who would not have thought him irresistible; even to Franzje he might have seemed so but one short week before.

She looked up at him, and the limpid loveliness of those guileless eyes had never struck him more forcibly than it did at that moment; but there was no response in them such as he had hoped for—only a kind of humble, brave regret, a sort of yearning over the past, which yet to her was too utterly past ever to be revived again.

"It would not make me happy now if it could all come back," she said; "I thank you, and I beg of you to forgive me; I seem to have done wrong to everybody —even to *you*."

He was scarcely to blame for not fully understanding her.

"I cannot comprehend what has changed you, Mademoiselle," he said, haughtily; "your coldness and your penitence alike are a mystery to me. Is it possible that you were only deceiving me when you let me pour out my heart to you, and answered me in words which, few as they were, seemed to mean more than a hundred protestations from the lips of shallower women? Can it be that you do not care for me at all? Or is it only that you have not courage to face your father's opposition, even

now when he has no longer the Dominie at his back, and
mean to play the dutiful daughter, and console yourself
with the calf-love of young Barentse when you have
driven me beyond recall."

He had poured out his words in an impetuous torrent,
but she had heard and understood them every one ; and
yet for an instant she did not speak, only looked up at
him once more with that innocent, sad appeal.

How could she make him see wherein her fault lay ?
How could she tell him that there had been delusion,
though not deception, that she had let herself love him
under a mistake, believing, because she wished to believe
it, that love and duty were not really at conflict, that in
some magical way all that barred her from him would
melt into air, and she be free to give herself to him without doing wrong to others ? Nay : and how could she
tell him too, that, with eyes opened by the shock of
sorrow, she was beginning to see that what she had loved
in him had not been so entirely his true self as what she
had imagined him to be, that the soft glamour which her
fancy had cast over him was being dispelled by the hard
light of truth, and that in the last twenty-four hours she
had learnt to understand in a measure why her father and
the Dominie so urgently desired to sever her from him.

So for that minute both were silent ; and he had leisure
to watch the delicate colour come and go, and to note the
fair, swan-like curve of the slender throat ; and to think
that even now, in her changeableness and perversity, this
was just the one most perfect woman that he ever had
seen, or should see—the one whom nature had formed to
shine as a star in whatever sphere she might be placed.
Oh ! how often did he see her in his dreams afterwards,
with that black ribbon cunningly twisted in her flaxen
hair, with that thick, sombre dress falling round her in

R

folds which no other Albanian girl could have made
graceful, and only seeming to set off her pearl-like beauty,
and enhance by contrast the vivid tints of her lips and
eyes ! The loveliness which had first attracted him kept its
hold upon him to the last, all the more so because Franzje
was at the moment utterly unconscious of her charms,
and evidently had not sought to heighten them by the
smallest adventitious aid. Not even the blue snood had
been donned in expectation of his coming ; and yet he
saw that she *had* expected him, and wondered to himself
whether he would have had a chance of a more favourable answer had he taken her quite unawares. He did
not know what to say to move her, for he had lost the
key to her mind ; all that lighter and more frivolous side
of her, that girlish vanity and romance which he had
known how to trade upon, seemed to have died out suddenly, and left her sad and earnest and resolute, with
nothing but her sweet, young beauty to bear witness to
her girlhood.

It was not really long, though it seemed so, before she
answered him.

"I have not meant to deceive you, Sir," she said
sorrowfully ; "only so short a time ago as yesterday I was
still trying to think that I might yield to your wishes and
yet not do wrong ; but I cannot think so now ; and when
we have seen the right we *must* follow it—there is no
other way."

She was as inexorable as Fate—this young girl, who had
ceased to listen to the voices of passion and of pleasure,
and to whom duty was becoming all in all ; but she was a
woman still, with a woman's sensitive faithfulness towards
what *has been ;* and there was a suppressed fire in her
voice as she went on, "I would not have you think, Sir,
that it is through cowardice I say so, or that I shall marry

any one else, even if my father presses it, which I do not
believe he will. I may not have made you a good return
for all that you have lavished on me, but you have shown
me what love is, and I can never play at it now with any
other person, nor forget what it has been to me in these
last few weeks."

She was not quite seventeen; and before them both, as
she spoke, rose up the long stretch of lonely years which
might come to test her resolution. She looked down the
vista undismayed, but he answered with scornful incredulity, " You say so, Mademoiselle, and I have no
doubt you mean it—*at this moment;* but should our regiment pass through Albany again when the campaign is
over, and should I then be still among my gallant com-
rades, and not lying stark on some battle-field with a
French bullet through my breast, I shall doubtless find
you the wife of some comfortable Dutchman, who has
enriched himself with the spoils of the poor Indians, and
can wrap you in the furs he has cheated them out of, and
make you the envy of all your companions by his store of
four-posters and crockery-ware. As for me, had I had
your love to cheer me on, I might have carved out fame
for myself with my good sword, and brought you those
distinctions which some women covet more than wealth
or ease; but it is useless to speak of that now."

It was a little too high-flown to be quite real, but she
was too young to detect that; he felt himself a sort of
unappreciated hero as he uttered it, and spite of his in-
justice towards her, she could scarcely help thinking him
so too, and was touched—as he had meant she should be,
—by that picture of him lying dead on the battle-field,
with a bullet through the heart which *she* had made
desolate. There came into her face a tender pathos and
pity, which yet was not relenting—a visible longing to

soften to him somehow the rejection which she *could* not turn into acceptance. He went on, trying to work upon her feelings with a moving description of the anguish to which she was consigning him, and the loss of faith in all womankind—in all truth and troth—which her defection would bring about in his soul ; and once in her emotion she rose up and stretched out her hands towards him, but drew them back again just as he was about to seize them and cover them with kisses. For a moment he almost fancied himself master of the situation ; but then again his want of that delicate chivalrous honour with which her imagination had invested him, led him astray. He committed the blunder of making a great point of what he called his honourable conduct in offering to marry her, and of her ingratitude in not appreciating this handsome treatment ; and then the innocent mind of the young Albanian, which had no experience of heartless flirtations, no knowledge of the then proverbial lightness of a soldier's love—which had never pictured to itself the possibility of a wooing of which marriage was *not* the object, revolted from him in utter surprise ; and a fresh gulf seemed opened between them just at the very instant when he was flattering himself that she might still be his once more.

It was that intense conviction of his own wonderful goodness in running all risks of scorn and ridicule from his brother officers, and lasting displeasure from his parents, by making her an offer of marriage, which made his rejection so peculiarly irritating to him. He had broken from M. Ryckman with bitter words of anger and insult, feeling as if his marvellous condescension had met with a most unhandsome return, and never even perceiving that after his open professions of love to Franzje, the offer he had made was simply her *due*. That he would

never have made it, if his over-mastering love for her had
not created a sort of necessity for binding her to him
permanently by the one only tie which in her case was
possible, was perhaps rather clearer to him; but he did
not think less of himself on that account. His love for
Franzje was only a higher form of the selfishness which
was innate in his character, he wanted her for his own
happiness, and was content to think that hers must follow
as a matter of course; but still, it *was* a higher form—a
something to lift him from the low level of ordinary self-
indulgence in which he had previously been content to live
—and it had raised his self-esteem and self-respect considerably. To find himself capable of so pure and unworldly an
attachment had been a sort of agreeable surprise to the
blasé man of pleasure; and there seemed to him a kind of
unfairness in its not meeting with a happy result. When
Franzje, amazed at his last argument, drew back from him
in all the majesty of maidenly pride, he reassumed the
injured air which he had worn when he first entered the
room, and dropped the ardent persuasive tone which had
tried her courage so sorely. It is perhaps in the great
eventful moments of life that ignoble natures reveal themselves the most clearly, and at the same time the most
unconsciously. All unknown to himself, he was destroy-
ing by each fresh word that fair ideal of him which had
filled Franzje's mind, and made her blind to his faults
and deaf to the accusations brought against him. But yet
his reproaches went to her heart in a manner, for she *had*
wronged him, though all unwittingly. Each answering
look, each answering smile that she had ever given him,
seemed to her now an irretrievable wrong; and it might
all have been spared had she been loyal to the Dominie,
had she but kept in the strict safe way of entire
obedience !

She stood before him humble and self-accusing, and yet wrapped round with a sort of steadfast dignity and purpose which made him feel at last that words were useless —that nothing was left for him but to go.

There was something a little melodramatic in the tone in which he began his farewell, something in his gaze the while from which she almost shrank; but the sound of his horse's hoofs on the gravel, and the sudden apparition outside the window of the round black face of the boy whom he had set to hold it, made him all at once natural again, and brought back his self-restraint.

" It is hard to have a spy upon our last moments together," he said ; " but there is nothing left for me to say. Adieu, Mademoiselle ; if we should meet when you return to the city, we shall meet, I suppose, as the merest acquaintances. I wish you a happier fate than wearing out your heart in waiting for the Dominie's return, or settling down into the wife of a stripling who is not fit to black your shoes. Have you no good wish for *me*, whom you are sending from you ? "

What she said was so low that he could hardly hear it; he thought it was "Oh ! you know that I have ! " But for the last time the star-like eyes spoke to him in that deep language which needs no audible words. It was not love, nor longing, nor regret, nor anything that could have lured him to a hopeless allegiance ; it was thanks for all he had been to her ; forgiveness, blessing—a message straight from her pure heart to all that was left of pure and good in the heart of the man whom she had loved.

She stood where he had left her till he was mounted and gone ; and when the brilliant soldierly figure faded away in the distance, she felt that the little brief romance had faded out of her life, and left rather a dreary blank in place of the old happy contentedness. Her thoughts flew back to the time before the regiment came into the town ; how light-hearted she had been then, and with what glad expectation she had looked forward to the future! Nothing could ever bring that time back again ; even if the regiment were to go, and the Dominie to return, it could never all be as it had been before ; *people* had changed as well as circumstances—she herself among the number ; and even going back to the old ways would not bring back the old feelings and the old calmness of heart. And yet she could not bring herself to wish that the last few months could be blotted out ; they had brought her much that was still precious, though mingled with bitterness, and she could not have borne to part with it, only she would have liked to live them through again, in a wiser, nobler way.

She did not quite know how long it was before Madame Schuyler came in, nor what there was in her own face to tell of the struggle she had passed through ; but when the good lady kissed her tenderly, saying, " My dear little maid, has it gone as deep as that? " she did feel it a relief to lay down her head on that broad, kindly bosom and shed a few quiet tears.

" I wish it had all been different," sobbed the girl, " and that I had never wounded, or vexed, or misled any-one. But, Aunt Schuyler, I did not know ; I did not see it all as I do now! "

Madame had heard of Mr. Vyvian's visit from one of the chattering little negro lads as she came up the steps ; and directly she saw Franzje, her quick intuition told her what the purport of that visit had been, and how it had ended. " My child," she said, kindly, " I don't wonder you were dazzled by him at first ; this old head of mine even was pretty nearly turned by him, and I encouraged when I should have checked. Your parents were wiser,

and so was the Dominie, though he did not go the best
way to work. He used almost to put *me* out of patience
with his prejudices, so no wonder young ears like yours did
not always give heed to his warnings. I never believed a
word against Mr. Vyvian till the Colonel—not his Colonel,
but mine, my Philip—told me one or two things on the
night of our sleighing-party, which he had heard from
M. Banker himself; and then it went to my heart to
think that this was the man that my poor little Franzje
was ready to take for a husband. The Colonel comforted
me by saying he would never ask you; but I could not
think so badly of him as all that."

Franzje raised her tear-wet face a little proudly, a little
indignantly, to rebut the Colonel's insinuation.

"He spoke to my father this morning," said she, with
the old innocent confidence in her tone, as if it would have
been quite impossible for *him* to act otherwise; and then
suddenly came over her a burning remembrance of the im-
mense merit which he had ascribed to himself for doing
so, and once more she bent down her head to hide the
blushes which scorched her cheeks.

But then again her mingled loyalty towards him and
the Dominie made her say a word for each, though speaking was an effort. "He could never have slighted or
wronged me, he has always been so good to me; he is
much better than the Dominie thinks; but still I ought
to have heeded the Dominie's warnings for *his* sake even
more than for my own, for now I have wronged *him*, as
well as helped to drive our Dominie away. I am very
young to have done so much harm, and harm that can
never be undone! Aunt Schuyler, please let me go home.
I will try to do all I can for Father and Mother, and never
grieve them any more. It is all that is left for me to
do."

Tender-hearted Aunt Schuyler kissed her again, and did not grudge her the relief of a few more tears, but presently said in a cheerful tone, "You must have courage, my child; God has plenty of work for you to do yet. He would not have dashed down your poor little castle of happiness if He had not something better in store for you some day."

And then she lifted the sad face between her hands and gazed at it fondly for a moment, reading on the calm wide brow and in the great spiritual eyes so sure a prophecy of a nobler holier fate than the one the young heart in its ignorance had desired, that she wondered how she could, even for a moment, have tolerated the idea of seeing Franzje the wife of that careless pleasure-loving soldier.

Franzje continued urgent in her desire of going home; and Madame, who fully understood the feeling which prompted it, and did not construe it into any want of gratitude for the kindness shown her at the Flats, half promised to let her go the next day; but when the Colonel returned, he told them that he had seen M. Ryckman, and agreed with him to keep Franzje till the Friday morning; and so the girl, in her new anxiety to be wholly dutiful, was fain to be content to leave the matter as her father had settled it.

"He still thinks, perhaps, that I should want to go to the theatricals," she said to herself, humbly and with shame; "but if I might have gone home he would have seen that I did not; and I might have helped to keep Evert away."

It so happened that the Colonel had promised to be in Albany very early on Friday, to confer with the elders and some of the leading inhabitants of the place on what was to be done with regard to services during the Dominie's absence; and the quaint high carriage was

brought round the first thing after breakfast, and Franzje
was hurried away from her last clinging embrace in the
very midst of her whispered thanks for Aunt Schuyler's
tender goodness, and bidden with kindly authority to
"Jump up at once, and not let Elder Jansen be put out
by having to wait."

She had not very much to say to her good old friend
as they drove along together, and could not keep her eyes
from straying out over the river, so changed already from
the clear frozen mass which it had been on the day of the
sleighing-party ; but she listened to his description of the
breaking up of the ice—which had been used to form one
of her annual excitements, but which had passed almost
unheeded in the course of this agitating week—and
showed sufficient interest to please and satisfy him.

They were just drawing near to the town, when the
notes of a military march struck upon their ears, and a
small advanced guard of soldiers came hurrying by ; and
when they entered the street, the band of Colonel
Trelawny's regiment came in sight, followed by what
appeared to be the whole body of soldiers.

The natural supposition was that they were coming out
for exercise ; and as there was no room to pass, Colonel
Schuyler drew up at the side of the road, just under the
windows of M. Gerritse's house, not ill-pleased to have
the chance of this little military spectacle, except that
he would fain have spared Franzje the meeting with Mr.
Vyvian. But in another minute loud voices from within
drew their eyes up to the windows ; and then, by the
anxious eager faces that they saw there, as well as by the
excited crowd that began to gather in the street, they
guessed that something had happened, and that this was
by no means a mere ordinary marching out.

At one of the middle windows were Cornelia and

Engeltje Banker, with their mother standing beside them; and to Franzje's amazement, it was little shy Engelt who on seeing her leaned forward and called out, "O Franz, Franz! they are going away! they are going to the war!"

Even amid the clang of the music, the shrill sweet tones reached Franzje's ears, and made her look towards the speaker. Engelt was all in her fairest apparel, her dimpled cheeks flushed with a bright crimson, her soft eyes gleaming with excitement; and strange to say, she had placed herself in the most prominent position, while the usually more forward Cornelia gloomed from behind her with an air of unmistakeable dudgeon.

As Colonel Trelawny rode by at the head of his men, there was a sudden scream from one of the upper windows, and the momentary apparition of a tear-swollen face, with dishevelled hair hanging about it, which Franzje with difficulty recognised as Anna Gerritse's. The sight of it gave her a pang; but in another minute her gaze returned to Engeltje's proud, flushed, love-lighted face. What could have happened to the little thing, so to transform her all at once?

The mystery was solved, when presently, in the rear of the last company, the handsome adjutant rode by. His glance lighted for one instant on Franzje sitting there motionless in the carriage, with wide absorbed eyes, and almost marble-like beauty—so pale had she become at his approach—and then it went up defiantly, ostentatiously, to the little radiant face that was watching him from above; and all his doffings of the hat, and wavings of the hand, and lover-like looks, were for Engelt—Engeltje! who to all appearance had never been to him anything till now but a pretty simple child, to whom he liked to drop a kind word occasionally. Franzje could not choose but see; but after the slight bow with which she had acknowledged his hasty glance, she never looked at him again, and neither spoke nor stirred; her cheek grew perhaps a shade whiter, that was all.

This was the man on whom she had been ready to waste her whole heart and life, for whose sake she had angered the one friend whose esteem she prized most of all.

As for good old Colonel Schuyler, he by no means took the matter so calmly; he would have liked to knock the sentimental dandy off his horse, and box little Engeltje's ears, and could scarcely keep his mutterings to himself, or refrain from brandishing his driving-whip in the young officer's saucy face. But yet, what right had he to say or do anything, since Franzje herself had dismissed her quondam lover—as he knew from his good wife's confidences—who was now of course free to make love to any other woman as quickly as his shallow feelings would allow?

.A minute more, and even the adjutant had gone by, glancing back still over his shoulder at Engelt, whose exulting radiance was fast melting into tears. Then came the rear-guard; and then Colonel Schuyler was about to drive on, when out came Cornelia Banker from the house and stopped him.

"O Franzje!" she said, eagerly addressing his companion, "Anna is fainting, and she has been crying out for you; do come in, if it is only for a moment! we don't know what to do with her, and Madame Gerritse does nothing but scold."

The Colonel was unwilling to leave his charge, thinking she had been tried enough already; but Franzje had not the heart to refuse the petition.

"She wants Colonel Trelawny to come back and marry her," went on Cornelia, as she drew her friend up the

stairs ; " but I do not believe that he will. Thank goodness, *I* have had nothing to do with these nonsensical
officers, beyond making game of Mr. Gardiner now and
then. Did you see that silly Engelt ? Mr. Vyvian went
on to her in such a way last night at the dance after the
theatricals ; and then in the middle came the order to
march, and the gaiety was all broken up. Then Engelt
cried, and he kissed her, and called her all the sweet names
you can think of. I never saw such foolishness—when
we all know it was *you* he really cared about."

" He does not now," said Franzje faintly ; but Cornelia
answered with easy disdain, " Oh, nonsense ! Didn't I
guess it was to the Flats he went when he galloped off in
such a hurry on Wednesday ; and didn't he come back fit
to kill himself with spite and ill-temper ? Of course, all
this with Engeltje is mere mockery and bravado ; I tell
her so, but she won't listen to me."

It was partly a vain jealous girl's way of pooh-poohing
the love affairs of a younger sister ; but still there was
sense and truth in it—more truth than Franzje's wounded
spirit would quite allow itself to admit.

Scarcely off with the old love before he was on with
the new ! Ah ! it was not only that *hands* were severed ;
poor little Franzje's *preux chevalier* was falling, falling,
falling from his throne in her *heart.*

CHAPTER XVI.

" Bon Voyage."

" HERE, Arij, stand out of the way, or I'll shoot you !—
Dirk, you run up to my room, and fetch the powder-flask
thet you'll see there—Albert, you be off and find Jan ;

I've heaps of things to say to him.—Killian, how can
you stand there gossiping with Franzje, when you have
all your preparations to see to?"

It was thus that Evert poured forth commands and remonstrances, as he sat on his favourite perch in the
window-seat, smoking a pipe for almost the first time in
his life, and cleaning his gun, while three admiring and
envious little brothers hovered about him, and Killian
stood somewhat apart, with his elbow on the mantel-
piece, talking to Franzje, who was busy knitting a new
heel to one of the young gentleman's stockings.

Dirk and Albert started off at once to obey his behests;
but Killian never even so much as turned his face in the
direction of the speaker. He was absorbed in watching
Franzje's flying fingers, and seemed to find the click of
her knitting needles very pleasant music, judging by the
contented expression on his dark brown visage. ·

"So you think I managed it well?" he said, in the
low tone which was only meant for her ears.

"Oh! so well!" she answered, looking up at him
with a beaming gaze of gratitude. "I should not have
been so unhappy at the Flats if I had known that you
would see to Evert. That was one of the things that
weighed upon me."

"Could I have helped in the other things?" There
was somewhat of eager longing in the tone, but not
enough of hope to make the response seem very crushing
when she said sadly, "No, thank you; no one could."

She went on knitting in silence after this; and for
some minutes Killian seemed satisfied to be silent also.
He was something of an Indian in taciturnity, as well
as in bearing and complexion; and as she was looking
at her work, and not at him, she did not see the
dumb faithful yearning in his dark eyes, which told

how much he wanted to comfort her, if he had only known how.

"I never did see anything like you two!" burst forth Evert again; "haven't you muttered together long enough? Franz does go on working—I will say that for her; and well she may, with all my things to get ready before six to-morrow; but as for you, Barentse, you are simply wasting time. I tell you what it is—if I am ready, and the canoe is ready, and you are not, I shall start without you. See if I don't!"

It was said with a gay good-humoured laugh, that made it sound a great deal more jocular than threatening, but still it was a tolerably saucy speech, from a young gentleman who but for Killian's kindness would have had no chance of starting at all; and his sister looked round at him with wondering reproof, while Killian merely retorted, smiling, "You impudent fellow!"

The merry lad who was whistling and singing and flinging out pert speeches this bright April afternoon, had come to Killian's window at the dead of night but a few days before, in such a state of despair and wrath and misery, as would have moved any one's compassion. Displeasure at the boy's audacity in announcing that he meant to go to the play in defiance of all commands to the contrary, joined to disgust at finding that he had been one of the ringleaders in the insult offered to the Dominie, had worked up his usually indulgent father to such a pitch of indignation, as to lead to measures of quite extraordinary severity. Madame Ryckman's motherly entreaties had averted the threatened cudgelling; but when Evert got up on the Wednesday morning, he had found himself a prisoner in his room, and had been informed that he was to remain so till arrangements could be made for sending him to his uncle at New York. To prevent his escaping from the window his clothes had been removed; but he had managed to disinter a quaint linsey-wolsey suit of his grandfather's, that happened to be in a press behind his bed, and favoured by darkness, had effected his escape in this marvellous apparel, though the clumsy padded breeches and cumbrous shoes with copper buckles had rather impeded the agility of his movements. His notion had been to get Killian to hide him till the following night, and lend him some garments in which to appear at the play, and after indulging in this piece of undutiful enjoyment, he had meant to make off to the woods, and lead a sort of savage existence till his father's anger had blown over; but he had not come to the right person to aid him in such a project as this. Killian had soothed and reasoned, sympathised and scolded, by turns; and though at first Evert had only raged, and lamented that he had not gone to Dirk Wessel's instead—to whom he infallibly would have gone had he not happened to have quarrelled with him the day before—he had gradually been brought to his better senses, and finally had consented to relinquish the playgoing, on condition that Killian would use his influence with M. Ryckman to prevent the fulfilment of that hated plan for consigning him to the drudgery of a merchant's office. Young Barentse, in his faithful love for Franzje, was nothing loth to do a good turn for Franzje's brother; and finding that the father had set his face against "having the boy hanging about idle any more," had offered to take him as a companion in the trading voyage among the Indians, upon which he was just going to set forth. To this, after a good deal of hesitation, M. Ryckman had consented; and so now, instead of being on his way to New York, Evert was getting ready for an expedition which was exactly after his own heart, since it promised a goodly share of adventure, and gave him some of the privileges of a man before his time.

" I wish the war had not begun again," sighed Franzje, as she finished off one stocking with a grand flourish of her knitting-pins, and began upon another ; " if that foolish. boy were really going by himself, we should not have a moment's peace about him. It is the greatest compliment that Mother could pay you, Killian, to trust him to you."

" Not the *greatest*," said Killian under his breath ; " that would be to trust some one else to me."

She would not pretend to misunderstand him ; but she turned her face away with a sort of sad impatience, that showed him he was getting on dangerous ground.

" I did not mean to vex you, Franzje," he pleaded ; " I will promise you to say nothing till I come back from my voyage."

" I wish you would promise me *never* to say anything ! " she answered in a voice of suppressed earnestness.

He looked at her, and half opened his lips to speak, and then looked again, and with a sort of inward fire flushing his tawny cheek, replied, " I cannot promise that ; I will wait, I will bide my time ; but it is hard to have nothing before me in the future, nothing to work for."

" Oh ! if you could but be what the Dominie hoped and wished ! " she said, suddenly lighting up into eager animation. " I shall never forget how he talked of it one day in the little chestnut grove near the Wendels'. It would make me so glad to feel that *one* of us had not disappointed him, that *one* of us was faithful to the vocation he had marked out for us."

" I know what you mean," said Killian meditatively ; " you want me to be a missionary to the Indians some day; but even if I did set that before me, I do not see that one hope need destroy the other."

"I think it would," she answered with grave gentleness; "the Dominie said a true missionary must be content to have 'the Lord for his inheritance,' and forego many things which fall to the lot of other men."

"Other men are welcome to everything else that I have cared about, but not to *you*," said Killian, with something of boyish sulkiness and defiance.

And she smiled at him as from some far-off height, as she made answer, in the soothing tone she would have used to Arij, "O Killian! you need not be afraid; I shall be proud to be your friend always, and I shall never be more than that to anyone now."

"How can you tell, when you are so young?" he said, looking at her with puzzled eyes, as if she were getting beyond his comprehension.

For one instant there came a mist of tears between her and her work; she felt that it was possible to have one's story out while that of others was but beginning. In another minute she had raised her head brightly, and answered with brave gaiety, "I am going to be like my great-aunt; she was the one single woman of Albany in those days, when it seemed just as much the fashion for everybody to marry as it is now. She brought my father and his brothers up, you know, when Grandmother died, and made it her boast that no one ever set a stitch in their clothes but herself. I believe that she made Grandfather's too."

"Not knowing that they would one day assist a young rascal of a grandson in making his escape from his father's house," said Killian, turning to Evert with a laugh, his jealous fears about Mr. Vyvian somewhat relieved by Franzje's determined assertion of her intended spinsterhood.

"What's that you're saying?" rejoined Evert; "do come and look at this gun. I wish Father would have given me a new one. I should like to have a good bang at the French if we meet them."

"We sha'n't," said Killian, mindful of Franzje's anxieties. "I am not going to take you into danger, young man. Our friends, the Mohawk scouts, will get us news of the enemy, and we shall be able to steer our canoe out of harm's way."

"Do you think much will be done in this campaign?" asked Franzje, and an indescribable something in her tone made him feel that she was not asking altogether for his sake, nor for Evert's either.

"I don't know," he answered, rather gloomily; "they talk of making a fresh attack on Crown Point, you know; and Messervé has been required to raise another New Hampshire regiment; and Colonel Waldron and Peter Gilman"—the two Commissaries who resided at Albany—"are just sending off a grand supply of stores. If it were not for Evert, I think I should throw up my voyage, and get employed in the Commissariat, or else go and enlist."

It did not look much like being a missionary; but Franzje saw that it was pique which made him speak thus; and Evert burst out, "Don't talk as if *I* kept you from the war; I should be only too glad to go to it myself if Father would but let me. You should have heard me describing what a battle is like to Engeltje yesterday. Didn't I make it a fine picture of horrors! and didn't I enjoy seeing her eyes start out of her head with fright!"

"It was very cruel of you," remonstrated Franzje.

"Not a bit. *You* don't pity her, do you, Killian? If you had seen her run crying to Franzje for comfort, as I did, you would have been as angry as I was. Making

s 2

eyes at Franzje's lover, indeed! and crying after him as if he were hers!"

It was not the custom to treat love-affairs as mysteries in Albany, and Franzje had no great reason to be surprised at her young brother's discernment; but a blush mounted to her very forehead, as rising and gathering up her work she said, hastily, "Evert, the thought of your trip with Killian has sent you quite off your balance. I will not stay to hear little Engelt mocked at. I shall go and help Mother make the pies for your supper."

"You will come and see us off to-morrow, won't you?" said Killian, hurrying to open the door for her with a courtesy which he had learnt from Mr. Vyvian.

"Yes, I suppose that saucy Evert will have us all out to see the last of him," she said.

She knew that was not the sort of answer the youth longed for, and even his Indian immobility could not hide from her the signs of his mortification; but she said no more except "Good-bye for to-day," in a cordial tone, and as she had both her hands full, she could not even shake hands with him.

She was bound for the kitchen; but somehow or other she went to it by way of her own room, and tarried there for a minute, with quivering face and heaving breast, thinking sad thoughts, which she was far too brave to utter in human hearing. They were not all about Killian, by any means; but at the end she said to herself, with a sort of wistful regret, "I should like to have been kinder; he is so kind to me, poor boy! but I must never deceive anyone again, nor let anyone love me, if I can help it."

She did not see Killian any more till the next morning, when, after an early breakfast, the whole family and household, with the exception of Uncle Jan, turned out

to witness Evert's departure, and wish both the youths
good luck in their voyage. One or two other young men
were going to start at the same time, so the river bank
was crowded with friends and well-wishers, some of them
cheery and hopeful, predicting a safe and happy return,
others—among whom was Madame Ryckman—anxious
and tearful, with scarcely courage to do more than pray
that their fears might not be verified. There was really
good grounds for their anxiety, for in steering towards
the Canadian frontier, there was no saying with what
dangers the young voyagers might not meet; and though
they had promised to avoid the track of war, and to seek
only the haunts of friendly Indians, the perils of the way
were sufficient at the best of times to make the hearts of
mothers and sisters tremble. The little bark canoes looked
almost too frail for their load of blankets, guns, powder,
beads, &c. ; and amid all this store of goods for exchange,
there seemed but little room for any provision for the
comfort of the traders. A small stock of dried meat and
Indian corn meal, and a keg of spirits, was all that they
had with them in the way of food ; and for further supplies they were to depend entirely on their own skill with
gun and rod, and the hospitality of the Indians.

Nevertheless, they all wore a most happy, satisfied expression, except one lad of eighteen, who was already
married, and who evidently found it hard to tear himself
away from the clinging embrace of his child wife, though
his parents—who had accepted the fact of his imprudent
marriage with the easy good-nature characteristic of Albany
—were comforting him with assurances that they would
take care of her, and counselling him to be sharp in his
bargains with the Indians, and bring back enough furs
to win the means of furnishing a house for her on his
return.

"I hope *I* shall get enough to buy a schooner," said Evert, in his gay, sanguine tones, "and then I shall go sailing up and down the river all summer, and be as happy as a king!"

In the slight, half-Indian garb usually worn by the traders, his fine muscular figure showed to great advantage, and already his blooming, boyish·beauty seemed to be getting a touch of manliness; but his speech was childish enough to make his father answer drily, "If you have earned the price of one by the time you are two-and-twenty you may think yourself lucky. You will be more trouble than profit to Killian this voyage; and so long as you bring home your own skin safe and sound, we won't ask how many moose-skins you have got to your share."

"Monsieur Evert going to be Monsieur Killian's black boy!" grinned Jettje, with friendly jocularity; and in truth, Evert was going to fill that place in his friend's canoe which in the others was occupied by the slave of the owner; but though a general laugh greeted the old negress's sally, Evert was not in the least disconcerted.

"I think I am the blackest of the two, Jettje," said Killian, who in his new apparel was scarcely distinguishable from one of the aborigines, except that there was more olive than red ochre in the tints of his complexion, and more sensitiveness than stolidity in the expression of his mouth; and then drawing near to Franzje, he said in a low voice, "I know you will bid me God-speed when I tell you that I have remembered the Dominie's horror of our tempting the Indians with 'fire-water.' I have no spirits among my cargo, except a small stock of it for Evert's and my own consumption when we have to cross swamps or sleep on damp moss. If I cannot be a teacher of good things, at least I won't tempt to evil."

Her eyes thanked and praised him, though she only said, " Have they got it in the other canoes ? "

" Yes ; and Jansen Bleeker says that it is madness to attempt to trade without it, but I am content to take my chance. Did you know that he came back from New York last night ? He has sold his furs well, and talks of marrying Cornelia at once. It is just as well he did not arrive before Mr. Gardiner departed."

" I am sure she cares most for Jansen really ; she has known him all her life," said Franzje, unthinking of the inference which might be drawn from the words.

" Does that ensure love ? " returned Killian, with something wistful, almost reproachful, in his beautiful, melancholy glance. " Look, Franzje," he added, without waiting for a reply, " Marte has his bride, and Dirk and Asa have each their sweetheart ; see how different it makes their setting-out from mine."

She looked as he bade her, and a little, bright blush rose to her face as she marked the demonstrative public farewells of the two betrothed maidens. Killian, as he stood there brave and solitary, without father or mother, without a single creature belonging to him to bid him good-bye, except a confidential slave of his old grandfather's, who was taking care of the canoe while he made his adieux on the shore, did seem to deserve a happier fate than to be sent forth without an encouraging word, with nothing to keep his heart warm amid dangers and difficulties but his own hopeless, unrequited love. And yet, what could she say to him ? She did love him after a certain sort, but not in the way he wished, and it seemed to be her fate to wound the very people for whom she cared the most.

She put out her hand to him, and her face was kind, sorrowful, almost tender, as she said, " Killian, I am so sorry ; if you would only not have cared for me ! I do thank you with all my heart for your goodness to Evert, and I do pray God to bring you safely back. If the Dominie should come back before you do, I will tell him how you remembered his teaching, and I am sure he will say that you have God's blessing as well as his."

It was sweetly and nobly spoken, and it was something to feel that trembling hand within his clasp, and to see a tear glisten in the soft azure of those matchless eyes ; but when she turned from him to Evert, and he saw the loving kisses that rained down upon the boy, who would scarcely so much as tarry to receive them, he might be pardoned for knitting his black brows with a sudden, bitter pang of envy, and striding away to his boat without remembering to bid good-bye to his staunchest ally, kind Madame Ryckman.

Another minute, and even the three happy lovers were off also, and away sped the four frail barks over the bright waters of the Hudson, shaping their course northwards, towards the waterfall which would prove the first difficulty in their arduous journey, but which, like most well-known dangers, scarcely troubled anybody in comparison with the undefined prospect of howling wolves, unhealthy swamps, trackless forests, poisonous rattlesnakes, unfriendly Indians, encounters with French traders, and various other by no means impossible perils which loomed before the imagination of mothers and sisters and sweethearts. Fathers and brothers for the most part pooh-poohed the mention of danger ; not that they could deny its existence, but because it was so completely a matter of course that an Albanian youth should encounter it in the pursuit of gain, as a preparation for that settlement in life to which they all naturally looked, that they could scarcely understand why their womenkind should make a fresh grievance of it from year to year. Had not those comfortable storekeepers, or masters of trading vessels, all done as much in their time? and had not they come back safe again and again from their summer expeditions, and sold their spoils prosperously in New York each winter, and married and settled, and surrounded themselves with " four-posters and crockery-ware "—to use Mr. Vyvian's contemptuous words—and would not the five· young adventurers of this morning be able to do the same, if only they had the good sense to keep out of the way of the French army, and resist the temptation of enlisting in the Anglo-American corps?

At tea that evening, Madame Ryckman let her tears run down over the huge delf tea-pot, ornamented like the one in Knickerbocker's History, with "paintings of fat little Dutch shepherds and shepherdesses, tending pigs, with ·boats sailing in the air, and houses built in the clouds, and sundry other ingenious Dutch fantasies," and informed Franzje that that had been her husband's first gift to her, and that she hoped Evert would some day present his bride with just such another, " If he should live to come back, and grow up, and marry, poor fellow ! "

" I don't think he has a fancy for anyone as yet, and there is not a girl in the Company that is really good enough for him," went on the warm-hearted mother, with true motherly partiality. " I have thought at times that Engeltje Banker would make a good wife for him some day—and though she is a little older than he, a baby face like hers is sure to *look* young always—but now she can think of nothing but that worthless Englishman."

" That will pass," said M. Ryckman tranquilly ; "she will find out sooner or later that it was only fooling, and then she will be glad to take up with an honest lad like our Evert."

Franzje had listened with parted lips, and a bright spot on either cheek; when her father had ceased speaking, and the children had run away to play, she said earnestly, "It may not have been only fooling. I do not think Mr. Vyvian has given *us* any reason to distrust his honourable intentions."

Decided as Franzje was by nature, and ready to think for herself, it was so seldom that she advanced an independent opinion, that her parents looked at her in surprise.

"Then you think, my maid, that a man may be ready to marry one lass on Wednesday, and another on Thursday," said her father in his slow, deliberate tones. "It isn't the way with us Dutchmen, but it may be with your fine, town-bred Englishmen. I don't pretend to understand them."

Franzje winced under this plain setting forth of the case; but not the less did she answer bravely, "I would rather think that he could change, than that he could play with Engelt and deceive her. Don't let us judge, Father; let us wait and see.—And, Mother, please let me have Engelt here sometimes, for Keetje mocks at her, and the child can hardly bear it."

A short while before, the parents would have laughed to hear their little Franz talking of a young companion with that air of tender, unconscious patronage; but somehow, in the last week they had learned to feel that she was a woman now, and to begin to treat her as such; so her father answered readily, "Ay, my maid, she shall come when she likes, and neither Mother nor I will taunt her, I promise you; but Keetje will be too busy with her own love-affairs now to think much about Engelt's. Jansen Bleeker has turned out as broad-shouldered, manly a fellow as you could desire to see. I wish that poor lass Anna Gerritse had such another sweetheart to come

and cheer her up. They do say her father curses the day
that ever the regiment came into the town."

"Well he may," said Madame Ryckman, pursing up
her lips, and. shaking her head with an air of mystery.
" I hope we shall have no more soldiers quartered here
but the Royal Americans. The mayor says we shall have
plenty of regiments marching through before the war is
done, but that if the rendezvous continues to be at
Number four, they will none of them stop here above a
night. How I wish we could let our Dominie know that !
If he could but have foreseen how quickly we were to get
rid of Colonel Trelawny and his crew, perhaps he would
never have gone away."

"I don't know but he did the wisest thing, though,"
said M. Ryckman, turning away from the table, and
puffing at his pipe. "People are beginning to find out
what he was worth to them, now that they have lost
him. It's surprising to see how the tide has turned
already. Scarce a soul has a good word for the officers
now, nor a bad one for the Dominie. Please God he may
come back soon !"

Franzje could not help thinking the general feeling
against the officers rather ungenerous, considering how
much some of the townspeople had made of them when
they were on the spot ; but she echoed her father's con-
cluding wish from the very depths of her heart. There
was a strange flatness and vacuity about her life, now that
the Dominie and Mr Vyvian, and even Killian, were all
gone away; and Evert's absence took much from the
brightness of her home-party, for his saucy gaiety and
enterprise had been wont to enliven them all. Jan was a
dull, quiet, plodding boy, with whom she had scarcely a
thought in common, and she had no girl friend to whom
she could turn for sympathy, for her quondam ally, Cor-

nelia, had shown herself too giddy and hoydenish during
the sojourn of the regiment in the town to be quite after
her own heart any longer, and was moreover absorbed in
the interest of her approaching marriage with young
Bleeker. Engeltje was loving and gentle as ever, and
humbly grateful to Franzje for not treating her as an obnoxious rival; but to listen to her innocent raptures
about Mr. Vyvian, and her apologies for having dared to
care for him, was not very congenial work, and of course
no word of wounded love or wonder at his changeableness
could be breathed to _her_. So Franzje took refuge in
silence; and while performing with careful minuteness her
duties as daughter of the house, and being more regular
than ever in her visits to the sick and suffering, especially
to the Dominie's favourite, old Vrow Dorckman, who was
still lingering in patient misery, she grew to be much
fonder than before of spending all her leisure by herself,
or in the silent company of her Uncle Jan. Sometimes
she would sit for a long while at his feet, turning over the
leaves of one of his favourite Psalm-books and now and
then reading a verse to herself; but more often she would
let the book fall on her knee, and her gaze would become
fixed and dreamy, and her thoughts would go wandering
away out upon the broad Atlantic with the Dominie, or
following the march of the troops who were assembling
for the attack on Crown Point. She could no longer
think of the young soldier as her chosen knight, her ideal
hero; if a word could have brought him to her side she
would not have spoken it. In the chapel, that memorable
Sunday morning, she had thought to part from him at
the cost of a broken heart; but now she recognized that
no heart had been broken in the parting, that her life
might be always a little desolate, and other men distasteful
to her, but that her strength was good for living and en

during, and the world by no means a desert, though the
magical Elysian brightness that once hung about it had
faded. She did not ponder as much as some girls might
have done on the question as to whether his sudden atten-
tions to Engeltje had been the result of pique or of inconstancy ; nor would she admit the supposition that they
had meant absolutely nothing, and the poor little one was
wasting her heart in vain. " No, he was not a deceiver,"
she said to herself, and she never sought to define exactly
what he was, only she knew with painful, miserable certainty that the noble qualities she had so loved in him
had been very much the work of her own imagination
—that her womanhood had begun with a mistake which
could never be undone.

And in these hours of disappointment and self-abase-
ment her heart turned . back to the Dominie, with something of its old filial, trusting devotion, mingled with a
new remorse and dread, for which, in earlier days, there
had been no cause. Would he ever come back ? and if he
did, would he ever forgive her, and not only forgive,
but condescend to be her guide in the higher, more earnest life, which she hoped to live for the future ? Mr.
Vyvian's words about his " cowardly departure " rang in
her ears. Had it been cowardly to fly from the pains and
difficulties of his position ? to leave his rebellious flock to
their own devices ? She would not let herself think so.
She had been too ready to judge him, to distrust his
wisdom, to ascribe his strictness to narrow prejudice ;
now, in her earnest repenting, she was ready to think
him wholly right, and herself wholly wrong. Oh ! if he
would only come back, and let her prove to him that she
was sorry !

Easter came—a dull, sorrowful Easter to the Dutch
congregation, which was left pastorless and forsaken,

and specially sad to Franzje, who had hoped then to be
admitted as a "Church member," and who now felt that
her admission must be deferred indefinitely. Something
was said about borrowing a minister from New York, and
her father and M. Jansen made a journey to the capital
to see what could be done, but came back unsuccessful.
There were but one or two ministers in the city, and
none of them could be spared from their post; moreover,
the New York "Kerke-raad" had heard of the dissipated
doings in Albany, and, instead of showing any sympathy
with the two elders, administered a public rebuke to them
for not having managed matters better, so that they returned crest-fallen, and rather out of humour. A sort
of lay service was to be held in the chapel, as had become usual on Sundays, but the crowning rite—the Easter
Feast—must needs be wanting; and the more serious-
minded among the community went about their business
silently and sadly, feeling themselves severely punished
for their want of zeal in the Dominie's cause. "If we
had all stood by him more bravely, we might have made
head against godless innovations," admitted some of the
candid-minded, sorrowfully; and then Elder Jansen turned
round on them with that unsparing "I told you so,"
which is calculated to give the finishing touch to poor
weak mortals' dejection.

It chanced that early on Easter morning Franzje received a summons to Vrow Dorckman's bed-side. The
old woman had announced that she had been "called"
in the night, and that she wished to speak to her young
friend before she died. What she said was not very
novel, nor impressive; but, coming from those pale,
trembling lips, it carried a certain importance with it;
and when she wound up by saying, "I should like to
have had our Dominie near me to-day, but I shall see

him again, never fear—perhaps long before you do, my
child," Franzje started, and felt as if the words were a
prediction, and as if the wonderful clairvoyance of
death were revealing to the sufferer things which her
own young heart panted vainly to know.

"Do you think the Dominie is going to die?" she
asked, holding her breath for the answer, as if it would
really determine the pastor's fate ; but the old Vrow only
murmured something unintelligible, and her nurse came
forward, and said she had talked too much already, and
that Franzje had better go.

So the girl went forth from the darkened room, with
her heart throbbing and trembling, and felt the glory of
sunshine in the outer world almost oppressive for the
moment, and longed for some quiet corner to kneel down
in, that she might pray for the departing soul, and ask
that the Dominie might be blessed and comforted, and
spared to come back to them, and that she might be forgiven for having helped to drive him away.

The outer door of the English church was open as she
passed it, and knowing that it was not yet the usual hour
for service, she felt a sudden impulse to take refuge there,
and retracing her steps, entered the porch, and, pushing
back the inner door with a gentle hand, stole softly in,
closing it after her. She had thought to find an empty
church, and by the deep stillness that prevailed, it might
well have been so ; but, on the contrary, it was the
fullest she had ever seen, and the congregation of the
strangest. Kneeling in profoundest reverence, with their
mantles drawn over their heads so as completely to veil
their faces, were upwards of two hundred Indians of
both sexes, as motionless as if carved in stone, and evidently wholly absorbed in adoration of "the Great
Spirit," Whom they had been taught to worship "in

spirit and in truth." The altar was vested in a fair
linen covering, and a white-robed priest was standing
before it, preparing to celebrate the Christian Mysteries.
To Franzje it was all strange and new, and beautiful,
and awful. She did not remark that the building was
small and mean, that the fittings of the Sanctuary were
of the commonest. She did not say to herself that these
were the Mohawks come into the town for their Easter
Communion, and that surpliced figure was Dr. Ogilvie,
the English minister, whom she had seen hundreds of
times before. A voice within her said, "It is Easter
here," and at the first sound of the "Our Father," she
dropped upon her knees in a dark corner near the door,
and remained a silent, breathless, motionless worshipper
throughout the whole of the service.

English was almost as familiar to her as Dutch, so that
she had no difficulty in following the words of the Office,
and their very novelty only made them more impressive,
more thrilling and appealing to her agitated spirit. Deprived of true Eucharistic teaching, and taught to look
upon the Lord's Supper chiefly as a commemorative rite,
she had yet been bred up in deep reverence for It ; and
now an instinctive faith which she could not have de-
fined, and which surely was of no human implanting,
made her tremble and adore, as she became aware of a
Presence which had come suddenly in the midst " when
the doors were shut."

Pleading, pleading, pleading, from the Altar as from
the Cross ! pleading for her His unworthy child, for the
dying woman close by, for the pastor out upon the wide,
wild ocean, for the soldier marching into battle, for the
two young voyagers in their frail canoe ; pleading in the
might of His finished Sacrifice, His glorious risen Life,
His Ascension to the right Hand of the Father ;—oh !

how all things grew possible in the consciousness of that
availing Intercession !

Once she lifted her head as slowly, softly, solemnly,
the Red Men rose from their places and gathered round
the Altar band by band; and then she saw that another
white-vested priest, whom she had not remarked before,
had joined the celebrant, and that it was from the hand
of their beloved teacher, " the Father of the Deserts,"
that these simple-hearted Christians were receiving " the
Cup of Salvation." O blessed priest, and blessed people,
true sharers of their Lord's Easter joy ! and not all un-
blessed she who was permitted to touch Him by faith, to
recognize him as "made known in the breaking of Bread,"
even though the Feast Itself were not for her. He loved
her, He was near her, her life was to be lived for Him ;
she could not feel desolate or forsaken any more.

She was almost lost to outward things when at last the
deep hush that followed the words of Blessing was broken
by the stir of the rising congregation, and presently out
filed the Indians in silent dignity, while she drew further
back into the corner behind the door and watched them
pass. Some were stately old chiefs, with grim, war-worn
faces ; some were striplings, though with nothing of boyish carelessness about them ; and of the squaws, the elder
had a weary, trodden-down air, as if life had gone hard
with them in the old days before Christianity came to
soften the hearts of their lords and masters, while the
younger were bright and prosperous-looking, and held up
their heads with an air of quiet self-respect. They were
going back to their good brother Philip, as they called
Colonel Schuyler, and would sleep at the Flats that night,
as they had slept the night before, accommodated in the
way that best suited them—in the porch and some surrounding sheds ; and then in the dawn of the morning

T

they would assemble before the portico to sing their hymn of thanksgiving, and be off to the woods to follow their own hardy, independent mode of existence, not surely without some happy, thankful thoughts of the Blessing which had fallen to their lot on this Easter Day.

As Franzje left the church the bell began its summons overhead, calling the few English people in the city together for their Easter service ; and she was obliged to walk on quickly to join her own home-party, who were advancing up the street.

The Dutch hymn-singing was flat and spiritless that day, and Elder Jansen expounded in a way that was more gratifying to himself than to his audience ; but Franzje's heart was in a glow of grateful worship. That solemn service, shared with the simple children of the forest, had left its impress on her ; she had learnt that even on earth there may be foretastes of the fulness of joy which His Presence gives.

CHAPTER XVII.

The Irretrievable.

"I wish you a happier fate than wearing out your heart in waiting for the Dominie's return," Mr. Vyvian had said, tauntingly, when taking his farewell of Franzje ; and often and often during the remainder of the spring and through the hot, tedious summer those words haunted her, for a strong feeling of expectancy grew and grew as the months went by, and still no word came from the absent pastor, no promise that he would come back, no tidings even of his having reached the land of his destination.

There was something ineffably dreary in this abandonment and silence; and other hearts besides Franzje's ached and drooped, and other eyes turned longingly in the direction of the deserted Manse, feeling it hard to be deprived of counsel and support just at a time when they had most need of them.

It was one of the saddest and most anxious summers that the good city had known for a long time; the war was pursuing its weary course close by, with continued ill-success on the Anglo-American side; and the frequent passage of troops through the town, the summary requisitions of supplies, and the erection of a hospital for the reception of the wounded, brought it home as a reality even to quiet, phlegmatic, unexcitable people, who were apt to be engrossed in their own concerns, and to care little for news of the outer world. The tidings of the loss of Fort William Henry, and of the massacre of part of the disarmed garrison by the Indians on the French side, excited universal consternation; and now, as autumn advanced rapidly towards winter, people were anxiously awaiting intelligence from Fort Edward, where General Webb and the remainder of his army had retreated, expecting daily to hear that he was attacked by the French, who would surely not fail to follow up their recent victory by a fresh attempt upon the British posts.

"We never have any excursions now, like we had last autumn," grumbled Dirk and Albert Ryckman to their sister. "Is it because Evert's away, or because of the French?"

"I don't know," replied Franzje, absently, her gaze fixed on the opposite porch, towards which a wounded militiaman was limping his painful way.

"Why are you so stupid, Franz?" proceeded one of the little questioners; "that's only poor Arrian coming home from his walk. He told me such a long story about Colonel Goffe yesterday. *I* shall serve under Colonel Goffe when I'm old enough : but I don't see why we shouldn't have any fun because we're not big enough to fight. Don't you care about us now, that you never make fun for us ? "

The girl turned round with her tender, beautiful smile.

" My little hearts, have I seemed to neglect you ? We have all grown stupid, I think, in these anxious times. I will ask Mother if we may invite your Company, and we will take them to drink tea in the chestnut wood near the Wendels.' Madame Wendel will give us some hot water and some fresh milk, and we will ask all the little boys to join us, and have such fun."

" If our Company don't object to having other children mixed up with us," said Dirk, with a dignified air ; but Albert seized his sister's hands, and jumped up and down in a sort of exuberance of delight, forgetting all his fancied injuries in a moment, and ready to vote Franzje the very best sister that ever lived,

The party came off not long afterwards ; and Franzje, though not belonging to the same Company as her little brothers, was graciously allowed to accompany them and preside at the feast, in consideration of her having taken all the trouble of it. Blithe and gay as she seemed on the occasion, it was not all pleasure to her by any means : the chestnut wood had associations which were largely mingled with pain ; and yet she was glad to be there— glad to sit once more where she had sat with the Dominie, and to watch the evening sun shedding its radiance through the rifts in the heavy foliage, just as it had done on that well-remembered day.

When the children had finished their meal, and had gone off in an exploring party further up the glen, she lingered to collect the fragments, and to pack up mugs and plates; and presently Madame Wendel came out to help her, not at all sorry to have an excuse for a chat with some one from the city.

"It was kind of you to fix your pic-nic here, Franzje," she said; "it makes a rare treat for my little boys, who see nobody but just the Bleekers from year's end to year's end almost. Gerrit Bleeker and his wife were finely set up at his brother marrying Keetje Banker, but they don't say much about it now. She drove out to drink tea with them once in the spick and span carriage that Jansen brought her from New York, and she was as fine as a popinjay, and as gracious as Madame Rensolaer herself; but I didn't think much of her, and I don't think they did either. If Jansen had married Franzje Ryckman, I said, that *might* have been something to boast of."

Franzje laughed, but coloured also, and wished that good Madame Wendel would not be so personal. She was stooping down picking up the tea-cups, and was particularly glad to be so employed, when her frank-spoken friend went on, "Not that you are quite in your best looks to-day, Franzje. I did think, when you came here last autumn with the Dominie, that there couldn't be your match in the whole city for health and beauty; but though you have a pretty colour of your own still, you are not nearly so stout as you were"—stoutness was evidently a charm in Madame Wendel's opinion—"and your eyes have a ring round them as if you lay awake o' nights. I hope you're not pining after those fine English officers."

"No," said poor Franzje, simply and truthfully enough.

"For my part," continued the young housewife, who

really had too much good feeling to pursue her attack upon her visitor, "I owe them a grudge for having so upset our Dominie. The idea of his going away! I should as soon have expected to hear that the Town-hall was gone. I could scarcely credit Marte when he came in and told me, and I don't believe old Pete ever looked up from that day. Marte said, what odds did it make to us, who did not see him above three or four times a year? but I know I miss him sadly; and now that Pete's dead, there seems nobody to speak to us about Heaven and the way to get there, nor to see after the children's Catechism, nor anything."

"Don't they say it to you?" inquired Franzje, as she heaped up the plates together in a lofty pile, and proceeded to tie them up in a cloth.

"Oh yes, sometimes on Sundays; but they don't take half the pains in learning it for me that they did for the Dominie. He was strict with them, you know, and yet he was kind too. Franzje, they all loved him, I do believe, even the littlest of them, though some of them would run and hide when he came if they thought they had not got their lesson right. I never saw anybody that made one feel so ashamed of one's faulty ways, and so anxious to be good. When he looked at me, I used always to think he could see right down into my soul."

"Oh, I wish he could have!" said Franzje, lifting her head with a sudden eager sigh. "Then he would have seen that we were truer to him than he thought—that he need not have despaired of us altogether. I don't mean you, who were safe out here; but we of the city, who got into temptation, and displeased him."

"He could never have thought much harm of *you*, I should think," said Madame Wendel, looking kindly at the young face, which, though it had lost something of its roundness, had gained in depth and sweetness of expression.

"Oh, but he did, and I deserved it—in part. Madame Wendel, do you think he will come back? I feel as if nothing will prosper with us unless he does."

"Come back? oh, of course he will!" she rejoined cheerily, leaning to the bright side, as was natural to her; "he's just gone away in a grand sort of pet—I say a pet, because I can't think of a proper word for it—but he'll no more be able to keep away than I should from my children, even if they'd been ever so naughty. I fancy it was partly not being well in his health that made him take things to heart so; he looked as ill as possible the last time I saw him, and I think he'd been sitting too much over his big books. He gave *me* a book that day, and I've a great mind to show it you, for I can't make it out at all. It's all about predestination, and reprobation, and 'the final state of the damned,' and it gives me the shivers whenever I open it."

She started off to the house to find it; and Franzje, who after this unattractive description felt no great curiosity to see it, was still not sorry to have the chance of a few moments' solitude in that beautiful, shady place.

The sunlight flickered down here and there on the long, soft grass, and in the far distance came a mirthful sound of children's voices; but there was an intense coolness and greenness and sense of seclusion about the spot, and memory and hope seemed to meet there, as Franzje pondered silently over the past, and then turned to the bright anticipations awakened by Madame Wendel's cheerful words.

"Of course he will come back." Oh! how ready the young heart was to echo the assertion. It was so natural, so delightful, to believe that the anxious gloom of the last few months was to disperse in brightness after all, that the Dominie would certainly return, and that better times would come back with him.

The boys and girls of the Company of the Yellow were in a state of almost uproarious merriment on the homeward way, but Franzje could not find it in her heart to check them. Why should not they be glad and gay, when all nature was steeped in radiance round them, and everything seemed to speak of hope and joy, and the burden was lifted from her own spirit as if by magic? What harm was there in the songs that rose upon the air as the two great waggons creaked slowly along, in the shouts with which each vehicle which they chanced to meet was greeted? It was all perfectly innocent mirth, such as not even the Dominie himself could have condemned. Oh! suppose he was embarking at this very moment on his way back to them!

A soft breeze came up from the river, and caressed her cheek as she leant forward to meet it; a golden transfiguring glow was upon everything, just as it had been on the evening when she had driven home with the Dominie and her mother by the very same road; and even the houses in the town looked something more than common wood and stone, with their walls all shining, and their windows all ablaze in the intense glory of that sunset. Franzje could never pass the Gerritses' house without a thought of Mr. Vyvian; but there was no regiment marching out to impede the progress of the waggons, only a few townspeople standing about, and ready to return with kindly greetings the merry shouts of the children. Other children clustered at the doors, or came running into the road, as they got further into the town; and some ran along by their side, and were pelted with flowers,

which they gleefully threw back again; till at length,
when the *cortége* reached the Ryckmans', where the Company was to sup, it had assumed the character of a
triumphal procession. All was fun and brightness and
jollity; there was not a cloud in the sky, not a murmur
in the air, not the least shadow of coming evil to dim the
golden splendour of the day. As Franzje sprang gaily
down, and went smiling up the steps with her arm round
two or three little necks, how could she guess that the
woe of her life was to meet her on the threshold?

She could never quite tell who formed the excited group
that were gathered in the hall; she never quite knew
who it was that spoke first to her, nor what were the
words they said. She had a vague impression of seeing
the Patroon standing up straight and stiff, holding a letter
in his hand; of M. Jansen gesticulating in the back-
ground; of her father and Jan bending over a convulsed
figure which she took to be her mother; who else were
there, and what they looked like, she never could
remember. But *somehow* her startled senses grasped the
fact that the Dominie would come back to them no more,
that he was dead—*drowned*, some one was saying; oh!
could it be true?—"dead, dead, as surely as you stand
there alive," some one else reiterated; drowned, yes, really
drowned, and lying still beneath the blue waters of the
Atlantic, while she stood there in the sunset glory, full of
life and youth, with her bright hair wreathed with flowers!

One of the little children who were clinging to her,
understanding well enough to be frightened, burst into a
loud wail; and roused to her accustomed thought for
others, she mechanically opened the door of the big
parlour where the supper was laid, and drew them in
there.

Then she met the others, who were thronging up the

steps, hushed their boisterous merriment, and ushering them also into the supper-room, shut the door upon them. In another moment she was bending over her mother. "I will see to her if you will go and take care of the children, Jan," she said, in a voice which sounded strange even to herself; and Jan went readily enough, leaving her to assist her father in guiding poor Madame Ryckman's steps to her own big chair in the accustomed sitting-room, where she might give way to her grief in comparative privacy, and find a support for her quivering frame.

"Is he really drowned, Father?" Franzje asked, as they went along.

"Ay, my girl," was the answer, in gruff sorrowful tones.

And then she could not find courage to ask anything more.

M. Ryckman went back to the group in the hall, but Franzje remained with her mother, kneeling on the floor beside her, and offering her tender breast as a pillow for the bowed aching head. She had not time to think of her own loss, her own grief, and the weariful remorse which was keenest of all; her whole heart was bent upon soothing the more demonstrative sorrow before her, and her soft kisses and low murmurs of love came in that natural spontaneous flow, which belongs by right to those chosen souls whose mission it is to be the comforter of others.

But a terrible shock was still in store for her.

"He can't have thrown himself overboard—it *must* be false!" sobbed the poor lady, with a sort of passion breaking through her heavy grief; "we who knew him, know he was the last person to be guilty of such a crime as that. I shall always deny it, whatever anybody says; and you must do the same, Franzje."

She spoke as if Franzje had already heard the report, and disbelieved it; but the girl started away from her with wide wild eyes, and cheeks that had grown suddenly white with a new awful terror.

"That is not what they say, is it?" she gasped. "Drowned! does it mean *that?* Mother, mother, tell me!"

There was not a tear in the blue eyes, but their strained fixed look of anguished appeal remained in the mother's memory to her dying day.

It was her turn to offer comfort. "Don't look at me like that, my child," she sobbed, drawing the girl's head down upon her own shoulder. "I forgot you had not heard the Patroon read the letter. It said the Dominie had either fallen overboard or thrown himself over, and that the sailors all believed the latter; but neither you nor I need believe it, nor anyone that loved him. It's easy for those sailors to say so, who did not know or care for him; but I hope he did not live a godly life among us for all those years and years without convincing us that *he* was not the man to put an end to himself in that wicked way. I thought I should have choked when I heard M. Jansen cry out that that was what we had driven him to, with our worldliness and our sinful pleasurings. *He* to believe it! he who knew our Dominie so well!"

"Did the letter say what made the sailors think so?" asked Franzje, in a voice so unnaturally calm as to contrast strangely with her mother's excited tones.

"Did it? I forget," said Madame Ryckman, all in confusion. "Where are you going to, my child?" as Franzje rose quickly to her feet. "To see the letter? Ah yes, you must be quick, or the Patroon will be gone; he is going to the Flats." And then, as Franzje left the room, she relapsed into a fresh paroxysm of grief, rocking herself to and fro as she sobbed out, "It's pretty near broken her heart, poor child! and well it may. To think that our Dominie should be drowned, and that people should be found to slander him even in his grave!"

Madame Ryckman's utter incredulity regarding the terrible reports of the manner of the Dominie's death, and her intense indignation against the "slanderers" as she considered them, were really a kind of support to her; so that, violent as her grief was, there was no such utter intensity in it as there was in Franzje's. All that the girl had heard of the Dominie's moodiness, of the strange state of hard despair in which he had gone forth from among them, flashed back upon her memory with agonizing vividness as she ran out into the hall to entreat for a sight of the letter which had brought all this woe to the house. "That is what you have driven him to!" Oh! could it be true? Did life really hold such possibilities of retribution for faults committed, like hers, in the mere thoughtlessness of youth?

She was too late; the Patroon had gone, and her father and M. Cuyler were descending the steps together; while M. Jansen, whom no grief could subdue, was lingering for a parting admonition to the weeping negroes, who had gathered from kitchen and stable to hear the sad tidings, and a few of the children, who had stolen out from the supper-room to learn more particulars than Jan would tell them.

"Take warning," he was saying, as Franzje came upon the scene; "take warning, all of you, and abstain for the future from all godless pleasurings." And then, as his eye fell upon her, his zeal waxed fiercer with the sense of having now got hold of one of the real culprits, and, in his harsh, cracked voice, he added, pitilessly, "And you, my fine wench, it is time you left off bedizening yourself

with flowers. Your fickle gallant will never leave Fort
Edward alive, I warrant you, and it will be poor comfort
to think it was for his sake you drove our Dominie to an
untimely end. 'Tis because of you and such as you that
he lies under the sea, and you may well go in sackcloth
for your sins till your dying day, and put off for ever those
gauds that so ill become a Christian woman!"

He was pointing with scornful finger to the rich
crimson flowers that the children had twined amid that
wealth of flaxen hair, to the gay yellow streamer that they
had pinned in sport to the little white tippet that covered
Franzje's shoulders; and she was fronting him with her
beautiful, sad face, and that same fixed look of anguished
appeal as she had turned upon her mother. How could
she care what he said to or of her, when all that she
wanted was to know the truth about the Dominie!

The negroes and the children, who were by no means
so indifferent, were gathering round as if to defend her;
and Jettje in particular was advancing towards the fiery
little Elder, with a determined, "You go 'long!" when,
gliding among them, came the unexpected apparition of
the recluse, who, in the general excitement, had been forgotten by everyone. He had been standing on the stairs
a silent listener, and now advanced to Franzje's side, and
cast his arm about her.

"Silence, my friend," he said, raising his other arm
authoritatively, and drawing up his usually bent figure to
its fullest height. "You do this maiden wrong by your
words, and still more do you wrong our Dominie when
you speak as if it were certain that he had brought his
fate upon himself. It *may be* that disease brought a cloud
over his brain, and that in a delirium, as it were, not
knowing what he did, he cast himself into the waves; but
still more likely is it that through some accident he fell,

and as none, it seems, were by to see, none have the right
to affirm that it was not so."

"The sailors all believe—" began M. Jansen, angrily;
but the grey beard stopped him with unwonted peremp-
toriness.

"Ay, I know; but a belief of that kind is a belief, not
a knowledge nor a certainty; we who knew him, among
whom he lived, have a right to *our* belief, and God grant
it may be the true one! Dear little children, and friends
all, this is the whole story, as the master of the vessel
wrote it to our Patroon, and as the Patroon read it here
in this hall scarce a quarter of an hour ago.—On the voyage to Holland, our Dominie was observed to be sad and
full of thought; he spoke little, and walked often on
deck alone. One evening, when he had gone above for
this solitary walk, he appeared no more; search was made
for him when he was missed, and a boat lowered, but no
trace of him was found. The sailors said at once he must
have thrown himself overboard; the captain thinks he
must have become giddy when he was leaning over the
vessel's side, watching the waves according to his wont,
and must have fallen accidentally. The man at the helm
neither saw nor heard anything, for the wind was loud,
and his whole attention fixed upon his work. This is all
we know concerning our dear minister's fate. Doubtless
the waves received him; but the exact spot where he
fell, and the exact manner of that fall, none can say.
God, Whom he loved, has taken him to rest, and it is with
him, as with Moses, "no man knoweth of his sepulchre
unto this day."

The speech, so strangely long for the silent old man,
was ended, and there was a hush, broken only by the un-
restrained crying of the negro women and children. The
little Dutch Americans were too awed and bewildered to

cry; it sounded to them like a story, a melancholy tale
full of a certain mysterious fascination, like those legends
that their mothers would sometimes tell them just at this
hour, when night was dropping suddenly down, and putting out the splendour of the day.

"Do you think," said one of them, at last, in a low,
awe-struck tone, "that God may have prepared a big fish
to swallow our Dominie, just as He did for Jonah, and
that so he may get to land, and come back some time to
preach to us?"

"I've got such a big gourd, all my own, for him to
sit under!" cried out a younger child, without the
slightest perception of the absurdity of the suggestion;
and then the negroes tittered even in the midst of their
tears, and M. Jansen gave a contemptuous snort, and
wrapping his cloak round him, prepared to go.

He stopped on the threshold, however, arrested by
Uncle Jan's voice, once more raised in clear, emphatic
tones. "Do not laugh at the children; God has strange
ways of deliverance for His servants even now. Since
none can say that they have seen the dead body of our
Dominie, I for one think it *possible* that he may yet come
back to us, that he may be hidden from us for a time
rather than taken from our head for ever. Let us each
pray that it may be so, and, in the visions of the night,
God may reveal to us whether it be so or not."

As he stood there in the gathering darkness, with his
tall, thin figure, and his flowing beard, and his thoughtful,
visionary face, he looked almost like some seer of old
enunciating some prophetic message. M. Jansen turned
on his heel and hurried away, snorting as he went; but
the slaves and the children gathered eagerly round the
speaker, full of excitement, and ready to embrace the well-
nigh impossible hope which had been suggested.

Franzje's two hands were locked tight round her uncle's
arm; now that M. Jansen was gone, she laid down her
head upon them, and silently in the darkness her tears
began to flow. *She* had no visionary expectations; she
knew with a calm, aching certainty, that the Dominie
would never come back, that not till the last awful day
would the sea give up its dead; but the great unutterable horror that had possessed her was lifted from her
soul. No, it was not with the guilt of self-destruction
upon him that the Dominie had passed into eternity:
sad indeed they had made him, broken-hearted perhaps,
but not desperate; he had lost faith in them, but not
in God, never in God! and so a merciful accident, a
delirium for which he was not accountable, a something
—no matter what, since it was no rash, sinful act, but
rather a putting forth of a Providential hand to draw him
to his rest—had taken him away for ever from the life
which he had found too bitter.

There rested on her—so she thought, poor, sorrowful
child!—and on all who had sinned with her, the guilt
of having wearied him out, of having broken his heart,
but not blood-guiltiness, not the utter misery of having
driven him to a doom which would have well-nigh wrecked
all hope for this world and the next, and wrapped his
very memory in unutterable darkness.

"Go in sackcloth!" yes, verily, when would the day
come that she should cease to mourn?—and mechanically
she put up her hand to pull the flowers from her hair—
but the mourning was all for her; there was peace now
for the Dominie, nothing could grieve or trouble him any
more.

The children came thronging out of the great parlour,
ready to disperse for the night; and Franzje went back to
her mother, whom she found sitting just where she had left

her, but quiet and composed now, as if the violence of
her grief were spent. For a little while they rested tranquilly in a mutual embrace, and then Madame Ryckman's
housewifely instincts re-asserted themselves, and she got
up and bade Franzje call for lights, and tell the maids to
be sure to have something nice ready for their master's
supper when he came home.

"He has gone round with M. Cuyler to tell the bad
news, I suppose," she said, " and a sad office it is for him,
dear good man! Put an extra lump of sugar in his Hol-
lands and water to-night, Franzje ; he has a sweet tooth,
my good man has, and we must get him to take his supper
as usual, if we can. We must eat and drink, whatever
happens, poor, weak creatures that we are!"

So things began to slip back into their usual course in
that natural inevitable way which sometimes seems hard
and heartless to the young and sensitive, but which older
people acquiesce in as being only one of the many incon-
gruities of this imperfect world, in which not even sorrow
can live on heroic heights, but must come down to attend
to everyday wants and trivial commonplace duties. To
Franzje the tedium of it all was very repugnant at first ;
what did it matter whether the churning turned out well
or ill, whether the four meals a day were served with their
usual regularity or not, whether the autumn preserves
proved a success ? what did anything matter, when the Dominie lay cold in his ocean grave, and regret for the past
was powerless, and hope for the future no longer possible ?

But after a while she grew to be glad that her mother
at least could find a solace in these little cares and in-
terests, and recognized that the continuance of the daily
routine did not imply forgetfulness ; that though the men
went to their stores or to their farms as usual, and the
matrons and maidens occupied themselves with their

U

wonted industry in household tasks, there was a general
heaviness of heart, which no industry could dispel.
Through his strong individuality, his real interest in his
flock, and his intense devotion to what he thought the
right, the Dominie had left his mark on the place in a
way which no one else had ever done. Even when his
people had been most out of humour with him, most
disposed to grumble at his love of power, and to try to
shake off his yoke, they had never ceased to respect him
in their secret hearts; and the intellectual gifts which
they had been so little able to appreciate, the enthusiasm
which had left their feelings unstirred, had yet made an
impression on such imagination as they possessed, so that
perhaps they had *admired* the Dominie all the more because they did not thoroughly understand him, because
he was so utterly unlike themselves. And now that he
was dead, now that the pathetic story of his fate had
been told from house to house, and commented on and
magnified till it had become the most dolorous of all
possible tragedies, there was but one universal feeling of
sorrow, largely mingled with self-reproach in the case of
those whose contumacy had helped to drive him from
among them. Few were found to blame his desertion of
them, few sat in judgment on his mistakes; had the Dominie come back in living presence, much might have
been said in self-justification, but before the accusing
shadow of their dead pastor nearly all tongues were
silent. He was dead, and in a certain sort their sins had
slain him; it was they who, by their frivolity, their dis-
obedience, their want of sympathy, had helped to send
him forth on this fatal voyage; they had had a prophet
among them, and they had not honoured him as such, and
behold, he was gone from them, never to return!

Out of the grief and the reverence there grew at length

something like a revival of hope. Wonderful stories began to be circulated—whence originating no one distinctly knew—of how the Dominie had been picked up by a passing vessel and carried off on a distant voyage, or had managed to swim to a neighbouring island and was living there as a hermit, passing his whole days in meditation and prayer; and however contradictory these legends might be in many of their details, they all united in the same conclusion—that he would some day come back to his people inspired with new wisdom, and that a golden era would then arise for Albany, in which all that was painful in the past should be forgotten. It was strange to see how minds not peculiarly imaginative by nature turned for comfort to these romantic possibilities, and how some in their simple faith were even ready to believe that God had worked a miracle in their Dominie's behalf. The accomplishment of predictions which he had uttered was pointed to as proof that he had been something more than a mere ordinary man; and people recalled his deep spiritual gaze, and the flights of religious eloquence in which he had so often soared above them, and said to one another that surely a life such as his could not have been cut short prematurely, that some providential interposition must have occurred to preserve him for the holy work which he might yet do on earth.

Franzje listened, and at times her eyes would light up as though a bright vision had passed before them; but young as she was, hers was not a mind that readily lent itself to illusions, and besides, there had been borne in upon her from the first an irresistible conviction that nowhere in this lower world was the Dominie to be found; that he had passed utterly away. She never forgot the chance words that had forced the truth upon her—" So surely as she stood there alive," with that passionate, trembling, loving, beating heart—so surely was he lying in the stillness of death, the grave, awful stillness, that no bewailings could break. Oh! how little her penitence availed; how all too late was the better mind that had come over his erring people! She was speechless, tearless, almost prayerless, as she realized it, crushed by that sense of the *irretrievable*, which is perhaps the most poignant cause of human heart-break.

He had warned her himself that the awaking might not come in time, but she had not heeded the warning; he had told her to remember when that day came that "the least expression of penitence would have been accepted had it been offered now;" and oh! she did remember it, with aching, sickening distinctness, when the remembrance was no longer availing, when that "now" had become the irrecoverable past. She was sorry, but she could never tell him so; she was ready to obey with the trusting filial obedience of her earliest and simplest days, but he would never again utter a command; she would have done anything in the world to serve him, but he needed service no more.

It was right, it was just; there was nothing against which she could rebel, nothing that she could say was undeserved; only she had not known that life could be so terrible, and justice so pitiless; her heart seemed frozen within her as she went about her weary way.

Her mother told her that she was growing white and thin, and lovingly begged her to get up her looks against Killian's and Evert's return, which was expected almost daily; her father's eyes rested on her anxiously from time to time, and he puffed away a great many doubts, and fears, and longings on her behalf together with the smoke from his evening pipe; but though they often talked

about the Dominie before her, they never seemed conscious
of anything which might make the loss of him more painful to her than it was to them or to Jan.   When her gaze
grew absent, M. Ryckman believed her thoughts had flown
to Fort Edward ; he had a great notion that love troubles
were the only ones a girl could have, or at least, the
only ones that could affect her deeply, and he believed he
had found a salve for her grief when he came home one
day with an important piece of military news.   Contrary
to all expectation, the French, instead of pursuingtheir
advantage, and attacking Fort Edward, had returned to
Canada, and there was therefore no fear of any further
hostilities till the following spring.   Colonel Trelawny's
regiment would probably return to Number four, or might
even be sent back to Albany for a while—in his secret
soul the worthy elder devoutly hoped that might not be
the case—and at any rate, Mr. Vyvian was safe from the
chances of war for the next six months.   He told it all
with good humoured elation and importance, and Franzje's
face did really brighten for a moment with a look of eager
interest which he mistook for delight.   He was pleased,
and yet he was a little frightened.   Was it well that she
should continue to care for Mr. Vyvian, when—even supposing that his heart was faithful to her, and that his love-
passages with Engelt had been nonsense—no alliance was
possible between them, since not even to make her happy
could it be admissible to give her in marriage to a worldling, and one, too, who had wrought such harm among
them all, and given such sore umbrage to their dead
pastor ?   He need not have been alarmed ; Franzje cared
for Mr. Vyvian in the way in which a faithful nature
always cares for anyone it has ever loved at all, and had
prayed for his protection in battle many a time, but more
for his soul's sake than because she ever hoped or wished

to see him again in the flesh; he had gone out of her life, and she had nothing more to do with him: it was not that she forgot or despised him, but that he seemed to belong to a past which could never revive—to that little bright foolish time of happiness, which had to be paid for with years of pain. She was glad, oh! heartily glad that he was safe, and that he would be out of peril for a while, but it was for his sake only, not for her own.

She spent some time in her Uncle Jan's room that afternoon, and by way of something to say, she told him the news, and when she had told it, she sank into one of those profound reveries which had become habitual to her in her hours of leisure. He seemed to be thinking deeply also, but for once his mind was occupied with her rather than with those abstruse meditations in which it was usually engaged. Those dreamy eyes of his, that seemed half closed to sublunary things, had pierced the veil of her gentle patient reserve more surely than any other eyes in the house; and though he had been content to keep silence hitherto, it seemed to him that the time to speak had come.

"My child," he said suddenly, "it is not for the young soldier, is it, that your heart is so heavy?"

"No, dear Uncle," she said softly, with her grave eyes turned upon him in a sort of awed wonder at his discernment.

"You are very young," he went on, "to bear your burden alone; why not let the old man share it? If the Almighty had taken our Dominie from us a year or two ago, should you have sorrowed as you do now?"

"No," she answered, almost inaudibly.

"And what has made the difference?"

She tried to speak, and faltered, and was silent. He waited with sweet, patient eyes, and a loving hand laid upon her head. Then out it came, in a burst of tears. "Oh, Uncle! because then I had never angered him, or only in such a way as could be forgiven the next minute; and now I have done wrong, and vexed and grieved him, and he has not forgiven me; and I am sorry, and he can never know!"

There was no immediate answer; and she grew ashamed of her vehemence, and was afraid that it had displeased him. "I did not mean to complain," she added, in humble heart-broken tones; "it is all right and just, and I have deserved it, only——" and there the voice died away in sobs.

"Only God's justice is very terrible? So it seems, my child, when we forget His love. Was it God or the devil, think you, that was nearest our Dominie at his death?"

She looked up at him with a startled, bewildered gaze, as she whispered, "God."

"Yes, surely, for what does the Holy Book say?— 'Because he hath set his love upon Me, therefore will I deliver him;' our Dominie loved God with all the force of a strong man's soul, and doubtless He Who gave the love rewarded it. Well, then, can you think if God was with him that he died unforgiving?"

"No; but he did not think I deserved to be forgiven."

"Does forgiveness wait for our deserts? There was one who came back to his father covered with sins, and 'when he was yet a great way off his father met him, and ran and fell on his neck and kissed him.'"

"But the Dominie did not know that I was sorry."

"Could that father have known unless God had revealed it to him? the embrace came before the prayer for pardon. You will say the Father in the parable means God. Well, be it so; but does not God give of His own loving-kind-

ness to His servants, to His shepherds? Our Dominie
went away despairing of us, but do you think he died
despairing of us? My child, I do not think it, though it
may but have been a lightning-flash at the last that
showed him his mistake."

"Mistake?" echoed Franzje, as if there were presumption in the sound.

" Yes, surely ; a mistake such as Elijah's, when he cast
himself under the juniper-tree, saying, ' It is better for
me to die than to live.' "

"But we drove him away by our sins," said Franzje.

Could it be a smile upon the old man's face! " Your
sins !" he said ; "poor child! so it is this that lies so
heavy at your heart. Could the Dominie see you now,
he would weep to see you weep ; but he is at rest, as we
trust, and be you at rest also. Are you thinking of him
as still bitter against you, as still angered and grieved,
that you mourn for him so much? Nay, earth's griefs
and stings are over ; he fears and frets and despairs no
longer, but is lost in the ocean of God's charity, and hopes
and loves."

Franzje's face was buried in her hands, and the low
gentle tones seemed to murmur on above her like something heard in dreams. They were as the very droppings
of balm to the bruised heart.

" If I could only see him again for one moment !" she
sobbed, but not in the crushed, hopeless accents in which
she had spoken before.

"And you *shall* see him. Have you forgotten the
great day of meeting, the day in which there can be no
more misunderstandings, for the secrets of all hearts shall
be revealed? Think of the pastor's joy, when he finds
some of the souls that he despaired of the brightest
jewels in his crown ! "

She did not take this to herself in any way, but the thought was comforting, even in its awfulness. In a few minutes she put her hand upon her uncle's knee, and said timidly, " Uncle Jan, help me to live so that I may not be a grief to him then ; I do not want my life to be like these last few weeks. I have nothing to look forward to, like other girls, but I will try to look *further* forward now. On Easter Day I seemed to see what life might be, and then this sorrow came, and blotted it out ; but it is coming back, coming out of my very grief ! "

She broke off, for her thoughts were growing too deep for words : how often the dawn of a new life has sprung from a *grave*, He whose Resurrection is the Church's hope alone can tell !

" You will live to comfort others," said the old man, tenderly ; " sometimes I fear that your lot has been cast in evil times. Our Dominie once said that this war was but the beginning of sorrows, and I seem to fancy that he was right ; but if so, there will be but the more work for those who live for God and their brethren, and are at the call of all who suffer. Your parents, I know, have other thoughts for you ; they think that in time Killian——"
She shook her head, and he continued, " Nay, then, I will not vex you by dwelling on their hopes ; it is more your mother's fancy than your father's, and will never be urged upon you against your will. I should have joyed to see you a happy wife, as well as another ; but I can well believe that one who has been formed by such a man as our Dominie, and who has had their fancy caught by a brilliant man of the world like Mr. Vyvian, could never be happy with a lad like Killian Barentse, single-minded and true-hearted though he be. God bless thee, my little one, and make thee happy in His own way ! "

She still felt as though happiness were not for her,

but she lifted her face up brightly for the old man's caress. Oh! how good it was that such comfort had been sent her through him just now, when she needed it so sorely.

She went about her daily tasks less sadly from this time forward, and seemed to put aside her own grief in care for the griefs and pains of others. Little Engelt was the first to claim her sympathy, for the regiment did not come to Albany; and, as time went on, and no letter or message came from Mr. Vyvian, the child began to droop sorely, and to feel that she had been deceived. "I thought all the summer he was too busy to write or even to think much about me, perhaps; but now that the fighting is over he must have plenty of time, and he might send me one word, at least, if he cared for me at all!" That was the piteous lament; and Franzje soothed and stilled it as best she might, finding after a while an unexpected assistant in Evert, who seemed to see a great deal more in his sister's pretty little friend now that he had come home, than before he went away.

With his bronzed complexion, and his sensible, thoughtful manner, he was like a totally different creature from the troublesome boy who had taken his departure in such giddy spirits. The trading expedition, with its toils and dangers, had made a man of him, and the shock of the news which met him on his return completed the sobering effect. Killian, after spending a day or two with his grandfather, went on to New York to dispose of his cargo; but Evert remained at home, and was his mother's great delight during that dreary winter, in which all attempts at gaiety seemed to stagnate, and which was marked by an unusual number of deaths among the elder citizens.

Saddest of all these losses was that of good Colonel Schuyler, whom everybody missed, and whose death left

Madame so desolate, that all her friends vied in offering
her attention and sympathy, feeling as if the childless
widow, whom everybody loved, had become the special
legacy of the whole town. Her sister and nieces were
much with her, but she had a craving for Franzje's company; and it was in ministering to this dear old friend—
the best she had ever had, except the Dominie—that the
girl began in earnest that tender mission of comfort which
the recluse had set before her as her life-work.

CHAPTER XVIII.

By the River Side.

"AND so we meet once more, Mademoiselle; and I lie
here and am tended by you, as if it were the most natural
thing in the world."

"And I am sorry that you have not a more skilful
nurse, Sir."

Certainly the little hands that were adjusting bandages
trembled somewhat; but the speaker was not so unskilful
as she called herself, and the occasion was one to draw
forth all her powers, and banish the awkwardness that
springs from self-consciousness.

It was the beginning of July, 1758; the unsuccessful
attack on the lines of Ticonderoga—where the young
Lord Howe was killed—had just been made; and the
hospital at Albany and the barns of some of the neighbouring proprietors were crowded with the wounded; poor
writhing, groaning wretches, whose piteous state evoked
the liveliest sympathy in the breasts of the kindly
Albanians. The great barn at the Flats had been fitted

up as a temporary hospital, and had proved a refuge for
those whose wounds were considered the most dangerous,
and who had therefore been sent on in boats the day after
the action, and conveyed with all possible speed to the
nearest place of reception.

Among these were Mr. Vyvian, and Killian Barentse—
a volunteer of a few months standing—and among the
nurses were not only the widowed Madame Schuyler and
her nieces, but Franzje Ryckman, who was now on her
knees beside the young officer's couch, applying a fresh
bandage to his wounded arm.

He had been shot through the left arm, and the bullet
had penetrated the side, so that at first he had been supposed to be mortally wounded, but after all no vital part
had proved to be injured, and he had been one of the
first to revive under the care of doctors and nurses, and
to find spirits and strength for talk. Killian was lying
insensible a little way off, and Franzje was surprised to
find how anxiously her heart turned to him even while
she was busied with other sufferers, and how compara-
tively indifferent to her was Mr. Vyvian's renewed cordiality. It was not that she was the least in love with
her old playmate, but that the sort of sisterly affection
she had for him was deeply rooted, and made her feel
almost as she might have felt if Evert had been in the
same sad case; whereas her girlish fancy for Mr. Vyvian
had been a transient thing, which his own unworthiness
had gone far to blight, and which had well-nigh faded
into insignificance since the great black cloud of sorrow
had swept over her life. She was a tender ministrant
to the wounded man, but the tenderness was more a part
of her womanliness than the result of any individual
feeling for him; it was not even quickened by the sense
of returning good for evil. She had ceased to think

his seeming fickleness an evil, and had almost forgotten
that she had anything to forgive.

When she moved away from him, and went to get
some water for some thirst-stricken patients whose
couches were opposite his, he managed to raise himself a
little on his right arm and watched her. How quickly
and noiselessly she passed up and down the pathway
which had been left between the double row of beds,
with what unconscious grace she stooped to bring the
refreshing draught to a level with the sufferer's lips ! Her
bright hair was partially covered by a small round cap,
often worn by young girls at Albany ; and instead of the
smart châtelaine that she used to wear by her side, she
had a large white dimity pocket, such as Dutch house-
wives delight in, containing linen and scissors and other
things that were likely to be needed for her present task ;
her dress was black—was it worn for the Dominie ? he
wondered—and short enough to show the pretty feet
cased in grey stockings and black shoes with silver
buckles. It was not a very elegant costume, but it gave
a touch of conventualism to her beauty, which harmonized
well with the surrounding circumstances ; except for the
silver buckles, it might have been the dress of a *sœur-
de-charité*. He went on watching her ; and she became
aware at last of the intense gaze of the dark, brilliant
eyes—which looked all the deeper and blacker from being
set in such a white face—and came back to him to see if
he wanted anything.

"Let me smooth the pillow, that you may lie down
again," she said ; "the doctor wished you to keep as still
as possible."

He let his arm fall by his side, and leant back his head
obediently, and turned up his eyes in a drolly pathetic
way to the raftered roof.

"There's nothing to see when one lies on one's back this way," he grumbled ; "where's all the hay gone that used to be in the open loft up there ? "

" It is made into beds, all of it that was left from the winter."

" And that was some of Madame's best damask that you wrapped round my arm just now, wasn't it ? and the man she is feeding with a spoon over there, is that scoundrel Lee, who victualled his men at her expense the other day, without so much as saying, 'By your leave.' Well, there is something in finding oneself among Christians after a battle, instead of falling among thieves. Have you heard the number of killed and wounded yet ? "

" More than two thousand, they think," she answered, fearful that she was giving him a shock ; but finding that he bore it very philosophically, she added, " Do you know about Lord Howe, or was that after you were wounded ? "

" Killed, isn't he ? Shot in the back. I heard them telling the news just before I swooned. He was a fine fellow, though he did commit the affectation of sleeping in a tent and cutting his hair short, and wearing a soldier's old coat, as a rebuke to Sybarites like me."

" He was a true soldier," said Franzje, fervently, as she turned to go.

" Did you know him ? " was the answer, in an eager, jealous tone ;—"a little of that water, please, before you leave me.—He used to visit at the Flats, didn't he, when he was encamped close by here a few weeks ago ? "

" Yes ; but I never met him here, though I have seen him pass in the city."

" And was he not seduced into joining any of the city tea-parties ? I suppose the Dominie's accusing shade does not frown upon feeble gaieties of that sort, though all such wicked pastimes as *we* introduced have been completely forsworn, I am told."

A strange thrill passed through the girl at that light mention of the Dominie ; but she held the cup quietly to her patient's lips as she replied, " I do not know much of what goes on, it has not been a time for thinking of pleasure lately."

" And you have not married young Barentse yet ? " he asked, taking little sips between the words as a device to prevent her leaving him.

She turned her head in the direction of Killian's inanimate form, over which a surgeon was anxiously bending. " He is either dead or dying," she answered, in a tone of sad rebuke.

The young officer gave a start which made her tremble for his wound. " You don't mean to say he was in the action ?   Has he joined the army, then ? "

" Yes ; he volunteered this spring."

" Driven thereto by your cruelty ? " was the further question, in a strangely exultant tone.

She might have denied his right to ask, but instead of the grand look of insulted dignity which he expected, there came a sudden rush of colour, and a crushed, self-accusing droop of the stately little head.   " I do harm to everyone," she murmured, as if the confession were made to herself rather than to him.

" It is not the first time that beauty has proved fatal ; but such harm as you have done me, Mademoiselle, you are making up for now.   It is not the time and place to say more ; but some day, perhaps, you will let me plead my cause again."

She started away from him now, her colour deepening, her eyes flashing.   " You are forgetting Engeltje," she said.

To her amazement he began to laugh.

"No, that won't do," he said, checking himself as a spasm of pain crossed his face; "to laugh in the present condition of my side is simple agony; but, Mademoiselle, you are really too amusing. So you thought those kisses of the hand were real inconstancy? I flattered myself you knew me better."

She was standing up straight now beside his couch, and she twined her hands together, and looked down at him with a strange, earnest, intensified expression, the meaning of which he tried vainly to unravel. She could not be cruel to a man in bodily torture; but if she had let herself speak she must have said, "I know you now, and I despise you from my soul, and I despise myself for ever having cared for you!"

The emotion passed; in another minute she said gently, with the staid manner of a real nurse, "You have talked too much; I am going to leave you, but I will come back presently, and see if you want anything."

And then she went away and joined the doctor, who was trying to force some brandy between Killian's lips.

"Are you his sister?" he said, looking up at her with a quick, scrutinizing glance. He was an army surgeon, and knew nothing about her.

"No, he has none," she answered; "but I have known him all my life, and will do anything in my power for him."

"Then I give him into your charge; he is not dead, and as we have extracted the ball successfully he may possibly recover, but the chance is slight. Much will depend on you." And in a clear though rapid tone he proceeded to give her full instructions as to what she was to do. "I had thoughts of asking Madame to see to him, but she has her hands full already."

" I will do my best," said Franzje, humbly, but resolutely. And then, as the doctor turned to leave her, she
added, "Will you tell the officer in the fifth bed from
this that I cannot come back to him as I promised, and
will you ask one of the other nurses to see to him ? "

The surgeon scanned the occupants of the beds, and
as his eye lit on Mr. Vyvian, he said, hastily, " The man
with the arm ! Oh, he'll do. His impudence will carry
him through. He would like to have all the pretty
nurses at his beck, but they've other people to think of,
fortunately."

So they apparently had, for Russell lay and grumbled
to himself unnoticed through the remainder of the hot
afternoon, till at last a very ugly old negress came to him
with some tea. Now and then he raised himself on his
right arm again, and watched Franzje, who was neces-
sarily absorbed with Killian ; but he could not see her
very well because of the intervening beds, and pain soon
forced him to resume his recumbent position. What a
bore it was that she had taken that idea into her head
about Engeltje, a silly little thing for whom he had never
cared a straw ! What dreadfully downright people those
Albanians were, that they couldn't understand how natural it was for a man to make violent love to one girl just
by way of piquing another ! As for Engeltje herself, he
did not give a thought to her : he only reviewed his past
conduct with reference to Franzje ; trying again and again
to fathom the meaning of that strange fixed gaze of hers,
which seemed to say so much and yet to leave so much
unsaid. It was not love, nor even the anger or jealousy
sometimes born of love, which had looked out of those
marvellous eyes ; was it, could it have been, scorn ? His
whole nature writhed at the thought. A little country-
bred Dutch girl to despise *him* ?. a simple soul like

x

Franzje's to read his through, and turn from it with disdain! Impossible, horrible! His self-complacency turned away from the notion, and deliberately refused to admit it. Only the year before she had hung upon his words, and greeted each witty sally with—oh, such innocent, bright appreciation; never could he forget the proud glory of the smile which had lit her face the night that he had kissed her. And even when the absurd scruples inspired by the Dominie had led her to refuse him, there had been no contempt in her manner; she had been calm and dignified, but with a sort of heart-broken calmness which had given him a very comfortable notion—comfortable to his self-love and his disappointed, irritated feelings—of the suffering to which she was condemning herself in thus parting from him. Was it possible that his hasty meaningless flirtation with another had sufficed to change her whole feeling towards him, and that now, when the Dominie was dead, and his other rival likely to be disposed of in the same manner, and everything seemed so favourable for the renewal of his suit, a new and hopeless obstacle would be found to it in the shape of her repugnance?

"Now that the Dominie was dead," he said that to himself so complacently, little guessing that the dead pastor was a far more powerful adversary than the living one had ever been. That little episode with regard to Engeltje, on which his thoughts dwelt so persistently, might possibly have been explained and forgiven had Franzje been the Franzje of his first acquaintance; but between her and the past, between her present self and the old self that had sought pleasure and novelty, and given up its heart in a sort of infatuation to the handsome, flattering, entertaining stranger, there lay a barrier never to be overpassed, a barrier formed by a grave. In the old days she had dreamed a pleasant dream, she had gone her own way, and enjoyed herself, and thought no harm ; but the shock of the Dominie's departure had sufficed to rouse her, and his death had brought so entire a waking, that it was not possible for her ever to sink down and dream that dream again. Henceforth her life must be lived on lonely heights—lonely as regarded this world's companionship ; the heart that was brimful of passionate penitence, of high resolve, of infinite yearning towards the future, had no longer in it any capacity for such love as Russell Vyvian wanted. She had helped to wreck a noble life by falling under the spell of an ignoble fascination ; how could she ever yield to it again even for a single moment ? As she stood beside Russell, looking down at him, she had felt as if she almost hated him, not for any one fault or failing of his, but because he had once bewitched her into loving him.

But as she kept her unwearied watch by Killian's couch, all feelings of hate and scorn died utterly away, or were turned only against herself ; and her thoughts shaped themselves into prayers, and her whole heart was filled with an unutterable longing to save his life even at the expense of her own. She did not reck of her own fatigue, nor count the slow hours as they passed away ; when her untiring efforts were rewarded by a faint movement of the eyelids and a deeply-drawn breath, she almost cried out aloud with joy and gratitude. Hope brightened her task after that, and she had no idea how late in the evening it was when Madame Schuyler came to her, and said, " My child, you must go to the house and get some supper. I will stay here till you come back."

Franzje's face was almost as white as her little cap, but she looked up beamingly as she said, " He has opened

x 2

his eyes once or twice, dear Aunt; I do not think he
knows me; but still, is it not a good sign? and see how
much better he breathes."

"Yes, and he does not look nearly so like death. My
patient is better, too, and has fallen asleep. God be
thanked for all His goodness! And now go, my dear
little maid, or your strength will be quite spent."

Franzje heard, but did not move; she could not care
for rest or food, while the life still hung upon a thread
which *she* had helped to send into peril; but Madame
was wise enough to insist upon obedience, and then, half
ashamed, the girl rose up, scarcely able to stand at first
for stiffness and weariness.

"I will not waste any more time," she said, as she
moved away, "I will come back quickly;" but she could
not pass Mr. Vyvian without looking at him, and the
reproach in his eyes made her pause for a moment.

"You knew that I did not come back because I could
not?" she asked, gently.

"I saw you had a more interesting case; is he better?"
was the reply, in languid tones.

"There is just a hope of life now. I am going to the
house for a few minutes. Can I do anything for you
before I go?"

Oh yes! he wanted his pillow made more comfortable,
he wanted something to drink, he wanted various things,
possible and impossible. He seemed to take a selfish
pleasure in detaining her; perhaps the imperfect light,
and his own weakness, hindered him from seeing plainly
the weariness and exhaustion written on the fair wan
face. And she was too generous to betray it even by a
sigh.

When at length she joined Catalina and Maria Cuyler
at the supper which they had by this time nearly finished,

it was only by force that she could make herself eat anything; and, as she hurried back to Killian, she glanced
rather nervously towards his rival's pallet, almost dread-
ing the fresh demands that might be made upon her.
But the services she had rendered him had really helped
him to greater ease, and he was asleep.

So she was free to resume her watch beside her childhood's friend, free to think her own thoughts, and to con-
secrate herself by fresh resolves to the life of self-sacrifice
of which this was the beginning. "It will not do for me
to be tired, or to mind anything," she said. "Now, I
know what it is to be thankful for health and strength.
Were they not given me to give back to Him?"

There came floating through her mind once more that
glorious sense of living for One who is Love itself, and
who accepts even the poorest oblations of loving hearts,
which had come to her so vividly on the Easter Day following the Dominie's departure, and which her uncle's
words had revived within her, when it had seemed to
perish, grief-stricken, in the shock of the Dominie's
death. It was sad to look back at the past, with its
poor little happinesses that had faded, and its little
foolish mistakes that had wrought such disproportionate
harm; but she was not afraid to look forward, though
she knew not what the future might hold for her of
trial and effort, or what the offering up of self might in-
volve. It was the second night she had kept vigil, and
already the fresh young bloom had left her cheek; but
she felt strong even in her weariness, and when the surgeon made his night round, and banished Catalina Cuyler
as evidently over-done, he did not banish *her*, though he
shook his head a little over her, and said, "This must not
go on."

Killian was reviving wonderfully, but the doctor did

not seem very hopeful about him; perhaps he thought it
the flickering up which often comes before death. As
he hung over the couch, lamp in hand, Killian looked
at him fixedly, and said, in a faint voice, " I don't
know you ;" and then his gaze turned to the sweet face
of the nurse, and his bright gleam of recognition showed
at once that he knew *her*, and was glad to have her near
him.

He appeared to doze for a while after this, but when he
woke, though the doctor and his lamp were gone, and the
light but dim, he seemed to know that it was Franzje who
was watching beside him, and contentedly took some food
from her hand, with his great hollow eyes fixed upon
her all the time, full of that dumb yearning which she
had often seen in them before, though never under such
pathetic circumstances.

" You *have* loved me a *little*, haven't you, Franzje ? " he
said presently, in the low whisper which she was obliged
to bend down to hear.

" More than a little," she answered, with the frank
tenderness from which he had sometimes almost shrunk,
but which was soothing now in his utter weakness, when
all life's passionate hopes and longings were fading away.
" Dear Killian, don't try to talk ; let me feed you ; I want
to bring back your strength, if I can."

" It does not matter much," he said, after a minute's
silence, " as I am not going to live ; but if I had not had
this fatal wound don't you think I might have won at
last ; don't you think you might have married me ? "

She did not instantly reply, but raised herself up and
gazed out into the dim distance, reading as in a vision
the story of what might have been. She saw that it
was possible ; that if he could have lived, his patient
persistence might at length have wrought upon her ;

that through her pity, through her dread of making others suffer, through her growing spirit of self-sacrifice, she might have been led to give herself to him, spite of the deep reluctance at her heart. An involuntary shudder passed over her, but she controlled it, and answered gently, " I think you might have won, as you say ; but, dear Killian, is it not harder to have a thing and find it not worth the winning, than to put it by altogether ? Do you remember the address that our Dominie gave at Mina Renselaer's wedding, and what a beautiful, holy, noble thing it made marriage to be ? Could we either of us be content with anything short of that ? Is it not better to be brother and sister always, than to play at something else which God never meant for us two ?"

" You were ready to play at it with the Englishman," said Killian, in his hoarse, faint tones.

It was the most bitter and the least generous speech that she had ever heard from him, but it came out of a deep heart-wound, and she could not resent it.

" That was earnest while it lasted," she said, with quivering lips and soft pleading accents, too humbled by the consciousness of having mistaken the false for the true, to attempt any other defence.

" While it lasted ! then it is over now ; you are not going to marry the Englishman after I am dead ?"

He little thought that his rival lay so close to him, and did not guess why she turned her head aside with a startled involuntary glance as she answered, " Never ! whether you live or die ; but, Killian, hush—"

She wished to draw his thoughts away from her and to himself, but he interrupted her. "Then, Franzje, my sister, if you will have it so, and my one dear love, what is your future to be like ? I cannot bear the thought of leaving you to a lonely, dreary life."

Even in that great, feebly lighted place, and to his dim uncertain gaze, the sudden radiance that transfigured her could not pass invisible.

"Not lonely," she said, "not dreary either, spite of all that has come and gone. God and my work here, God and my rest *there;* the day coming when the sea will give up its dead! Killian, I can hope and I can wait; only pray for me that I may persevere, that I may not fall away."

"And does your heart never droop?" he questioned; "do you never wish that you were as near death as I am now?"

"Yes, I know what you mean," she answered, "and almost I could wish that I might creep into the grave with you—perhaps I should then know where *his* grave is."

Her head was thrown back as if listening—she seemed to hear the plash of the Atlantic wave upon that undistinguished spot.

"But oh! I can wait," she said again, with brave lips that would not let themselves quiver; "and Killian, God may yet have work for you. Do not let us throw away your chance of life by this agitating talk. Do you remember the prayer that the Dominie taught us when we were little children standing at his knee—'that we might glorify God by our lives or by our deaths'? I only thought then what long words there were in it, but I have loved it since. Let me say it for us both now; and then try to sleep once more—I shall be close beside you all the time."

He did not attempt to speak when the softly murmured prayer was ended, only took possession of her right hand with his feeble fingers, and at length dropped off to sleep still keeping it locked in his.

He was wounded almost to the death, and as weak as a

child ; but his heart was not so sore within him as when
he had rushed away to the war in sudden anger and disgust. He felt now, with more absolute conviction than
ever before, that Franzje could never be his even if he
lived, that it would not be right to tempt her to do
through pity what she would never do of love and free-
will ; but yet the distance between them did not seem so
hopeless, nor the sisterly affection she proffered him so
utter a mockery ; bride or not, she was, in a *certain* sense,
his after all, for were they not both God's ?

"If I live," he said to himself, "I will try to work for
God, and hope and wait as she does ; it is living for self
that has made life bitter. Thank God for having showed
me that, in time at least to *repent* of it."

Ah ! could the Dominie have seen them that night,
these two young souls whom he had taught and guided,
and fired with that divine ambition which may smoulder
for a while but which rarely dies out, would he have still
believed that he had " spent his strength for naught," that
he had cast his nets in vain ? He had gone forth in
despair, believing that Franzje was utterly given over to
vanity, that Killian had lost in a passionate earthly aim
the bright purpose of his boyhood ; and behold, the clear
eyes of angels had seen that the heavenly love still
burned in the young hearts, and an unseen Hand had
drawn them back to the path of single-minded devotion,
with spirits quickened by the earnest repenting that had
come out of their brief mistakes.

The short-sightedness of human judgment, of human
despair ! volumes might be written upon it, but we shall
never know it fully till we stand face to face with "the
God of Hope," and have learnt from Him who is Love
the deep charity which "believeth all things, hopeth all
things, endureth all things."

And Killian did not die. Spite of all he had gone through, spite of the surgeon's prognostications, spite of that agitating talk which Franzje blamed herself for permitting, he struggled back to life, and was good Madame Schuyler's pet and pride and triumph throughout the weary time of his recovery.

"I do not believe he has been saved for nothing," she said one day to Dr. Ogilvie, who frequently visited the wounded, and read and prayed among them. "Our Dominie always thought so much of that lad ; and he will not make the worse minister for his little touch of soldiering. The state of his right arm disables him from further service in *that* way, but I tell him he will yet do his country good service in other ways ; and I think as soon as he is well enough he will go somewhere to study for the ministry. He has set his heart on being a Missionary to the Indians, like our good friend Mr. Stuart, and my little Franzje encourages him with all her might. She may well have a voice in the disposal of his life, since it was she who helped to save it."

Russell Vyvian—a captain now, through the severe losses which his regiment had sustained in the late action —was one of the first to recover from his wounds and to leave the temporary hospital, which had afforded him so timely a shelter. He spent about a week in Madame's summer mansion before rejoining the army ; and during that week he was constantly seeking opportunities for a *tête-à-tête* with Franzje ; but there was no corresponding anxiety for it on her side, and she was still too much occupied with her duties as a nurse to have a great deal of time or thought to spare for other things. One sultry evening, however, Madame Schuyler, seeing her look white and wearied, peremptorily insisted on her taking a stroll by the river-bank ; and there, in a shady spot, not far from the Flats, she came upon Captain Vyvian seated on the grass, leisurely contemplating the scene before him.

"Look, Mademoiselle," he said, rising, and lifting his hat with languid grace, "is it not lovely?"

So lovely it was, that she could not but turn and gaze, forgetting him and herself and her weeks of toil in a momentary sense of exquisite delight.

The river, more than a mile broad at this place, reflected the pine-crowned hills opposite on its shining surface; and not far from the bank lay a beautiful little fertile island crested by tall graceful sycamores, and fringed by bending osiers and weeping-willows whose branches dropped lovingly into the water. Hundreds of white divers were sporting around it; and on a long narrow sand-bank which stretched out at one end stood a quaint row of larger birds, bald-headed eagles, herons, and ospreys, busily engaged in fishing for perch, while around them swam a crowd of saw-bill ducks with scarlet heads, which glowed and gleamed in the sunshine. The sky above was deep cloudless blue, and a soft lazy stillness rested upon the land, where the day's work was done, and orchards and corn-fields lay basking in the golden light, with not a sound proceeding from them save the ceaseless chirp of insects.

It was all so bright and full of fruitful life, and yet so silent, that Franzje felt her heart swell with an undefined emotion, which seemed to need utterance, but for which she could find no intelligible words. Captain Vyvian was the first to speak.

"It reminds me somehow of that day when we watched the waterfall together. You began by only enduring my company then, yet we parted good friends, I think. Do you remember how it dawned upon you for the first time

that plays were meant to be acted, and what bright fresh
interest you took in my schemes? You have learnt to
think it all very wicked since then, I fear."

"I don't think it need be wicked," she answered, looking down.

"You don't condemn amusements wholesale, like your
worthy Dominie? Well, that is something. Mademoiselle, may I not hope that some of the narrow rules by
which he bound you have ceased to be in force now that
he is dead?" There was no response in her face; and
he went on hurriedly, "Do not think that I expect you
to feel, as I feel, what a deliverance from bondage you
have had. I dare say you cherish his memory with
tender gratitude; and it is very natural, and very charming; but as time goes on you will realize your emancipa-
tion."

"Do you mean that I shall become unfaithful?" she
said, with her face lifted, and the large beauty of her eyes
turned full upon him.

"Unfaithful to what? To narrow-minded traditions,
which were never meant to fetter souls like yours? Yes,
I fervently hope so; but be faithful, I beseech you, to
your own sweet self, to the self which allowed me to love
you, which returned my love—that self whose image I
kept enshrined in my soul through all the weary months
that we were parted. You dread your father's opposition,
no doubt; but trust me to overcome it. I do not believe
he has the power to part us; the one real obstacle has
been taken out of the way."

As he uttered the last words, the face which just before
had been so tender and beseeching wore for an instant
that dark vengeful look which she had seen on it the
night when he had said to her, "I *hate* whatever comes
between me and the objects on which I set my heart;"

and she knew, as clearly as if he had spoken his thoughts aloud, that his hatred reached beyond the grave, and that the deepest sorrow of her life was to him a cause of rejoicing, of selfish triumph.

Where was the love of which he had spoken—that love of hers for him ?　Dead, and he had slain it ; and this was the final stroke.　But it was not horror, or scorn, or indignation, which looked out of her eyes now, only an intense pity—a wonder and compassion so deep, that unawares it smote him to the heart.

" How shall I make you understand ? " she said, as she had said once before, but with a more earnest trouble in her voice.　" It was for no selfish ends of his own that the Dominie wished to part me from you ; it was because it would not have been *right* for me to marry you.　I did not comprehend his reasons then, but I think I do now ; and once more I ask you to forgive me, Sir, for having in any way misled you."

" You mean that he thought me not worthy of you ? I do not blame him for that ; no man is fit to mate with an angel.　Yes ; do not shrink away from me ; this is not the language of flattery.　I have not a very high opinion of human nature in general ; but I believe that here and there upon the earth may be found souls as spotless as the heavens above us, and I believe that yours is one of them."

" It only shows that you do not know me," she answered, as a burning blush overspread her face.　" And indeed, Sir, you must not fancy that the Dominie thought me good ; it was not *that*.　But he knew that I had been taught the way to become so—that God had given me the longing to live for Him, and that it was unfaithfulness in me to give a place in my heart to anything which might lead me away from Him."

"Then he wished to make you a sort of nun, in fact," said Russell, with the sneering thought, which fortunately he did not utter, that this was the kind of dog-in-the-manger policy which clerical despots in all ages have been apt to follow ; but Franzje shook her head. A marriage "in the Lord," a holy union of hearts upheld by mutual love, inspired by the same faith, and struggling towards the some blessed end—this was the ideal which had been set before her from her childhood up. The Dominie's ascetic turn of mind had made him content to lead a single life, but he had never sought to induce anyone but Killian to follow his example in this respect, and Franzje, like every other maiden in Albany, had been taught to look forward to marriage as her rightful destiny. That she no longer looked forward to it was more Captain Vyvian's fault than the Dominie's, though he did not know it.

"I do not pretend to be what M. Jansen calls a true believer," he said ; "but I can respect the belief of others. Do not fancy that in wedding me you would expose yourself to mockery or to persecution ; I vow there is not a woman living more honoured or more happy than you should be as my wife. O Franzje ! if you loved me you would trust me and try me ! Why will you not ?"

She put her hand up to her head, as if his vehemence stunned her ; and he saw her lips quiver as she tried to speak. How could she tell him the hard truth that she loved him no longer ? she ! to whom it was so sore and bitter to wound anyone.

"I cannot !" she said ; "I have no love of that kind to give now, and I do not think the sort of happiness you speak of is meant for me ; but you, Sir, will be happy, I trust, and some day, perhaps, the joy of belief will come to you. I will pray that it may."

It was strange how her words carried conviction with

them, the very simplicity of her manner helping to give them reality. All his protestations and entreaties seemed to die away unspoken after that one steadfast "I cannot."

She held out her hand as if to bid him farewell; but just then the rattle of wheels was heard on the high road, which swept along close behind them, only a few yards further from the river's edge, and turning, they saw one of the quaint little carriages of the country, with Evert and Engeltje sitting therein.

Evert drew rein when he perceived them, with an eager "O Franzje!" while little Engelt looked from one to the other with anxious, doubtful, frightened eyes, that said, as plainly as eyes could speak, "So you two have come together again—then perhaps I am only intruding. Do not mind about poor foolish me."

Captain Vyvian merely lifted his hat without approaching, and could scarcely conceal his annoyance at the interruption; but Franzje went close up to the carriage, and kissed her little friend. "Dear Engelt," she said fondly, "it seems years since I saw you!"

"Mother sent me to see when you are coming home, Franz," said Evert. "She gets fidgety about you sometimes, though Uncle Jan always comforts her, and says, 'The child will come to no harm; she is doing a good work, and He Who put it into her heart will take care of her.' There is a report that a fresh pastor is coming out to us from Holland, so that has diverted her mind a little, and she doesn't miss you quite so much as she would if Engelt were not so constantly with us;" and he looked down at the pretty creature beside him with a gallant appreciative air, which augured favourably for the fulfilment of Madame Ryckman's wishes regarding her son's destiny.

"It is very good of Engelt; and you must tell Mother

that I hope to be home in about another week, as nurses will not be so much needed then. Captain Vyvian was one of Madame's patients, and you see he is already about again."

She turned a little to where Russell stood gloomily flicking his boot with his little cane, and looking at none of them; his left arm was still in a sling, and he was rather pale, but otherwise he was quite his own handsome distinguished self. Engelt smothered a little sigh as her gaze followed Franzje's; it was a blow to have to give up all thoughts of so grand a gentleman, but no doubt he was *too* grand for her. Once face to face again with Franzje's loveliness, how could he have eyes or thoughts to spare for a poor little thing like herself? She drew a little nearer to Evert, as if he were her chosen consoler and protector; and, lad though he was, he could bear comparison even with Captain Vyvian, as far as physical beauty and pride of bearing went. No doubt his figure was rather clumsy, and his grey frieze coat not so becoming as uniform, but what of that? Engeltje was not very critical; he was so kind to her, and he had never cared for anybody else, and there was no danger of *his* forgetting her, even if he should go away to the war.

"Aunt Schuyler has sent me out for a ramble; won't you put up the horse at the Flats, and come and take a stroll with me?" Franzje said to them both; and Evert caught at the idea, and asked if he should drop Engeltje then and there, and come back to her when he had disposed of his vehicle.

But little Engelt protested against this arrangement; and as they drove off to the house together Franzje heard her say, "Oh! don't leave me; keep by me all the time, if we do go for a walk," and saw Evert bend his head down to her with a quick, impulsive movement, which looked very much as if he were consoling her with a kiss.

Evidently she had dreaded that Captain Vyvian would form one of the walking-party; but Franzje had rightly judged that in inviting these two young companions she was giving him his dismissal. Best to part before she had wounded him any further; they must go their several ways, and perhaps they might never meet again—but at least her prayers would follow him, for he had been dear to her once.

Possibly that sense that it might be a final parting lent softness to her voice and glance as they stood together for a few brief minutes before the others returned. There was nothing to raise false hopes, nothing that he could construe into encouragement; but there was a something that would make it impossible for him ever to look back with *bitterness* to her rejection of him. He was a proud man, and she had rejected him twice, and yet he lingered beside her, and found it hard to go. At least he was not leaving her to any rival; the one he had most feared slept under the waves, and the other was self-devoted to a career in which marriage could form no part. He was not even troubled by the thought of other suitors, actual or possible; it did not enter his head *now* to taunt her with predictions of one day finding her the bride of "some comfortable Dutchman." He saw that she had found her vocation; and a dim perception came over him that she would be happy in it—not with the tame content which he had seen and despised in some of her worthy townsfolk, but with the intenser happiness which belongs to hearts that "love and will strongly," and yet have learnt to beat responsive to that Divine Love and Will, in harmony with Which is their only true life.

Not till he saw the two young figures coming down the pathway from the Flats did he turn to leave her, and then he sent one swift glance out at the beautiful, shining river, and up at the blue sky arching over it, before he took his last look at the perfect face which had been the one bright vision of his dreams ever since he had first known her. A strange thought came to him—to him, stained with vice, and practically almost an unbeliever—that he should see her again in *Heaven*, a presentiment perhaps of better things to come. And ever afterwards there lived before him that image of her as she stood by the river-side, with her hood thrown back, and all the glory of the sunlight falling on her flaxen hair, on the pure, wide brow, and the parted lips, and the beautiful, calm, regretful eyes. It is something for a bad man to have loved worthily ; it is much if this love have given him a sense of his own unworthiness. As Russell Vyvian stood and looked at her for the last time, he recognized all at once—without anger, without rebellion even, for the moment—that he had lost her by his own fault, that the Dominie had done well—ay, very well, in severing her from such an one as he. It was the beginning of conviction—conviction which might be smothered for a while, but would work its work some day, all unknown to Franzje, but not unknown to the good mother in England, to whom alone the story of the love of his youth would ever be told.

"Farewell, then," he said ; only just those words ; and she answered nothing but "Farewell ;" and they heard the soft plashes of the divers in the river, and the whirring of an eagle's wings as it rose up into the sky, and slowly the clasp of the hands was loosed, and she was alone. Alone—alone always, in one sense, and yet not lonely. Oh, how sweetly the river flowed, in the stillness and sunshine, reflecting not only the steep, rugged hills behind it, but the broad, blue heavens above! Oh, how peacefully life flows on in the light of God's love, even though shadows from a painful past may cross it now and then!

THE END.

LONDON: R. CLAY, SONS, AND TAYLOR, PRINTERS.

WORKS BY CHARLOTTE M. YONGE,

Author of " The Heir of Redclyffe."

ABBEYCHURCH : OR, SELF-CONTROL AND
SELF-CONCEIT. Second Edition. And the MYSTERY OF
THE CAVERN. In One Volume, fcap. 8vo, cloth extra, with
Frontispiece, 4s. 6d.

SCENES AND CHARACTERS. Sixth Edition,
fcap. 8vo, cloth, 3s. 6d.

THE SIX CUSHIONS. Second Edition, royal 18mo,
with Frontispiece, 3s.

NEW GROUND. Second Edition, fcap. 8vo, cloth,
with Frontispiece, 3s.

COUNTESS KATE. Third Edition, royal 18mo,
cloth, 3s. 6d.

THE STOKESLEY SECRET. Second Edition, royal
18mo, cloth, 3s. 6d.

FRIARSWOOD POST-OFFICE. Sixth Edition,
demy 18mo, cloth, 2s. 6d.

THE CASTLE BUILDERS ; OR, THE DEFERRED
CONFIRMATION. Fifth Edition, fcap. 8vo, cloth, 3s. 6d.

LANGLEY SCHOOL. Fourth Edition, demy 18mo,
cloth, 2s. 6d.

THE PIGEON PIE. Fifth Edition, demy 18mo,
cloth, 1s.

THE CHRISTMAS MUMMERS. Second Edition,
demy 18mo, 1s. ; cloth, gilt edges, 1s. 6d.

BEN SYLVESTER'S WORD. Eleventh Edition,
demy 18mo, 8d. ; cloth, 1s.

LEONARD, THE LION-HEART. Ninth Edition,
demy 18mo, 6d.

THE RAILROAD CHILDREN. Ninth Edition,
demy 18mo, 6d.

MOZLEY AND SMITH,

6, PATERNOSTER ROW, LONDON.

JELF (Rev. G. E.) THE SECRET TRIALS OF
THE CHRISTIAN LIFE. By George Edward Jelf, M.A.,
Vicar of Blackmoor, Hants ; and sometime Student of Christ
Church, Oxford. Third Edition. Crown 8vo, cloth, red
edges, 5s

"The author is probably known to many of our readers by a volume of Sermons, favourably noticed in the 'Guardian,' which is, like this, devoted to the
complete development and consideration of one important subject. He now
addresses a less general audience, those who are in earnest striving to 'make
up for lost time,' and find their path beset with unforeseen obstructions. He
assumes that the secret trials of the Christian life are felt, and the hindrances
which arise from them deplored ; and he offers here just that instruction as to
their origin and nature, and the 'way of escape' from them, which is most
helpful, and, at the same time, most consoling in the hour of need, distress, or
peril. The work is full and searching, and has a pervading manliness of tone
and sentiment, which is preserved even when the immediate aim is to soothe
or win."—The Guardian.

JELF (Rev. G. E.) MAKE UP FOR LOST TIME:
A Course of Sermons. Second Edition, crown 8vo, cloth, red
edges, 4s.

"These twenty sermons are a worthy filial tribute, by a worthy son to a
worthy father, and we do not doubt that Dr. Jelf wisely and correctly thought
(as his son says in the dedication) that they would prove of some 'help to a
troubled soul.' We can recommend them safely to souls either troubled or at
rest."—English Churchman.

JELF (Rev. G. E.) HOW DOES THE CHURCH
HELP US TO LIVE ACCORDING TO THE RULE OF
THE GOSPEL ? A Paper read before the Clergy of the Rural
Deanery of Alton, December 2, 1873. Published by request.
Crown 8vo, 6d.

JELF (Rev. G. E.) OUR TREASURE OF LIGHT:
Eight Addresses delivered at St. Michael's, Highgate, during
the London Mission of 1874. Published by request. Fcap.
8vo, cloth, 1s. 6d.

JELF (Rev. G. E.) BLESSINGS FROM THOSE
WE BLESS : Words of Counsel chiefly for Masters and Men,
spoken at a Festival of the National Deposit Friendly Society.
18mo, 2d., or 14s. per 100.

JELF (Rev. G. E.) THE UNION OF BISHOPS
AND PRESBYTERS A DIVINE SAFEGUARD FOR THE
CHRISTIAN LAITY. An Appeal to Holy Writ. 8vo, 6d.

JELF (Rev. G. E.) THE CURE OF SOULS: Its
RESPONSIBILITIES AND ITS LIMITS. A Paper read before the
Clergy of the Rural Deanery of Alton, October 22, 1874.

MOZLEY AND SMITH,

6, PATERNOSTER ROW, LONDON.

RIDLEY (Rev. W. H.) SERMONS IN PLAIN
LANGUAGE, adapted to the Poor. By the Rev. W. H.
RIDLEY, M.A., Rector of Hambleden, Bucks. Fifth Edition,
fcap. 8vo, cloth limp, 2s. ; cloth boards, 2s. 6d.

By the same Author.

THE HOLY COMMUNION: Its Nature and
Benefits. With an Explanation of what is required of them
who come to the Table of the Lord. Cheap Edition, cloth
limp, 7d., or 24 copies for 12s. ; Fine Edition, cloth, red
edges, 1s. ; roan, 1s. 6d. ; Persian morocco, with cross, 2s. ;
morocco, 3s.

A PLAIN TRACT ON CONFIRMATION, Explain-
ing the Two Parts of that Holy Ordinance. 2d., or
14s. per 100 ; fine paper, with covers, 3d. ; 12 for 2s. 6d.

A SECOND PLAIN TRACT ON CONFIRMA-
TION. Fcap. 8vo, 1d. ; or 7s. per 100.

A PLAIN TRACT FOR THOSE WHO HAVE
LATELY BEEN CONFIRMED. 1d. ; or 7s. per 100.

PREPARATION FOR WEEKLY COMMUNION:
Being a Supplement to "Holy Communion." 18mo, 2d. ; 12
for 1s. 9d.

MOZLEY AND SMITH,
6, PATERNOSTER ROW, LONDON.

ROBINSON (Rev. W. P.) AIDS TO THE BETTER
RECEPTION OF THE HOLY COMMUNION, suited to the
Use of Schoolboys; with an Introduction on Confirmation.
Compiled and Arranged by the Rev. W. PERCY ROBINSON,
M.A., Warden of Trinity College, Glenalmond. 18mo, cloth
boards, red edges, 1s.

ROBINSON (Rev. W. P.) PRIVATE PRAYERS
FOR THE USE OF SCHOOLBOYS. 18mo, cloth, 8d.

ROBINSON (Rev. W. P.) DAILY SERVICES FOR
THE USE OF PUBLIC SCHOOLS. With Introductory
Notice by the Very Rev. E. M. GOULBURN, D.D., Dean of
Norwich. 8vo, cloth boards, red edges, 1s.

EVENING REST; OR, CLOSING THOUGHTS
FOR EVERY DAY IN THE CHRISTIAN YEAR. By the
Author of "Morning Light." Third Edition, pott 8vo, cloth,
red edges, 2s. 6d.; calf limp, 5s.; morocco, extra, bevelled
boards, 6s.

A CHEAP EDITION, for Distribution, is now ready, 18mo,
cloth limp, 1s., or Twelve for 10s.

MOZLEY AND SMITH,
6, PATERNOSTER ROW, LONDON.

Milton Keynes UK
Ingram Content Group UK Ltd.
UKHW040139160224
437928UK00003B/29

9 783382 831288